The old-fashioned silk gown swirled about Isabeau as though it had been created for her. It was as if she had shed a chrysalis, and whirled out, suddenly a jewel-bright butterfly in some kind of fairy-spun finery.

"My god," Griffin rasped. "Isabeau, you look so beautiful . . ."

Their eyes locked for long seconds that seemed to spiral out into eternity. Despite herself, Beau drew nearer to him. This need that flowed through her, to the very tips of her fingers, this vast emptiness filled with heady-sweet anticipation was a wondrous surprise.

Then, as if he, too, felt the shattering temptations, as if he, too, held no power to resist, Griffin groaned and pulled her into his arms.

She had not known what to expect, but whatever fleeting thoughts she may have entertained could not even touch the reality of Griffin Stone's kiss. Beau couldn't breathe, couldn't think, mesmerized as she was by the power of his hunger. Of their own volition, her hands charted a path up his chest as she savored the feel of him, the taste of him.

And she ached to have him touch her, touch her in ways that made blood rise, hot, to her cheeks . . .

Books by Kimberly Cates

Crown of Mist
Restless Is the Wind
To Catch a Flame

Published by POCKET BOOKS

TO CATCH A FLAME

KIMBERLY CATES

POCKET BOOKS
New York London Toronto Sydney Tokyo Singapore

This book is a work of fiction. Names, characters, places and incidents are either the product of the author's imagination or are used fictitiously. Any resemblance to actual events or locales or persons, living or dead, is entirely coincidental.

An *Original* Publication of POCKET BOOKS

POCKET BOOKS, a division of Simon & Schuster
1230 Avenue of the Americas, New York, NY 10020

ISBN: 0-671-68494-9

First Pocket Books printing May 1991

10 9 8 7 6 5 4 3 2 1

Printed in the U.S.A.

To my daughter, Kate,
who taught me everything I know
about the temperament of royalty.
I love you, your ladyship!

TO CATCH A FLAME

Prologue

ENGLAND, 1768

The night roiled with fury, gnarled tree branches tearing at the darkness like greedy fingers hungering for some unseen prey.

The moon, a single ghoulish eye, leered down from the heavens, casting eerie shadows over the mounted figure racing wildly along the perilous ribbon of road. Jagged stones and twisted roots snarled across the crude pathway beneath the magnificent animal's thundering hooves, threatening to plunge both horse and rider into the devil's outstretched palm.

The devil . . .

The rider shuddered, casting a glance over one broad shoulder as he attempted to see what lay behind him. It was as if he could feel Lucifer's own breath hot upon his nape, could feel the claws of death curling inexorably toward him—and, more terrifying still, toward the son he treasured above his own life.

For he had seen . . . witnessed—

"No!" He drove his heels deep into the horse's ribs, and the beast surged forward as if it, too, sensed the suffocating evil all about them. "It is madness . . . impossible . . ."

But his mind would give him no peace. The darkness

seemed to twist into images from his worst nightmare—the folds of an ebony cloak, a face lead-painted, white.

The devil's own . . .

The rider reined his mount to the west, where the woods thinned slightly. Slender fingers of light flickered in the distance, beckoning, welcoming.

He urged his horse forward, dizzy with relief as he neared safe haven. But suddenly his mount whinnied in fright, rearing as an apparition was conjured from the very mists.

Horrified, his eyes locked upon the figure that stood stark against the night, a cape whipping back in the wind like the wings of a fallen angel. Even in the meager light of the moon the apparition's eyes burned, twin pits of hate, turning the rider's blood to ice.

Desperately he groped for his pistol while struggling to cling to his mount's back, but it was as if the horse itself was possessed. He felt himself driven back from the saddle, his knees tearing loose from the horse's barrel, the reins ripping from his hands.

Laughter echoed through the night as he hurtled through darkness. His soul reeled, raw terror lancing through him, not for his own life, but for his son's.

His son—

There would be no one . . . no hope to save him now. Except . . .

Maybe but one . . .

One man, one chance—

He screamed the name as the gates of hell yawned wide beneath him, plunging him into death's embrace.

"Griffin!"

Three months later Lord Griffin Stone sailed back to England, the lazily arrogant mouth that had bewitched a hundred ladies now hard with grief, and his eyes, the blue-gray of a tempest-tossed sea dark with the pain of loss. . . .

Chapter One

The brace of pistols appeared ludicrous in Molly Maguire's small-boned hands, and she stared down at the weapons pillowed upon her lap, her huge eyes somber, her lips pale. "Beau, this is madness." Her warning echoed softly about the tiny inn room. "You cannot ride tonight."

"Don't be a gudgeon, Moll!" Isabeau DeBurgh tossed her flame-red curls, her bright summer-green eyes snapping with excitement as she retrieved the weapons, her most cherished possessions. "It is a perfect night for raiding."

"A perfect night to get yourself hanged."

"Molly, can't you see it?" Isabeau made her most ghastly demon face, her voice dropping into the low, eerie tones that she knew sent shivers up her friend's spine. "There is moon enough to cast sinister shadows." She fluttered her fingers, drawing nearer to Molly. "And the wind whispers like hauntings through the branches . . . It makes those pompous, jewel-encrusted oafs who travel the highroads quiver down to their diamond shoe buckles even before they've left the safety of their fete or musicale."

"Beau," Molly said pleadingly, shrinking back against the crude wooden chair. "You know I loathe it when you make your voice that way!"

But Beau ignored her plea, unable to resist such a susceptible audience. "And the 'ristocrats," she continued in a low purr, "they'll have filled their coachmen with ominous warnings and be clinging to their treasures like a mammy to its babe. I'll wait . . . wait in the darkness while they shiver with images of night dragons and specters, and then—whoosh!" Beau leaped toward Molly with an ear-splitting howl. *"I'll spring from the shadows like a nightmare come real."* Molly's squeak as she skittered from the chair, filled Beau with glee.

With a jaunty grin Beau straightened. Skirting the narrow bed and slant-topped table, she strode toward the looking glass to arrange the froth of ruffles tumbling down her shirtfront. "And then, Molly, me girl," Beau observed, giving her black breeches a pat of infinite satisfaction, "those port-bellied curs will *hurl* their pretties at me—and gladly, relieved that it is not the devil himself come to steal away their souls."

"Pray God they don't hurl something else at you. Like a musketball or a sword." There was an unaccustomed edge to Molly's usually gentle voice, and it stung Beau more than she would admit even to herself. "It is no game you are playing at, whether you believe it or not. Look how many highwaymen have been taken to Tyburn Fair. And the gibbets, they line the roadside . . . everywhere."

Molly's slender form was racked with shudders, and Beau's own mind filled with images of the ironbound structures dangling tarred corpses like grisly fruit—a sinister warning to any who would dare take to the High Toby.

But she brushed the sobering thoughts away as though they were no more than butterflies clustered upon a gilly-flower. Her eyes danced like twin devils as she grinned. "They would have to catch me first. And no mere mortal could ever cast into chains the bold Devil's Flame."

"You cannot know that for certain," Molly cut in, wringing her hands. "It was bad enough before, when it was just Bow Street's runners you had to fear. But ever since—since that grand duke was found . . ." Molly nibbled her lower lip.

"The only reason you've given half a thought to the Duke

of Graymore's demise is that it is splashed all over the *Spectator* that his scoundrel brother is returned to England. The infamous Lord Griffin Stone—duellist extraordinaire, heartless rogue. No doubt he is greedy to pick his brother's bones."

"I care not a whit about Lord Griffin, nor about any of those silly writings! I tell you, there's been something afoot for months now. Something wicked."

"The only thing 'wicked' afoot that night was Graymore's bloody horsemanship. He deserved to snap his fool neck, bolting about on those roads in the middle of the night."

"But you race about all the time!" Molly blustered. "Darkness has never stopped you! And you know as well as I that the duke didn't merely tumble from his saddle. The streets have been abuzz ever since—"

"It takes precious little to set these streets astir. Graymore *fell from his horse,* and—"

"Then what about Lily Tymmes? And Rebecca Mathers? Neither of them ever touched a saddle in their lives."

Even Beau could not stem an inward shiver at this last. It was rumored that the corpses of the two low-born women had been discovered within the dense woodlands skirting the Blowsy Nell Inn. But it was whispered that even their mothers could not have recognized their faces, knife-slashed as they were with symbols that could have been from Satan's own hand.

Stiffening her shoulders, Beau forced a dismissive snort. "It was awful, what befell those women. But there is no proof the victims were Rebecca or Lil. And furthermore, the murders had nothing to do with Graymore, and still less to do with me. I am no dainty wildflower to be crushed beneath some nightstalker's heel. I am the bold Devil's Flame—highwayman, brigand—"

"What you are, Isabeau DeBurgh, is a fool if you believe yourself immune! I know you think me a coward, and maybe I am, but this time, Beau, this time it is different. I *feel* something is amiss—feel it to the marrow of my bones."

"What? You fear some monster lurking in your imagination will swallow up the Devil's Flame? I think not." Beau's eyes glinted with amused arrogance. "Have you not read the pamphlets of late, Mistress Maguire? 'The Flame is a monster of a rogue, with blood-hued eyes and fists the size of anvils. His horse is as swift as death and thrice as daring'."

Beau scooped up her jaunty cocked hat, adjusting its dashing crimson plume. Her irreverent gaze flicked from the headgear to her own petite form mirrored within the silver plane of the looking glass. "It must be the hat."

Despite her best efforts, the corners of Molly's mouth twitched in the barest hint of a smile. "If it were that simple, I'd take the thing and stuff it in the fire so you would make an end to this idiocy. I swear—"

"No, you never swear," Beau replied, warming at the very real concern in her friend's voice. "You are entirely too sweet and good to keep company with a reprobate like me."

Molly looked away from Beau and caught her pale lower lip with her teeth.

Beau watched as she paced to where a black velvet cloak—prime pickings from a snipe-nosed baronet—was spread upon a narrow bed, the richness of the garment oddly contrasting with the humble chamber. Molly smoothed a tiny wrinkle from the fabric.

"Beau, I can't—can't help but blame myself for . . ." She faltered. "For driving you to ride. It is because of me you need risk again so soon, I—"

"Bah!" Beau denied gruffly, but she could not meet her friend's eyes. "Was I not the daughter of Six Coach Robb, one of the greatest brigands ever to ride? It is but another grand adventure, and I revel in 'em. I only wish you had"—the bantering tone faded from her voice "—wish you had told me things were awry again before . . ." Beau's voice trailed off. She hated the flush that sprang to Molly's thin cheeks as they both recalled the previous night. Beau had returned from a fortnight's amusement at Medlenham Fair only to find Molly painfully absent . . . at Old Nell's bidding.

"He—he was not *so* odious a man." Molly rubbed her

fingers upon her petticoats as though to cleanse them of grit only she could see. "And it was over . . . quite soon."

Beau's heart twisted. There were darts of shame in her friend's brown eyes, shame and a fear that seldom left them for long.

"I think I shall become used to it after a time. Old Nell claims—"

"Old Nell is a shriveled-up bag of nonsense, and you're a goose to listen to her. You'll *not* become *used* to any such thing with me around, and now Owen . . . Owen will be riding, too, and will be able to help you." The thought of Molly's fifteen-year-old younger brother soured Beau's mood, but she forced herself to conceal her misgivings.

Owen Maguire was five feet of bumbling, awkward trouble, with a temper too quick by half and a pistol aim so poor it was whispered he couldn't hit the Tower of London if he had his nose smack on Traitor's Gate.

And tonight the Devil's Flame, the highwayman rogue known throughout London for cunning and daring, would be joined by that green lad. Madness, Molly had called Beau's rides earlier—but Beau knew it was softness in the head indeed to lug along a boy whose temper was tinder to a brushfire. And yet . . .

Beau's lips compressed with an uncustomary grimness. Last night when Molly had returned from her assignation with one of the brothel's patrons there had been stark fear in the girl's eyes. The timid Molly could scarcely speak to strangers without going white in the face, and to steal away with them to a room upstairs, endure their pawings and gruntings was a horror beyond Beau's imaginings.

The mere thought of that fate made Beau's skin crawl. She had wanted to rail at her friend, furious that the girl had not warned her that she needed more coin to pay her way at the so-called "inn." But one look at the suffering in Molly's face, and Beau had been unable to stay angry.

She had merely drawn out her pistols and told Owen that tonight he would begin to learn the highwayman's trade.

"You are taking him tonight?" Molly's nervous quaver

broke into Beau's thoughts. Beau drew her soft leather boots over the tight black breeches she always wore.

"I'm taking him tonight."

"Beau, he . . . he's not the steadiest sort, Owen isn't. I fear—"

"I know it's hard, but he must learn some skill with which to support the both of you, else you'll be trapped at the Blowsy Nell forever." A defensive note crept into Beau's voice. "I wish I could school him in a printer's trade, or perhaps a solicitor's, but I can't. I can only teach him what I know." And pray he becomes decent enough at it that if anything should befall me, you will both survive, she thought. "I know it is not the best solution," she said aloud, "but I'll take good care of him for you, Moll."

Molly's dark-lashed eyes flashed up, a sweet, sad smile on her lips. "Of course you will. And as for . . . for what you are schooling him in . . . Beau, no one knows better than I how generous you've been with the two of us. Without you we'd not have survived a month in this city. Do you remember when you found us? That awful old baker had me by the petticoats, and Owen—"

"Owen looked like a starved rat." Beau shook her head, remembering the scrawny pair the two had made, crofter children whose parents had been killed by a runaway coach. London had been a labyrinth of terrors and cruelties for the orphaned Maguires. They had been cowering before a flour-spattered baker who had discovered them pawing through the refuse heap behind his shop—Molly a wide-eyed eight-year-old, Owen five.

The baker had threatened to see them clapped up in Newgate for their thievings when Beau came upon them.

All of ten she had been, nettlesome as a briar patch, all swagger and snap. Hands on hips, she had stomped up and let fly a string of curses so blue they made even the grizzled old man blush. Then, with an already well-honed instinct for discovering the weakness beneath one's armor, she had warned the old man that if he persisted, she would bring down upon him the wrath of the most feared highwayman in all of London—Jonathan Everard Ramsey, known throughout the city as Gentleman Jack Ramsey.

The baker had roared with laughter until he had peered into Beau's crystal-green eyes.

"It is you, then," the man had said to Beau as he let Molly loose with a surprising gentleness. "The girl Jack tends. Daughter o' Six Coach Robb."

"No one tends me," Beau had flashed back. "Jack but keeps me 'round 'cause I be so blessed entertainin'."

"Gentleman Jack keeps you around 'cause you be child of the greatest highwayman that e'er lived. Take these two whinin' pups, if you've mind to, your ladyship." The baker had reached out, ruffling Beau's wild curls with a smile. "Your pap, he robbed me once, an' one wi' finer manners I never did see. Made it seem near a privilege that 'e chose us, 'e did. 'Membered him always. Do 'im honor, girl. Do honor to the memory of Six Coach Robb an' his most beautiful lady."

Beau had puffed up with pride as she remembered the father who'd taken her on wild rides perched upon his glorious night-black horse, the father whose scarlet satins and ringing laughter had delighted her, the father who had meant the world to the beautiful, gently bred woman who'd been Beau's mother.

A twinge of grief beset Beau as she thought of her mother's porcelain-delicate face as it had been when last she saw it, the laughter, life that had ever bubbled in Lady Lianna ebbing away, as though the hangman who had dealt her husband death had opened her veins as well. They had buried Lady Lianna at his side, but a fortnight after Robb's friends had cut him down from the gibbet.

Frightened, the seven year old Beau had been then, for the first time in her life, frightened and furious with her parents for having left her alone. Yet she had not been so for long. *He* had ridden up, astride a blooded sorrel, his plumes a splash of color upon the drizzly-gray sky. The devilish-handsome face that made countless women swoon had been astonishingly still, solemn.

He had swung down from his horse in a flurry of sapphire cloak and had strode toward the cluster of mourners about the new-dug grave. Straightaway, he had come to Isabeau, and had swept the cocked hat from his head, bending down onto one knee before her.

Your most obedient servant, my lady Isabeau, he had said softly. *My name is Gentleman Jack Ramsey. I rode with your father. It is I who will take care of you now.*

And he had—that young man with his flashing smile, and his ready wit. He had schooled Beau in reading, in ciphering, had her tutored even in the classics which she loathed. And manners, he had struggled to gift her with, reluctant as she was, in memory of her gently bred mother. Yet even then she had been too much Robb's issue to play the budding lady for long—and the swagger, sparkling eyes, and bold ways that had winged her father into legend delighted Jack Ramsey, in spite of himself.

"Remember how poor Mr. Ramsey looked when you dragged Owen and me into the inn?" Molly's voice shook Beau from her unaccustomed foray into the past.

Smiling ruefully, Beau again met her friend's eyes. After a moment both girls broke into grins.

"It was a sight worth a king's purse," Beau said with great relish. "Gentleman Jack nearly swallowed a leg of capon whole."

"One can hardly blame him! You breezed in with the two of us in tow and told him you were keeping us as pets—like his current light-o'-love's infernal pugs."

Beau tugged at one of Molly's yellow curls. "At least you didn't keep poor Jack awake with your yapping all night long. And I kept the both of you in my chamber, so you didn't sleep at the foot of his bed. Remember how he loathed those curs? He might have wed that empty-headed Miranda if it hadn't been for those dogs."

"No." There was a soft wistfulness in Molly's voice. "I think even then he was waiting for another."

Beau whirled around, swooping up the ribbon she used to bind her hair. But instead of catching back the flame-hued tresses she merely fingered the wisp of satin. "Moll—"

"No more, I promise. I didn't intend to—to plague you. I only wish Mr. Ramsey were here to stop this foolishness."

"Jack is still off at Medlenham trying to charm the Lady March out of her pannier. It is a good place for him, too. Ever since that idiot Sir Mandelay bragged to the *ton* that the minuscule scar on his cheekbone was the mark of bold Gentleman Jack, half the knaves in London have been out after getting their face carved up to impress their ladies. It's most annoying. Of course, I suppose I could come up with a mark of my own. Or perhaps I should put a ring in my victims' noses."

"This isn't a jest, Beau, or some grand adventure. I can't bear the thought of you riding again on my account. I'm not eight years old anymore, Beau. I'm not a green country girl adrift in London. I have to take care of myself now, and you can't keep charging in, trying to rescue me."

"Why not? If I choose to—"

"I don't choose to let you hang for me, Beau—no, nor Owen either."

"Ah, she'll not be hangin' girl," a wheezing voice cut in. "It will be a far worse end the spiteful hoyden'll come to." As the girls turned their eyes to the doorway Beau sensed Molly's sick dread. Molly wrung her hands within the shelter of her petticoats as Nell Rooligan shuffled into the room.

The old woman's opaque blue eyes were rapier sharp as they peered out from pouches of sagging flesh. A net of wrinkles quilted her jowls despite the cork plumpers she used to attempt to hide her sunken cheeks. Liberal swipes of rouge had been swabbed with a haresfoot over lead-painted skin, and a preposterous-looking wig perched askew upon her low brow.

Yet despite her ridiculous appearance Nell Rooligan was seldom dismissed as a pathetic crone. She seemed to carry a mantle of mysticism about her hunched shoulders, a mysticism incongruously mingled with starkest practicality.

It was as if she could see to the core of one's very soul, and upon viewing the secret vulnerabilities within she jeered like the devil himself.

Most people who crossed the aged lightskirt's path sought her favor with near-desperation, but Beau had always regarded the old woman with contempt. This emotion was returned tenfold by the whore-mistress, who would never forgive the fiery, beautiful girl for escaping the lucrative calling Nell had planned for her.

Nell lumbered forward, a dented pewter tray heavy with meat pasties held in her fists. She set it down upon the trestle with a thud, smacking her lips as she eyed Beau. "You're goin' t' ride. Take that worthless Owen with you."

Beau started at the old woman's words. She never told anyone but Molly when she took to the road, and as for her plan to bring Owen along—she'd certainly never betrayed that. Despite the smile she forced to her lips, Beau couldn't help the stirring of unease that crept through her.

"Listening at walls again, Nell?" Beau asked, sauntering over to the tray and helping herself to a rich meat pie.

"I need not stoop to so common a trick. I have other ways of knowing . . . of seeing . . ." Nell's tongue curled about the words, her tone intended to unsettle. "And I have seen far more than just your foolish plottings, Isabeau DeBurgh. Something be afoot this night—something evil . . . deadly evil. I heard the night a-whisperin'."

"Save your Banbury tales to scare the babes by the fire."

"A Banbury tale, is it?" Nell cackled, and the sound prickled the fine hairs at the base of Beau's nape. "Dismiss it as such if you be a blind fool. I warned Lily Tymmes about the lurkings before she disappeared, but she'd have none of it neither. An' they swooped her off—the hauntin's did, just like I said they would."

Beau heard Molly's gasp, and the sound renewed Beau's courage.

"The only thing that swooped Lil off was some handsome soldier," Beau said breezily. "The chit was ever slavering after anything in regimentals. Even now she's most likely ensconced in her lover's room, being petted and spoiled with fans and silks and such frippery."

"Nay, she be deep in the cold earth, a-rotting. Whatever's left of her. Remember that I warned you, when *they* be feastin' upon you."

"They? Who in thunder are *they?* Dragons in the forest? Flesh-eating monsters?" Beau let her voice drop to a mocking, eerie tone. "Ooooo . . . Beware, little girl, else the harpies feast upon you."

"It won't be harpies, my fine miss. It'll be something more sinister still. And you—you'll run afoul of it this night, mark my words. It is dangerous upon the road."

"Ah, my eternal thanks, my sage and wondrous sorceress! Your revelation rivals those of the prophets! It is dangerous upon the road!" Beau struck her palm to her brow with all the drama of a Drury Lane actress. "I had no notion it was real pistol balls those knaves have been firing at me these many months!"

The old crone's face remained enigmatic. Her expression gave Beau the strange sensation of teetering upon the brink of some unseen chasm.

"Come now, Nell." Beau was stunned at the cajoling tones in her own voice. "Even demons wouldn't dare draw fire from these pistols. Of course, I could strap on one of Jack's swords for good measure, but considering what a clumsy oaf I am with a blade, it would only give my foes unfair advantage."

The old woman straightened, and Beau felt another twinge of forboding steal over her. Nell drew nearer, her breath reeking of garlic and onion as it blew hot on Beau's face.

"Aye, go ahead, Isabeau De Burgh," Nell said. "Laugh at my demons. But the hauntings winging about this night will not fall beneath your pistol fire, nay, nor Jack's blade. You'll see. Aye, as Rebecca Mathers did. And Lily, when she failed to heed my warning."

Beau tucked her pistol in her sash with numb fingers, the weapon suddenly too heavy to hold. The tiny inn room rippled away like her reflection in a crystal pond, everything melting into a blur as Beau's eyes locked with those of Nell Rooligan.

Never before had Beau dreaded the darkness in the thick woods, or what lay within any man's soul.

Yet for an instant, just an instant, bold Isabeau DeBurgh tasted fear.

Chapter Two

The post chaise careened through the night at its wide-eyed driver's command. At the sides of the road, trees clawed at the bruise-colored sky, and in the distance thunder rumbled ominously.

"'Tis crazed he is, Adley," the spindly postilion choked out to the driver as he clung, white-knuckled, to the edge of his seat. "Mad, wanting to set out upon the road at such an hour. 'Tis suicide, I say. Aye, pure and simple. And you . . . you're no better, drivin' like a bloody whip. Should've stayed in my own bed, I should've. Let the two of you go t' the devil!"

The grizzled driver cast the man a bleary smile, eyes rheumy with gin. "Think of it this way, Tavish. If we do overturn, at least we won't need to worry about being set upon by those highwaymen you quake over every time we make a trek. Maybe me and his lordship'll be doing you a favor."

"Bloody hell!" Tavish yelped as the vehicle struck a stone and lurched sickeningly to one side. "I'd take my chances with an honest brigand any day rather than be at the mercy of you, you drunken sot—aye, or that madman below."

The driver barked a stiff laugh. "Don't be lettin' milord

Stone hear your blathering, or you're apt to find yourself skewered upon his spit. He's killed men for less, so I'm told. Finest swordsman in all England, he was, before he was banished to the colonies."

"'Tis a fine place for the likes o' him, full of wild red Indians an' such," Tavish said. "So why the devil did God send 'im back to plague us civilized folk?"

"It's because of his brother." All jesting fled from the coachman's rough voice. "The good duke died upon this very road."

As he spoke the dirt track narrowed.

"Ye'd best . . . best take up old Bess, Tavish," the driver said. "'Tis Rogue's Row ahead."

"Rogue's Row," Tavish echoed, unable to quell his fear. He groped with chill fingers for the firearm at his feet. "You should drag your Lord Stone up here, if he's such a wonder with a blade. Let him fend off the brigands he's so eager to tilt with."

"Nay, Tavish, Lord Stone and his like don't match their sacred blades with raw brigands. They hire us t' bloody our hands and take the musket fire."

"May he rot in hell!" Tavish said prayerfully. The darkness grew deeper as the woods closed skeletal fingers about the lurching chaise until even Tavish drifted into silence. No man dared the perilous stretch of road known as Rogue's Row without feeling death's cold blade whisper near his throat.

No man save Lord Griffin Stone.

Griffin lounged against the worn squabs of the chaise as he watched the violet shadows of the trees pass by. No mist of danger haunted him, no trickle of dread crept up his broad-muscled shoulders.

The stark branches held a fascination for him, a kind of terrible beauty that set his blood pounding hot in his veins, tightening every nerve in his body with anticipation. But it was no phantom brigand that drew Griffin's attention, no fear of blazing pistols or gleaming blades slicing into flesh.

He watched the land, which even now, wreathed in mist, seemed as though it were but a figment from his most secret dreams.

England.

His lips curved with cynical amusement as he fought the odd urge to reach out his gloved fingers and brush away the darkness that shielded the countryside from his sight. But he could picture it clearly in his mind: the tangle of hawthorne and oak, the jewel-bright wildflowers that grew about the trees' snaggled roots and scaled the scattered hedgerows that wove the landscape into a most exquisite patchwork.

It had been ten years since he had last seen Norfolk. Ten years since he had plunged recklessly down this same road, fleeing disaster, betrayal, and heartbreak. Fleeing all that he was. Back then the far-off American colonies had been his only hope, exiled as he was for the consequences of his fiery temper. At the time he'd thought it was the end of the world, but the world had a way of spinning relentlessly onward.

And the gods who presided over the fates of mankind bore a sense of mischievous irony. Were they laughing even now, those dark gods, as they watched this prodigal son wing his way home, mysteriously summoned by the very brother who had cast him out so long ago?

The smile upon Griffin's lips faded as he reached into the pocket of his gold-embroidered waistcoat to finger a stiff edge of vellum, its broken wax seal still dangling along its edges. Despite the darkness he could picture the precise script that flowed from the pen of his brother and the lion saliant crest that had graced the seal of the dukes of Graymore since Richard III. The Duke of Graymore's last will and testament.

Griff felt a dull twist of grief mingled with the disbelief that had tormented him since he had broken the letter's seal.

William. Griff closed his eyes, his mind filling with images of pale brown curls crushed into obedience beneath stern brushings, solemn eyes and shoulders that had seemed to bear the weight of the world. Until . . .

Until death had reached down its merciless hand and swept up the one person Griffin Stone thought to be invincible.

William, the strong, the ever-sensible. The elder brother who had dragged Griffin out of a score of childhood scrapes. William, who had stalked the length of his study at Darkling Moor that night ten years ago, furious, frustrated, yet strangely broken as he banished Griffin from England.

Griff had hated him then, as William had let loose anger pent up over the years.

"You fool! You cursed fool!" Griff could still hear William storm. "Do you not see what you have done? You've ruined your life over a woman you won't even remember in a year! A harlot who has served as mistress to half of George's court—"

Griff winced at the memory of how he had lunged for his sword hilt, seething with fury. "You'll not insult Elise. I've killed one man on her behalf! Another will scarce make a difference!"

"Oh, yes, your grand duel!" William had laughed sickly as he forced Griffin's sword back into its scabbard. "Your grand and glorious duel. Her husband! You killed her husband! An old man—"

"Who abused her! He struck her, and—"

"While she was out dangling after a train of green pups such as you? I only wish Sir Lionel had struck her before she infected you with her poison! But it is too late now. Too late, Griff. Sir Lionel is dead, and this time there is nothing I can do to save you from yourself."

"Bloody pompous bastard!" Even now, ten years later, the hasty words seared Griffin with regret. "What would you know of a man's passions? Your blood runs so cold, it is a miracle you got an heir at all! And as for me . . . as for Elise . . . I will remember her forever! Forever!"

"Then I pity you, Griff." William had turned away, and Griffin had detected the slightest catch in his brother's voice. "For Elise Devanne has forgotten you already . . ."

Griffin swore under his breath now, raking his long fingers through unruly locks that were dark as sin. He wished he could scatter the shades of the past, drive back the hauntings of his words and his cursed stupidity. But the shadows would not be banished, and the gnawings of remorse ate away inside him.

If only he'd been able to tell his brother that he was right. Elise Devanne's fading beauty had vanished from his mind almost the first moment he had stepped upon the raw, bustling shores of Virginia. In his ignorance Griff had thought never to feel joy again, but hope and renewal had seemed to bubble like a spring within the virgin lands. The New World had held the kind of adventure Griffin had always craved.

He'd soon understood the wisdom of his brother's harsh words. Yet it had been far more difficult to admit the truth to William himself. And now it was impossible.

"I intended to do it . . . meant to . . ." Griffin spoke the words aloud. "Christ, where did the time go? Ten bloody years!"

His heavy dark brows slashed low over his aristocratic nose, his sensual lips compressing in a pale line. "Yes, and because of my accursed pride it is now too late."

Iron bands seemed to crush Griffin's chest, and his throat felt thick. He had been stunned by the news of his brother's accident, but he was even more dazed when he learned that the wise, cautious William had entrusted all that he owned to Griff's hands.

Control of all my estates and guardianship of my son and heir, Charles Edward Arthur Stone, I leave in trust to my beloved brother. . . .

Beloved brother? Bedeviling brother, perhaps. Infuriating brother. Scoundrel brother. That was all Griffin had ever been to William—tormenting him, teasing him, and defying him at every turn, until even William's formidable store of patience had soured.

Griffin peered up at the silvery moon, which seemed distant and chill this night. Maybe things had not needed to come to such a pass. If things had been different.

But their fates had been written the day their father had been killed in a duel. That day every one of their indulgent, adoring servants had been swept away by the indomitable lady who had come to take the two Stone boys in hand—Lady Judith Stone, dowager duchess of Graymore, a lady of such awesome will it seemed that even the towers of Darkling Moor bowed down before her.

She had descended upon the halls she had once ruled, driving out every vestige of her pleasure-loving son and his gentle, long-dead wife. Like a general she had mustered her own troops about her, intent upon crushing any rebellion mounted by her grandsons.

"You are the heirs of Edward Stone," she had told the two children, her gray eyes boring into their round faces. "The blood of royalty courses through your veins. And you will take the name of Stone out from the gutters into which your father flung it and hold it up as a shining example of honor and nobility, if I must crush you within an inch of your life to see that you do."

Griff's mouth curved into a grim smile as the gray-tressed martinet's image rose in his mind. She had managed to bring William to heel almost immediately, bending him to her will with her diatribes about duty, layering him with guilt and more than a little self-importance.

But in Griffin even the daunting Lady Judith had met her match. She had endeavored to break his will through countless thrashings and punishments, but all she had managed to do was to fray her own nerves to the snapping point, while Griffin continued to be not the scion of the nobility his grandmother had desired, but rather the wastrel duke's son in face, form, and spirit.

Griffin braced one long, booted leg against the chaise's floorboard as the vehicle jolted over a particularly deep rut in the road. If there was one pleasure in this bittersweet homecoming, it would be seeing Judith Stone's expression when he strode into Darkling Moor, trustee of the grand house and newly appointed guardian of the noble name Stone.

She had tried to sever the bond between the brothers with her meddling, and Griffin had let his love for William wither under the weight of his pride. But his final gift to William would be to honor the bond they had once shared.

He arched his head back against the squabs. He was a far different man than when he'd left. His cheekbones slashed in hard bronzed planes to a patrician nose, heavy dark brows shadowing eyes stunning in their intensity. It was his father's face, a bewitching mixture of raw masculinity and bedeviling amusement. In many ways his face held the strong lines of Lady Judith's own.

His return would be the woman's worst nightmare come real—Griffin snatching the heir to Graymore from her clutches. Griff struggled to picture Charles Stone as he must be now—his chest thin, his cheeks shadowed with a sparse beard. A boy yet a man at nineteen, no longer the imp with huge brown eyes Griffin had bid farewell to that long-ago day in the east meadow.

Griff had knelt before the quiet, frail child, Charles's too-pale lips quivering with tears he was trying manfully to stem.

"Don't go, Uncle Griffin," Charles had sniffled. "Please don't. Grandma and Father—they'll never let me run in the fields or swim in the stream if you go away."

"I have to, little man," Griffin had said, hating the pain in the child's innocent face. "Something . . . something happened, and . . ." He surrendered to the futility of explaining dueling, jealousy, death to the child. He said only, "I'm counting on you to be strong. Steal away to the stream if you want to. Be yourself, Charles. Don't let them own you like the manor houses or the hedgerows. Don't let them carve you into some stodgy statue to deck their accursed gallery."

The child had stared at Griffin, eyes solemn with promise. "Won't. Won't let them make me into marble."

Griffin had given the boy a ring carved in the shape of the mythical creature he himself had been named for. His throat rough with enotion, he thrust it on the child's middle finger.

"I cannot . . . cannot take it," Charles had managed between hiccups. "It's your favorite."

"This way you'll not forget me, boy."

"I could never forget you!" The child had flung himself into Griffin's arms. And when Griffin finally walked away he felt as though he'd left behind a piece of his heart.

Griff reached down to where a bundle of his most treasured possessions lay upon the chaise's floor: A quillion inlaid with rubies protruded from the carpetbag's end. A sword, formed in Toledo, would be a fitting gift for the man Griffin hoped his nephew Charles had become.

Soon Griff would know—would see whether Lady Judith had worked her will upon the boy. God knew she had broken far stronger spirits than Charles Stone's. But her reign over Darkling Moor would soon be over. And even Griffin's would be but a short one.

In two years Charles would reach his majority, but Griffin had no intention of languishing about Darkling Moor that long. He would set the estate's affairs in order, then engage someone trustworthy and eminently suitable to tend things in his absence—maybe Tom Southwood, the boyhood comrade Griff had run wild with in the streets of London. The friend who had married respectably and still kept up with Griff through yearly letters filled with the news of England. And then, once those arrangements were finalized, Griff would leave England and the vast Stone fortunes for good.

Griff's jaw clenched, his eyes hardening. It was what he wanted after all, was it not? What he had always wanted? To be free of the yoke that revered name had placed upon him? It was infinitely sensible, entrusting the estates to someone levelheaded and responsible. Someone already in England. So reasonable that William himself should have made the arrangements. Why then had the unerringly sensible William summoned Griffin home? Had he sensed death's dark horse riding toward him?

A chill trickled down Griffin's nape, the cloak tossed carelessly over his greatcoat failing to deflect the cold night wind that wisped through the chaise's window. He had heard of premonitions in men's dreams, but he had never given credence to such tales. And William was even less superstitious than he.

It was impossible that William had suspected he would meet his death. Impossible.

Shadows sucked the chaise deeper into darkness. The light of the moon now scarcely reached through the trees. Even the wind seemed colder. Griffin stared out into the mist-shrouded landscape. Even after ten years' absence he recognized the strip of land.

Rogue's Row.

He remembered the spindly postilion's voice as he described the perilous stretch of road. Griff recalled that the man had fought mightily to dissuade him from traveling through the night woods, his own terror evident in his shaking fingers and round, bobbly eyes. "It is a devilish evil place, your lordship," he had warned, "filled with haunts of the men murdered there, and the brigands who cut 'em down. Dark as a grave it be, and ye'll be buried there within it if you dare to cross."

Griffin jammed his foot against the floorboard, levering himself upright as he drove the man's fearful ravings from his mind.

"Yes," he said aloud. "That is what I need to chase these maudlin thoughts away. Some daring knight of the road to try my skill against."

His grin widened. A brigand . . . yes, that would prove a diversion. Some devil borne of night, all swashbuckling courage and elegant manners, armed with a pistol or sword. Griffin leaned forward in his seat with a prickling of anticipation.

His fingers brushed the jeweled hilt of his own sword lovingly. Ah, England! The one thing the colonies lacked was brigands with a brilliant splash of style.

Griff started to lean back after a moment when suddenly the world seemed to explode.

Tavish shrieked; the blunderbuss thundered. The horses plunged, and the coach pitched wildly as another weapon blazed orange against the darkness. The chaise lurched one more time, wood splintering as a pistol ball found its mark, the wheels grating sickeningly to a halt.

Griff stared for a moment in disbelief. Then a slow smile spread across his features. A moment later, he lunged for his sword, his hard laughter echoing through the night, laughter that had chilled the blood of countless adversaries who had seen death dancing upon the shining point of Griffin Stone's blade.

Chapter Three

The waiting was always agony for Beau, but Owen Maguire's presence honed even that exquisite torment into a torture worthy of the Spanish Inquisition. Beau gritted her teeth, running a soothing hand down her stallion's glossy neck as she glared at the boy beside her.

His lanky frame sat awkwardly upon a horse too spirited by half, his face so greedy for excitement that Beau doubted that even a cudgel could drive caution into his thick skull. Yet her palms fair itched for a smooth length of wood with which to try it.

"It is no game we play here," she whispered, echoing Molly's words of earlier that day. "This night's success, our very lives, depend—"

"I know, I know!" Owen's impatience rippled through his voice as he fondled the shiny new pistol Beau had given him. "My ears are numb with your instructions! We ride down upon the coach. I block the road and hold the drivers at bay while you get the fun of slitting the passenger's purse-strings."

Owen leveled his weapon at an imaginary target, mimicking a soft popping sound as he pretended to squeeze off a shot. "Take that, you rich scum," he said. "Your purse at once, else I blow your blasted head off."

"The only thing you are going to blast," Beau snapped, "is this raiding, if you don't leash yourself! There will be no shootings. No killing. The Devil's Flame—"

"Never takes a life," Owen trilled in a sing song voice. "Well, I don't know why. You might as well shoot the aristocrat curs! It will be hanging for us whether we kill 'em or not, and they can serve as witnesses against us if they live."

"They'll not have to serve witness against you," Beau ground out, "for I'll drive a pistol ball through you myself!" She tried to calm herself so that she might reason with the willful boy. "Owen—"

"I'll fare all right, Beau. Truly," he said. But a moment later his eagerness burst through again. "Was there ever such a night? With the wind and the darkness? And my pistol, it gleams—"

Beau sighed, taunted by the memory of her own sense of invincibility on her first night—that wondrous sense of power, adventure that had raced through her veins like the headiest of wines.

Yet in the time that had passed since that first night even *she* had learned to face a night ride with caution.

A bead of sweat trickled down Beau's neck; the mask covering her face felt stifling as it blocked out the night breeze. "Owen," she said, "I am trusting you. Putting my fate in your hands, even as you are doing the same with me. There is no room for arrogance, no—"

The words suddenly stilled, Owen's long-suffering sigh cut off. "Beau, look!" the boy gasped. His arm flashed out, his horse skittering sideways at the sudden movement.

Beau glimpsed a bobbing point of light racing toward them from the road below, heard the pounding of hooves as four dark horses thundered along the rutted ribbon of earth. Close. The equipage was too close, moving too fast . . . but there was no knowing whether another unwary traveler would happen along this night. And unless they snagged a purse, Molly would again be at old Nell's mercy.

"Now!" Beau drove her heels into her stallion's sides. In that instant the image of Owen's face seared into Beau's mind—the boy's bravado and arrogance had vanished, leaving behind the peaked countenance of a frightened child. Wrong, it was all wrong—the certainty spiraled through her as she fought the horrible sinking sensation in her stomach. But it was too late to do anything but pray things came aright as her pistol blazed fire.

She clutched the reins of her stallion as it hurtled down toward their prey, her own tension mirrored in her mount's sweat-sheened muscles as she struggled to jam her spent pistol into her high-top boot. Her other pistol was inches from her hand as she reined the spirited black MacBeth toward the oncoming coach. The sound of Owen's horse charging awkwardly behind her drummed dread through her veins, but Dame Fortune seemed to be with them, and one of the chaise's team swerved, its traces splintering. The coach would have to stop.

Even as she felt the familiar surge of triumph it turned brassy with doubt as she caught a blur of Owen and his ill-controlled beast charging wild within the narrow strip of road, driving the coach-horses into renewed frenzies. A wail of alarm breached the youth's lips as he failed to catch up the lead horse's bridle, failed even to hold his own mount in check. The reins slithered from his grasp to trail perilously upon the ground.

Beau wheeled MacBeth in a tight circle, fighting to control the situation. But Owen's fear-crazed mount and the postilion's shriekings were driving even her well-schooled stallion to restiveness.

With an oath Beau yanked back upon MacBeth's reins, hating the roughness she was forced to use, yet hating more the unfamiliar sting of panic she felt.

"Hold!" In a guttural voice she bellowed the command, ripping her other pistol free, but the coachman and postilion had already sprung from their seats and were dashing into the dense vegetation beyond.

"I—I'll stop them!" Owen screamed. "Shoot—"

"No! Don't—" Beau flung her arm to deflect the boy's

pistol, but she was too late. The leaden ball whizzed directly over Owen's mount's head, winging one bay ear.

Wild-eyed, the gelding reared, crashing into MacBeth with bone-jarring force. Beau battled to cling to the horse's back and felt her own weapon flying free as MacBeth crashed into the chaise's curved side. The wood tore at her breeches, battered her thigh. Pain streaked up one leg, yet she managed to hold on.

Just as she was righting herself Owen's horse charged beneath MacBeth's nose in a crazed flight to the woods.

MacBeth reared in fury, kicking out with massive hooves as Owen's gelding raced by. For an instant Beau feared MacBeth would crash to the ground, so wild was his panic. She felt her beloved stallion struggle for balance, felt her knees tearing free of the saddle. The reins burned her gloved hands as the leather whipped from her fingers.

She cried out, fighting to grasp something, anything, and failed. She slammed into the hard-packed earth with a force that drove the breath from her lungs. Her head spun as she struggled to cling to consciousness.

As though from a distance she heard what could only be the coach's door being flung open.

Beau shook her head, trying desperately to clear it, as she scrambled toward the underbrush. But she had not even managed to reach the side of the road before something hard and heavy pinned her to the earth.

Beau gritted her teeth against the pain. A sudden awful stillness engulfed the clearing. By force of will she turned to face her assailant.

Moonlight glinted upon a glossy boot, planted firmly upon the folds of her cloak. Polished leather clung to a well-muscled calf, the boot then giving way to breeches that molded perfectly to thighs honed to a hardness to be found only in the most excellent of riders. Beau's gaze flew upward past a flat stomach and massive chest to shoulders so broad they seemed to dwarf her with their power. Then her eyes locked upon a slash of white in the darkness—a sinister, terrifying flash of teeth framed within a smile as grim as the pair of unsheathed swords clasped in the man's hands

—swords that were pointed almost carelessly at Beau's chest.

"Leaving our little fete so soon, Sir Rogue?" The voice sliced through Beau's courage. "I would be devastated if you were to trundle off to whatever nest of thieves has spawned you bearing the tale that Lord Griffin Stone had proved a poor host."

"Stone . . ." The memory of the *Spectator's* tale spun about Beau as she repeated his name in a husky voice. She cringed inwardly, recalling the gruesome tally of deaths accredited to this man's blade, but she clung to defiance. "Go to the devil!"

Moonlight gilded his rich, dark hair; the dim light from the chaise's lamps lit the planes of the notorious rake's face. Beau stared, frozen, her heart thundering in her breast as she braced herself for the death-thrust she knew would come. But the accursed nobleman only stood there, his eyes glittering, a low, deep laugh emanating from his chest.

"It seems, my friend, that you already attempted to dispatch me to Hades but moments ago. Tried and, I must add, failed—most regrettably for you."

Beau cast a fleeting glance toward the break in the woods where the horses had bolted. Perhaps Owen even now was riding to her aid. But that thought brought renewed despair. The inept fool was most likely halfway to London by now.

"Go to hell," she blazed at her assailant.

"Temper, temper! Your language is most appalling, even for one of your occupation. Here I have been longing to clash with an honorable English blackguard, have been pining for the . . . *elegance* . . . the knights of the road possess, and you sprawl there, swearing like a fishmonger. It is most disconcerting."

"Disconcerting?" Beau burst out, trying to rip her cloak from beneath his boot. "I'll bloody *disconcert* you, if you'll let me the blazes up."

The man swept her a courtly bow, removing his boot from her garment as if he had not known it was there.

"How clumsy of me," he said, again leveling a gleaming blade at Beau's throat. "I most humbly beg your pardon."

Heedless of the weapon, Beau scrambled to her feet and planted her hands upon her hips as she faced him. "You can beg pardon until you turn purple, and I'll not forgive—"

"Forgive me for witnessing a grand rogue like you bumbling about like some fair-day jester? I must admit that, were the tables turned, I would be most ashamed."

"The Devil's Flame does not play jester!" Beau spat, groping desperately for some way to fend off this daunting nobleman's attack. She grasped one wild, reckless hope. "I warn you," she snarled in her most frightening tone, "a dozen of my men wait to swoop down upon you. Even now their pistols are leveled at your cowardly belly. I have but to give the word—"

The nobleman's grin grew wider, and Beau fought the urge to slam her fist into that arrogant face.

"Then by all means do so, Sir Flame," Stone urged. "Call down your wolves upon me. I shall attempt to shore up what flagging courage I possess to meet this blood-crazed horde."

Beau felt tears of frustration sting her eyes. This man was exposing her as a fool. One mocking, dark brow arched up, the low, despicable chuckle again rippling from that broad chest. "What? You are too merciful to consign me to your cohorts' fury? I must protest your goodness of heart." His voice boomed. "Men of the Devil's Flame, I hold your leader at bay. Though I tremble in my boots, I have no choice but to suffer your wrath . . . musket balls, swords, whatever you hold available."

Beau longed to drive those bright, white teeth of his down his aristocratic throat.

"Shut up, you bloody bastard! You—"

"Still your tongue!" One of the sword points jabbed closer and a tiny, stinging cut burned upon the soft flesh of Beau's throat. She skittered back a bit, staring at the man as though he had gone mad.

"Brigands, you may commence! Or is it that your leader is not worth the precious lead in your pistols?"

Beau gritted her teeth in fury, her face burning with humiliation. Despite the peril, she could no longer bear being made to look like an idiot. "Maybe they're chasing your cowardly servants," she said.

"Ah, I see." The nobleman's mocking grin made Beau squirm. "This army of brigands hied off through the woods after my scrawny postilion and half-drunken driver. What riches they might discover this night! Filthy breeches and a flask of Blue Ruin."

"Maybe they've already caught them. Maybe they're riding here even now."

"And maybe the earth is going to split and send you skidding into hell for lying." Lord Griffin made a *tsk*ing sound in his throat.

"No man makes a fool of me and—"

"I am quite sure *that* statement is truth. But then, you need no one to aid you in making *yourself* look the fool."

The combination of Stone's sneerings and Beau's own raw pride made her take a step toward him, eyes blazing. "If you were half a man, I'd—"

"You'd what? Blast me into eternity? Pierce my black heart with a sword thrust?" Lord Griffin shook his head with feigned regret. "Ah, I know!" His eyes shone with hard amusement. "*Gentleman* that you are, you would demand satisfaction. Very well. I believe, then, it is proper etiquette that I choose the weapons."

"I don't want any bloody satisfaction! I'm not an infernal gentleman, and your *etiquette* can go—"

"Swords." Lord Griffin said as if he had truly been mulling it over in his mind.

"Swords?" Beau gasped, taking a step backward.

"Accept? Most civil of you."

"No. I most certainly do not! I—"

Stone cocked his head at a dismissive angle, his sensual lips pulling into a sneer, his voice silky soft. "What ails you, Flame? Does a coward lurk beneath that mask?"

Beau seethed, uncertain as to whether it was raw terror or blind fury turning her blood to fire. Her temper flashed like the powder pan of her pistol, all caution and wisdom seared away in that single instant. "I be no coward! I think it only fair to warn you that my skill is notorious throughout England."

"Then prove it." Mocking laughter jabbed at Beau's nerves. Stone's dark eyes glinted as his gloved hand swept out, dropping one of the swords to the ground.

"This weapon is to be a gift for my nephew," Stone said. "Think how much more the boy will treasure it when he hears it was wielded by such a dread swordsman as the Devil's Flame."

Dread swordsman? A wild little laugh bubbled in Beau's breast as she glanced down at the weapon that shone eerie blue in the lantern light. Dreadful, maybe!

She felt a momentary twinge as she realized the weapon's worth, and that she'd not live long enough to steal it.

But as she raised her eyes from the jeweled hilt to the unyielding face of her tormenter all thought fled, her stomach pitching.

"Take it." His voice was unsheathed steel, his eyes piercing hers. "This time, milord rogue, you will fight face to face, like a man, rather than skulking about in the shadows."

The shadows . . . Beau glanced at the inky poolings beside the road, her heart pounding. If she could fight this pompous oaf, hold him off long enough to reach the edge of the woods, she might manage to escape. She was fast, agile, and she could find her way through the night with the uncanny skill of a cat. Maybe she could melt into the darkness, slip away.

Slowly, so slowly, Beau reached down, her fingers feeling chilled as they brushed against the metal hilt. "Very well, milord," she said as her hand closed about the weapon. "Prepare to die."

She scooped up the sword, astonished at its weight as she flung it up in an awkward swipe. Her clumsy action caught her other hand, and the razor-honed blade cut a stinging slice in her skin. She bit her lip to stop from crying out. Lord Stone now stood in a swordsman's pose with the innate grace of a stalking panther. Beau's eyes fixed in horrified awe upon the sword point, which was flashing against the night like a will-o'-the-wisp.

A master. Beau felt her heart turn to a hard lump of ice in her chest. She had seen Jack often enough at his practice to know skill when she saw it.

Her palm slickened with sweat, and she felt the terror of a rabbit in the jaws of a cat. A cat who would torment its prey until it became bored with the creature's struggles and close in for the kill.

"Are you certain you wish to cast yourself into such foolery?" Beau tried one last time to brazen it out. "Considering the rare courage you have shown, I might even be willing to allow you safe passage."

Those intense eyes seemed to strip away every veil she possessed, giving her the sensation of standing naked, vulnerable before this daunting man. "I would not think of so imposing upon your generosity." The deep, velvet tones drove into Beau's stomach as the man sketched her a bow. Her final effort had failed miserably.

Boldly she clutched the sword hilt, the fierce pride of the daughter of Six Coach Robb pulsing through her, her mouth settling into a grim smile that would have made her father proud.

Beau raised her weapon in a tolerable imitation of Jack facing an opponent. *"En garde."*

Griffin Stone raised his sword in a graceful salute, flexing his wide shoulders as if to loosen them. His whole body seemed fluid, like quicksilver, dangerous, mesmerizing. His hair fell in glossy waves, rich as chestnut above the arrogant planes of his aristocratic face.

Beau struggled to remember something, anything Jack had said those long ago days when he had tried to teach her swordsmanship, but her mind was empty. She would have no choice but to draw upon her own wits. Jaw thrust out with resolve, Beau sent one more longing glance at the woods, then met Griffin Stone's gaze with a hard one of her own.

She tensed, then made a wild lunge at Stone's flat belly with her blade, but the nobleman merely danced out of her way, deflecting the steely point easily. Set off balance, she stumbled, her nose slamming hard into the nobleman's breastbone.

Her eyes smarted, blurred with stinging tears, but instead of ramming his advantage home the nobleman flashed a hand out instinctively to steady her.

"Ah, now I see the source of your . . . *generosity,* milord Flame. A swordmaster?" She saw his brow rise archly, sensed the twinkle in his eyes. "Methinks you should have found yourself a more apt teacher."

"Bastard!" Beau grated. "Scurvy bastard!" She tried to clear her befuddled head as she skittered away from her tormenter, but Stone's blade flashed out, relentless, its point sweeping but a whisper from Beau's throat. She expected to feel it burn a path across her skin, expected the rush of blood, but she heard only the subtle ripping of fabric, felt the swirling folds of her mantle slip from her shoulders as Stone slashed its fastenings free.

The night wind bit her skin through its shielding of waistcoat and linen shirt, but the trembling of Beau's hand had nothing to do with the sudden chill.

"It will be easier by far to fight without that monstrosity encumbering you," Lord Griffin advised with a sageness that made Beau half mad with fury. "Consider it your first lesson."

". . . Don't need . . . your bloody . . . lessons. . . ." Beau's breath caught in short gasps as she attempted to break through the man's guard, Stone easily blocking every thrust. Beau hated him. Her mask stuck to her face, plastered to her skin with sweat, while Lord Griffin appeared completely unruffled.

"Oh, but I fear that you are in sad need of instruction," he taunted her. "You hold your blade like a crofter wielding a scythe—no, that comparison would do injustice to the crofter."

Beau slashed with her sword, the weapon nearly flying from her fingers in her zeal to draw blood. "Amazed . . . popinjay like you . . . knows what a scythe . . . is. Honest labor . . ."

"Like yours, milord Flame?" The nobleman's blade struck again, Beau's neckcloth dropping free, the froth of lace tumbling to ensnare her fingers. She ripped it away with her other hand, the delicate webbing tearing upon the jeweled hilt.

Beau's breath caught, her heart threatening to beat its way from her chest as she retreated. Fear bounded within her as she tried to blot out what would happen when Griffin Stone at last turned the full force of his expertise upon her.

"Thievery . . ." Beau challenged, "more honest . . . than having gold showered on . . . from birth." She thrust, parried with increasing grimness. "Bleeding dry . . . common folk . . ."

Lord Griffin winced as though her blade had struck some part of his iron-honed body. "And you?" There was real anger in the man's voice now, enough to make Beau flinch. He dashed his sword against hers in a bone-jarring blow. "I suppose that you rob only from the rich, eh, Robin of the Hood? Do you shower your booty like largess upon the starving masses?"

Molly Maguire's face flashed across Beau's mind, the sick feeling in her stomach deepening as she scrambled back toward the encroaching underbrush.

"Do . . . what I have . . . to do . . . to . . . survive. . . ." Her arm was so weakened by his powerful blows that it trembled, the muscles feeling as though they might snap.

"That is what is in question, my fine Flame, is it not? Survival? How many innocents have you murdered on this road? How many—"

"I've killed no one!" Beau blazed, despite her fatigue.

"How does it feel to be the one on the other end of the sword?" Griffin Stone's voice was suddenly as cold as a fresh-dug grave.

She cried out, wheeling in a futile effort to shield herself as his sword flashed, but the weight of her weapon made her stagger, and the fabric of her shirt gave with a sickening sound.

She heard Stone swear in surprise, felt him yank his blade away in what seemed an effort to spare her, but it was too late.

Agony exploded in her left shoulder. She gritted her teeth against a scream, the black robes of unconsciousness swirling about her like a shroud.

Chapter Four

"Blast! You bloody fool!" Griffin bit out an oath. Stunned, he yanked free his weapon, casting it aside in one fluid movement as he instinctively attempted to break the highwayman's fall. "Damn you, I didn't mean to—"

To kill him? A voice echoed in Griffin's head. What the devil were you planning to do? Escort him to Darkling Moor to pilfer the silverplate?

Griffin lowered the limp figure gently to the turf, furious with himself for his sudden surge of conscience.

In truth, he *had* planned to dispatch the villain—when it pleased him—after a contest of skill and daring. The rogue deserved to die. He had most likely dealt death to others. Griffin had meant to clear the highroads of one more scoundrel.

Yet once he had seen the brigand's awkwardness, sensed his desperation, any thirst for the kill had palled, replaced by a raw sense of mischief and the undeniable desire to prick the bumbling rogue's pride.

Griffin had just meant to toy with him, teach him a lesson, when suddenly the witling had all but flung himself onto Griff's sword. Why? God's teeth, he had only slashed open the thief's shirt!

His mouth thinning in aggravation, Griffin hastily yanked off his own neckcloth and pressed the white fabric against the wound. Disbelief jolted through him as his palm compressed not the hard, flat plane of muscle that sheathed a masculine chest, but rather a welling softness.

No!

His gaze flashed down, his hand closing roughly on the fabric of the mask, ripping it away from the highwayman's face.

What he saw smothered him in waves of horror. In the moonlight the felon's features were achingly fragile, childlike, framed in a fall of vivid red hair. Her thick lashes were pillowed upon ashen cheeks, while full lips swelled beneath an arrogant little nose.

A woman.

Sweet Christ, he had almost killed a woman.

Griffin reeled inwardly.

"Don't die, damn you!" he railed at the figure who suddenly seemed devastatingly small. "Curse you, don't die!"

His gaze flashed to the coach-horses, who were hopelessly entangled in their harness. Frustration drove him half mad. It was but a small wound, but God knew it could prove lethal.

At that moment Griffin heard a rustling in the woodland nearby. "Damn your eyes, Adley, Tavish! If that's you, get your carcasses out here before I murder you myself!" The rustling stilled, and Griff's impatience fired hotter. "And if you're one of the Flame's men, show yourself before your leader spills the last of her blood upon the ground. Blast you—"

His words were cut off by the sound of a soft whicker, his eyes catching the intelligent gleam of an equine eye within a night-black face. The horse stepped from the sheltering woods, and in the glow of the lantern light Griffin recognized it as the magnificent beast the girl had ridden.

"It's all right, boy," Griff said in a soothing voice. "All right."

The stallion took a tentative step forward, then another, shaking his massive head as if in warning.

"Please," Griffin whispered to some unseen deity. Slowly he reached toward one trailing rein, knowing that if the horse shied, the girl's life could be in peril. And, blast her, this girl was going to live. Live long enough for Griff to shake her until her teeth rattled.

The powerful beast eyed the stranger warily, its ears flattening, head tossing. But before it could dance out of reach Griffin's hand swept out, clutching at the thin leather strap. And at the most fragile of hopes.

The inn room reeked of lye. The bandy-legged surgeon bent over the lumpy bed, scowling at Griffin, his bushy brows meeting over a bulbous nose.

"*Do* something, curse you!" Griffin entreated. "There must be more you can do." His eyes locked upon the girl's waxen face, her features seeming heartrendingly fragile, wreathed as they were in the riotous fall of flame-hued hair spilling across the pillows. "She looks so small . . . weak . . ."

"She's a damned sight stronger than you give her credit for. Tough as a Barbary mare, in spite of her size. And the wound, I vow to you, it is scarce a scratch—"

"A scratch?" Griff burst out. "I carried her here on my saddle, holding my hand over the cursed wound. She was bleeding. . . ." His fingers clenched as he recalled the sticky wetness beneath his palm, the moans of pain that had grown softer, weaker with each mile. He half believed the reason she'd survived was because he had raged at her foolishness throughout their flight through the woods.

"I vow to you she'll be hale before the week is out," the physician said calmly. "I have stitched the wound, poulticed it. The only other treatment I might prescribe would be bloodletting. But that would seem redundant." He waved one hand toward the stained cloth at the end of the bed.

Griff's stomach lurched as he thought of the grim treatment—the lancet gleaming, the bowl beneath filling with the dark flow of crimson. "Maybe it would help her . . . a bleeding . . ." Griff jammed his fingers through unruly hair, hating the desperation in his voice.

"More likely it would finish the job that sword-thrust started." There was cold challenge in the physician's voice, and the older man's eyes bored into Griff's. "Would you like that, sir? To watch her bleed?"

Bile rose in Griffin's throat. "Of course not! You sick bastard! I brought her here for you to heal!"

"So you did." The physician maneuvered himself between Griffin and the girl. "A most singular affair, is it not? A grand personage like yourself—traveling alone, no less—taking a wounded waif to your bosom?"

"Contrary to what the masses believe, there are those of us among the aristocracy who do not trample babes beneath our feet!"

"And there are also those among you who see them as nothing but fodder for your twisted, brutal games."

Griffin frowned at the man's unyielding expression; the physician was bristling up like a bantam rooster. Griff had the unsettling sensation that he had just stumbled into an unfamiliar theater during the third act of a play.

"Baronet, duke, whoever you may be," the medical man continued, "I warn you that I will not stand by and watch another poor lass crushed."

"Another?" Griff shook his head. Outrage and confusion were roiling through him. For some reason the physician was taking a very real risk, verbally sparring with a peer of the realm. In spite of himself, Griff felt a sharp tug of respect for the surgeon.

"Do you think I'd do the chit harm?" Griff peered down into her ashen face, surprised by his desire to skim his fingers across her blaze-red curls. "She has nothing of value to recommend her, and if you fear I would take her as mistress, I assure you even *I* am not desperate enough to bed women who thrust pistols in—" Griff cut off the words.

"Pistols?"

"It is nothing. We just met upon the road, and had an, er, difference of opinion as to who should serve as keeper of my purse." Griff squirmed beneath the weight of the older man's gaze. "I didn't mean to hurt her," Griff bit out defensively. "Didn't even know she was a blasted woman." Outrage over the brigand's duplicity surged through him afresh. "You cannot let her die before I have the chance to thrash the very devil out of her for what she has put me through!"

The corners of the physician's mouth twitched, and suddenly the dour old man surrendered to a bark of laughter. "So the girl . . . and your lordship . . ."

Griffin ran a finger beneath the neck-edging of his shirt, the garment suddenly seeming too tight. "It was not the most uneventful journey I've ever experienced. Suffice it to say that I'll be bloody glad to get back to the colonies, where women are *civilized.*"

"The colonies? Ah, you must be the Lord Stone we've been reading about of late. Gone these ten years." All the hostility drained from the man's red-flushed face. "My condolences upon your brother's death. He was a good man." The physician turned away. "And there are few enough of them left about."

Grief stirred deep in Griffin's chest.

"Things are different hereabouts since you left, my lord," the doctor went on in a low voice. "Different. And of late"—Haversham shuddered visibly—"being a physician, I've seen the ugliness."

"I don't understand."

"You will, I fear. And it'll wrench your stomach inside out when you do. Forgive me for blazing at you about the girl. It is just that there be something astir with some of the grand swells hereabouts."

"Astir? What do you mean?"

"Some sort of hocus-pocus, nonsensical thing. Thought it harmless enough. But I've buried two waifs the like of this child the three months past. And God knows how many more lie waiting to be discovered."

"I'm sorry." Instinctively Griff knew the man felt loss at those deaths.

The old man shrugged. "Of course, it has nothing to do

with your lordship," he said. "But it makes one wary, I vow, after you've seen . . ."

Haversham paced to the bed, smoothing one blue-veined hand over the girl's pale cheek as if to assure himself that she was alive. "My youngest, she is just this age. Off and married a sea captain from Cornwall, has a cottageful of wee ones. Every time I look at a lass thus, helpless, hurt, I see my Rachel. And since this new scourge has beset us my nightmares are filled with her face."

"It is hard, I know. But rest assured, good Haversham, this girl is safe from whatever perils you are tilting with. And as for her being helpless . . ." Griffin smiled at the thought of the Devil's Flame hurtling down upon the chaise, pistols blazing, cape flowing. "I promise you she is more skillful with her talons than a falcon." His last lingering fear for her eased as he recalled the girl's bravado, the flash in her eyes.

"You will see to her then, my lord?"

"I should turn her over to Bow Street."

"Aye, sir." The doctor slipped his instruments into his bag, his lips crooking into a grin. "Methinks you'll wish you had before you've done with her. Rachel has red tresses as well, and her temper—"

"I've already run afoul of this lady's temper, and I have never yet come up against a woman I could not bend to my will."

The doctor glanced up, his face alight with a knowledge that made Griffin uncomfortable. Haversham was not laughing at him, but from the glint in the surgeon's eyes he might as well have been. "I would advise you to keep your sword close at hand," he said with barely suppressed amusement. "I am surprised that the girl is not awake already. And when she does awake—"

"When she does she will have plenty to answer for," Griff said, his tone hardening with resolve as he peered again at the woman's pale face. Her lips were the hue of ice-frosted roses, and she moaned softly. He burned afresh at the knowledge that he, Griffin Stone, had cut down this delicate waif.

"She will recover? You are certain?" he asked.

"As certain as one can ever be in such cases." The man bustled over to the table upon which he'd set his bag. "If you need me, you've but to send word. Mr. Quimby, here at the inn, knows how to reach me." Haversham started toward the door.

"I nearly killed her," Griff said softly, his gaze resting upon the shallow rise and fall of her breasts beneath the thin sheet.

"No." Haversham's gravelly voice broke through his musings. "You spared her life. Most men would have left her to die upon the road."

Griff shuddered inwardly at the image the surgeon's words invoked—that supple body still forever, the lips that had hurled defiance at him stiff, cold.

He looked at her rich lashes, which fanned upon porcelain-smooth cheeks, a pale hand gripping the coverlet as if, even in unconsciousness, she needed something to cling to. She shifted, restless as a babe, and the sight wrenched at something deep inside Griff.

The old doctor cleared his throat, and Griff was astonished to find the man was still in the room. "Farewell, Lord Stone. Methinks you are not half the heartless rogue the *Spectator* would have us believe."

Griffin gave a rumbling laugh, the sound raw in his throat. "If you have any doubts regarding the fact that I'm reprehensible, you need but converse with my grandmother."

When the doctor finally left, the chamber suddenly seemed achingly empty, quiet. In an effort to drive away the prickings of guilt, Griffin ordered up the innkeeper's finest port.

Later, tankard in hand, he sank down upon a hard oak chair, his long legs stretched out before him. His boot soles pressed upon the edge of the bed as he tipped the chair backward at an angle, his dark head resting against the wall. He sighed, sipping the drink slowly, watching the girl's face as the first rose-shaded ribbons of dawn unfurled through the tiny window.

Haversham had assured him that she would be well, and though she showed no signs of stirring, a wisp of hope went through him.

"Yes, you will awaken," he murmured as the port began to warm his stiff limbs. "And then, milady rogue, the question will be what to do with you. Newgate? Bow Street? And a trip to Tyburn Fair? It is what you deserve for your thievery. A right just punishment. And yet . . ." A drowsy smile kissed Griffin's lips as he thought of the brigand-sobriquet the girl had flung at him in the shadow of the chaise. "Such a fate seems an unforgivable waste for a devil who bears the face of an angel."

Isabeau battled to keep her body limp against the soft feather mattress. Sweet Mary, would that infernal dolt Griffin Stone *never* go to sleep? Or at least leave the accursed chamber? Even aristocrat curs had to answer a call of nature *some*time, didn't they?

It seemed as though she had already been lying there for an eternity. She felt the sun filtering through the window grow warm, then cool with the passing of time, and her temper began to chafe.

Her right leg twitched, and she felt the urge to kick one massive bedpost in frustration. If that bloody lord didn't move soon, she might erupt in a fury and bludgeon him with the nearest weapon. But even the Devil's Flame could scarce hope to hold off the likes of Lord Griffin Stone with a goose-down pillow.

Beau couldn't keep her fingers from clenching; her palms itched for the feel of her pistol's smooth grip. She felt a twinge of loss as she thought of her firearms, abandoned, no doubt, upon that twisted road. She'd oiled the pistol's metal with the care most women reserved for Sevres china, and now they lay rusting from the morning dew.

But though robbed of those weapons, Beau had discovered that she possessed another, far more devastating blade.

Guilt.

Somehow she managed to keep the smug grin from her lips as she remembered how the nobleman had pleaded with the surgeon. Stone had sounded desperate. And once, when Beau had dared steal a glance through her slitted lids, she had seen his stunningly handsome features twisted with remorse.

At that instant she had let a pathetic moan slip from her lips—and at strategic intervals thereafter. And the effect, she had to congratulate herself, had been even greater than she had hoped.

Stone had cursed himself because of her "pain," and it had given Beau intense pleasure to feel her nemesis burning with self condemnation. No doubt it had blackened the nobleman's honor to have cut a woman down. But Beau had no delusions. Griffin Stone would feel no such nigglings of conscience if Tyburn's executioners took her life.

She moved her shoulder a little to test it; the surgeon had done his work well, so well that Beau was certain she could make good her escape if only Stone would *go the bloody hell away!*

Then she could just slip into the inn's stables, get astride MacBeth, and escape Stone's noose.

She held her lips stiff, stifling a grin. When she had awakened after the debacle on the highroad feeling her beloved stallion's familiar gait beneath her, it had felt like a plum too sweet to be real. She had held herself still in Griffin Stone's steely arms, thanking the fates for her good fortune.

She had bided her time then, waiting for the first opportunity to escape. But with each passing moment Beau felt more anxious, until now the very air within the inn chamber was choked with desperation.

She gritted her teeth, silently cursing Griffin Stone with words that would have made a fishmonger flush. Then suddenly a slight sound made her breath snag in her throat. Her heart slammed to a stop as she strained to decipher that faint noise. Then her pulse almost sang with elation as she heard again the soft rumbling. He was snoring.

Asleep! Beau thought jubilantly. By St. Stephen's arrows, it was about time!

She opened her eyes, and the unfamiliar room seemed to spiral slowly, then it slid into focus. She was in a wide bed with thick-hewn posts. A pewter branch of candles was by her side, its once-tall tapers globby lumps of wax within their holders. But her gaze locked on the door. It beckoned to her to flee.

Cautiously she moved herself higher upon the pillows, watching the sleeping man who was only an arm's length away.

His stubborn chin rested upon his chest, and his eyes were firmly shut. The lips that had mocked her, were parted, and his deep, even breaths stirred the lace that tumbled down his shirtfront.

He looked so restful, so patently unconcerned, that for an instant Beau felt an urge to kick his booted legs away from the bed's edge, and send him tumbling backward in his infernal chair.

It would be the richest of joys, and the most foolish. For despite his deceptive languor, menace lurked beneath his hard, bronzed visage.

She could still hear that mocking drawl. *And now, my lady rogue, what to do with you? Newgate? Bow Street? A trip to Tyburn Fair?*

She pressed her fingers against the thick wadding of bandage about her shoulder, remembering her terror. But only for an instant. There was no time for weakness, no time for fear.

The Devil's Flame would not wait docilely for *his lordship* to decide her fate.

She glanced around her, alarmed to discover one side of her bed flush against the wall; only the edge upon which Griffin's glossy boots rested held any chance of escape. She eased herself toward the foot of the bed, her panic eating into her courage like acid droplets. As she slipped her feet over the side her breath caught in her throat. Her legs were only a hand's breadth from the dozing nobleman.

Her bare feet touched the chill boards, and every muscle in her body tensed as she grasped one thick bedpost with her good arm. She pulled herself to a standing position, her knees suddenly watery, her heart bounding.

Now. It was now or never.

She swallowed hard, drawing in a deep breath as she forced one foot forward.

"Forgetting something?"

Beau wheeled toward that hateful voice and glared into eyes the color of a summer sea—eyes that were snapping wickedly. In one crooked finger he dangled one of Beau's precious pistols just beyond her reach.

Instinctively she lunged toward it. Then she froze, stricken, as her movement opened the front of the shirt that was three times too big for her. Her hand flew to her throat, but too late. The cool air of the room wafted over the bare skin of her breasts, and she knew the burning force of Griffin Stone's gaze fixed upon those vulnerable swells.

With a tiny cry she yanked the garment closed, but the nobleman's gaze trekked lazily along the pale sliver of flesh peeking between the fine linen edgings.

"You needn't fear for your virtue," Stone observed as he rocked lazily back and forth upon the chair's rear legs. "I make it a practice never to ravish women who will bleed all over my linens. Of course, I've never bedded a hellcat brigand who tried to rob me. It might be worth inconveniencing the laundress to sample—"

Rage and desperation erupted in Beau. She loathed him, loathed the smug arrogance in that handsome face, loathed the laughter that always threatened to rumble from that broad, dauntingly male chest.

Her eyes narrowed, jaw knotting, as she threw what small sense of caution she possessed to the winds. She reached out, catching the nobleman's booted foot, and wrenched it upward.

Lord Griffin cursed in surprise as she overbalanced him. Beau's wound burned, but feral joy tore through her as he crashed to the floor in a tangle of long, muscled legs, flailing arms, and splintering wood.

Lightning-fast, she dove toward the door, but at the last moment her eye caught a gleam of polished silver. Her pistol was a keg's breadth away from her hand. She knew she should leave it behind, but she couldn't. Her fingers swept down to capture the weapon. She had scarce touched the gleaming metal when a strong hand manacled her wrist, imprisoning her. Pain shot deep into Beau's shoulder, and she ground her teeth to keep from crying out.

"You idiot!" Stone blustered, scrambling to his feet. "You probably ripped your wound open! If you're bleeding again—"

"If I'm bleeding, it is your infernal fault! But I vow it will have been well worth it to see you on your arse."

"On my . . ." Griffin's jaw tightened. Even though she could feel all chance of escape slipping through her fingers, Beau reveled in the grand nobleman being brought low.

His eyes shone with fury. "You bloody rogue! Haversham was right! You were fine all the time! Duping us!"

"There was precious little glory in duping the two of you," she replied scornfully. "It was simple as stealing a blind man's cow." She brushed an imaginary speck of dirt from her sleeve. "But I must admit, your concern on my behalf near brought a tear to my eye."

"I'll bring a tear to your eye, devil take you! I should have left you by the side of the road, you ungrateful little wretch!"

"Why, pray tell, didn't you?" Beau mocked him. "Did the high and mighty Lord Griffin Stone want the glory of turning the Devil's Flame over to Bow Street? Was I to be a trophy to impress your accursed Cyprians?"

"I very much doubt *you* would impress anyone." Stone's voice held the temper of a sulky boy. "But I'm beginning to think I could damn well dance at your hanging!"

The blood drained from Beau's cheeks as fear again wrapped its clammy folds around her, but she struggled to still the quiver in her lips.

"I imagine you'll enjoy it right enough," she said, but her voice bore a hollow ring. "You can hold a picnic within your fine carriage that day, bring your ladies, all garbed in their silks to watch the merriment. And after—after you can watch the surgeons fight over my corpse, unless it is to be dipping in tar for me. Dance—yes, Lord Griffin, I'd wager you'd love to dance at such a civilized diversion."

"Hold." The softness in his voice made Beau meet his gaze. She wanted to hate him, this man who had made her reveal the fear she despised in herself. But Griffin's smoke-blue gaze had lost its sulkiness as he watched her face. His eyes softened.

"In truth, I've never had much stomach for hangings," he conceded. "And as to dancing, I must confess, your swordmaster and my dancing master must have been of one school."

Beau's tongue flicked out to dampen her lips, and she hardly dared speak. His words raised a fragile hope within her. "You—you would not attend—"

"And neither will you, if I have anything to say concerning it, milady . . . er . . ." He paused, seeming to grope for something to call her, then grinned. "Your name," he said. "What is your name? I can hardly run about calling you 'Devil', though I admit you have Lucifer's own temperament."

"Your temper is *much* fouler than mine!" Beau snapped.

"True, but at least you know what name to curse me by. It is only fair that you give me a like advantage."

"So you could use it against me? I think—"

"Believe me, Mistress Flame, I have more than enough information to use against you already, if I so choose. Your mere name would not prove half as useful as a full description of the face the Devil's Flame has so skillfully hidden behind that mask. Of course, if you persist in being stubborn . . ."

Her fingers clenched, and her nails dug into her palms. She was racked with indecision. For an instant she thought of giving him a false identity, but one look at the unyielding light in Stone's sea-blue eyes made her swallow her rebelliousness.

"Isabeau," she admitted through gritted teeth. "It is Isabeau DeBurgh."

There was no triumph, no gloating in his unwavering gaze. And she was surprised as his head tilted a bit to one side.

"Isabeau." The syllables rolled from Griffin Stone's tongue sounding like the sweetest of music, lilting, soft, feminine in a way hoydenish Beau had never been. "It is a wood sprite's name, or that of a fairy princess," he mused. "Not a name for a rakehell thief who goes tearing about the countryside with pistols."

"I had little to do with its choice," Beau said, stung by his apparant criticism. "My mother was a grand lady and she saddled me with the bloody monstrosity."

"And was it this fine lady who abandoned you to the savageries of the open road?"

"Savageries?" Beau bristled. "She chose the open road over your pompous mansions, chose my bold father. And she reveled in the life he carved for her until he was . . . captured." There was the slightest hesitation upon that last word, but it was enough to betray her. Her chin thrust up at a stubborn angle, as if daring him to say something.

"Captured." Griffin mulled the word over. "And after your father was . . . *captured* . . . why did your mother not return you to the bosom of her family?"

"She was the love of Six Coach Robb." Pride rang deep in Beau's voice. "And in London that honor was greater than being the blasted queen."

"Robb . . . Six Coach Robb." Griffin's brow creased in thought, then his gaze snapped up to her face, recollection dawning. "The highwayman Lady Lianna Devereaux eloped with. I well remember that scandal." The corner of his mouth curled up in wry amusement. "It was one of the few social tempests *I* was not belly-deep in, although I must admit I was but a scruffy schoolboy back then."

He braced one shoulder against the wall, crossing one booted foot over the other at the ankle. "She was beautiful, your mother. Fragile as a calla lily, with a smile so sweet it broke the heart of any who saw her. When she ran away it was said half the bucks of the *ton* went hieing off to rescue her."

"She didn't need to be rescued! She loved—"

"Loved your father. So much she followed him into the grave."

"It would have served his memory better if she had lived!" Beau flung out, then stopped in stunned silence, aghast. She had lived with the pain of her parents' deaths for years, had grieved for them and railed at the fates. But she'd never realized until this moment that her anger was not directed toward the fates, nor at the Bow Street Runners who had cut her father down. Rather, it was directed at her mother, the gentle Lady Lianna, who had faded like a flower trampled beneath some heedless boot heel. The woman who had left Beau alone.

Her stomach clenched with remembered pain; the knowledge that she had revealed to this arrogant stranger that most secret, hidden wound raked her spirit. She glanced at Griffin Stone. She saw no mockery; his face was suddenly solemn as he watched her.

She had not known that the voice that had tormented her could be so achingly gentle. "Come, Isabeau. I hardly think poor Lady Lianna *chose* to die. All the Devereauxs were of a precarious constitution, and most," he added with a wry grimace, "were of an abominable humor. There is not one of their line left save the dowager countess, and she is well past seventy."

The ghost of a smile tipped Griffin's lips. "Last I heard, the dowager was flitting about the Continent, neck-deep in revels now that that wastrel of a husband of hers has died. As for your mother, her love's death must have been a fearsome shock. And she was most delicate."

"She was the wife of Six Coach Robb! The boldest highwayman ever to ride! She should have ridden through London like a peer of the realm, daring any to speak ill of him! But instead she wept and wilted away. She didn't even watch him die. Wouldn't let me—" Beau's voice cracked, and she loathed herself for that show of weakness.

"Attend your father's hanging? Isabeau, you were a child. She could hardly have let you witness such a horror."

"I should have been there! *Wanted* to be! There was no one there for him—to see how bravely he met his fate. No one who loved him."

Griffin cleared his throat at her impassioned words. He reached toward her, his knuckles skimming the curve of her cheek as if in comfort. "Having you there would only have made it worse for your father."

She jerked away from him, her eyes blazing with scorn. "Bah! What do you know about it, my fine lord? What do you know about the code that rules the highroads? It is a game we play—all of us who ride—a grand masquerade full of swirling capes and sweeping plumes and rakehell courage! And in that game the size of the plunder matters far less than the style with which you gain it. We are actors upon the most dazzling of stages. And the scene at the hanging tree is our final curtain call."

"And what good is an actor's trade without an audience?" Griffin said the words slowly, peering into that pale, defiant face, eyes that were glittering green pools of pain.

Instinctively he knew that Isabeau DeBurgh would fly into a rage dark enough to set Beelzebub to cowering if he mentioned her sorrow.

Yet there was something within him that longed to stretch out his hands, entangle his fingers in the riot of flame-hued curls that tumbled about her narrow shoulders. Something in those mutinously compressed lips that filled him with a sudden, intense need to soften them with a brush of his mouth.

This girl was nothing like Lianna Devereaux with her angel-gold loveliness. Yet though Isabeau DeBurgh gleamed like a too-bright sun, all fight and fire and steely defiance, Griff sensed in this woman a vulnerability so deeply hidden that he felt its tug in his own well-guarded heart.

"Isabeau." He said her name, just her name, feeling some silken web spin out from her, entangling him in something he didn't want, dared not have.

It was as if she felt it, too, sensed what was happening inside him, and those huge green eyes changed, their jewellike brilliance misting with hope.

"Let me go." The words fell, relentless, like stones in Griff's stomach.

"Isabeau, I—"

"You say you don't want me to hang. If you surrender me to the authorities, it will be a gibbet for me. You know what they do to highwaymen. You've seen the corpses rotting at the roadsides."

"Blast you, of course I have!" Griffin felt a sharp surge of fury, and he spun away from her. "Sweet God, who could not know—see—"

"They would send me there. A grand trophy of Bow Street. As the Devil's Flame I would be notorious enough in my own right, but when they discover who my father was . . ."

Griffin felt his scalp prickle as though her fear were a palpable thing. He felt his resolve waver, and was almost tempted to hurl his cloak over her, hide her from the authorities. Then he realized she was smiling faintly with satisfaction. Her green eyes held a lurking wisp of smugness.

Griffin tensed, knowing that he had seen the look in those eyes before—in jewelers attempting to barter glass for diamonds, polished tin for the finest silver. And in his nephew Charles's features when the boy had been wheedling to get his way.

Griff's jaw knotted, brows slashing low over his eyes as he glared into that wood-sprite face. The brazen chit was trying to yank him about like a puppetmaster's moppet upon silken strings—*him,* Lord Griffin Andrew Arthur Rivington Stone.

"So," he said with deceptive mildness, "you would have me open my hand and let you fly as though you were some bright-winged butterfly I had plucked from a flower?"

"Yes. Forget you ever saw me, forget my face—"

"Until I see it splashed upon a wall by some pamphleteer? Or see news of your hanging in the *Spectator?"*

"It will be none of your concern then!" the girl said eagerly. "You will have done all you could."

"Perhaps I should wait longer still?" Griff's voice snapped like the crack of a whip. "Until you bungle another robbery and blast the life out of some poor innocent?"

Isabeau flinched. "I've never . . . would never kill anyone!"

"No, milady?" Griffin laughed as his hand grasped the front edges of her shirt, drawing her toward him. There was no gentleness in the curl of his arrogant lips, his face bare inches from her own. "Ah, now I remember. It is all a game with you! A grand jest, is it not? Well, I regret to inform you that there are those among we 'aristocrat curs' who are fool enough to take it seriously when someone thrusts a pistol into our face!"

Griffin expected the girl to cringe from his fury, a fury from which battle-hardened soldiers had fled. But any uncertainty Isabeau De Burgh had felt a moment before had obviously disappeared. Her chin jutted out at a pugnacious angle, her flame-colored tresses a riot of glistening color—the perfect foil for the greenest, most belligerent eyes Griffin had ever seen.

"Send me to hang, then, my high and mighty lord!" She sneered, her gaze raking his fine clothing in scorn. "For next time I go raiding, I *might* be tempted to blast whoever lurks within the coach—rather than be tortured by the whinings of an old woman the likes of you!"

"You little witch!" Griff gritted his teeth against the urge to wring that graceful white neck. "I should—"

"Should what, my beneficent lord? All-powerful, so bloody wise. I await your verdict with bated breath!"

Griffin glared down into her face, feeling suddenly as though he were a peregrine being attacked by a sparrow. And he had to crush the incongruous surge of laughter he felt building in his chest. "I should have damn well stayed in America!" he snapped. "The savages there were far preferable company to what I'm finding here."

"Then go back! I hope they take your bloody scalp! I hope they roast you upon a spit! I hope you—"

"You needn't elaborate further. I have a most vivid imagination." Griffin loosened his hold on her, astonished that this woman—that *any* woman save his formidable grandmother—had been able to break through his shield of lazy amusement to fire his temper. "But since I did not have the good sense to fall beneath some Iroquois's lance, I fear I need to find another solution to this coil. I can hardly turn Lianna Devereaux's daughter over to Bow Street. And I most certainly cannot allow you to go on terrorizing unwary travelers."

"It is my life! I do as I choose!"

"Not anymore, mistress blackguard." Griffin reached up, tangling his fingers in her hair, forcing her to meet his steely gaze. "You are mine, Isabeau De Burgh, body and soul. A cursed millstone slung about my neck, whether we will it or no."

"Pompous swine! I won't be bludgeoned into—"

"Ah, but you will, though it might send us both to Bedlam. You will come to Darkling Moor. And you'll stay there until I decide what the devil to do with you."

"I'll not!" Beau cried, very real alarm whirling within her. "You cannot make me!"

"Would you care to lay a wager upon that, my lady? You will do as I bid you—*whatever* I bid you from this moment on. If not, I will hurl you into Newgate with no more thought than I would give to casting away an irksome neckcloth."

For the first time he saw the girl falter. "You would not dare."

"Try me, milady," he said in arctic tones. "I am not a patient man."

"No, you are a—"

"You will leave off your unflattering appraisal of my less-than-admirable qualities. It is most unseemly in a lady of substance."

"I'm no bloody lady, you thrice-cursed dog!"

"I vow you're not! But you will endeavor to mime one when you are in my presence! And the first thing I command you to do is *bloody well stop swearing!* My grandmother, the dowager duchess, will not tolerate—"

The words died upon Griffin's lips as a crystalline image formed in his mind. An image of the haughty, steel-spined pillar of the nobility, Judith Stone, confronted with this snarling, flame-tressed girl.

A slow smile spread across his face, and he felt laughter rumbling deep in his chest. Griffin flung his head back, surrendering to it, until tears of mirth flowed down his cheeks, and Isabeau DeBurgh gaped at him as though he had at last succumbed to madness.

Chapter Five

Insane. The man was insane. Isabeau scrunched into the corner of the lurching coach, straining to keep from bumping the long masculine thigh stretched out negligently beside her. Time and again she had heard whispers regarding the strange humors of aristocrats. She'd often heard that generations of interbreeding had made the nobility's blood so thin that their sanity snapped. Yet until now she had never set much store by the tale. Outwardly Lord Griffin Stone seemed to carry only the finest traits of his ancestors. But Isabeau knew full well that she was in the hands of a madman.

She glanced at the profile angled away from her: the straight, finely chiseled nose, nostrils flared with just a touch of haughtiness, the mouth full, sensual, bracketed with lines carved by laughter.

Despite herself, Beau could not crush a stirring of admiration. He would swash a fine buckle upon the High Toby, were he so inclined. It was a pity he was merely a nobleman, encumbered by society's strictures.

Yet from what she had witnessed, Beau knew Stone was capable of any irreverence. The man was an enigma that infuriated and intrigued . . . and terrified.

Bah! Beau scorned herself inwardly. What pudding-pated foolery! She had thought herself above such nonsense. Still there was danger in the man who lounged beside her, the graceful, latent power of a panther sunning itself upon the edge of a cliff. Drowsing, true, yet ready to attack anyone foolish enough to pass beneath.

Beau couldn't stop the chill that prickled the back of her neck, her gaze stealing again to Stone's beautifully honed countenance.

During the two days her wound had kept them confined at the inn Griffin Stone had been given to odd moods. He had alternately brooded and laughed, paced the floor and jested, scolded her roundly and then lounged within the chair, teaching her to play chess as though he would be content to remain there forever.

Whenever Beau had attempted to bait him, to enrage him to the point that he must let her go, he had merely gotten a strange look in his eyes and tried to strangle his laughter.

Beau drew the folds of her newly acquired mantle closer about her shoulders. There could no longer be any doubt about her plight. She was in the clutches of a bloody Bedlamite.

"Is your wound paining you?" His question startled Beau out of her thoughts. "Or are you merely sulking because we left behind that man-crusher of a horse you're fool enough to ride?" His tone was so solicitous she wanted to scream. Instead she merely cast him her most fearful scowl and scooted further away upon the narrow seat.

He feigned a wounded expression. "I promised you earlier that I would not have the beast sent off to the renderers as long as you behave yourself. I've been most generous considering the trouble you've put me to already."

"I'd like to put you to a deal more trouble!" Beau snapped, seething beneath his amused gaze. "I'd like to—"

Stone gave a mocking shudder. "Such a hideous face you are pulling!" he said. "If you do not take care, it will freeze thus, and you'll spend the rest of your life frightening small children."

"There is nothing wrong with my face that your falling off some battlement would not cure."

"You may well have an ally in that quest once we reach Darkling Moor." His white teeth flashed into a grin so lazily sensual it could melt the most frigid of hearts.

"What? Have you abducted other women and chained them up in your accursed castle?"

"I regret to say that you will be the first prisoner we've held there since Cromwell. I can only hope that my ancestors have left some diverting trinkets about. Thumbscrews. Iron maidens. I have read that they had metal instruments called 'shrew's muzzles' to leash feminine tongues that grew too sharp." Griffin raked fingers through his hair, and the rich, dark strands tugged free of the ebony ribbon that bound them at his nape. "Of course, I fear that was just idle talk, for if such things had still existed, I am certain my poor grandfather would have put them to good use."

"Your grandfather? No doubt he had the same fcul temperament you do, and your grandmother had no choice but to defend herself."

Beau started as Griffin's laugh turned cold, his lips suddenly thinning. "Judith Stone has more defenses than a blasted fortress, and she possesses a wit so withering it could make half the king's army flee for shelter. No doubt the two of you will get on famously." His voice was bitter, and Beau was suddenly uncomfortably aware of how warm his voice had been moments before.

He was her tormenter, her jailer, and she despised him. Yet he was also the man who had whiled away the endless afternoons in the inn room by teaching her chess. In fact, he'd taught her with far more patience than Jack had shown when instructing her in swordplay. And when she had stolen his rook Stone had smiled at her, and he had been almost tolerable—for a puffed-up popinjay.

She cocked her head to one side to peer into his face, but he had turned away, watching the verdant English countryside.

"If your grandmother is such a shrew, why drag yourself

across an ocean to endure her company?" Beau asked. "Do you take pleasure in torturing yourself?"

"Only with red-haired witches who fling themselves upon my sword. As a rule I am wiser about avoiding family disturbances. But this time . . . this time there was no escape for me." A sigh breached his lips, and he paused, his voice dropping low. "My brother died."

"Oh. I remember now." Beau faltered. "I read about it in the *Spectator*. I didn't mean to—"

"To bring up painful memories?" Griffin turned toward her. The face that could be so disarmingly boyish suddenly seemed terribly old. It was like the face of an eager young knight who had battled far too many dragons, only to discover that the enemy he sought lurked within his own breast. "How now, Mistress DeBurgh, I didn't know you possessed such a soft heart."

Beau smiled broadly. "Jack claims it goes hand in hand with my soft *head.* But my tongue is sharp enough, and my will stubborn enough to make up the losses."

"I can attest to that." The laugh lines deepened about his mouth. "This Jack, he must be a wise man. Is he your husband? Your love?"

Beau felt her cheeks burn and her denial burst out too hastily. "No. He is but a friend. A good friend who taught me all I know."

"Highway robbery?" Griffin scowled. "What kind of a scoundrel would teach such a trade to an innocent girl?"

"One that didn't have any other choice." Beau couldn't keep a smug smile from her lips. "I duped him into it, you see."

"What? You stowed yourself beneath his saddle? Tucked yourself into his pocket?"

"I beat him in a game of dice. First, I won his favorite brace of pistols. Then I wagered them against his promise to take me on a night raid. Never, in anyone's memory had Jack lost twice in one evening's wagerings, so he felt quite safe, I am sure. He turned pure purple when I beat him again."

"I can well imagine."

Beau smirked. "Of course, *I* knew I would win from the beginning."

"Confident, were you?"

"No. Shameless. You see, the dice were weighted."

Griffin gave a reluctant laugh. "You were that determined to learn to be a thief?"

"A *highwayman.* There is a vast difference. And Jack, he is the boldest of them all, save my father. Maybe you have heard of Jack even in those barbaric colonies you come from. It is said that Gentleman Jack Ramsey is the greatest swordsman in all England."

Griffin grinned, cuffing her gently upon the chin. "If that be so, my fine rogue, it is evident he lacked much as your teacher."

"I fear it was my own fault. I . . . ah . . . I am a trifle short on patience at times. Given to fits of temper."

"Surely not!" Griffin's eyes widened in feigned disbelief.

"I know it will be hard for you to believe." Beau found herself giving him an answering smile. "But one day, when things had been going particularly poorly, I . . ." Her voice trailed off for a moment. "Jack had this sword he was inordinately proud of. Some Spanish thing, all silver, and—well, I got angry and slammed it into the side of a wall."

The nobleman shuddered visibly. "You slammed a Toledo sword into a wall?"

Beau shrugged. "I could not see what all the fuss was about. It could not have been very well made, for it snapped in two like a piece of kindling."

"Sweet Christ! It is a wonder you are yet alive! Remind me never to let you near my blade." His fingers trailed lovingly over the dress sword he wore at his waist. "William gave me this on my eighteenth birthday, and he nearly made me vow in blood that I would"—pain flickered across those arresting features—"would not be careless."

Silence drifted between them, and Beau squirmed, uneasy at their confidences and his palpable sorrow. The chaise jarred over a rut. A throbbing pain pulsed within Beau's shoulder, then mercifully faded. She felt a need to say something comforting, something wise, soothing, as Molly would, but she lacked her friend's ability to salve inner wounds.

She glanced at Griffin's face, saw his lips twist into a grimace of self-loathing. "I wonder what William would say now if he knew that I was bringing a common thief into his precious Darkling Moor."

Beau winced, strangely hurt by his hard words. The softening she had felt toward Stone dissippated. "He would probably think you a fool. As I do."

He reached into the pocket of his frock coat and withdrew a jewel-encrusted flask. He opened it with an impatient twist, then raised it to his lips to take a long drink. The tension about his broad shoulders eased only slightly. "A fool?" he said, his eyes narrowing to slits. "Yes, and if you judged me so, you would both be right. A fitting heir to my father, the wastrel duke, am I not, Grandmama?" He lifted the flask toward the coach's window in a mock salute, and its silver glittered as it picked up the last rays of the sun.

Beau's gaze locked upon the huge manor house that stood in stony majesty at the crest of a welling hill. It was a monument to generations of nobles, rulers of their own land. Yet though she gaped at the unabashed richness, at wonders she had never thought to see, she could not enjoy the spectacle. For as the equipage's driver guided his team through the sweep of coachway that wound about Darkling Moor's fantastical parklands, Beau was struck by an odd certainty. Lord Griffin Stone was as much a stranger here as Isabeau herself.

Griffin clenched his hand to keep it from trembling, stunned at how deeply the mere sight of Darkling Moor's Palladian marbles and soaring Ionic pillars affected him. The vista of mock wildlands stretched out in a glorious sweep, as perfect and beautiful as a painting. The lake William's workers had created glistened, jewel-bright; the newly constructed folly, patterned after a Greek temple, gleamed white amidst a carefully nurtured tangle of thriving vegetation.

Memories of the past swept through him as he surveyed the grounds. It was in the shadows of those contrived ruins that Griffin had kissed his first serving wench, wooed his first woman. And it had been upon that tiny emerald island set within the crystalline lake that the child Griffin had sobbed in desolation the day his grandmother had meted out his cruelest punishment, giving away his cherished pony in the wake of some childish defiance. For Griffin it had been the day all hope of ever being loved by that steely-eyed martinet had died forever. The day he had first allowed himself to hate her.

Though he had loathed Judith Stone and all she stood for, he could never bring himself to hate the lands, the manor house, the rolling hills. Griff felt a tightness in his chest.

The land—it was the same. Yet it was defiled. Defiled by the loss of the master who had tended it so lovingly. And to Griffin that seemed the gravest injustice of all.

He closed his eyes, disbelief stealing through him once more. Perhaps this journey was some sort of nightmarish jest, and he would awaken at his plantation, the rustle of tobacco in the wind drifting through the windows of his bedchamber, the hot, heavy air trickling the scent of magnolias across his senses.

But if it were a dream there would be no crushing grief, no hurt, confusion, no resentment from childhood scars. And there would be no rebellious hoyden sniping at him from the lumpy seat of a coarse hired coach.

The wheels of the equipage ground to a halt, the driver's muffled command penetrating even the bowed wooden walls of the coach. Griffin slammed the portal open, not waiting for the servants to fling wide the door and let down the step. He leapt with graceful impatience from the vehicle. He flung Isabeau a careless glance and was irritated to see her hanging back against the threadbare velvet like a child.

A wary child, a belligerent child. One that yanked at Griffin's frayed nerves, and at his beleaguered conscience.

"Get down here," he snapped. "For God's sake, the carvings will hardly devour you alive!"

He was challenging her by calling her coward, and he

knew it. Her emerald gaze met his, and for a brief moment there was hurt in her face, gone as quickly as it had come.

She muttered an expletive and stormed out of the carriage in a whirl of outrage, and a moment later her feet thudded upon the ground. Her fingers briefly reached toward the thick bandage at her shoulder, and for an instant Griff had a pang of remorse. Then the girl tossed her curls and stared down her nose at the estate spreading all around her.

"I know you 'ristos think that you're gods," she sneered. "But bloody Zeus himself would lose his stomach over this melee of Greek and Roman atrocities."

For a moment Griff was surprised that a street waif could identify such architectural wonders.

"I'd keep your opinions regarding my brother's home bottled up in that infernal mouth of yours if I were you."

"Why did you bring me here? Why put yourself to so much trouble?" she blazed back. "Why not just let me—"

Griffin's hand flashed out and caught her chin and he pulled her face within a whisper of his own. "Goad me once more about releasing you, you little cutpurse! *Just once more!*"

No threat followed the words, no list of consequences, but suddenly Isabeau was silent, and she looked away from him. He wanted to continue to bait her, to find release for the pain ripping through him. And he wanted to feel the sharp lash of her temper against his own.

But even that relief was denied him. With an oath he wheeled away and stalked up the broad stairway with Beau following in his wake. The massive doors swung wide, opened by a skittery footman. The servant's Adam's apple leapt in his scrawny throat as he tried to bar their entry. "Your business here, sir . . . may I inquire . . ." But Griff charged past the stammering servant into the great hall beyond.

He heard Beau's gasp of astonishment, the soft sound of her tread behind him. But all his thoughts were caught up in the sight of what had once been his home.

Heraldic leopards still snarled their defiance upon the newels, and the ceiling still held a profusion of beautifully wrought plaster roses and vines, each tiny petal and leaf so perfect that as a child he had made a mountain of tables and gilded chairs in an effort to pluck one of the tantalizing blooms.

Griff's fingers almost stretched toward the delicate flowers, but at that instant a door in the far corner flew open. The figure that burst from the portal was as lanky and clumsy as a colt, a mane of pale brown curls tumbling about a face still more boy than man.

Charles.

Griff stared, mesmerized by the changes in his nephew. Yet Charles stood looking at his uncle with no sign of recognition.

"Y—your grace," the footman stammered. "Forgive me. These persons, they pure charged past me. I tried to stop them, but—"

The young man's pale brown eyes skimmed from the servant to Griffin, and Griff was bitingly aware of the bedraggled figures he and Isabeau cut in their travel-stained clothes. The younger man's full lips pursed with displeasure.

"Bring my horse around at once, and the marquess's," Charles ordered the footman, as though the two newcomers were beneath notice. "And see that you hasten, or it will be off without a character for you, man." His brown eyes glinted with satisfaction, as if he were a boy playing pranks on his elders. The servant cast a panicked glance from his master to where Griffin stood, then bolted off toward the stable. Charles smiled with the obvious relish of one unaccustomed to power.

Griff shook his head, trying to reconcile this gangly youth with the shy, round-cheeked boy he had given his ring to ten years ago. There was an almost frantic eagerness about the lad, a wild sense of defiant freedom odd in one who should still be raw from the pain of so recent a loss. Shouldn't his father's death have left a deeper mark?

Charles's white hand flicked to brush dust from a ridiculously elaborate riding habit. On his hand he wore the glistening griffin-head ring tucked among his many less tasteful treasures. Griffin felt a tiny spark of cheer. Perhaps some vestige of the boy he knew remained.

Charles's gaze again swept from Griffin to Isabeau.

"If you've come seeking a situation," Charles said, self-importantly, "I suggest you go to the servants' entrance. They may be able to find you something."

"I already have a situation," Griff managed through the odd thickness in his throat. "At least I did when you were a boy. I was master villain of Darkling Moor wood—the sheriff of Nottingham, a bloodthirsty infidel, Launcelot the betrayer to your King Arthur."

"My . . . no!" The youth's mouth popped open, his eyes wide. "Uncle Griffin? Never say you are Uncle Griffin!"

Griff's own voice was gruff with emotion. "Yes, Charles. And you—you had the ill manners to grow up whilst I was away."

The boy flushed with delight, drawing himself up to his full height. "I'm near to six foot now, the tallest one in my set, and—oh, devil take it! It's dashed good to see you!"

For an instant Griff hoped that Charles would fling himself into his arms, as he had when a boy.

But this Charles stifled any such unmanly urges. He merely closed the space between them to clap Griff uncomfortably upon one shoulder.

"It is wondrous grand to see you again! I've been regaling my club with your exploits, and they are all agog to tip a glass with you—the notorious Lord Griffin Stone," Charles said awkwardly, his tone becoming a bit too bluff. "A score of duels, *grandes passions,* and enough wagerings to make any sane man a Bedlamite—it is what they say of you. And that grand gesture when you rid Lady Elise of her brutish husband."

Griffin felt awkward at his nephew's ecstasies. "It was the most addle-witted thing I've ever done," he said, wanting to dash any glaze of heroic glamour from the boy's eyes. "Elise Devanne was a scheming baggage, and her husband an old man. Your father—"

"My father cast you out." A look of resentment shadowed Charles's eyes.

"It was right of him to do so. And in truth"—Griff's voice softened—"much as I missed you, Charles, it was the wisest thing William could have done for me. I was going straight to the devil as fast as I could manage."

"It is much more entertaining in hell anyway, is it not, Uncle? I vow heaven must be brimful of dull-witted saints floating about with their somber faces as they look down upon us poor sinners." Charles laughed thinly as he walked over to a gilded table to finger a porcelain bowl. "No doubt Father is even now enthroned upon some cloud, staring down at us with that look in his eyes—you know the one—as if I am yet five years old and scribbling in his ledgers."

Griffin's jaw knotted, and a feeling of betrayal stirred in the pit of his belly. "Yes," he said. "I know the expression you mean. And I would give every scrap of wealth that I possess to see it with my own eyes once again."

He saw the boy stiffen, Charles's lightly freckled cheeks darkening red. "I—I—of course I would, too. Poor old man. It's only that it is a raging pity he never had any revels while he was alive. Just musty old books, and statues."

"He had you," Griffin said, his voice holding a quiet certainty. "It was all he wanted. To leave you an estate you could be proud of."

For an instant Charles looked ill, his fingers catching uncomfortably at the folds of his neckcloth.

"Then our Charles is twice blessed, is he not?" a masculine voice dangerous as thin ice commented. "An industrious father who left him great wealth, and a blackguard uncle who showed him the pleasure that could be had with it."

Griff turned toward the voice. A reedlike figure leaned against the oak-panelled doors. His thin face was lead-painted, and his snowy powdered wig made the man look as though he'd just emerged from an ice palace. Hooded amber eyes glittered with recognition, colorless lips pulling back from uneven white teeth in a mockery of a smile.

Griff recognized the disturbing man immediately.

Malcolm Alistair, marquess of Valmont.

The years had done nothing to soften the stark cruelty within that harsh face, nor to ease the loathing it inspired in Griffin's chest. As if it were but yesterday, he could remember the last time he had seen the vicious nobleman.

Griff and Tom Southwood had been taking their pleasure in the most exclusive brothel in London. It had proven a most diverting night—until Griffin had come upon the Marquess in a dark, deserted hallway. The innocent serving girl who had waited upon the courtesans had been trapped in Alistair's arms.

Even now, Griff's mouth hardened as he remembered the girl's violet eyes, wide with fear in her pinched face, a face marked with the fiery-red slashings of Alistair's riding crop—evidence of his displeasure upon her resistance. Displeasure? Bile rose in Griff's throat at the memory—no, there had been nothing but pleasure upon the marquess's face.

God alone knew what would have happened if Griff had not heard the poor wench's screams.

He shuddered inwardly, the memory making his palm ache for the hilt of his sword.

Only Tom Southwood's intervention had prevented Griff from calling the man out. That and the fact that Griffin had been exceedingly deep in his cups.

"Valmont," Griff acknowledged, his dislike for the nobleman evident.

"It is overwhelming fine to see you again," Alistair purred. "Charles here has been most eager for you to—er—shall we say *reason* with your brother's solicitor—if, indeed, it is possible at all to reason with one of his limited intelligence. It seems the esteemed Howell is proving a trifle recalcitrant in his dealings with our new young duke."

"Recalcitrant? Septimus Howell?" The gentle old man had served the Graymores for two generations. "He has shaped the fortunes of this family since you were in short pants, Alistair."

"Aye, and it is high time he retired to his country house where he belongs!" Charles cried. "He's a tight fisted old fool who refuses to give me what is mine. Uncle Griff, I told Alistair that I could depend upon you to come to my aid. Force Howell to let loose of my pursestrings."

"And I," Malcolm Alistair said silkily, "warned Charles that you would not. As I recall, beneath that rakehell facade of yours you are as prudish and dull as your brother was."

"Hold, Alistair." Charles's voice held a quaver. "I'll not have you speaking of the old fellow that way."

"Ah, yes, dearest Charles, I'd forgotten how bosom close you and your father were before his untimely demise. So close that when I heard of the old duke's death I wondered for an instant if you might be responsible."

Charles's hand trembled, and the base of the china bowl clinked against the table. If Griffin had doubted that his nephew grieved for his father, it was clear in Charles's stricken face now.

"Damn your eyes, Alistair," Griffin ground out, his hand grasping at the hilt of his sword. "I should—"

"Griffin." Strong, insistent, yet touched with dulcet tones, Beau's voice broke through his rage. Her small fingers grasped the dusty sleeve of his frock coat.

For an instant confusion surged through him, then suddenly his mind cleared. Isabeau. Sweet Christ, he had all but forgotten her.

"Who the devil—" Charles began unsteadily as Alistair's knowing laugh echoed in the hall.

"It seems your uncle has not waited to arrive at Darkling Moor before he began to stir up scandal."

"With a servant?" Charles said uncertainly, raking the coppery-haired figure with his eyes. "The boy is—"

"The *boy* is a *wench,* unless I miss my guess. And a comely enough one, beneath those breeches and that dirty face."

Griff could feel Beau tense, her voice dripping challenge. "In your eye, you white-faced son of a pig."

"Isabeau!" Griffin's voice was sharp.

Her fiery green eyes flashed to his. "Well, I suppose that snipe-nosed weasel would look much better if he'd been skewered and locked in a coach and—"

"Enough!" Griff bellowed. Even heedless as Beau was, she sensed his wariness.

"A wench? Who talks like that, and is rigged out in boots and breeches?" Charles's mouth gaped open. "Sweet thunder in heaven." He emitted a low whistle. "You must forgive me, milady, but I had no idea my uncle was . . . ah . . . thus accompanied."

"This is Mistress Isabeau DeBurgh," Griffin bit out. "My *ward.* Mistress DeBurgh, my nephew, the viscount . . ." He stopped, wincing at the pain the next words caused him. "No, I stand corrected. The Duke of Graymore."

"Ward?" Alistair echoed, arching one thin brow. "You are becoming a veritable papa, are you not, my Lord Stone? A most imposing figure of respectability. Or maybe you are not so dignified as you would like certain people to believe."

"Grandmama, for instance," Charles piped up with a faint grin.

Disgust and anger welled within Griffin. For an instant he wished that he had finished the duel he had begun with Alistair so many years ago, and that Charles was yet young enough to receive a sharp thrashing.

"You will accord my ward the respect due her, your grace." A muscle in Griff's jaw tensed. "She has a questionable enough opinion of the English aristocracy without your confirming her worst suspicions within moments of our arrival."

"They didn't have to bother, Stone," Beau snapped. "You already—"

"Damn it, Isabeau, you will go over there and sit down, or I'll—"

His threat was cut off by her snort of disgust. She tossed her red curls and stomped off, not to sit down as he had commanded, but rather to eye a pair of magnificent silver candelabra as if she were figuring their worth and plotting some way to steal them.

Griffin turned back to Charles, noting that the boy had moved closer to Alistair, as if seeking shelter from his uncle. The young duke's narrow chest swelled beneath his pea-green frock coat, and he fingered the trim at his cuff. His lips curled in a jaded hopelessness that stunned Griffin.

"So this well-bred ward of yours has a questionable opinion of us aristocrats, does she?" Charles sneered. "In that case, her stay with the Stones of Graymore should be most illuminating, should it not? For a more *aristocratic* family you could never find. We have had the noble patriarch, the wastrel younger brother, the disappointing heir, and what with Grandmama . . . it is rounded out nicely with an adder-tongued—"

"Enough!" Griff's voice boomed like cannon fire, leaving them all in stifling silence. "I have had a long and most trying journey and am in desperate need of a glass of claret and a bath so hot it will sear the grime from my skin. And I fear"—he cast a scathing glance at Alistair—"my patience for polite conversation is quite exhausted. Charles, if you will have the servants tend to Mistress DeBurgh's comforts, and if you will excuse me to the dowager duchess, I will wait upon the lot of you when I am refreshed."

"It will be pleasure indeed to tend to such a lovely lady's needs"—Charles sketched Isabeau a bow—"but as for our cherished *grandmère—"*

"I fear you shall have to wait considerably longer to pay your regards to her grace, my lord." Alistair drew a scented handkerchief from his waistcoat pocket, holding its folds at his long nose as he pointedly flicked his gaze over Griff's travel-stained garb.

"I don't understand."

The look of a man recently pardoned from the gallows crossed Charles's face.

"Annie has carried Grandmama off to Bath to take the waters. The old girl was so stricken with grief."

Griffin sucked a deep breath into his lungs and let it out slowly. Despite a lifetime of resentment, a threading of compassion stirred within him. "Aye. She would grieve for him. It is one thing we both share." He arched his neck in an effort to drive the tension from his stiff muscles.

"Of course, I also encouraged her to go." Charles's voice took on an annoying eagerness. "Wagered it would give us the best opportunity to set things right with the solicitor. I was overjoyed when I discovered you were guardian—knew we were of one mind regarding the meaning of life. Wenching, good claret, and plenty of coin to lavish about. No sense letting it molder in the family accounts."

"Charles!" Griffin's voice silenced the boy's babblings. "I'm bloody exhausted, hell's own demons are pounding in my skull, and *my brother is dead! Dead,* curse you! At the moment I don't give a damn about your lights o' love, your liquor, and especially not your desire to gamble away the Graymore fortune. And if you and Valmont expect me to be an ally in destroying what it took my brother a lifetime to build, then you are a fool."

Griff saw Alistair's eyes flash with triumph as the boy's breath whistled through his teeth.

"How—how dare you—" Charles started to sputter. It was not the fury of a man, but rather that of a willful child reined in when he expected his elders to laugh at his antics.

Griffin was immediately sorry, yet before he could soften his harsh words Charles snapped back. "So Alistair was right about you, eh? You, who did exactly what you damn well pleased when you were my age, think that you can merely yank upon poor spineless Charles's leash, and he will come to heel. Well, since the day you left Darkling Moor I have been caught in Grandmama's and Father's chains—propriety, duty, grinding away studying accursed books and worse ledgers. I hated it! Just waited for the day when I would be a man—the duke—whom none but the king himself could say nay to." Charles's chest heaved, his lips trembling, his eyes over-bright with what Griff suspected were tears.

"I *will* have that money. I *must* . . ." Charles took a shuddering breath, and Griffin could almost see the boy struggle to calm himself. After a moment Charles's lips curled in a pathetic mockery of a man's scornful sneer. "Play the dull-spirited drone, Uncle Griffin, if you will. Levee your orders, keep all beneath lock and key. But when I reach my majority there will be no one who can stop me from doing exactly as I please, will there, Valmont?"

"Charles," Griffin began in a warning tone.

"It is *mine,* this house, the Graymore wealth." Charles's voice almost cracked as he rounded upon Griffin. "I thought *you* at least were different! All these years I wished that you would come back. Now it would please me mightily if you were sucked straight down to hell."

Griffin's eyes locked with those of his nephew. The boy he had once regarded with such affection had become a stranger. Griff dragged a weary hand through his hair, not bothering to stop Charles as the youth charged past him out into the crisp country air.

Griff saw the boy vault up into the saddle of the horse the footman had brought around and rip the reins from the beleaguered servant's hands.

"Hurry Alistair," Charles called to the marquess. "Let us seek the company of those who know how to live."

"Even you cannot halt the march of time, Stone," Alistair's voice whispered in subtle challenge. "In three short years he's going to be a man. And then you are going to lose him. Lose him as your brother did. In truth, Charles is already beyond your grasp."

Griff stood silent, stiff, as the nobleman swept from the hall, mounting his own night-black stallion.

Griff watched Charles slam his heels into his horse's barrel, jarring it into a run, and he had the strange sensation that he was watching his nephew hurtle his mount toward some unseen abyss.

Behind him Isabeau cleared her throat. "It is true, you know," she said quietly, "what that iceman of a marquess was blathering about. You will lose the boy if you try to chain him."

Griff hated the look in her eyes—a strange mixture of defiance and empathy. It was the empathy that drove Griff mad.

"Chain him? William should have taken a switch to the idiot years past! Did you hear him? Sweet Christ, his father is scarce cold, and—" Griff stopped, suddenly aware of the weight of her stare. "What *are* you gaping at?"

"You asked me if *I* heard your nephew. Did *you?* Really hear him? He was hurting."

"So much he can't wait to squander the Graymore fortune."

"I suspect it is just his way of handling . . . his grief. If you would—"

"Enough!" Griff roared. "It is none of your concern. You will bloody well forget what has transpired here, milady Isabeau, before I decide to give *you* the thrashing my nephew deserves. Now get the devil abovestairs and scrub the filth off yourself! It is not the London stews here!"

"No," the girl agreed in frosty accents, peering down her pert nose. "In the stews we have better manners. Yes, and we are kinder by far to those we love."

With that Isabeau DeBurgh swept toward the grand staircase, ascending it as regally as though Charles, Valmont, and Griffin were coarse villeins and she was their blasted queen.

Chapter Six

The tapers illuminating the richly appointed study guttered in their silver holders, and the faint light made the columns of figures swim before Griffin's burning eyes. He raised his fingertips, rubbing them against his throbbing temples. But the pain thrummed on relentlessly, mingled with the sharp, fresh sting of grief.

Sweet Jesu, how long had he been here, trapped in a maze of William's precise notes? It seemed an eon had passed since he had thrust Isabeau DeBurgh into the hands of a bevy of maids and stalked into this chamber, resolved to delve into the mind-numbing task of familiarizing himself with William's business affairs.

He sank back against the carved mahogany chair and bit out a curse. Griff knew his plans to entrust Charles and the estate to others and return to the colonies were futile.

All of Graymore was in disarray, and even if it were not, there was still the girl to consider. Lianna Devereaux's daughter. Granddaughter to the Dowager Countess Sophie.

Ten years ago he would have shrugged, resigned to letting the headstrong Isabeau run headlong into the executioner's arms if she so chose. Or, more likely still, he would have dumped her, kicking and swearing, on the Devereaux doorstep. He would have judged that it was far better for the unfortunates at Devereaux House to deal with the mayhem than to suffer the inconvenience himself. But he'd changed. Responsibility—a yoke that had never proved much of a bother to Griffin before—now seemed to chafe relentlessly against his shoulders. Now, whether he willed it or not, he felt responsible, for his brother's lands and his brother's son, as well as for the girl who, despite her lowly upbringing, had a family heritage that rivaled Griffin's own.

No, there was only one thing to do. He would have to fashion the girl into some semblance of a lady. He didn't want the chit to give her esteemed relative apoplexy. And furthermore he would have to try to find some way to free the Dowager Countess Sophie of responsibility for the girl.

It would be too cruel to destroy Sophie's well-deserved peace now that her snarling dog of a husband had died.

If Griffin could fix Isabeau up a bit, polish her manners, her dress—and, pray God, curb her infernal cursing—perhaps he could free them all from this coil by arranging a suitable marriage with an unsuspecting male. That way the dowager countess would only need to give the girl an appropriate dowry, and she could wash her hands of the chit forever.

Finding Beau a husband should not prove to be such an impossible task. In her way she was handsome enough, he supposed. Although she did not fit the current milksop-pale fashion. But she did possess a certain dash. Surely he could find *someone* to wed her, especially if he added some of his own funds to sweeten her dowry.

Still, even if he did manage to find a suitor for her, there was Charles. And this accursed pile of stone that William had so loved.

Truth was, he had changed from the scapegrace Griffin, the man who was able to dash off, heedless, to indulge in his own reckless adventurings. And the knowledge terrified him.

* * *

It was hours later when Griffin exited the study, bone-deep exhaustion driven into his very core. He ached for a steaming hot bath, food and a soft bed where he could find peace—in sleep.

But he had barely reached the corridor to the family's private apartments when he heard an ungodly racket.

Curses. Griff was almost certain he heard curses—as black as any that could spew from a sailor's tongue.

It could only be . . . Isabeau.

Fury tore through him. How dare she set the house in an uproar! He stalked down the hall from the serenity of his chamber toward the noise. Suddenly the door to the gold room burst open and a brawny maid rushed out. She was soaked from head to foot with water, her bobbly eyes bulging from their sockets.

"What the devil?" Griff barked.

With a screech the servant wheeled to face him and stumbled against a mahogany table against the wall. A figurine teetered, and only a miracle saved it from smashing to the floor.

Yet though the figure did not topple, a loud crash reverberated from the chamber the maid had just exited, and the woman all but jumped from her skin.

"Gor' save us! 'Tis a demon she be! Mad! Pure mad!"

"I swear I'll send her to the devil that spawned her!" Griff muttered, but his voice was lost in the fresh spate of cursing that shook the walls, another, more desperate voice piercing through it.

"Nay, mistress! You must not—not her grace's Ming—"

With an oath Griffin stormed past the quivering maid, through the half-open doorway.

The three other maids were wailing as they stood trapped in the far corner of the room. One of the women was clinging desperately to a bundle that could only be Isabeau's clothing. The rich Tabriz carpets were drenched with sudsy water, rivulets from the half-full bathtub upon the hearth trickled past shattered bric-a-brac and overturned buckets.

Amidst the mayhem stood Isabeau, her damp hair clinging to cheeks flushed with fury, her naked body gleaming wet from its recent soaking.

Griff's rage froze in his throat, the image before him branding itself forever in his mind. Fragile coral nipples crowned small breasts, narrow ribs sweeping to a waist so tiny he could have spanned it with his hands. Hips almost boyishly slim gave way to long, sleek legs while candlelight glistened on the droplets of moisture that beaded the dainty flame-red down that arrowed between her thighs.

Griff swallowed hard, trying to drag his eyes away from her rose-blushed, ivory-satin skin, its perfection marred only by the half-healed wound upon one shoulder. He was almost astonished to discover that the girl who had seemed as frail as a child in the inn was in fact a woman. A woman whose nakedness set a new throbbing to pulse inside him, his loins clenching painfully, his heartbeat quickening in a way that infuriated him.

He tore his gaze away from her, forcing himself to look at her hands—hands that were clamped about one of Judith Stone's most prized Chinese objets d' art as she took a threatening step toward the maids.

"Give them to me," Beau snapped, oblivious to Griffin's presence. *"Now,* or I vow I'll break this over your thick skulls!" The Ming jutted out before her, as threatening as one of her pistols.

"Don't you dare!" Griff commanded as the maids' screams pierced his eardrums. "That vase is worth a queen's ransom."

Beau spun toward him, blazing with outrage. She'd been humiliated, bullied, skewered and bellowed at since the moment she'd faced the point of his rapier on the dark night road. But this—*this*—was bloody well the outside of *enough!*

"You!" she raged, murder in her eyes. "You craven dog! You son of a swine! How *dare* you order them to take away my clothes! You tell them to give back my breeches or I swear I'll smash this monstrosity into a million shards!"

"When hell freezes over, you little barbarian!" Griffin

stormed. "You will cease this infernal racket and do as you are bid. And the first thing you will do is *bloody well put that vase down!*"

Eyes the hue of emeralds flashed green fire, and berry-red lips tautened into a devil's smile. Griff guessed her intentions in that instant, and tried to lunge toward her as her slender fingers released their hold upon the priceless artifact. But it was too late. The object that had survived four hundred years of war, revolt, and countless natural disasters was demolished in a heartbeat by Isabeau DeBurgh's temper.

"Damnation!" Griff roared as the girl darted lightning-fast behind the tub, evading him as easily as if he were some clumsy oaf. He stormed toward her, fully intending to wring her blasted neck, but as he charged the toe of one polished boot snagged on an overturned bucket.

He pitched toward Beau, his outstretched hand grazing sleek damp skin as he hurtled toward the tub. Then he plunged headlong into the tub. Soapy water filled his nose and mouth and drenched his hair.

Griff jammed himself upright, gripped by the most savage fury he had ever known, a fury that deepened as he heard Isabeau DeBurgh's laughter.

"Witch!" he bellowed. "You infernal little—"

"You condemned me to a scrubbing. It is justice indeed that you suffer one as well!" There was a jauntiness beneath her anger that drove Griffin mad. "Now tell these blithering idiots to *give me back my breeches,* or I'll—"

In that instant what little rein Griff still held on his self-control snapped, and he charged at her, his hands closing in a bruising grip about her upper arms. "Break one more thing in this room, and you'll be in Newgate so fast your head will reel!"

She tried to break away, and though her struggles were surprisingly strong, Griff held her fast. He gritted his teeth and yanked her against him, his arms banding her as he battled to subdue her. The soft swell of her breasts was crushed against his chest, his wet shirt no barrier against the pebble-hard tips of her nipples. They burned into his flesh, torturing him, but he dared not ease his hold upon her.

"Out! All of you!" Griff bellowed at the maids, knowing that the whole house, from gardener to the lowliest spitboy, would be abuzz with this tale before an hour passed. "And as for Mistress Isabeau's breeches—burn them."

"No!" Beau shrieked, kicking him in the shins, battling to tear free. "Damn you—"

"Now!" Griff roared at the trembling servants. "And if I hear the slightest of whispering as to what transpired here, the three of you will answer to *me.* Do you understand?"

"Aye, your lordship!" "Never, your lordship! Not a word!" the servants babbled, yet they still hung back against the wall, eyeing Beau as though she were a fiery dragon.

"Leave us!" Griff commanded. "For Christ's sake, I'm holding on to her! She cannot harm—oof!" Her knee slammed dangerously close to his groin. As if they feared the monster would indeed break free, the women made a mad dash across the chamber, spilling out the door, slamming it behind them. Griff would not have been surprised if they had shoved a heavy table up against it.

Once they'd left he dragged Beau three steps to the massive bed that graced the chamber. Its regal elegance dated from before the Restoration, but still he slammed Beau down upon its softness, pinning her there beneath the weight of his own body, her curses deafening him as she warred against his grasp.

"Damn you, you little fool!" He shifted himself so that his hips crushed against hers, his legs twining with her flailing ones in an effort to restrain her. "Be still!"

"Let go of me, blast you!"

"And let you unman me? I think not! Now you will *bloody well listen to me, woman,* or I vow I'll cast you into Bow Street's hands without a pang of conscience!"

"You'd not—"

"Wouldn't I?" Griff snarled. "It is but right justice to kill mad curs, is it not, milady? And you have most certainly been acting like an animal."

"And what of you? Grabbing me? Pawing me?"

Griffin nearly choked upon his laughter. "Pawing? Do you think I am so desperate as to want a starveling cat the likes of you clawing at me? No, thank you. I prefer women who do not draw blood every time they touch me!"

"Then get . . . the hell . . . off . . . me!" She bucked up her hips in an effort to dislodge him, the pressure of that damp triangle of curls against his shaft putting the lie to his seeming indifference. In that moment he wanted to crush his lips to her impudent rose ones, subdue her with his mouth in a way he could not with his hands.

But the knowledge that she had moved him made Griffin feel somehow vulnerable, and the thought of being vulnerable to anyone—especially Isabeau DeBurgh—seared him like an open wound.

Abruptly he released her, rolling to his feet. A moment later the stunned Beau struggled to right herself amid the tumbled coverlets.

"There, milady, you are free," he said, danger threading his voice.

Her green eyes held his, wary, yet with the untameable spirit of a wild stallion. Tentatively she reached up and touched her shoulder as if the half-healed wound pained her. "If you expect me to thank you," she said, "you can go to the devil."

"I expect nothing of you, milady, except that you do exactly as you are told! It is obvious I was too gentle—"

"Gentle!" Beau roared.

"—in explaining to you your exact situation here at Darkling Moor. To obliterate any further misunderstandings, I shall put it in language you can comprehend. You, Isabeau DeBurgh, are going to conduct yourself as befits a daughter of Devereaux blood, and one who is Lord Griffin Stone's ward. You are going to wear women's clothes, learn to dance, to flirt, and to hold a fan and every other wile a woman can employ to ensnare some poor, hapless man. The greatest gift I can give poor Lady Sophie will be to find some suitable fool to wed you so she can be rid of you for good."

"You can both be rid of me right now! Just give me back

my breeches, and you and the pompous old sow can go on as if I'd never existed."

"A moment ago you struck a blow that made me patently aware that you exist, Mistress DeBurgh. Though I might wish to high heaven that I had taken any other road in Christendom save the one I found you on, there is no way to change the fact that we are agonizingly acquainted."

"You cannot force me to make a fool of myself."

"No? Watch me, Isabeau. If you defy me just one more time, or if you dare even contemplate an idiotic scheme like running away, your face will be splashed across the wares of every pamphleteer in England. I'll make certain your name is upon the lips of every runner at Bow Street. I will hurl all the might of the house of Graymore behind the search for you, and when they drag you to Tyburn Tree I will come to glory in your hanging."

He saw the girl's face pale. He hated himself for losing his temper, and he hated himself even more as the vibrant veil of tumbled hair wisping about her body started new pulsings of desire within him.

"You'll never make me into a lady!" she flung at him, but her defiance was edged with a kind of hopelessness. "I cannot be—"

"Oh, yes, you can," Griffin bit out. "I will give you three days to rest your wound, Devil's Flame." His voice dripped with scorn. "But when that last evening comes, Mistress Isabeau DeBurgh will present herself at dinner. It is past time she learned to eat like a civilized person."

Beau watched as he spun and stalked from the room, the bronze skin of his broad shoulders showing through the clinging dampness of his shirt, his breeches already tight, molding to powerful thighs and iron-honed buttocks—and cupping, as well, that part of him that had ground into her softness when he had pinned her upon the bed. Her cheeks burned, and she wanted to kick him, hurl something at him. Wanted to dash that infernal aristocratic arrogance from those sinfully beguiling features.

But for once caution made her hesitate. Griffin Stone's harsh promises and the steely light in his eyes quelled her thoughts of open rebellion. She had confronted enough men upon the highroad to know whether they were bluff and bluster or in deadly earnest. And Lord Stone had meant every threat he had made.

Calmly she turned her gaze toward the window, the sunlight making the mullioned panes of glass sparkle like diamonds. While she was in the tub she had planned to escape through that window.

Now she would have to bide her time, wait for some other opportunity for escape to present itself—some method that would dash Griffin's threats of vengeance while securing her freedom. Perhaps Molly or Jack were already searching for her. Even the hapless Owen could have found his way back to the Blowsy Nell by now. She would just need to wait, watch.

Yes, that was it. She would be canny enough to concede to her captor this single, fleeting victory. But then . . .

She smiled grimly.

Then she would make bloody certain that it would cost him dearly. She would do everything—*anything*—within her power to turn Griffin Stone's life into pure, unadulterated hell.

Chapter Seven

Two long days had passed since Griffin had battled with Isabeau. Two days in which he'd ignored the taunting red-haired witch tucked in her bed above stairs and had buried himself in work. But in the end, the countless business matters had only made the sinking sensation in his stomach tighten, deepen, ruining one of the few pleasures he had looked forward to upon his return to England—seeing Septimus Howell once again.

The elderly solicitor had handled the Graymore affairs since before Griffin was born. He had been friend, confidant, a family mainstay. Never had Griffin suspected that the kind old man would also be a harbinger of doom.

Now in William's study, Griff stared into Septimus Howell's myopic eyes in disbelief as his fingers ripped loose a neckcloth that suddenly seemed tight.

"Why?" Griff asked, his hand crumpling the edge of the parchment upon which the older man had just scribbled. "Why would William take such ruinous sums of money from Graymore estates? And then mark them with these infernal vague notations in the ledgers that are bloody worse than nothing? 'Miscellaneous.'" Griff jabbed a finger at

William's notation. "What the blazes does that mean? It is insane. Blasted impossible—"

"I'm sorry to say that it is quite possible, your lordship. I know . . . know how difficult all this is for you." Howell shook his head, long jowls wobbling with regret. "God knows I've prayed for your return often enough. I had hoped that you and your brother would make your peace. But now, coming home to this . . ." Howell raised his hands palms-up in a gesture of hopelessness. "I swear to you, Master Griffin, I tried to be the most responsible of solicitors—did all that I could to sway his grace from this path—"

"You should have chained him to his chair until he came to his damned senses! William slaved his whole life over these accounts. Suffered over them. I cannot believe that he would squander so much of his fortune. If you had only—"

"Only tendered my resignation *before* I cast the Graymore fortunes to the winds?" Howell stiffened his slumping shoulders. "Your grandmother, the dowager duchess, offered that same opinion after his grace died. And the young duke could not wait to be quit of me. I only awaited your arrival. Thought that you"—the gravelly voice cracked—"you might have need of me. I see that I was mistaken. If you'll excuse me, your lordship, I'll not encumber you with my presence any longer."

There was an air of defeat in Howell's lined face. In an instant all anger and frustration drained from Griffin, leaving him heartily ashamed. "Howell, wait," he called softly. "Please. It's been the devil of a day, and I fear my temper is foul as it ever was."

Seconds ticked by before the solicitor spoke in a gruff voice. "I suppose I should be grateful I am not saddled with a title, else I'd be compelled to challenge you to a duel for slighting my honor. And despite the muddle the world is in at present, I'm not yet ready to abandon it."

His attempt at humor touched Griffin as nothing else could have. "Your integrity was never in question, Mr. Howell." Griffin spoke with a rare solemnity. "No one knows better than I how much the Stones owe you. It is just that this seems like such madness." Griff swept his hand over the accounts spread before him. "Prudent William mortgaging estates. Huge discrepancies in his record keeping. I don't understand."

The solicitor's rheumy gaze brimmed with compassion. "It is difficult to make sense of it, I know," Howell said. "His grace—you remember how exacting he was, how precise. From the time he was a stripling everything regarding the dukedom was his highest priority. I never thought to see that change."

"But it did?"

"When one's son is taken up in a sponging house for gaming debts, a father as loving as William Stone is scarce likely to let the boy rot there—no matter how foolhardy the youth has proved."

"Gaming debts? William bled the estates dry over Charles's gaming debts? I doubt one boy could have caused so much damage."

The solicitor's lips thinned. "I fear Master Charles has little understanding of the value of coin, your lordship. And the company he keeps has only made a difficult circumstance worse. The Marquess of Valmont—"

Griff's lip curled in distaste. "I don't give a damn if the idiot has been trailing about upon Satan's own coattails! It is still no excuse for such idiocy. Valmont could hardly have been holding a pistol to Charles's skull when the fool diced his inheritance away. And William—it was insanity for—"

"For a father to be overindulgent with his only child?" Howell interrupted gently. "Especially when that father was laboring under considerable guilt?"

"Guilt? By God's wounds, what did William have to feel guilty about? Perhaps he was a bit stern with the lad, allowed Grandmama more influence over Charles than I would have liked. But William adored the boy. He built his fortune for him."

Septimus started to speak, then hesitated. After a moment he shrugged, surrendering the words with a visible reluctance. "It was never enough for Master Charles," Howell said. "Never enough wealth, never enough prestige, never enough freedom. I fear that the boy went through a period most youths do—one in which they turn their noses up at their fathers, feeling as if their sire must be the sternest, stodgiest, most unyielding man ever to bedevil a son."

"Of all the addle-pated things I've ever heard! William was the most noble, honorable—"

"I fear that nobility and honor of the duke's sort does not set young hearts pounding. His grace did not cut a dashing enough figure, and he was not the type of man a young boy could brag about. There were no tales of adventure or battles or love affairs about the duke to impress Charles's set."

"Then he should have told the lot of them to go to the devil. And William should have had the sense to ignore the ungrateful brat."

Septimus ran his ink-splotched fingers over a broken quill. "You know, your lordship, I spent years in this room with your brother. He would come here before dawn most days and not leave until night was half spent. We managed disaster after disaster, struggling to make them right. And always succeeding." A wisp of pride threaded through Howell's sorrow.

"I know that you did. The two of you should be raised to sainthood, you worked so many miracles."

"But it didn't matter," Howell said. "Not to the one person his grace loved above all others."

"Charles? William should have dragged the boy into this study and buried him neck-deep in the workings of the estates. Maybe that would have kept the young fool out of trouble."

"His grace tried. But Charles did not have his father's gift for such pursuits. The young master could seem to do nothing to his grace's satisfaction. And though William tried to be patient, I know his constant reprimands hurt the boy. In the end, both gave up trying. His grace buried himself still deeper in his work, while Charles drowned himself in an orgy of drink and gaming and lights o' love. It broke his grace's heart, I think. For two years I watched him fade. Knew he was weary of grinding away all the time. Knew he was lonely. God knows, he could have used a sweet, gentle soul of a wife like my Susannah. And as Master

Charles's escapades grew more frequent, more serious, the duke was at his wit's end."

"And William had already had a belly full of escapades with what I put him through." Griff winced inwardly at the memory of his own countless scrapes. "It is a pity he had to endure more of the same."

"Even at your most incorrigible, Master Griffin, you never scorned your brother. He always knew how much you loved him, respected him. I am certain that in time Charles would have come to appreciate the man his father was. But I regret to say that Master Charles's scorn seeped into the very marrow of his grace's bones. It was painful for both of them, I know." Howell locked his hands behind his back, pacing across the carpets. "At any rate, in the months before his grace's death I felt that things were reaching the shattering point. Whatever bad blood lay between the two of them was surging near the surface. Charles was so edgy it drove me mad to be in the room with him. And the duke's eyes were dark with trouble. Time and time again I heard servants whisper about their battles. And that last night, the last time I saw his grace alive . . ."

Septimus turned to face Griffin, his face clouded with anguish and confusion. "We were tending to the estate's accounts as usual, your lordship, when I noticed that his grace had mortgaged one of the lesser estates, and drained what little was left of the Stone assets."

"But why, Howell? Why?" Griffin slammed the flat of his hand against the desk, confusion and frustration warring inside him.

"I know precious little for certain," Howell said. "Master William was a private man. It was not fitting for a duke to lean upon any man, even me."

"You loved him like a father." Griffin sought to offer comfort despite the cold dread in the pit of his stomach. "If anyone held a clue to William's secret pain, Mr. Howell, it would be you."

The eyes that could be so canny misted.

"Someone needed to love the brace of you after your own father went to his rest." Septimus walked toward an oval gilt frame on the dark-paneled wall where the merry countenance of Griffin's sire peered jovially out upon the ruin of the estates.

"I'll never forget the night before your father's fatal duel. Took me aside, he did, with a grin upon his face. He told me 'I full intend to stride from the field, Septimus, but if fortune dices against me, you'll tend to my boys.' "

Grief touched the man's face. "I wanted to do more for the pair of you once your grandmother came," he went on, "but her grace would not have it. A common lot the like of myself soiling those of her noble blood. I watched William. Watched both of you. But I failed to carry out your father's wishes. Failed you. And now failed your brother."

"You never failed in being our friend." Griffin skirted the desk, his hand curving about the older man's shoulder, giving it a bracing squeeze. "If not for your labors this tangle with finances would be a much deeper muddle. And because of your interference we will be able to make it come right in the end."

"Do you think so? I mean, yes. Of course." A small smile lightened Septimus's face, and Griff could feel the man's gratitude. "You were always a most stubborn boy, hurling yourself into anything that you turned your hand to. The dukedom would not dare crumble if it is your will that it remain."

"It is." Griffin steeled himself, glad Howell had taken comfort, yet knowing that he had no choice except to probe deeper into the elderly man's painful remembrances. "But if we are to raise the Stone holdings from the ashes, I need to know everything—*everything*—you can tell me of how it was brought low."

"The Stone family was brought low by generations of wastrels and profligates," a feminine voice said acidly. "And with you as its trustee, we will be crawling in the gutters again before a fortnight is out."

Both men wheeled toward the door, the solicitor's face pale, Griffin's a stony mask.

Even the relentless march of time and the searing of grief had not bowed the haughty carriage of the dowager duchess of Graymore. She stood in the doorway like an aging goddess, cold, distant, and splendid. Her astonishingly supple skin was stretched taut over her fine-boned face, and a wealth of ice-white hair was piled atop that regal head like a crown. At seventy-five her only concession to age was a gold-handled walking stick. She used it not to ease her gait, but rather to wave in the faces of terrified housemaids and to clap about the shins of footmen who were not spry enough to suit her.

Griffin was stunned to discover that she still made him feel the yawning chasm of emptiness he remembered from his childhood.

"Grandmama." He spoke the name mockingly as he swept her a scornful bow. "I am overwhelmed by the warmth of your welcome."

"Come now, your grace," Howell said. "It has been ten years since we've had the boy home. He's grown into a man—a fine one, whose ventures in business are thriving. He's a man to be proud of."

"Proud, Mr. Howell?" Judith Stone's nostrils flared as though scenting something particularly malodorous. "Pray, what have I to be proud of? The fact that he was forced to flee England because of a duel over some harlot? Or should I be proud of the fact that he managed to scrape together some sort of consequence in a swamp somewhere, with moneys my William drained away from the Graymore estates?"

Septimus bristled. "Master Griffin never accepted any stipend from his grace. He financed Marrislea with his own coin."

The dowager duchess closed upon the older man's words like a shark upon a blood scent, and she turned upon Griffin.

"With your own coin you bought this tobacco farm Howell makes so much of? Is that what you would have people believe? You had no moneys of your own—no legacy. All you possessed was William's charity."

"And my skill at the gaming tables," Griffin countered with feigned amusement. "Pray, don't forget, Grandmama, I was as notorious for my abilities at dicing as I was for my hand with the ladies. I accrued almost as substantial an accounting in both areas as my father."

"Your *father—"*

"Didn't give a tinker's damn what you thought of him, and neither do I," Griff observed blandly. "But William"—Griffin paced to where a crystal decanter caught the rays of the sun and poured himself a glassful of amber liquid—"William's good faith in me is another matter entirely. He obviously felt that I had some merit, despite my flaws, for in the end he entrusted me with his beloved estates, Grandmama. Entrusted me with his son."

The duchess's face mottled with fury and grief, but Griff didn't regret his words.

"William was distraught. Not himself." Judith Stone faltered. "Else he would never have cast Charles into the hands of a worthless blackguard when I stood willing, ready to—"

"To what? Curse Charles to a life of misery as you did William?"

The duchess's eyes snapped up to Griffin's, and they were filled with loathing. "It was you who made William's life a misery. I loved him! Helped him!"

Griff laughed bitterly. "God preserve me from your love!"

A sharp breath hissed between the duchess's teeth, and her bony hand clenched the handle of her cane. For an instant Griff thought she would strike him with it. "My love? You've never had it! Never will! William was worth ten of you—"

"Do you think I don't know that?" Griffin turned away from her and drained the glass of claret in one gulp. "But William is dead. We shall all have to limp along as best we can without him."

Griff slammed the crystal goblet onto the edge of William's desk, then started to sweep past her and stride toward the open door, but Septimus Howell's gnarled hand flashed out, catching at his sleeve.

"Wait . . . Master Griffin . . ."

Griff stopped, turning to look into the loyal man's face.

"It is all right, Mr. Howell." Griff sought to soothe him. "I but need a breath of air. I fear I've not yet developed William's stamina for entombing oneself indoors for days on end. I think I will take a ride through the estates. Clear my head until it is time for dinner."

Griffin cast a glance toward the dowager duchess's gun-barrel-straight spine. "Come now, Grandmama, surely that prospect should cheer you. Think of the possibilities. My horse might shy and fling me into a wall. A coach might run over me. Brigands might set upon me." The slightest of grins quirked at this private joke. "You may even be fortunate enough to have me break my neck," Griffin observed with a sudden strange amusement. "Then everything would be under your control again. Graymore. Charles. Yes, even my ward."

"Your ward?" The duchess's thin brows arched.

"Mistress Isabeau DeBurgh," Griff said with a devil's grin. "I regret to say she has been suffering from a malaise for the past two days, but tonight will mark her full recovery."

Griffin felt a niggling guilt that he hadn't even glanced in upon the patient. But his nerves, already frayed by William's ledgers, had not been up to doing battle with a disgruntled highwayman. He resolved to make it up to her as best he could.

"I will be presenting Mistress DeBurgh to you at dinner this evening," he said breezily. "And, should I perish in the interim, she will be my vengeance upon you from the grave. Even roasting in Hades I could take joy in watching the pair of you rend each other limb from limb."

"I'll not be saddled with any common—"

"Mistress DeBurgh is far from common, Grandmama. That much I assure you. And she loathes me as much as you do. Think how entertaining it will be for the pair of you to plot my demise."

Chapter Eight

A hundred candles lit the vast dining hall, and each tiny tongue of flame seemed to bore into Griffin's skull like a gnome king's trident. If he *had* found some peace during his hard ride across the parklands, any serenity had vanished the moment he had recrossed Darkling Moor's threshold.

He peered down the length of the mahogany table with its scores of vacant carved chairs. The dowager duchess sat at the head, ensconced in regal splendor. Swathed in deep black mourning clothes, with her face set in harsh lines, she looked ready to burst with indignation and outrage.

Her grace had been annoyed when Charles had informed them he was traveling to London for a few days; Griffin had been none too amused himself, since he suspected the boy was avoiding their confrontation over finances.

But the duchess's mood had become black as the gates of hell when her precisely ordered schedule was disrupted even further.

Isabeau was late.

Griffin's own temper was held only slightly in check. Beau should have been in the dining room nearly half an hour ago, he thought, and she bloody well knew it. He had warned her to be prompt or prepare to face his considerable wrath.

Yet with each movement of the minute hand on Griff's golden pocket watch he saw nothing of the fiery-tempered young woman, nor of the quavering maid he had sent to fetch her.

He almost ground his teeth in aggravation, but he refused to give his grandmother the satisfaction of knowing he was annoyed. But despite his outward composure, his anger grew.

Restive footmen lined the frescoed wall like an impatient army awaiting its general's command. A dozen elegant dishes emitted heavenly scents from beneath their silver covers. Griffin knew that soon they'd lose what little heat remained within them.

The delicate concoctions that the dowager duchess's French cook, Alphonse, had slaved over were deteriorating with each second that ticked by, the sauces thickening into lumpy masses, the butter melting, the once yeasty, warm bread hardening into cold slabs.

The dowager duchess's discomfiture was the single fact in which Griffin could find a grim modicum of pleasure.

"That *person* is late." The sound of her voice in the suffocating silence almost made a gangly young servant drop a salver full of roasted capons. Griffin's eyes widened in mock surprise as he regarded his grandmother.

"Late?" he echoed. "I had not noticed."

"No doubt a civilized meal is far beneath your concern, since it has nothing to do with gaming or wenching. However, I do not intend to lower myself to your barbaric standards, despite your *position* in this household. If that *ward* of yours does not present herself at once—"

"Then we will both be eating our meal a good deal colder than Alphonse intended." Griffin glared at his grandmother, his jaw knotting. "I commanded Mistress DeBurgh's presence."

The duchess snorted. "You? Commanded?" She gave an ugly laugh. "Well, that explains it. We shall sit here until we are starved to death."

Griff's lips hardened in a brittle smile. "I warn you, madam, not to bait me further. Though I'm not a youth, my temper remains unchanged. And I promise you I will take whatever steps I deem necessary to maintain my sanity while I sort out this mess you and my nephew have made of William's estates."

"Indeed!" The dowager duchess huffed. "Of all the insolent—"

"I shall even crawl so low," Griff said with steely accents, "as to banish you to your dower house for the duration of my stay if you test me."

"You wouldn't dare!"

The corner of Griffin's mouth lifted in a taut smile. "Nothing, Grandmama, would give me greater pleasure."

Their eyes locked for long seconds, as though the dowager duchess was gauging the mettle of her hated adversary. The sensation raked white-hot claws of anger within Griff, but he revealed nothing in his gaze. He was well aware that any display of weakness would prove a lethal weapon in Judith Stone's hand.

A score of times she had glared at him thus, until he had at last looked away. But this time it was she who ended their contest, offering one small surrender.

Even that tiny victory was hollow for Griff. He yawned as though unaware of her withdrawal. "For all that I find your opinions tiresome, your grace," he said, waving one hand toward the food, "I fear that this waiting is becoming even more wearying. Perhaps poor Isabeau is daunted by the idea of dining in the midst of such august company. I fear she is . . . er . . . afflicted by most delicate sensibilities."

"Maybe if you had had the manners to introduce me to the girl before now, she would not be off hiding in her rooms! How I despise cowardly milksop chits!"

Griffin turned away from the duchess in an effort to hide his smile. But when he glanced out the open door he saw one of the maids who had been subject to Beau's temper.

"Ah, Allison," Griff called to her. "Come forward."

The servant froze, cornered, her hands clenching her duster. "Yer—yer lordship," the woman whined, bobbing him a curtsy, "I mustn't . . . I don't . . ."

"Do you not think Mistress DeBurgh bears a most . . . original temperament?"

"Original?" The servant choked. "Aye, sir."

"I am most eager for her grace to make my ward's acquaintance. You will hasten to Mistress DeBurgh's chambers at once," Griff said with deceptive mildness, "and you will tell her that there is nothing for her to fear here below."

"F-fear, my lord?"

"Just so, Allison. Tell Mistress DeBurgh that I have said she needn't shrink from dining with her betters. That we will make allowances for her . . . timidity."

For a moment Griffin thought the maid would fall into apoplexy rather than face Isabeau again.

"You tell Mistress DeBurgh *exactly* what I said, mind," he bade the poor quivering maid in unyielding tones. *"Exactly."*

"A-aye, milord," the woman answered faintly. She turned toward the grand staircase and Griffin glimpsed her making the sign of the cross as she disappeared behind the marvelously wrought carvings.

As though from a great distance, Griffin heard his grandmother's continued grumblings, but all his attention was focused on the open doorway. Anticipation raced through his veins as he awaited Isabeau's appearance—the same wild excitement and danger he used to feel when taking up his sword against some skilled opponent.

For Isabeau DeBurgh was as much of a challenge as any duel he had ever fought. And Griff knew full well that his words would flush Beau from her lair.

It seemed bare seconds before sounds of some disturbance reverberated through the corridors, drifting down the staircase like the alarums of battle. Griffin's muscles tensed, and he fingered the signet ring that glinted upon his left hand.

A high-pitched wail pierced the air, followed by shrieks and pleas that seemed to set the very prisms upon the chandelier tinkling against each other.

Then the deeper voices of the male servants joined in, their protests peppered with Isabeau's most colorful curses.

Griff glimpsed the dowager duchess's face. His grandmother was almost seething with aristocratic outrage. "Griffin!" she railed, addressing him by his Christian name for the first time since he'd returned to Darkling Moor. "What is the meaning of—"

Crash!

Griffin didn't even flinch at the sound of shattering china. He leveled his gaze at his grandmother and fought to maintain an aura of solemnity. "I fear Isabeau is a trifle clumsy with bric-a-brac."

"Out of my way, you gutter scum!" A voice rife with fury lanced through the room. All eyes snapped to the open doorway. The sharp hiss of a dozen people catching their breath echoed through the chamber as a small but mighty figure struggled in the midst of a cluster of agitated servants.

Griff caught the flash of fire-red hair and snow-white cloth. Then a burly underfootman thudded rump-first onto the floor, knocking over the beleaguered lad who had been balancing a trayful of capons. With a cry of dismay the boy let fly the heavy serving dish, raining roasted fowl upon the footman, the floor, and Isabeau's feet.

Her feet. Griffin's gaze locked upon the rose-blushed bare toes upon the chill marble floor. Disbelief streaked through him as he focused on thin white cloth pooling in disarray upon the polished stone. His gaze flashed upward to the meager veil of cloth that outlined her long legs and slim hips, the fabric anchored above firm but obviously unbound breasts by Isabeau's clenched fists.

Her shoulders were thrown back in defiance, her flowing hair cascading well past her hips, while her eyes—those huge, magnificent eyes—were alive with fury and courage and a challenge that made Griffin's loins fire with a fierce, wild need.

Desire and a grudging respect for her daring surged through Griffin as she stood defiant before him garbed in . . . what was it? A bedsheet?

"Mistress DeBurgh," Griff intoned ominously, uncertain as to whether to strangle her or kiss her, "I scarce consider bed linens proper attire for dinner."

"Well, you would have considered the alternative a damned sight less proper!"

"The alternative?" Griff rose to his feet. "Something original? Like clothing, perhaps?"

"Clothing?" Beau sputtered, stalking toward him. "You *burned* my bloody breeches, if you recall! My *favorite* breeches." She brandished one small fist inches from his nose. "You should be bloody *thanking* me for not setting your infernal grandmother on her ear by trekking down here naked as a newborn babe! Though I vow it was tempting!"

Naked, Griffin thought, astonished. Dear God, had the girl been imprisoned in her bed these past three days without a stitch to cover her? Considering that she'd all but unmanned him in their last encounter, it almost seemed a just revenge.

An apology half formed on his lips as he glanced from her flushed, indignant, strangely beguiling face to that of his grandmother. But the words died as he stared, stunned.

At the end of the table the dowager duchess stood, mouth gaping. Her eyes were wide with such a singular expression that Griffin knew he would never forget it. And at that moment he was certain that Isabeau DeBurgh had worked a miracle.

Judith Stone, Dowager Duchess of Graymore, had been struck dumb.

The absurdity of the situation sent pure, raw delight through him, and he sank into his chair, roaring with laughter.

Through his merriment he saw Isabeau's cheeks flush, her mouth setting. Then a small bare foot slammed into his shin with surprising force. Pain shot up his leg, but he only laughed harder still as Beau yelped, grasping her bruised toes with one hand.

"You son of a jackass! You hurt—"

"A th-thousand pardons for placing my shin in front of your f-foot!" Griff leaned against the table for support, swiping the dampness from his eyes. "Next time you attack, I'd suggest you wear . . . shoes. . . ."

His stomach ached from laughing, and he wanted to go on

so forever, but as he struggled to catch his breath he heard the quelling swish of velvet skirts, the dowager duchess's militant step as she stalked toward them.

When his vision cleared, his grandmother's face was close to his, her features distorted with anger. "I cannot believe this debauchery, even of you!" she railed, fairly quivering with rage. "It is heinous to bring this—this person to your family's home. This common doxy to play at bed games with—"

"I'm no whore!" Beau rounded upon the duchess. "And even if I were, I'd sooner sleep with my horse than with your precious grandson!"

Griffin choked and pounded on his chest with one fist in an effort to clear his lungs. "Your—your flattery puts me to the blush, milady. But I fear I intend to play no games with you save polishing you up to become a gem of the *ton.*"

"The *ton?*" the duchess shrieked.

"Yes, Grandmama. And *you* will have the honor of presenting her."

"I'd as soon rig out a swine to be presented to my peers!" Blue veins pulsed beneath Judith Stone's skin.

"You can take your snuff-nosed society and stuff it in a chamber pot, *your worship!*" Beau blazed, instinctively hating this haughty witch of a woman with her fish-cold eyes.

"Your grace, Beau." Griffin put his hand to his mouth to stifle a grin. "The correct form of address is—"

"I don't care if she's the Blessed Virgin!" Beau raged on, infuriated at his amusement. "I don't need her greedy-fisted, pinch-nosed 'ristocrat friends. I'm the boldest highw—"

"Isabeau!" Beau was stunned into silence by the death-grim warning she read in his unbearably handsome face. When her eyes met his, what she saw there rocked her to the center of her being. Fear. Of all the emotions she had expected to see, she had never expected to see fear.

Judith Stone's sharp scrutiny turned upon Beau, and she felt as though some malevolent god was inspecting her. And at that instant Beau silently pleaded with every saint she had ever blasphemed to shield her from the dowager duchess. The saints must have listened, for after a moment Judith Stone turned again upon her grandson.

"I'll not have this savage beneath my roof a moment longer," the duchess said. "Mark me, Griffin."

"Ah, but you keep forgetting"—Griffin gave an eloquent shrug—"this is no longer *your* roof to deny. *I* am trustee now. And you'd best pray that I am able to pull this dukedom away from the abyss, for if I don't, there will be no more Graymore left."

"Pray?" The duchess laughed. "Yes, when I heard you were returning to England, I vow I prayed—prayed every night that your ship would carry you to the bottom of the sea!" Her words snaked out like the cruelest of whipcords. "*You* should be dead! *You* should be dead instead of my William!"

Silence fell in suffocating waves over the room. The shock of the servants mingled with Beau's own sick horror. Ever since she had attempted to rob Stone's coach she had hoped for any manner of calamity to befall the high and mighty lord. But now . . . now she was astonished to discover that she ached for the man.

She wanted to touch his clenched fingers, wanted to shield him somehow from the old woman's viciousness. But she feared that to do so would strip away his pride.

Just when she thought she couldn't bear the crushing tension any longer Griffin's sensual mouth tipped into a smile that burned into Beau's very soul.

"I'm sorry to disappoint you, Grandmama," he said, in low, throbbing accents, "but then I always did."

Beau watched as the duchess spun away, sweeping from the chamber like some velvet-clad kestrel wearied of her prey. There was a soft shifting sound as Griffin lowered himself again into his seat, his broad shoulders slightly bowed, his eyes hooded.

"I find I am not as hungry as I thought," he said to the servants. "You may . . . offer my apologies to Alphonse."

Glad of the excuse to escape, the servants hastened from the room, leaving Griffin and Beau alone.

Beau started to edge toward the door, wanting to offer Griffin the only gift within her power—solitude. But he raised his fingers in a gesture to stop her.

"Beau . . ." He did not look at her, but she could feel his anguish and his humiliation. "I'll have a tray sent up to your chambers. You . . . you're scarce recovered from your wound, and—"

"It troubles me not at all," she interrupted, stunned at how desperately she wanted to ease his hurt.

"I'm glad," he said. "Forgive me for . . . for subjecting you to this . . . debacle. And for neglecting to secure you some gowns. It was most rude of me."

"You are always unforgivably rude, my lord," she said, her throat thick. "But . . . but it makes you almost tolerable for an aristocrat cur."

Griffin's forced laugh was devoid of amusement, devoid of life.

She caught her lip between her teeth to stop it from quivering, then turned to flee. At the doorway she hesitated, wishing she could offer some small comfort, but the words faded on her lips. Her eyes burned as she saw the dauntless Griffin Stone bury his face wearily in his strong bronzed hands.

Chapter Nine

The night was black as a brigand's cape, the moon a thin crescent that glimmered like the edge of a finely honed sword. Beau pressed her hand against the cool pane of glass, wishing she could slip into the darkness, far away from the rich brocade that hung about the vast bed, far away from the thick carpets, the elegant china figurines, and far away from the man who made her feel such strange, haunting emotions.

Griffin . . . She closed her eyes, trying to banish his image: his hair rich and dark and silken caught at the nape of a tanned neck, his blue eyes that twinkled with a devilment that matched Beau's own, and a mouth—a mouth so beautifully molded that it would have driven any doxy in Blowsy Nell's to pure ecstasies.

Beau's fingers clenched upon the window latch, and she unbolted it, flinging the casement wide, hoping the night wind would banish the heat stealing through her body.

How long had it been since she had experienced this kind of tugging at her heart? This sensation that some silken thread of kinship linked her to another's soul?

Since her father's death Isabeau had viewed emotional entanglements as a disease like the pox or the plague. And though she had friends, she had always kept part of herself hidden safely away.

She and Molly had always possessed a bond of understanding, but Beau had credited it to her friend's ability to burrow deep into other people's hearts.

And Jack had been her merriest comrade from the time she had been a child. They had rollicked and romped and raged and stormed with and at each other. Yet there had always been a comfortable distance in their relationship—a shared reluctance to get too serious about anything—life, death . . . love. . . .

Even recently, as Beau had become aware that the handsome highwayman wanted to forge a far deeper bond between them, she had managed to avoid entangling herself in emotions that she found more perilous than all the dangers of the High Toby. And more frightening.

Why, then, had Griffin Stone—an arrogant, mocking scoundrel of an aristocrat, the man who had wounded her, threatened her, all but imprisoned her—suddenly inspired feelings of . . . of emptiness, and an aching need to share?

"Share what, you bloody fool?" Beau asked herself with a sneer. "You already told him every secret from your past at that infernal inn, whining and wailing over your mother's weakness and your father's fate. Why, then, shouldn't his grand lordship be positively *chafing* to sit at your feet and tell you of the horrors that witch of a grandmother has wrought upon him? He'd no doubt be weak with gratitude as you dealt him out gems of wisdom from your vast stores."

She sucked in a frustrated breath, cinching the sheet she still wore more tightly beneath her arms. But she could not escape the sudden chill that went through her as she remembered the scene in the grand dining hall.

There had been such acid scorn in the dowager duchess's voice as she had raged at Griff, such loathing in her stingy cold lips and her ice-queen bearing.

Yet, though Beau had been struggling for two days now to examine every fault she could possibly find in the man who was her captor—though she had wanted—*needed*—to loathe him for making her feel helpless, she had found many attributes that had wrung from her a grudging yet sincere sense of respect. Qualities that would have made her proud, if he had been in her family.

She paced across the chamber, hating her realizations, feeling more trapped than ever. In the past she had unashamedly duped countless adversaries, but she had always been ruthlessly honest with herself. And the truth was that Griffin Stone would have had every right to send her to the devil for attempting to rob his coach. Most men would have left her by the roadside to die. Even the best of men would merely have continued on his journey and sent some lackey back to fetch her up and take her to the constable.

Yet Griffin had bloodied his own cloak, dirtied his own hands, carrying her back to the inn. He had summoned a surgeon and hovered over her, willing her to live. Beau had the grace to flush at the memory of his impassioned orders and the guilt that had laced his voice. Even when he had discovered her faking the severity of her wound, he had not called in Bow Street.

Instead he had taken her to his family's home, had her bathed, made sure she was warm, fed. Safe. Safe, to his way of thinking, from the world, and . . . from herself?

"Bah! I've done right well on my own!" Beau said aloud, thrusting out her chest. "And if he had but cooperated like the others and handed over his pretties without getting quarrelsome, we both could have saved ourselves this infernal tangle."

. . . there are those amongst us "aristocrat curs" who take it seriously when someone thrusts a pistol into our faces. . . . That mocking deep voice rang in her memory, and Beau felt a bittersweet wrenching in her chest. For while Griffin Stone mercilessly mocked the world around him, he mocked himself as well. Not with the brutal, sneering, cynical scorn of Judith Stone, but rather with a genuine amusement and acceptance of the world and all its foibles.

Bile rose in Beau's throat, at the thought of the dowager duchess's raking claws. How had he survived her cruelties as a boy and become the man he was? Not bitter, not hardened by rejection and life. But rather a proud man, a giving one.

A strong man, but a gentle one. A man with a temper as daunting as Isabeau's own, yet with a very real sense of justice.

"Sweet Jesus, next thing I'll be nominating him for bloody sainthood!" Beau groused to herself. "It is just that he is able to laugh . . . to see the absurdity in it all."

But how? The question again reared its head. "Madness. The man is either too mad to be miserable, or he is just plain stupid."

The door latch clicked, and Beau wheeled around. She almost tripped on the trailing sheet, and the swath of fabric slipped from her breasts. With a curse she yanked it up again, her face burning with embarrassment.

Griffin stood in the doorway, resplendent in amber velvet. His coat glowed like an ancient crown; his ivory breeches molded to his heavily muscled thighs. The candlelight from inside Beau's chamber picked out the golden threads among his rich brown hair. In his arms he carried a bundle.

"Isabeau. I'm sorry. I should have . . . have knocked before I flung open the door."

"Where I come from we're somewhat lacking in the amenities," Beau said with forced lightness. "Everyone barges in whenever they want. I barge in, too. With great regularity."

"I imagine you would," he said with a smile. After a moment he cleared his throat.

"I needed to speak with you about what happened tonight," he said at last. "It was unforgivable of me to leave you stranded beneath your coverlets without a stitch to wear. It was thoughtless and rude and unconscionable, even for one as churlish as me. I wanted to beg your pardon."

His eyes glowed softly as he watched her. "Of course, I wouldn't blame you if you told me to go to the devil."

"It would not be the first time," Beau said, but there was no edge to her voice. "And it will probably not be the last."

"No," he chuckled softly. "I suppose not."

"But I must admit, I so enjoyed seeing that rabid old witch near faint into her pudding, I can almost find it in my heart to forgive you, Stone. I've been considering adopting a sheet as my permanent wardrobe while I'm a guest here. I shall trail about, endeavoring to cross the hag's path. Her bellowings should prove most amusing."

She had hoped to see a twinkle of amusement in his eyes, but he sighed. "Believe me, Isabeau, you needn't go to such lengths to court my grandmother's wrath. The mere sound of my name has the power to make her face turn the color of blackberry jam."

He turned, walking to the open window as if he, too, felt the pull of the night. "It is beautiful," he said. "The sound of the wind, the stirrings of the night creatures, and the shadows of the trees reaching up toward the moon. It is as if the branches are trying to grasp something they can never have. And it's sad, because they don't know it is impossible."

His voice trailed off, and for a long moment they were both silent. "My mother was like that, I am told," he said softly. "Always wishing, dreaming. I often think of her on nights like this."

"Your mother?"

His voice held a forced lightness. "Contrary to your belief that I crawled out from beneath some rock, even blackguard scoundrels like me had mothers."

"I know that, you dolt." Isabeau looked away. "I was just curious, I guess. Wondered how . . . why . . . you became cursed with that harpy grandmother of yours."

"My mother died when I was six, and there was no one else to care for William and me." He chafed his thumb across the silk he held. "She was good and kind and beautiful, my mother. I miss her still." He hesitated for a moment. "This was hers. It would please me greatly if you would wear it."

Isabeau gasped as ever so gently he unfurled folds of peacock-blue satin, silver tissue, and ecru lace embroidered with gold thread. It was a gown. A gown so beautiful Beau couldn't keep her fingers from stroking one tantalizingly rich frill.

Surely he could not mean for her to don this magnificent garment, this treasured keepsake he had of his mother. It almost seemed blasphemous for him to give such a wondrous gown to her. She who was accustomed to swaggering and stomping and swearing.

"N-no," she stammered. "I . . . thank you. But I—I cannot. I'd snag it or tear it or dump a vat of sauce on it the moment I put it on."

"I much doubt that. You move more gracefully than any woman I've ever seen—even in your breeches." The slightest of twinkles stirred beneath Griffin's lashes, and Beau was shocked to find herself drinking in the sight. "I would like to see you in this, Isabeau," he said softly, extending the garment toward her. "Please."

Beau's pulse lurched, and her fingers trembled. She felt herself drowning in his sea-blue gaze, and she found that she could deny this solemn, sad Griffin nothing. She reached out tentatively, her callused palm snagging on the elegant cloth as she took it from him.

The dress was warm where it had pressed against his taut body, and it smelled of dried lavender and lemon blossoms. Beau suppressed the childlike urge to bury her face in the sweet-scented cloth. He must have treasured it, cherished it all these years.

And now he was giving it to her.

There was an odd pricking beneath her eyelids, and she turned away from him, hurrying behind a wooden screen to slip the garment over her head.

For some reason she could not name it was suddenly vitally important that she don Griffin's mother's gown, sweep out before him with the beautiful silver tissue molded about the bodice, the peacock silk draping elegantly down to the floor. But donning women's garb was far more complex than putting on simple breeches and sensible waistcoats, and after a leviathan struggle with corsets and ruffles, lacings and tight sleeves, Beau felt her frustration expand until finally she allowed herself one particularly colorful muttering.

She heard the quiet tread of boot soles on the floor, sensed rather than saw Griffin behind her. Then his strong calloused hands deftly tightened her laces, and untangled the fabric until it drifted down about her like the petals of some exotic flower.

When Beau's head emerged from the melee of silver tissue she caught her breath. She found he had shifted to stand before her, his devilishly handsome face bare inches away from her own. His breath was hot, sweet as it touched her skin, and his fingers were gentle as they tugged her tumbled curls from beneath the fabric.

Did she imagine it, or did his hands linger in the coppery waves, as if savoring their texture?

She felt hot blood surge to her cheeks, the flush spreading to where the tops of her breasts were exposed by the low-cut bodice.

Wordlessly he worked the intricate fastenings of the peacock silk stomacher, his knuckles brushing the fragile swells of her breasts as she struggled to steady her ragged breath. And her memory taunted her with vivid images of the way he had felt the night he had tumbled her back onto the bed to subdue her after her bath.

She remembered how heavy and hard his body had felt as he lay on top of her. And she knew the mere feel of his body could be more dangerous than any Bow Street runner.

Her heart skipped a beat, and she was suddenly, agonizingly aware that his hands had stilled. The gown swirled about her as though it had been created for her, the old-fashioned lines delightful. It was as if she had shed a chrysalis and was suddenly a jewel-bright butterfly in some kind of fairy-spun finery.

She saw her reflection doubled and redoubled in the polished windowpanes, but even so Beau could not believe what she saw—in those mirrored images or in Griffin Stone's dark-lashed eyes.

"My God." His voice snagged low in his throat. "Look at you, Isabeau. Look at you."

Beau held her breath, suddenly willing to endure forever the pinching stays, the binding sleeves, even the unsettling sweep of the low bodice to see Griffin Stone stare that way.

He looked at her with wonderment. Almost reverence. But most of all hunger.

Beau's stomach fluttered, her lips parting with a shaky laugh. "Th-thank you. I—I'd have been buried in silks forever if you hadn't . . . helped me. It was like a labyrinth in all those flounces and such, and I'm far more accustomed to dealing with the fastenings of breeches." Of their own accord her fingers brushed the creamy fabric encasing Griffin's thigh. A muscle jumped beneath her hand, the careless gesture and her bumbling words suddenly taking on an unexpected significance.

Her face flamed as she snatched her fingertips away. She turned, needing to put distance between herself and the dauntingly masculine figure before her. But her bare foot snagged in the underpetticoat, and only Griffin's firm hand saved her from crashing into the wooden screen.

"Perdition!" she blustered. "It's like walking among tree roots at midnight!"

His rich, welcome laugh rang out. "You'll grow used to it," he said. "In fact, soon you'll be sweeping gracefully about ballrooms."

"The devil you say," Beau grumbled, intensely aware of the heat of his hard palm burning through the thin silver tissue of the gown. She drew away from his touch, tossing her head with a carelessness she did not feel. "I've never even been able to learn to wield a sword. If I couldn't master something I needed to learn—something *useful*—how the blazes am I supposed to school myself to—to flit?"

"Flit?" Griff formed his lips into a censorious line, but his eyes brimmed with amusement. "Milady, a member of the *ton* does not *flit.*"

"Well, they look like bloody grasshoppers the way they skitter around, waving their snuffboxes and their fans and their infernal ribbons in a body's face. Makes my brain ache just to watch 'em."

She pursed her lips and fluttered an imaginary fan in the sugary-sweet way of the schoolroom misses she had seen about the confectioners' shops. "Lud, sir, you fair take my breath away," she gushed, then dropped her voice into a stage whisper. "Maybe it is because you reek of Hungary water."

Griffin strangled a laugh as he battled to capture the aura of a stern guardian. "Your manners, milady, are appalling."

"You flatter me, sir." Beau flashed him a smile and plopped into an awkward curtsy.

"I'd like to flatt*en* you most of the time. But maybe it would serve us both better if I were to teach you to curtsy in a way that would not inspire one to knock you into the next county for your insolence."

"Insolence?" Beau pressed her hands to her heart with an expression of feigned injury. Griffin dissolved into laughter. "Are you accusing *me* of *insolence?"*

"Yes. And I am accusing you of the far greater sin of having the most disreputable curtsy I've ever seen. A *lady* does not fling herself upon the floor like a squashed pumpkin. She holds her gown thus." He curved his hand over hers, demonstrating the proper manner in which to sweep up the voluminous petticoats. "And thus." He settled her other hand into place. "And then she drifts down gracefully, regally."

"I might have a bit of trouble being regal, Stone. It is my red hair, you see, and—"

"Try it," Griffin urged, his eyes dancing. "Once you master curtsying with the proper respect, I shall show you how to do it in a manner that will show your enemies that they are well beneath your notice."

"You mean you will teach me how to insult."

"How to insult someone most elegantly," Griffin agreed with a nod. "Think of the fun you could have."

"It would be more fun just to dump a keg of ale over their heads." Beau sniffed. "But if my lord insists . . ."

"He does." Griffin sketched her his most dignified bow. "Now, to curtsy properly you will need to know the rank of the person to whom you are being presented. If that person is a lord you would dip down so." He demonstrated.

Beau pressed her fingers to her lips, giggling at the sight of Griffin's muscled body moving in such a feminine gesture.

"If you are confronted with a duke or a duchess," he

continued, patently unruffled, "you will sink down farther still. You find this amusing, milady?"

"No, it is just that I cannot wait to discover how one insults a duchess. I plan to do so with great regularity." Beau muttered the last words beneath her breath, but Griffin heard her, and his blue eyes softened.

Beau felt again the bounding sensation in her middle, and she clutched up her skirts in her fists, hastily flopping into a curtsy in an effort to diffuse the tension. "L-like this?"

"Isabeau." Griffin caught her stiff hands in his, smoothing over the taut tendons until they felt soft as butter, her fingers seeming to melt into his callused palms. "Look at me," he said, his voice low, compelling. Her knees felt as wobbly as the day she had rolled down Tower Hill in a barrel, but Griffin only continued smoothing his thumbs over the vulnerable pulse point at her wrists.

"Isabeau, you look so beautiful here . . . now . . . garbed in my mother's gown. You should be proud, milady Flame. Show me."

Laughter had fled the room, leaving only echoes. Beau gazed into the compelling eyes of Griffin Stone, and slowly, with a grace she had not known she possessed, she sank into a curtsy.

Perfect it was not, and yet, as the flowing yards of her petticoats pooled about her in glistening waves, she looked to Griffin for approval.

Their eyes locked for long seconds that seemed to spiral out into eternity—an eternity of swirling heat, secret needs. Beau drew nearer the flame, her breath catching in her throat as she drank in the scent of him—fine leather, blooded horses, hot passions. Passions that flooded Beau, enveloped her.

She had scoffed at the tales Nell's girls had told of such soaring emotions. She had jeered at Molly's beloved stories of knights so bold and their ladies fair. And the more earthy side of sensuality . . . that had seemed to her at best an embarrassing inconvenience. But this . . . this need that flowed through to the very tips of her fingers, this vast emptiness filled with heady-sweet anticipation was a wondrous surprise. And a frightening one.

"Isabeau . . ." Her name rasped from between Griffin's lips. Then, as if he, too, felt the shattering temptations, as if he, too, held no power to resist, he groaned and pulled her into his arms.

She had not known what to expect, but whatever fleeting thoughts she might have entertained could not even touch the reality of Griffin Stone's kiss.

His hot mouth fixed upon hers as if he were starving for the taste of her. He crushed her against the unyielding plane of his chest, but this time it was not to bend her to his will; rather it was as if he were trying to draw something from her, something he needed with a desperation that stunned her.

Beau gasped, and her fingers clung to his shirt front, her knees weak. And as her lips parted, Griffin's tongue plunged past their trembling barrier, delving deep into the secret recesses of her mouth.

Beau couldn't breathe, couldn't think, mesmerized as she was by the power of his hunger. Of their own volition her hands moved up his chest, along the corded muscles of his throat. The honeyed satin of his skin tantilized her, tempted her.

Wisps of his dark hair brushed against her hands, and she buried her fingers in the midnight-hued locks at his nape. The black ribbon that had bound the thick waves loosened beneath her hands, and the length of satin drifted unheeded to the carpet.

She ached to have him touch her, touch her in ways that made blood rise hot to her cheeks, touch her in a way that would ease the fierce questing that knotted in her secret places.

His hands moved over her back, restless, seeking, and though she had never known the touch of any man's hands in the confines of Blowsy Nell's, she had witnessed enough to enlighten her despite her innocence.

He arched her neck back, his lips taking nips from the

smooth curve of her throat, the creamy skin of her shoulder. Stinging with embarrassment, yet devoured inside by her own raging hunger, Beau shifted in his arms so that his moist, fervent lips skimmed the tingling swells of her breasts.

Her lips parted soundlessly, and her nipples puckered with desire as Griffin's hand swept up her ribs to cradle and caress her breasts beneath their veiling of silk. And Beau held her breath, waiting, wanting that first brush of his lips on the aching crest. But suddenly Griffin grew still, and he slowly raised his head to look into her face.

"Did I—did I do something wrong?" She whispered the words, catching her lips between her teeth. "I've had about as much practice at this as I have at—at doing curtsies, and—"

"No, you are . . . sweet. Tasted so sweet." There was a tremor in his voice, and his fingers reached up to trace the vulnerable curve of her lips. "But I . . . we shouldn't. Can't."

"Why the devil not? If we bloody well want to." Beau suddenly looked away from him, remembering who he was, what she was. But she couldn't keep herself from whispering, "You did . . . want to. Didn't you?"

His laugh was harsh in his throat, but it held no amusement. "Yes, Isabeau. I wanted to." He smoothed the tumbled curls away from her kiss-dewed cheek. "But ladies . . . ladies do not allow gentlemen such liberties."

"I'm no lady! And you're sure as hell no gentleman. Stone, I—"

"Griffin. Call me Griffin. And you are wrong, Isabeau," he said earnestly. "You will prove to be a most formidable lady one day if you will but allow yourself the freedom to be one."

"I can't, Griffin. Even if I wanted to, I—"

"Promise me."

She was taken aback by the sudden solemnity in his voice. "Isabeau, promise me that you will at least attempt it." He looked away from her, his expression touched with a sudden melancholy that made her ache for him. "I've not done much right in my life," he said softly. "Not done much to be proud of. Of all the men in England, I am probably the least fit to be your guardian. But I vow I'll try to do my best by you. I'll try." He caught up her hands in a silent plea that humbled her, hurt her.

"Stay with me, Beau. For one month. Let me give you the life you were born to as a Devereaux. Let me prepare you to take your place at your grandmother's side. If you find you hate society's strictures, I promise that I will release you. Unconditionally, without saying a word to your family. And if that is your decision, I'll give you a purseful of gold that will keep you from having to dare the High Toby for the rest of your life."

"I love the High Toby," Beau said faintly.

"One month," he repeated. "If you choose to leave after the time is out, it will be your right to take to the High Toby again with a vengeance. But I trust, I hope, you will want to remain."

"I—I'll have to check my list of social engagements." Beau tried and failed to brush his words off with a quip. "It is busy upon the road of late, and—"

"Your word of honor, Isabeau." His voice was so soft it seemed to caress her. No jests, no barbs, only the tenderest of pleas.

Beau pulled her hands free of his grasp, whirling away from him in an effort to hide how much his words had affected her. "Oh, why the hell not?" she said with a toss of her head. "I've nothing better to do at the moment."

She heard the sound of his boot soles crossing to the door, heard it open partway, then stop.

"Thank you, Beau. For trusting me," he said. "And about—about what almost happened between us. You needn't fear—"

"I'm not afraid of anything," Beau said with a laugh, but it had a hollow sound to it, for she was afraid. Terrified. And mesmerized.

The bedchamber door clicked shut, and she turned

around, wishing she had done so in time to catch one more glimpse of those steely, broad shoulders, his thick, dark hair. The flash of his wondrous, solemn smile.

But he was gone, leaving behind him only the echoes of his words and the tingling sensations his hands had evoked upon her skin.

Chapter Ten

Beau stared at the door long minutes, listening to the sound of Griffin's stride as it grew fainter, more distant, until at last it ceased altogether. What had happened between them might have been nothing but a dream except that the gown's bodice still pinched her and its petticoats snaggled about her legs.

It had been real. Blazingly real.

From the first sorrow-kissed moments to the firing of their mutual passion to the soul-shattering tenderness she had seen in Griffin Stone's face. And he, a grand, high-and-mighty lord, had turned all those wild, raging emotions on her. Her. Isabeau DeBurgh. Hoyden Beau, who could ride or shoot or swear as expertly as any man born.

Why? The question raged inside her, tearing at her with an odd mixture of pleasure and pain, self-doubt and tremulous pride.

She rubbed her arms as if to warm them, turning back to the window. She watched her reflection in the window, following the image of the flushed, coppery-tressed figure as though it were a stranger. What had Griffin seen in her that had brought that hot light to his eyes, that had spawned in him that hunger and that tenderness?

Who was she? This slender woman draped in the finest silks, her hair tumbling in wanton abandon down her back. Her lips were kiss-reddened and moist. And she was trembling. Trembling and uncertain as she confronted emotions that were totally new and unexpected.

Beau watched the reflected woman, then slowly, carefully sank into a curtsy. A tiny smile played about her lips as she watched herself in the glass. But she quashed it, making a face as she fingered the elegant silver tissue of the over-petticoat that had belonged to Griffin's mother. Then she grimaced, glancing at her own rein-toughened hands.

"His poor mama," Beau said aloud. "She must be writhing in her grave at the notion of someone like me traipsing about in her things."

Despite herself, Beau's vivid imagination stroked pictures of the woman Griffin's mother must have been. Beautiful, blessed with the dazzlingly handsome features she had given her son. Gentle and so loving that Griffin's face had been filled with loneliness and loss, even after so many years.

Beau remembered her own anguish at her parents' deaths. Yet she had been lucky, treasured and pampered by Jack Ramsey and the rest of her father's family of renegades. It seemed that no one had showered such affection on Griffin.

"But his brother must have loved him," Beau said aloud, suddenly hating the echoing silence. "It's clear that Griffin adored his brother."

But in spite of that love Beau had detected a bittersweet shading of regret, a veil of anger. The legacy, she was certain, of Judith Stone's cruel favoritism. Beau's heart twisted with the certainty that other, more painful emotions must have tarnished the love between the two brothers. Resentment. Jealousy. Self-doubt.

And now William Stone was dead. And Griffin was left to carry the burning guilt.

Beau turned to the window, peering at her reflection again. But this time the image of the awed, uncertain woman who had smiled at her shyly moments ago was gone.

This time she looked like a jongleur's fool, tricked out

like a lady to ape her betters. Beau reached up a hand in an effort to smooth the defiant waves of her hair, but the curls still cascaded in a riotous halo as if daring her to tame them.

What would William Stone have thought of the stray brigand his brother had brought home? What would he or Griffin's delicate, high-born mother have thought of a red-haired, foul-tempered rogue of the road swaggering about their beloved Darkling Moor?

And what would they have thought of the way she had flung herself into Griffin's arms, willing, almost aching to devour his hard-muscled body, burning to drive away the torment that lurked beneath his rakehell grin?

Beau sighed, flopping wearily down upon a crewel-worked footstool, the petticoats that had swept about her so gracefully moments before bunched up like a washerwoman's bundles. How many times had she told Molly that the dead peered down at the earthly world from heaven's gates?

If it was true that phantoms stalked the living, Griffin Stone's loved ones were most likely swirling around Darkling Moor in an uproar, eager to get their ghostly hands about Beau's throat.

She glanced out at the black velvet curtain of the night, feeling an unfamiliar prickle at the base of her scalp.

It was idiocy. She did not believe in phantoms. But in this room, in this gown, it almost seemed as though she could feel the fingers of the past skim over her, entrapping her in some web that they alone could see.

"Bah! You're worse than Molly!" Beau said aloud. "Next thing, you'll be waiting for some demon, some banshee to plunge through the window and carry you off to—what the devil?"

Beau's heart plunged to her toes, and biting, deep terror engulfed her as a blur of misty gray and swirling black filled the open window. The figure seemed the embodiment of every specter she had ever created. She dived toward the fire iron. A feeble weapon, she feared, against a ghost.

But as she ran toward the window, her makeshift weapon poised, whatever had lurked upon the stone ledge came whisking through the open casement, devil's wings and horns and ghostly robes shifting into a whirl of cloak, divinely tailored breeches, and a most dashing tricorn with a cherry-red plume.

At the last possible instant she threw the fire iron away, driving it against the stone ledge instead of Jack Ramsey's face.

She froze, unable to move, stunned into silence by shock and sick horror at what she had nearly done.

Ramsey's eyes twinkled, and his lips curved into the careless smile that had made feminine hearts flutter on every highroad in England. An immaculate frock coat of biscuit-colored brocade swept back from a sapphire waistcoat, and the snowy folds of his neckcloth foamed about his square jaw in what could only be described as perfection. Despite his perilous climb up Darkling Moor's walls, he carried a beribboned walking stick tucked beneath one arm.

With a jaunty grin he leaned it against the armoire and crossed to stand before her.

"A thousand pardons, milady," he drawled, "but I must be in the wrong chamber. Surely this cannot be . . . the hoyden Isabeau DeBurgh."

The delicately mocking insult released the words horror had dammed up inside her. "You bloody jackanapes!" she cried, rushing over to lock the chamber's door. "How—how did you find me? What the devil are you doing here? Leaping through windows, and . . . and scaring me out of my skin! Don't you know it's dangerous climbing walls and lurking about, and—Christ, if I'd had my pistols, I'd have shot you myself!"

"Don't tell me you were *frightened,*" Jack whispered with infinite satisfaction. "Well, it'll be our secret, Flame. Though it's just like you to grouse about the modus operandi of your own rescue."

"My . . . rescue."

"Yes, after the debacle with the infamous Owen. Though I must say you put me to considerable trouble, Impertinence. I was beginning to wonder if saving your skin was worth the bloody snarls I had to uncoil. It was bad enough having to dash off in the middle of the night, expecting to find you dead by the roadside. And then seeing the blood and a sword . . . Once I saw the sword, I knew full well who got the worst of the encounter."

"My pistols misfired!" Beau cried, stung.

"I always told you they would." Ramsey's sage nod nearly gained him his death at her hands. "Dashed unpredictable, pistols are, not to mention noisy and dirty. In my opinion—"

"I don't give a damn about your opinion."

"Which is why you were wounded by my lord Stone's blade. It is fortunate he but grazed you in the shoulder."

"My shoulder." Beau gaped at Ramsey. "How . . . how did you know?" A sudden sick memory of the mystical Nell Rooligan and her supposed powers of sight rose in Beau's mind.

Jack flashed her a blinding grin. "It would be amusing to let you flounder about believing me to have bonds with the supernatural. However, I fear I came by my knowledge in a far more prosaic fashion. After I found the wrecked coach I tracked you to the inn. There I fortuitously happened upon a most loquacious serving wench. She was a country lass, quite fresh and innocent and new to the world away from her mama's knee. And she was fair bursting with the excitement of it all."

Beau ground her teeth, burning beneath Ramsey's superior aura. "She'd better pray she's not bursting with something else before nine months fly past." Beau shot a scathing look in the region of Ramsey's skin-tight breeches.

The highwayman's laugh rumbled low in his chest. "The lass has nothing to fear, though I must admit she was a tempting morsel. And, of course, all dewy-eyed and willing."

Beau gave an inelegant snort.

"However," Ramsey continued, ignoring her, "once I gained the information I had sought I bolted from the inn like the hounds of hell were at my heels, determined to pluck you from the grasp of the depraved nobleman who had taken you captive. Of course, once I saw this place I figured you would have the goodness to spare me the trouble of having to mount a rescue. Even that quaking friend of yours, Molly, would be able to slip from this noose."

"I could have escaped anytime I chose!"

Something flickered in Jack's eyes. "But you did not *choose.* Rather, you decided to parade around like a lady of leisure, sweeping about in fine skirts and drinking ratafia. If I hadn't happened to be below when you crossed before the window, I'd still be searching for you." Jack's eyes darkened with reproach.

"I can bloody well take care of myself, and you know it! I didn't ask you to forsake your latest mistress's bed to chase after me!"

Jack's eyes twinkled. "As a matter of fact, I *was* rather pleasingly occupied when Owen came charging in all astir. And yet"—he shrugged, his mouth twisting into its accustomed lazy smile—"despite your lack of proper gratitude, I am uncommonly glad to see you all in one piece."

The levity in Ramsey's voice was shaded with a very real relief, and his hands, gloved in the finest embroidered leather, reached up to chuck her beneath the chin. "Here the Maguires and I have been positively weak with fear for you, and you are flouncing about hale and hearty and . . . dare I say it?" His eyes skimmed down to her décolletage, one brow arching. "Looking like a *woman.*"

With an oath Beau drove her bare heel down upon Ramsey's instep, but he did not even make a satisfactory yelp. "Blast you, this is no time for jesting!" she railed. "You must leave—"

"I was hardly planning to stay and take tea." Ramsey's grin faded. "I but await your pleasure. Of course, it would most likely be more expedient to change into your breeches before you attempt to climb down. But if you want to pinch the dress, it is all the same to me."

"Steal the . . . of course I don't want to steal the dress!" Beau said with a quick stab of outrage. "It was his mother's!

And I gave my word of honor, I . . ." Beau bumbled into silence beneath the questioning light in Jack's gaze.

"Your word of honor, is it?" Jack said. "I wasn't aware you were over concerned about . . . ah . . . pretty speeches. Most especially when you were casting them out to swells like those who live in this monstrosity." He cast a scathing glance about the room. His eyes, when they returned to hers, held a hardness she had never seen before.

"He's not a swell!" Beau defended. "At least not—not like the rest of them. He—" She rubbed her throbbing temple. "It is hard to explain, Jack."

"I shall endeavor to stretch the meager powers of my intellect."

"He—he—" Beau raised her fingers to her elegant sleeve, toying with a bit of the gold trim. "There is—is a kindness in him, Jack. A goodness."

"Which a common rogue like me would not understand?" Tempests now raged in Jack's usually cool eyes, but Beau plunged on.

"Most noblemen would have left me to die. I would have been beneath their notice at any time, and after having tried to rob them . . . they would most likely have trampled me beneath their horse's hooves and gloried in it." She spun away, haunted by the memory of Griffin's rough voice as he had railed at her not to die, his strong arms as he had cradled her gently, so gently upon MacBeth's back.

"He took care of me, Jack," she said. "Even when I railed at him and baited him and tried to crush his pride. And after—even after all I had done, he didn't turn me in to Bow Street."

"Such nobility! It fair humbles me to listen to the recounting of such an unselfish, honorable act!" Accusation, jealousy, and hurt flashed across Jack's features, mingled with a bitter twist of betrayal. "You are a woman, Beau. Sweet Christ, it shouldn't be so difficult to figure out why this blasted nobleman dragged you off to his lair."

"And why, pray tell, was that?" Beau tossed her head with false bravado, her fists planted upon her slender hips.

She flinched as Jack's hands closed hard about her upper arms. "Damn it, Beau, you *know* why! Don't play the witling with me. Before Lord Stone fled England—banished because of a duel over a woman—he was a notorious rake with legions of mistresses to his credit."

"Then he must've begun indulging in amours in the cradle, for he was scarce nineteen when he sailed."

A dull flush mounted in Ramsey's cheeks. "Plague take it, Beau, what has he duped you with? Tales of how he, a poor innocent, was maligned by rumors? Stone and I are almost of an age. From the time I was fifteen I heard of his exploits."

"Curse you, Jack, I don't want to—"

"You don't want to know? That is most unfortunate, lady mine. For you're going to hear it. All of it." Beau could feel the tremors of anger racing through Jack, an anger such as she had never seen. For it was mixed with searing pain. And love. The truth she had been denying for so long lanced through her. Jack loved her.

But before she could deal with the crushing emotions within her, Jack loosed more venom upon the man he saw as a rival.

"Griffin Stone was the pampered darling of so many *ton* harlots I cannot even begin to list them," Jack snarled. "He was a profligate like his father. And he left more than one woman devastated in the wake of his waning attentions. It is rumored that one poor girl even took her own life rather than wed someone else—someone her father had chosen for her."

"Even if that Banbury tale were true, the wench must have been a poor-spirited drab! It is scarcely Griffin's fault if she had not the courage to defy her father." Beau chafed beneath the memory of the gentle, pained light in Griffin's eyes as he spoke of his parents. "I don't believe Griffin would wound someone that deeply."

"When will you believe?" Jack blazed. "After Stone has filled your belly with his bastard? After he casts you back into the streets, wearied of his pleasures? You won't be able to ride the High Toby, Isabeau, when you are swollen with child. And after you bear it, will you dare to take the chance of riding and leaving it an orphan?"

"It is pointless even to consider it," she said with searing honesty. "For it will never come to pass. I already kissed him. He thrust me away."

She had meant to demonstrate that Lord Stone held honorable intentions toward her. She had meant to soothe away her mentor's fears, to take some of the anger from Jack's handsome face. But at that instant she realized she had made a fatal mistake. The blood drained from Ramsey's features.

"You cursed little fool! For once, don't hurl yourself into the flames! Christ, girl, you deserve better than to be some rich nobleman's plaything! You have enough beauty and courage for ten women! It would do honor to any man were you to grace his bed—bear his sons." Jack's voice caught, and his lips contorted in anguish. "Damn it, Beau, listen to me for once in your benighted life!" Then suddenly his expression shifted, and he cursed, shaking his head. "Why the hell do I bother? Perhaps the time for words between us is past." His hand shot out, tangling in the fall of her hair.

Beau knew his intent. Now there was nothing of the elegant cavalier within the bold highwayman's face, none of the gallant knight of the road who had caused even his victims to tumble head over hindmost into love with him.

Jack's mouth was hard, angry as it closed upon hers, yet instead of the passion she'd felt with Griffin she felt only a kind of regret, and a sadness that dragged her spirit down like weights of lead. She forced herself to go limp in Ramsey's arms, her own feeling of stark betrayal leaving her torn and bruised inside.

Jack swore, shoving her away from him, his fists knotted, his breath ragged.

"Jack." She reached out a hand, wanting to ease his pain, yet knowing she could not. "I—"

"Sweet God, I mauled you like an accursed beast. Hurt you." His hand trembled as he reached out to touch her bruised lower lip. "Isabeau . . ."

She reached out, catching his rigid arm. "It is forgotten."

"We can never forget it, either of us," Jack said softly, his eyes abrim with misery and loss. "It will never be the same now between us two. For we cannot ignore . . . ignore the truth of it any longer."

"The truth?"

"That I love you, Isabeau DeBurgh. Have ever since you grew into a woman. But you . . ." He turned away, and a harsh laugh tore from his throat. "You seem to be the one woman in all Christendom who is immune to my legendary charms."

"Blast it, Jack, you are my best friend. Without you I'd not have survived."

"You would have fought your way through life if you'd been dumped in a desert, Isabeau. I don't want your gratitude! I want—"

Your love.

Though Jack didn't voice the words, they hung between them, an invisible barrier that could never be breached. The knowledge slammed into Beau brutally, ripping from her the shield of security she had always known in her friendship with Gentleman Jack Ramsey.

The silence yawned between them, endless minutes filled with the things they wanted to say. Things they dared not. And Beau wanted to rage at the injustice of it all—that she could not give this man, whose friendship she had cherished above all others, the one thing he desired in return.

"Beau, please. Don't—don't stay here. Come back where you belong."

She sighed wearily. "In truth, I don't belong anywhere anymore, do I, Jack? Lord Stone—he knew my mother. And it seems I have a grandmother. The dowager countess of a family named Devereaux. Hardly the usual patrons of Blowsy Nell's. But considering that I am also the get of Six Coach Robb, I am scarcely a fit ornament for a *ton* ball either. However, Lord Stone intends to attempt to restore me to my birthright."

"The Devereauxs don't want you, Isabeau! After your

mother died I went to their fancy estate, talked to the earl himself. I told them you were orphaned, all but begged the old bastard to take you in. In answer he had six of his footmen fling me off of his estate."

Isabeau chewed at the inside of her lip, uncertain, strangely hurt by the rejection she had never even known about.

"Damn it, Isabeau, listen to me," Jack pleaded, attempting to press his advantage. "These stiff-necked nobles will never accept you, and you—you'll suffocate under all of their blasted rules. It will kill you after a time—more certainly than one of Bow Street's pistol balls."

"I know that. But I gave him my word."

"And you intend to keep it?"

"One month, Jack. No more." She gazed steadily at her friend's face.

"I should knock you over the head, and drag you from this bloody chamber."

"I would only return." She walked to where a beautifully wrought silver candelabra graced a gilt table. The wood nymph fashioned by an artist's hand held the melancholy aura stealing over Beau herself. "You could not keep me prisoner forever, Jack. But if it is any comfort, Lord Stone will not be able to do so either."

Ramsey's shoulders sagged beneath his immaculately tailored coat, and he rammed his fists into his pockets with an alarming disregard for the crisp lace at his cuffs.

"I know," she said, "that in the light of all this I haven't the right to ask anything of you. But I must ask this one last favor. Molly—I fear for her. What with me unable to provide for her, old dame Rooligan will be casting her to those curs of men that dally about Blowsy Nell's. Jack, please take care of her, and of Owen, for just a little while. I swear as soon as I am free of my promise to Lord Stone I will find some way to repay you."

Ramsey rounded on her with an oath, and Beau took a step back beneath his piercing gaze. "You don't have to repay me, damn it! I'll do it for you. Freely. I wouldn't take your coin in payment if I was bloody starving to death!"

His words were like a knife twisting in Isabeau's belly, but she quelled the urge to go to him, knowing she could offer him nothing but more pain.

Jack wheeled and, retrieving his walking stick, stalked to the window. The breeze wafting in from the night plucked at the edges of his mantle.

"Jack," Beau called suddenly, beset by foreboding. He looked over his shoulder at her, his lips set in a tight line.

"I'm sorry," Beau said in a low, shaky voice. "I never meant—"

"It is scarcely your fault I ran blindly into an unsheathed blade," Ramsey bit out. "Take care, Isabeau, that you do not do the same."

In a heartbeat he was gone, leaving only the open window and the mournful sounds of the night. Beau crossed to the casement and closed it slowly, feeling for all the world as if she were shutting away a part of her life as well.

Chapter Eleven

The glossy hunter tensed its massive hindquarters, skimming over the stone fence with the dangerous grace of a soaring eagle. Griffin leaned low over the gelding's neck, the silky ends of its mane whipping back against his face, the heat of the rippling muscles between his knees warm and vital and alive as he urged the horse to even greater speeds.

Yet even if Brutus had sprouted wings and flown like some mythical steed into the new-risen sun, Griffin would not have been able to elude the demons chasing him this morn. Demons that would give him no peace.

Charles had returned. Griffin had heard him arrive hours earlier, and since then the youth had set the household topsy-turvy with his demands. Griff had wanted to confront the boy at once, about the troubles between him and his father. But Septimus Howell's description of Charles's pain—however difficult Griffin found it to discern—made Griffin curb his own impatience.

God knew he'd caused enough disasters in his own life. He did not want to be the one who pushed the scatter-brained youth beyond his endurance.

No, he decided, he'd wait until Charles was settled comfortably in his rooms, wait until his own emotions had cooled. Yet even the difficult prospect of dealing with Charles seemed like nothing compared with other chafings in Griffin's spirit, chafings that had left him sleepless the past night.

He shifted in the saddle, his hands clenching the reins as the glorious parklands of Darkling Moor blurred before his gaze and became green eyes wide with wonder, and riotous waves of red hair.

She had burned him . . . Isabeau . . . had seared her image into his soul forever with one kiss. A low ache throbbed in Griffin's loins as he remembered the taste of her, the feel of her crushed against him, eager, so eager.

He had kissed more than his share of women, women who had refined the play of lips upon lips into an art form. Yet never had he been struck through to the heart by a single kiss.

The pressure in Griff's loins twisted tighter still. The cravings that had tormented him through the night clamored again. Christ, he had wanted her. He had wanted to devour her with his hands, his mouth, wanted to take the sweet gift she had offered with her heart-wrenching blend of innocence and defiance.

She had looked so beautiful garbed in his mother's gown—a tumbled angel God had cast down before him as a jest, or one of Satan's own come to bewitch him. But if it was the gate of hell toward which Isabeau DeBurgh had been luring him, Griff knew full well he would have plunged through it to lose himself in the sensations she had stirred within him.

Yes, except that he could not forget the look of trust that had shone in her face.

Griffin cursed, leaning even closer to his mount's neck, driving the gelding to bolt faster still. Trust. Had he ever seen that emotion in the face of someone he had cared about—a trust untarnished by doubts or scorn?

But in spite of everything that had happened between him and Isabeau—despite ragings and railings and dragging her to Darkling Moor under the threat of calling in Bow Street—she had placed her life in his hands with all the faith of a child—a stubborn child, true, and maybe a reluctant one. Her reluctance had made it more precious still, for Griffin had known it had cost her a portion of that fierce, swaggering pride.

His horse cleared a bramble hedge, the impact of hooves striking earth scarce jarring Griffin, poised as he was in the polished iron stirrups.

Resolve roiled through him. He had vowed to do his best by Isabeau. Reunite her with her family and introduce her into society. *And,* he had added to himself, secure her a fitting marriage. A man to cherish her, to temper the recklessness that constantly threatened to plunge the girl into calamity. A man worlds away from rakehell Griffin Stone.

He smiled wryly, imagining for a moment he and Isabeau married. In his mind he painted images of Isabeau astride her midnight-black stallion, the beast keeping pace with Brutus, Beau's hair streaming back from her face, her face flushed as she tried to best him.

He could see her green eyes snapping with delighted challenge in the fencing room as he schooled her supple, lithe body into the graceful poses and swift moves with the rapier that he himself had learned so long ago.

As if you would bring her anything but misery, Griff could almost hear Judith Stone's acid voice. You would make her even less fit to take her place at her grandmother's side.

Griffin's smile faded, his whimsical musings slipping away, leaving only a gray, empty void.

But even robbed of his imaginings, Griffin knew the voice of caution whispering inside him was right. For Isabeau DeBurgh he would be the worst possible choice.

She needed someone who would nurture her, pamper her, pet her, without flying into a fury every time she opened her mouth. She needed someone who could hide his smiles at her antics, a man of more sober temperament who could guide her. Not someone who would urge her on to even greater absurdities, delighting in the mayhem she created. Not someone who would make her even less acceptable within the confines of polite society.

Griffin was stunned to realize how much he wanted for her. Wanted her safe, cared for. Loved. And he wanted it not with the detachment of one fulfilling a tiresome moral obligation, but rather desired it with a depth that made him willing to do anything, everything necessary to gain her such safe harbor.

He reined in Brutus. Silence engulfed the parkland, even the wood creatures seeming to pause and listen. "Isabeau." He said her name, his throat tight with regret and a very real longing. Then he tucked away the fantasies he had woven of the time they could spend together, locked away the memory of her mouth, soft and wet beneath his, her eyes, alight with a vibrant, glowing enthusiasm for life he knew he could never share.

He would be her friend during the coming month. Drink in her warmth, her sparkling gaiety, her fiery temper. Drink of the life he now knew he had shut away beneath a facade of bored arrogance and reckless ways.

Desire fled, replaced by an emptiness even colder than before as Griffin turned his horse back toward Darkling Moor. But try as he might, he could not drive from his mind the vision of Isabeau trembling in his arms upon the brink of discovering what could prove the most delightful adventure of all.

Griffin combed his fingers through his wind-tousled hair and stalked into the study, knowing how a condemned man must feel approaching a gallows. The servants had not drawn back the curtains, and the room had the aura of a tomb. Only the meager flickerings of a fire upon the grate cast any light about the study, but the flames did nothing to drive back the damp chill clinging about the chamber, nor did it chase away the shadows groping up the walls.

Griff's jaw set hard, and he wanted to go anywhere, set himself to any task in order to escape burying himself once again in the estate's morass of paperwork. But he forced himself to stride into the room, knowing that he needed to comb through the figures one last time. Check the numbers and then collect his thoughts before mounting the back staircase to confront his nephew.

Griff grimaced, taking a taper from a silver candlestick and plunging its tip into the embers upon the stone hearth. The flames flared at the disturbance, and the warmth trickled over Griffin's fingers with the same welcome sensation as Isabeau's hair. His hand clenched upon the silver as he made his way to the desk that was covered by an even more daunting pile of correspondence and ledgers than there had been the night before.

With an oath Griff swept one palm across them, attempting to clear a space for the candle holder, but the pieces of parchment scattered across the floor in total disarray.

Griff wanted to drive his boot into the polished wood desk in total frustration. But instead he thumped the taper down in the tiny space he had cleared and dragged his burning eyes down to the topmost layer of parchment.

On the first paper he recognized the instructions as having been written by the steward at one of William's lesser estates. Most of the others were inked in other unfamiliar hands. Yet suddenly Griff's gaze locked upon one other bit of parchment. This one bore a bold scrawl he had seen not only in England, but at Marrislea as well. Those rare, precious letters he had taken out to read and reread, that fed that part of him hungry for news of England and the life he had left behind.

It was from Tom Southwood. And, most astonishing of all, it was addressed not to William, nor to Charles, but to Lord Griffin Stone himself.

Griff took up the sheet, a faint smile playing about his lips. Thunder in heaven, how did Tom always know when Griff desperately needed a bit of cheer? In every crisis, whenever things appeared the bleakest, a note would be delivered bearing the seal of the Southwoods of Myddleton.

Flopping down into William's leather chair, Griffin broke the seal of wax, cheered by the prospect of being diverted by his friend's ever-amusing tales.

But when Griffin unfolded the parchment and scanned

the first lines his anticipation dimmed. Instead of Tom's customary jovial greetings and amusing anecdotes, the missive was a warning.

. . . regret the mess that awaits you . . . urge you not to do anything rash . . . Charles so flighty, I feared to confront things until your return . . . will arrive from France in two weeks . . . I shall send word and meet you in London and we will figure out what to do. . . .

"What to do?" Griffin swore aloud.

What incident had triggered Tom's words of caution, his plea for patience? Nowhere did he enlighten Griffin as to what the devil it was he was supposed to remain calm about.

Griff frowned as he examined the cryptic note again. His patience with this ordeal was growing thin. "How the devil can I figure out what to do if I don't even know what the blazes I'm supposed to be doing something *about?*"

He came to his feet, crumpling the letter in his fist. "If it is something with Charles . . . by God's wounds, the gudgeon has done enough damage to Darkling Moor already. No matter how much pain the boy is in, the dukedom can't afford three more bloody weeks of coils." Griffin's jaw clenched. The one thing he'd discerned after hours in William's study was that whatever strange accounting William had made had been for his son.

. . . urge you not to do anything rash . . . Southwood's plea echoed in Griffin's mind. All the anger, confusion, pain, and passion he'd tried to suppress since his arrival on English shores erupted into pure fury.

Maybe he could do nothing about his desire for Isabeau or the ugliness between him and his grandmother. But Charles —Charles and the fool disasters the boy was indulging in—now, that was an affair Griffin could damn well deal with, swiftly, even ruthlessly, if the cursed dolt would not see reason.

Fists knotting, Griffin stalked from the study. "Where the devil is his grace?" he snarled at a snipe-nosed servant.

"H-his grace? Why, I believe he is abovestairs, being attired by—"

Griff did not allow the man to finish. He charged up the stairway and down the winding corridors to the far wing, where Charles's apartments were.

Without knocking Griffin charged through the bedchamber door. Inside the room looked like a battlefield, strewn with casualties of the finest laces, gem-hued velvets and brocades, waistcoats, stockings, shoes, and jeweled shoe buckles.

A snuffbox that had apparently offended the sensibilities of its owner lay rejected amid a pile of cast-off wigs. The whole chamber reeked of soured wine.

In the midst of the mayhem Charles sat draped in a white sheet, his entire face engulfed in a powder cone as his valet busied himself with pomatum and powder, attempting to arrange the intricate curls of his ornate wig.

"It is about time you brought my tray, you lazy wench!" Charles complained, blinded as he was by the white cone. "It would drive me mad to have to suffer the company of my infernal grandmother and my hypocritical oaf of an uncle."

"Y-your grace . . . no," the flustered valet tried to caution his master. "It is—"

"The hypocritical oaf," Griffin snapped.

Charles emerged from the powder cone sputtering, red-faced, and as guilty-looking as a boy caught slipping pepper into his tutor's tea. "U-uncle Griffin . . . I mean, my lord . . . I . . ."

But Griff ignored his nephew's stammerings and glared frigidly at the valet who seemed comically to be shielding his master with the powder cone. "You are dismissed," Griff said, gesturing toward the door.

"My lord . . . his grace . . . he needs . . ."

"What his grace *needs* is . . ." Griffin's furious words trailed off as he thought that if the duke were a child he would take grim satisfaction in applying a willow switch to Charles's backside, or relieving him of his riding privileges.

But Griff swallowed the harsh words, unwilling even in his fury to humiliate Charles in front of a servant.

"His grace needs a few moments alone with me," Griffin

said in dangerous, measured accents. "We have had precious little time to converse since my return. And I am most eager to hear of all his adventures."

"A-adventures?" Charles choked out, his face flushing with unease as the valet skittered from the room. "I . . . I . . . don't understand."

"Neither do I. Perhaps you could enlighten me." Griffin thrust Tom's letter forward. The boy flinched as though he half expected to be dealt a leveler, but then his anxious gaze saw the paper.

"I say now. It is the outside of enough, charging into my very bedchamber, ordering out my servant! I tell you, I had nothing to do with—"

"With *what,* pray tell? You've not even glanced at the letter, let alone read what it says. Not that it says much, by God. Only that I should keep my temper and not do anything rash."

"I—I think that must be good advice." Charles licked his lips nervously, taking the note as gingerly, as if it were a dead rat.

"You do?" Griffin said coldly. "I wonder what Tom considers rash. It is all in one's definition, you know. For myself, I'm beginning to be tempted to thrash you within an inch of your life unless you tell me what the devil is going on here. After the muddle I've found in your father's account books, thrashing seems a mild punishment."

Charles scooted out of the chair, feigning bravado, but his sheet slithered to pool upon the floor, setting up a cloud of powder. "I—I . . . How would I know what your addle-witted friend is babbling about? I've done nothing."

"Nothing more than cast your inheritance into the Thames. I'll not stand by and watch you fritter away so much as another farthing on gaming, Charles. Mark me. One more penny and you'll spend the next three years barred in a sponging house—"

"I've not been gaming for over a year now," Charles cried, "not since—"

"Since you broke your father's heart?" The words were

too cruel, and Griffin knew it the minute they were spoken. The boy's face turned ashen.

It was as if in that instant time had spun backward, turning the gangly youth into the child Griffin had loved. The child Griffin had wanted to comfort, to soothe after suffering Judith Stone's harsh words, after William's iron dictates.

Griffin turned, raking his fingers through his hair, as the last of his fire-hot temper drained away.

"Charles. Boy, listen to me," Griffin said, self-loathing making his stomach churn. "I didn't—didn't mean that. What I said about your father. You were the most important thing in his life. He would have laid down his life for you."

Charles's face contorted with grief and anguish, and a horrible, sick sound came from his throat. "What do you know about my father? About me? You charged back in here as if you were master of Darkling Moor—raging at the servants and at Grandmama, and at me! You lock yourself up in Papa's study, hatching your plots with Howell standing over you like some accursed guard dog! You pretend to care about Darkling Moor and my father. Pretend to care about me. But the truth is, you don't belong here any more than that street urchin you dragged in with you."

"Charles," Griffin struggled to find the right words. The boy needed calming, soothing.

"I *loved* my father! *Loved* him! Perhaps I wasn't the most dutiful son. Perhaps I—I did break his heart. But at least I was *here* to do it! At least I wasn't an ocean away, letting him believe I still hated him even after ten long years had passed!"

Griffin paled as if Charles had run him through with a sword. For a moment they stood silent, the words they had wielded blanketing the room in raw anguish.

When he could speak Griffin kept his voice low and quiet. "Whatever you think of me, Charles, even if you should choose to hate me, this conversation is not over yet. I need to know what happened here between you and William. I need to know what caused him to drain the dukedom's treasury dry. I didn't come to gloat over my brother's bones, Charles. I came to help."

"You're too late to help now. Too late. My father is dead, and I . . ." Charles stopped, slamming his fist against the wall. "Why don't you just sail back to that barbarian plantation of yours and leave me to go to the devil? It is what I deserve! What I—"

With an oath Charles stalked over and snatched up one of the frock coats lying on the dressing room floor. "I have nothing more to say to you, Uncle Griffin. Now or ever. If anyone comes looking for me, you may tell them I am staying with the marquess of Valmont."

"Valmont?" Griffin echoed. He tried to think of something, anything, to bring some sense to this madness. "Is he responsible for what has happened? Even before I left England he had led more than one man down the path to ruin. *Talk* to me, boy, for God's sake!"

Charles roughly put on his coat. His face held loathing and disillusionment and despair, and he seemed at once young and agonizingly old. "You may be in control of my fortune for the time being," Charles said, his chin jutting up, "but I'll be damned if you can forbid me whatever company I choose to keep! I choose my own friends, I do, and—"

"Dammit, boy"—Griffin gave a vicious kick to a pile of garish waistcoats—"it looks to me as if you choose your friends with about as much taste as you use in selecting your wardrobe."

"And you? What about *your* companions?" Charles flung out. "What about that girl you dragged here who was tricked out in breeches?"

"You have all you can manage handling your own affairs without concerning yourself with mine. Now talk to me, boy! At once!" Griff took a menacing step toward him.

Instinctively Charles drew back, stuffing his fists in his voluminous coat pockets. "Why should I waste my breath?" Charles cried. "I can see they've already turned you against me!"

"*They?*"

"That withered-up old man, Howell. And that sanctimonious Tom Southwood! A regular prig he's turned into." Charles's lips were trembling, his body shaking. "I'll not stand for it, Uncle Griffin, not stand for being slandered and falsely charged with no evidence against me! Even felons are told of their crimes before they are dipped in hot tar!"

"Three weeks hence Tom will return to England. And then"—Griff paused to pin his nephew with a glare—" then, if you have anything to answer for, you will deal with me."

Charles tried to keep his hands from shaking as the broad shoulders of his uncle disappeared through the doorway. He leaned down and picked up Griffin's discarded letter, eyeing the inked lines as though, by will alone, he could somehow strip away the mysterious scribings and reveal whatever lay beneath Tom Southwood's cautious words.

Could it be that Southwood knew? Had discovered . . . ?

Charles swallowed hard. His fear almost strangled him as he thought of Griffin's steely-cold eyes and unyielding features.

How many times in the past year had Charles wished desperately for the return of the bluff, bold uncle who had been his champion as a child? How many times had Charles dreamed of the notorious Lord Griffin breezing into Darkling Moor to sweep him away from the abyss he'd been teetering upon for so long?

Charles had even begun letters more than once, trying to ask for help, trying to explain . . . but how did one explain something so dark, so horrible? Something that would be inconceivable to a man of Lord Griffin Stone's ilk?

In the end, even when Charles had confided in his father, it had only tightened the noose of horror around William Stone's throat as well, snuffing out his life like the flame of a wind-kissed candle.

He closed his eyes, trying to drive away the image of vine-shrouded ruins tucked deep in the countryside's woodlands. That pile of gray stones felled by time seemed to thrust its arms skyward as if in supplication.

No, it was too late now for his father, for himself. Too late to do anything besides fling himself deeper into the darkness.

He could only pray that soon it would consume him.

Chapter Twelve

In her dreams someone was tightening a cage about Beau's waist, driving the breath from her lungs and setting them afire. She tried to wriggle away from the bindings, tried to sink more deeply into the heavenly softness beneath her, but something thin and irritating bit into the soft flesh beneath her armpits, a plate of stiff material mashing her breasts and chafing at their tender curves. . . .

Blood and thunder, what torture device had she fallen prey to? Beau wondered groggily as she came awake, one hand scraping across the scratchy galon trim and hard, faceted gemstones that pressed into her stomach. Was she bound in an iron maiden? The scavenger's daughter?

She rolled over, and lumpy, tangled lacings ground into her back. Beau grimaced wryly. No, it was the most modern form of torture—an accursed woman's gown.

She struggled to open her eyelids. The sunshine streaked through the windows and warmed her cheeks, but the piercing rays were too hot. She dragged one of the feather pillows across her eyes, blocking out the light.

It had been the very devil of a night! First the scene in Darkling Moor's dining hall. Then there had been the even more devastating moments with Griffin when his sadness had robbed Beau of her defenses, leaving her spirit naked. And then . . . then, when she had still been stricken with uncertainty, with emotions she had neither desired nor expected, *he* had come. Jack, his jaunty grin vanished, his eyes black with betrayal.

Surely a night fraught with so much turmoil must have chiseled a millennium or two off of her sentence with the devil. And yet, when it had seemed that even fate could not summon up another misery, there had been the coup de grace.

She had been unable to undress! The lacings that Griffin had managed to fasten with such ease had been beyond the reach of Beau's own fingers. Her arms had almost been fused to her sides by the bodice's tight sleeves. And as if that were not enough, when she'd attempted to catch the end of one of the lacings, she'd snaggled them, so now it would take a knife to free them.

She had struggled for over an hour, swearing, stomping, and finally kicking the bedpost with her bare foot. Her throbbing toes had forced her to admit to herself that her attempts to get free were futile.

She had considered sneaking into Griffin's room and enlisting his aid until she had realized that she had no idea where his lordship was staying. Saints knew, she could hardly have wandered about the mansion in the darkness, peeking in each door, searching for him.

Despite a grinding pain in her left side, Beau chuckled into the pillow. It would have been worth a night's purse just to see Lord Griffin's reaction.

But she feared stumbling into the room of that wizened, nasty-tongued harpy. What would her grace have thought were she to see the girl she had treated so callously looming there above her?

"Maybe the old witch would think I meant to cut out her tongue," Beau mumbled with sudden satisfaction. "She might fall into apoplexy, or her heart might slam right away to a stop. Just think of the debt of gratitude Griffin would owe me then."

Beau giggled. If she were to rid him of that plague, he would most likely kiss her feet.

But the mere thought of Griffin Stone's sensual lips playing anywhere upon her body brought a rising tide of heat to Beau's flesh, a tingling sort of breathlessness akin to the sensation of tumbling from the stable's ridgepole.

A tremor worked through her as she remembered the feel of his hard body against her, the scent of him—fine leather, wild winds, mingled with a sharp tang of danger. His touch had been worlds apart from Jack's desperate kiss, worlds different from anything she'd imagined.

Griffin had fitted her body to him with a swift mastery that had made her feel fused to his long frame, that had made her long to bury herself further still in the wonder of him. And his mouth . . . there had been none of the awkward groping the women at Blowsy Nell's spoke of, no sickeningly wet bruising of her lips by his. Rather, he had taken her mouth with a hunger and a skill that had left her starved for more.

More . . .

Beau tightened her fingers upon the downy pillow, hating the ache that stirred deep in her secret places. She had wanted so much more from Griffin Stone. Wanted to hurl herself into the fires he had lit within her.

She'd never shied away from risk or from dashing headlong into any adventure she might choose. And she'd been ready—no, eager—to drown herself in what Griffin had offered her with his mouth, his hands. Never had she desired anything with a more compelling, more relentless strength.

And she had told him so . . . all but pleaded . . .

If we both want to . . . want this . . . then why should we not . . .

Her words echoed back to haunt her, flooding her with the heat of raw embarrassment. He had put her aside as though she had been a spoiled child wanting to make herself sick upon sweetmeats.

The thought stung, and yet, even through the waves of humiliation, Beau could remember the expression that had been on Griffin's face. He'd looked at her with such need.

She'd seen such vast loneliness in those storm-blue eyes that it had stolen into her heart and made her want to stomp into Judith Stone's bedchamber and break something over the cursed harpy's head.

She wanted to go to Griffin, hold him, soothe him.

Beau swallowed hard. She was sure the mighty Lord Stone would see her actions as pity, and she knew full well it would wound his fierce pride. She knew this because in that, at least, they were much alike. No, it would be much better to, say, kidnap his grandmother and sell her off to a band of sailors as a gift for some sultan in Turkey. Just think, she could help Griffin and bring an end to the Ottoman empire all in one fell swoop!

Beau grinned, pleased with her imaginings, suddenly eager to arise and greet the day. Perhaps she could do little to solve Griffin's problems, but the one gift she could offer—the one thing that he would not reject or see as a battering to his pride—would be laughter.

From the first they'd shared a quirky sense of the ridiculous. Helping her out of this predicament with the gown would doubtless cause him no end of amusement.

With that she flung the pillow off of her, ready to spring to her feet. Yet the instant her eyes flew open they all but popped out of her head. For looming above her like some spectral phantom was the dowager duchess herself.

Beau's heart plunged to her toes, but she didn't betray her discomfiture. She merely leveled upon her grace a most frigid stare.

"Blood and thunder! There is more traffic in this cursed bedchamber than there is in Covent Garden at high noon!"

The dowager duchess's mouth soured, and something in those pale-lashed eyes built a deeper wariness within Beau.

"You must excuse my intrusion," Judith Stone said, the warmth in her tones failing to reach her eyes, "but I must confess I've spent a most troubled night."

Despite herself, Beau grimaced. "It must have been something to do with the phases of the moon. It seems the affliction was incredibly widespread."

The duchess arched one brow, glaring down her nose in obvious displeasure. "I did not come here to be mocked, Mistress DeBurgh. Nor to be subjected to a tart tongue. Granted, we did not start on a favorable footing. Nor shall I insult your intelligence by denying that I do not want you here in my home."

"Griffin's home, for as long as he is guardian to his brother's estate," Beau put in.

The noblewoman's eyes narrowed further still. "Regardless, my dear, I fear that your loyalties to my grandson are most misplaced. Dangerous, in fact. You think me cruel, heartless. I see it in your face. But what can a child like you know about a man who is as deeply flawed as my grandson? What can you know of the pain I have suffered at his hands?"

Beau's chin jutted upward, her fingers still holding the counterpane snuggled about her shoulders. "Oh, I assure you, I can see *exactly* how much *you* have suffered, your grace." She crinkled her nose in disdain. "You think you're a bloody queen, dealing out commands, trampling on any who dare to defy you. But Griffin didn't lie crushed beneath your heel like the rest of the world. He dared to get up and spit in your eye!"

"Spit in my . . . you little hussy!" Judith Stone's porcelain-pale cheeks turned purple with outrage. "How dare you!"

"I'm renowned for having more daring than is considered healthy, *your grace."* Beau flung back the coverlet and stood. "It is one of my innumerable faults."

But instead of the harsh rejoinder Beau expected, Judith Stone gasped, her eyes locked on the somewhat crinkled folds of the silver-tissue gown.

"Where—where in God's name did you get that?"

Though Beau did not know why the woman was so agitated, she gripped the other's weakness with an instinct learned in the London streets.

"The gown?" Beau said, smoothing the elegant fabric. "It was a gift from my lord Stone. Do you not think it lovely?"

"L-lovely?"

"It seems it belonged to his mother," Beau said, flouncing the fall of ruffles in a deliberately careless manner.

"That is impossible. I burned it . . . burned everything."

Her words deepened Beau's confusion, but she charged on. "Well, apparently this gown rose from the ashes," Beau said. "It is a garment befitting a great lady. Do you not agree?"

"Lady . . ." The woman almost strangled with rage. "If you are fool enough to think for a moment that you—you would ever defame this family by . . . by . . ."

"By what, your grace?" Beau asked with poisonous sweetness.

"My grandson would never stoop to marrying so far beneath him! You are a barbarian of a wench, and lord knows how he was saddled with you! A doxy who would parade about naked as a Fleet Street strumpet!"

"I was wearing a bedsheet," Beau corrected. "And, in all fairness, it was not my fault. I was summoned to dine, and no one had bothered to give me any clothes."

"No, I would imagine my grandson much prefers you without them." An ugly snarl twisted Judith Stone's features. "And it is obvious you've not the wit to deny him! What has he promised you? Silks? Satins? Jewels? Heaven knows he's lavished a king's ransom upon more women than I can count. And after he has taken his fill of them he has thrown them aside with no more thought than he would give a torn neckcloth."

"He is going to make me a lady," Beau said, hating the older woman for echoing Jack's dire predictions.

"A lady?" Judith Stone flashed a scathing glance at Beau's disheveled hair, her crumpled gown, her bare toes, visible beneath its hem. "Look at yourself, girl." The duchess grasped Beau's arm, wheeling her toward a small cheval glass in the corner of the room. "God's own hand couldn't mold you into a lady! And as for this supposed link to the Devereaux family, I promise you that if you attempt to foist yourself upon them, they will hurl you out into the street with the rest of the slops."

Beau winced. The woman's words dredged up all her hidden doubts, all sense of her weaknesses. She glanced at her reflection in the mirror, remembering Jack's trip to Devereaux House and their blatant rejection.

The magic that had transformed Isabeau into a fairy princess the night before vanished like a dream mist. She was no longer the wide-eyed wraith of last night trembling upon the brink of something akin to beauty, but rather the belligerent, flame-haired termagant from whom every man in Blowsy Nell's had fled in fear.

Judith Stone's voice dropped into low, sneering tones. "You possess not even enough beauty to entice my grandson for a fortnight, Mistress DeBurgh. I promise you. However," she said, considering, "it is possible for you to emerge from this unfortunate incident, shall we say, most profitably. Yes, more so than you'd ever imagined."

Her clawlike hand closed over Beau's fingers, turning her palm ceilingward. The duchess held a purse above it, upending the container over her palm. Coins, gold and silver ones, rained down.

"Look at it, girl," Judith urged. "Take it. And if you need more, you have only to send word, and I—"

Beau cut her off with an oath, yanking her hand from the old woman's grasp. "I don't need charity, your grace. Nor do I accept bribes. And I assure you, I am quite capable of securing wealth like this for myself whenever the bloody hell I choose." Beau spoke the last words between gritted teeth, then flung the coins against the wall. They clattered and clinked with a deafening racket, scattering and rolling to the far corners of the room.

"Now, if you'll excuse me," Beau said. "I've lessons to attend to. I've mastered the curtsy, you see, but Griff promised he would teach me how to do it in a way that would insult whomever I was greeting. And I assure you, your grace, that is *one* lesson I am *most* eager to learn."

Clenching her teeth, Beau scooped up her voluminous skirts, her eyes spitting scorn as she dipped into a curtsy so exquisitely insolent that Judith Stone blanched with fury.

"Ah, perhaps that is one lesson I will not need," Beau

said, turning her back on the duchess and starting to sweep from the room.

"Girl!" Judith Stone's voice rang out. "Do you know with whom you are dealing? What power I wield?"

Beau grinned. "Fortunately, I am ignorant enough not to care, your grace." With that, Beau left the room, slamming the door with a resounding crash.

Chin held high, she stomped down the grand staircase, heedless of her untidy hair, immune to the gaping stares of the servants as they skittered out of her path. She preferred that they give her wide berth, for ever since she had arrived at Darkling Moor it seemed that she had been forever tripping over the witlings.

Yet when she reached the bottom landing it was as if there was a maze of doorways. The mansion was so large that a dozen people could live in its confines and never be forced to run into one another. Considering Judith Stone's disposition, it was a most endearing feature, Beau thought. Yet this morning it made finding Griffin all but impossible.

"You!" Beau barked, suddenly spying the underfootman she had knocked upon his backside the night before. The young man all but flattened himself against the wall. "Thunder in heaven, you gudgeon, I'm not going to black your cursed eye! I just want to know where Griff—I mean his lordship—is."

The servant's fingers grasped his shirt as if he did not wholly trust her promise, and he wet his lips with his tongue. "I—I . . . his lordship left orders that he not be disturbed."

Beau laid one finger along her jaw in consideration, eyeing the underfootman. The man started to tremble visibly. "On second thought, I may black *both* your eyes unless you—"

"No! No, don't!" The youth flung up both hands in surrender. "He—he's in the study again. Been there nearly all morning, 'ceptin' for his ride . . . and . . . and seeing the young duke. And—and breakfast. He had a bit of beefsteak."

Beau raised her eyes heavenward. "I'm not concerned about his lordship's menu, but I am at a loss as to how to find this infernal study you say he's buried himself in."

The footman waved one shaking finger toward a door at the far end of the hall. "There. But he—he left orders not to be disturbed. And his lordship's in a most fearful temper."

"Well, so the bloody hell am I," Beau said, brushing past the youth. She swept down the corridor, the footman stumbling in her wake, fighting desperately to reach the door before she did. She half expected the lout to bar it with his body, but instead the quaking youth grasped the door latch, opening the portal for her.

"My lord, Mistress DeBurgh," the youth choked out, his voice cracking with terror.

"Blast it to hell," a voice snarled from within the dim depths of the room. "I told you I was *not to be disturbed*—"

"He isn't disturbing you," Beau said. "I am."

She stepped inside the chamber, trying to adjust her eyes to the shadowy interior. "I threatened him with grave bodily harm if he did not lead me to your sanctuary at once."

She waited for some response, expecting a reluctant chuckle or at least a snarl, but she heard nothing, saw little, able only to discern the silhouette of broad shoulders scarcely touched by what meager light filtered through the gap in the curtained window.

"Isabeau," Griffin said with hopelessness in his voice that made her want to reach out to him. "I fear I am even less fit company than usual. You should ape the servants and flee to the far ends of the house."

"It would be a cold day in hell when I would cower from the likes of you, aristocrat cur," Beau said, closing the door.

A strained laugh broke from Griffin's lips, but he didn't turn toward her, didn't look. "You would do well to rethink your position," he said. "You need only ask my grandmother, or my nephew to discover what a villain I am. A regular Lucifer garbed in a mortal's clothes. It would be wise to run from me."

"Bah! I tend to be a bit on the . . . *devil*ish side myself. Jack gave me my highwayman's name, and believe me, it had more to do with my temper than my hair."

She was rewarded when Griffin faced her, the corners of

his lips tipped in the faintest of smiles. "I believe you," he said at last, crossing the room to stand before her.

With aching gentleness he took up a strand of her tumbled curls, winding it about his finger. "If the devil's flames are indeed this hue, I might willingly lose myself in them, and welcome," he said softly. "But you must be careful, Isabeau. Cautious. For if it was discovered who you are . . . what you were . . . even I might not be able to protect you."

The old Beau would have bristled at such a warning. God knew she'd all but skewered Jack with his own sword whenever the highwayman had attempted to protect her. She had always prided herself on being strong, insisting on fighting her own battles.

But she had never known how much courage it took to trust a corner of your soul into another person's keeping, until now.

There was something devastatingly endearing about the earnest tenderness in Griffin's face, in his touch. Something she sensed was as rare for the rakehell Lord Stone as it was for the hoyden Beau.

She swallowed hard, mesmerized by the gentle light in Griffin's eyes. "Even . . . even if I did slip and babble the truth," she managed to say, "who would believe it? The—the Devil's Flame is a monster of a man, with fists like anvils. . . ."

She fell silent. Griffin reached down and took up one of her hands, cradling it in his own. "I think the *Spectator* exaggerates a little," he said. "Your hand is more the size of a full-bloomed rose, and nearly as soft. Yet I can attest that it wields a pistol with much skill."

"I'll match myself against you any day you might name," Beau said with forced sauciness.

"Only if we pit ourselves against each other with swords as well."

She made a face, making him smile again.

"But now," he said, "for the purpose of this intrusion. Even you would not charge into the dragon's lair without reason, Isabeau. What is it? Did I neglect to see to your breakfast? Clothes . . . those I provided last night, if I remember."

"Yes, and then abandoned me trapped within them. I had to sleep trussed up like a partridge, my lord. Have you any idea what it feels like to attempt slumber in a bloody stomacher?"

Griffin stared, taken aback. "Sweet Mary, I—oh, Lord, Beau, I did not intend . . ." He cursed, and Beau was stunned at the embarrassment streaking across that handsome face. "First I practically dragged you down to the dining hall in nothing but a bedsheet, then I left you stranded in full regalia the night through. It is an infamous guardian I make, milady."

"And I make an infamous lady," Beau said softly. "Your grandmother came to my bedchamber this morning to tell me so in no uncertain terms. She said that God himself couldn't make me into a lady. And she was willing to pay quite handsomely to make certain that you never had a chance to try your hand."

Beau saw Griffin's mouth tighten. "And what, Isabeau, do you say?"

"I say I'm going to be the most pinch-nosed, cursed elegant lady the thrice-damned *ton* has ever seen." Beau tossed her head, eyes blazing defiance. "Teach me."

"Teach you?"

"Yes. Lady nonsense. Fluttering and fan-waving and swooning and such like. Though if you cannot teach me how to swoon without bruising my hinderparts, I don't intend to try it."

A faint smile played about Griffin's lips. Isabeau glared at him. "Well, if I'm going to make a fool of myself, I might as well make a thorough job of it," she said with a wounded sniff.

His hand swooped up to curve along her cheek, the brush of his calloused palm sending sparks hurtling through her veins. "Ah, Isabeau, Isabeau. I predict that you will set the *ton* on its ear. Despite us all."

Beau caught her lip between her teeth, her heart thudding

against her ribs as Griffin's hand fell away. He turned, crossing to sweep the velvet hangings from the window, and sunlight spilled into the room. In that instant she knew that she would do anything he bid her just to see that beguilingly tender smile again.

Yet even as he turned back to face her wariness poured through her, an instinct for self-preservation making her hide the confusing emotions.

"What is it to be?" she demanded brusquely. "Shall I flatten myself upon the floor? Wave painted chicken skin in your face? If so, you must provide me with a fan."

"I fear that your poor body has already been savaged enough by your sleeping attire. Perhaps we should postpone tutoring you in the social graces until you have the appropriate wardrobe. Today we'll turn you over to the mercy of the seamstresses, have them fit you out in everything a lady of quality might need."

"Pistols and breeches?" Beau asked with a saucy grin.

"But of course." Griffin's smile almost reached his eyes. "Dueling pistols, the finest to be had. Still you'll need someone to help you in and out of your weaponry—a lady's maid, perhaps?"

"Oh, no, Stone! I'll not have one of those sniveling baggages that dissolve into tears every time I come near 'em!"

"I'll have to find one suited to your . . . special needs," Griffin said, his eyes warming. "Perhaps one that is a master with the stiletto or dagger."

"Those traits would make us compatible, I should think. Between the two of us, we should be able to plot the demise of your grandmother quite nicely. But if this maid and I are to go off on such adventures, I think you should commission some slippers. Either that or return my boots. It is damnably cold in this drafty old place, despite all these great marble fireplaces."

"Cold?" Griffin's smile died, his gaze flicking down to where her toes peeped from beneath the hem of her skirt. "Poor moppet. I am the most reprehensible of rogues."

He scooped her up and set her down in a mammoth

leather chair. He knelt before her. His hands slipped beneath the hem of her skirt, and he cupped one small foot in the palm of his hand, drew it from beneath the veil of silver tissue.

"Sweet Christ, Isabeau, your foot is like ice," he scolded, attempting to chafe warmth into the skin by rubbing her foot between his palms.

"It is not so bad now that your hands are there to warm them."

"You shall have the finest slippers in Christendom before nightfall. I promise. But your foot is so small . . ." He seemed to take its measure, the pale length of it lost in his big hand.

Beau's breath caught as he raised her toes to his lips. A jolt of fire seemed to race up her leg as he brushed his mouth across the delicate arch of her instep. Wisps of his hair that had come loose from the ribbon tickled her skin, the shadowing of stubble upon his chin a delightfully rough contrast to the moist softness of lips, the silky cool whisper of his tumbled locks.

"I'll do better by you from now on, Isabeau," he said low in his throat. "I swear it." His thumb traced a circular pattern upon her skin, and she thought she might die of the pleasure of it.

She knew she would always remember this vision of the bold Lord Griffin kneeling at her feet, his face as full of tenderness and passion as any knight errant of old.

Chapter Thirteen

Valmont House was draped in curtains of mystery. The aged hallways and vast chambers were bursting with strange curios collected by generations of Alistairs who had devoured anything that whispered of dark magic, mysticism, or the netherworld. Every available space was filled with ancient tomes from Turkey and crystals claimed to possess powers that made most men squirm. Statues depicting Lucifer's fall from heaven and Eve's temptation in the garden were tucked within nooks in the walls.

Even the elegant moldings on the ceilings held savage scenes. Instead of grinning cherubs and voluptuous goddesses, Delilah sheared Samson's hair, and Mary Magdalene, unrepentant, tried to seduce Christ.

For what seemed the hundredth time, Charles tore his gaze away from where a black-liveried servant had disappeared an hour before. The servant had bade him to wait, saying Valmont was being attended to by his valet after having spent a late night at his revels.

It was a habit of Valmont to keep his visitors waiting in the midst of his macabre collection. From their first meeting Charles had suspected the man enjoyed startling people with his human skulls and bats' claws. Valmont liked making people confront the macabre within themselves. But he needed to go to no such lengths with Charles. Charles had already seen the void within his soul.

Charles now tugged at the frill about his neck, growing steadily more anxious. Once he had found Valmont's castle amusing, and he'd enjoyed the obvious contempt the current marquess held for these ancient trappings.

Back then Alistair had seemed so bold, mocking the grim sobersides who ran in fear of the devil, of dark magic and demons. In the beginning it had been a lark to listen to the older man blaspheme with such relish, to hear him say things that Charles would never even dare to think.

Charles used to watch from the outside of the circle of friends while Alistair and his exclusive set fairly drowned in mocking laughter over hobgoblins and witcheries. Their select band had swaggered about London and the countryside, jeering at anything that reeked of established society or its strictures. They had seemed somehow invincible, not swayed by the opinions of their elders or their betters.

Charles had watched them with wistful admiration as he had chafed beneath his father's rule, wishing he could be as daring and bold and reckless. And when the marquess had shown a most decided interest in Charles Stone, he'd scarcely believed his good fortune.

For the first time in his life Charles had felt that someone approved of him. That someone was actually heeding what he said. And the more outrageous his words became, the more rebellious he acted, the more Malcolm Alistair had approved of him. Until at last Alistair had taken him into the circle of his favorites. Alistair had promised him entry into a most elite society, a wondrously diverting secret society formed solely to amuse its members.

It had been heavenly. His new friends had given Charles the strength to stand up to his father, to throw off a good measure of the old man's chains. Charles had reveled in the attention they paid him as he followed them to the city and back. More and more he had avoided his father while slipping deeper and deeper into a world of gaming and wild, reckless diversion.

He remembered the first few meetings he had attended—gatherings that had proved to be every bit as diverting as Alistair had promised. Revelings in which Charles enjoyed the finest wines and foods, meetings where a dozen courtesans satisfied other appetites, some of them performing acts that were so remarkable Charles had been stunned.

The celebrants had indulged their every whim, within the walls of the ruined abbey, gorging themselves upon sweet, pure pleasure. Charles had gloried in it, reveled in the laughter, the amusement, reveled in his defiance as he tried always tried to imitate the rakehell uncle his father had banished from England so long ago.

It had all seemed perfect, so perfect, until . . .

Charles paced toward the fire, extending his hands toward the flame, but the bright tongues did not warm him.

Everything had seemed so perfect until the disastrous night when his whole life had crashed in around him.

It had been the night of his initiation. The night Valmont had mocked church rites, offering up what he had claimed was the "lamb of the world." That night he'd slashed the throat of a newborn sheep while the others looked on, muttering strange incantations that had made Charles's skin crawl.

He'd been stunned, his stomach churning at the sight of the crimson blood gushing from the slash, the strange light in Alistair's eyes as he had let its warmth run over his bejeweled fingers.

Though outwardly Charles had laughed with the others, he'd been sickened, wanting only to return to his bedchamber at Darkling Moor and drive the scene from his mind. He had resolved to quit making trips to the abbey, had even begun making excuses. He might have stopped altogether, could have stopped, were it not for the disaster that struck him that last night.

Charles wiped his damp palms on his doeskin breeches, bile rising in his throat. A tall, gangly youth had appeared, wanting to drag his sister away from that night's revels. Who had goaded Charles into taking up the sword against the youth? Charles did not know.

He'd been drunk on fine liquor and beautiful women and stinging with the knowledge that he must soon surrender the only place he'd ever felt he belonged.

He'd killed a man that night. And though he'd not been the one who died that night, he had lost everything when the youth fell under his sword. Even though Malcolm Alistair had proved himself the most loyal of friends, disposing of the corpse with remarkable haste, Charles had taken the first step into an abyss.

Three days later Charles had received the first note demanding a ransom to be paid for its author's silence. More missives followed, demanding greater and greater sums, each message containing a damning scrap of information about the death of the farm boy and the abbey rituals. The information had unnerved Charles, making him feel as if the demons Alistair had tried so hard to summon really were watching over him, waiting for him to fall into the everlasting pit of fire he deserved.

Desperate, he had gone to Alistair, demanding to know if one of their brotherhood was behind the horrible scheme, or if Alistair might think the missives a sick prank. But Alistair had looked him directly in the eye, reminding him that the other revelers had been almost unconscious with drink. He'd said that none of the others would remember the happenings clearly enough to describe them in such minute detail. And Alistair himself would never stoop so.

Surely Charles could see that it would be most inconvenient for Alistair, as well, should word of their little fetes escape.

Charles had left Valmont House sick with fear and dread, unable to confide in anyone in the weeks that had followed.

He had stopped eating, starting to waste away in terror, until at last his father had confronted him, refusing to let Charles leave until the boy told him the truth.

The pain, the terror, and the regret Charles had felt over the accidental killing had burst from him, and he had sobbed like a child in his father's arms, feeling for the first time how much the man loved him. But it was that precious, fragile bond of love that had kept Charles from telling his father the full details of what had happened at the abbey. The debaucheries still filled Charles with sickness and shame.

The duke had paid the ruinous sums that were demanded, culling them from every resource at his command. And he had vowed that he would not sacrifice his son into exile as he had his younger brother, even if the Stones lost everything they possessed. William Stone had tried valiantly to find the fiend who was blackmailing his son, but in the end it had been futile. The demon seemed to have vanished back into hell.

Charles shook away the memory, fingering the objects on a small claw-foot table. Sick dread washed over him at the thought of his uncle Griffin discovering anything about the bloody mess, the horrible secret that Charles alone was responsible for the ruin of Darkling Moor, responsible for his father's death.

For if the duke had not been so obsessed with saving his son, so preoccupied in keeping Charles from harm, William would not have been so careless. He would not have tumbled off of his horse. A second horrible accident. A hideous waste. All because of Charles.

He shifted his gaze to his fingers and snatched them back, horrified, as he saw that his hand had been fondling the dried head of a mammoth python, its skin shrunken upon its frame of bone.

"You do not like my grandfather's little pet?"

The sound of a voice made Charles nearly leap through the ceiling, and he spun about. Alistair stood bare inches away.

"Is—is it not enough that you have kept me waiting all this time? Must you also be so rude as to creep up behind a guest?"

"And *frighten* him?" Even without lead paint the marquess's face was pale, as though it had never known the kiss of the sun. His lips curved in a most charming smile. "You must forgive me, dearest. My tardiness is inexcusable."

"It is all right. I'm afraid I've been a trifle preoccupied."

"Preoccupied?" Alistair questioned with concern. "And I thought we had managed to drive all tiresome worries from your head. Pray tell, what can be of enough import to so trouble one of my own?"

"It is my uncle. Lord Griffin."

Alistair emitted a sneering laugh. "Ah, his illustrious, most respectable lordship. Scion of the infernally boring. Surely, Charles, you are not child enough to pay him any heed."

"I—I would not, except this morning he barged into my bedchamber enraged."

"What grave crime were you guilty of? Taking a shilling without his permission?"

"I don't know. I am not certain what it was about." Charles slipped his fingers into his waistcoat pocket, withdrawing the crumpled bit of vellum therein. "He but stormed in and waved this missive beneath my nose, demanding to know what devilment I was about."

Alistair reached out his bony fingers, plucking the letter from Charles's hand. The boy shifted from one foot to the other, twisting his ring as the marquess skimmed the lines. His eyes shone with keen interest.

"Ah, so Tom Southwood is nosing about in other people's concerns."

"I fear that—that he has somehow discovered what happened that night, when there—there was the accident."

"Accident? As I remember, it was quite deliberate, my sweet. A brilliant thrust to—what was it? The heart?"

"Damn it, Valmont, don't!" Charles cried in a sick voice. "It is no jest to me, no grand lark. It was murder, pure and simple. The boy scarcely knew what end of the sword to hold."

"I fear I cannot understand these subtleties of honor you seem prey to. If you'd not dealt with the ragged wretch, he would have been quite happy to kill you, I am certain. Then you would be rotting in the bottom of Killey's well, and he would be off grubbing potatoes or whatever that sort do."

"Alistair, I do not take this lightly. A boy died that night, and someone is threatening to tell."

"Not as long as you keep humoring them with money, boy. Of course, you could always go off to the wilds of the colonies, or else take up residence at Newgate with the rest of the cutthroats."

Charles felt the blood drain from his face, and he gripped the edge of the table to steady himself.

"Now, now, don't go off into such a taking," Alistair soothed. "Believe me, dearest, there is nothing to fear from men like Tom Southwood or your uncle, nor from the author of these mysterious notes. You are one of my own, now, Charles, and I will protect you."

Charles shifted beneath the weight of those odd amber eyes. "I just want this to be over. Finished. I want the nightmare to end."

"You are just feeling a bit overwrought, Charles. Why, it was not that long ago that your father took that most unfortunate fall from his horse. It is little wonder you are so skittish." Alistair grasped Charles's trembling arm with his cold hand, guiding him toward the doorway. "You must go home now, my dearest, drink a decanter full of port, and vent your loins on some hot-mouthed serving girl. You will feel much better in the morning, I suspect."

"N-nothing will ever make me feel better," Charles whispered, drowning in hopelessness as he stumbled toward his coach. "It will never, never end."

Alistair's brow arched as the boy clambered into the dark coach. "Ah, my poor, misguided pet," he muttered to himself with a gloating smile. "Nightmares never do end. Therein lies their power."

Chapter Fourteen

The day was bright as a new guinea. Sunlight streamed across the bedchamber from the windows Beau had flung open at dawn.

She perched on the narrow stone window ledge, her new gown of blue watered silk a bright splash of color against Darkling Moor's stone walls. Her feet dangled, encased in tiny blue satin slippers with glittering diamond shoe buckles that sent reflections of rainbows spilling across Beau's skirts.

Griffin had promised to do better by her, and in the past few days he'd proved to be as good as his word. A few mornings ago she had awakened to find a dozen seamstresses lost in a sea of brocades and taffetas, silks and satins. Costly laces had crested the waves of fabric as if they were no more than sea foam, and jewels, from translucent pearls to flashy, bold emeralds and diamonds, had been scattered about like seed for a flock of hungry chickens.

The band of seamstresses had had Beau at their mercy for three days. It had been hard to keep from snapping and snarling at them when they accidentally stuck her with pins or left her standing for what seemed like hours but in the end she began to enjoy seeing their glorious creations.

Although she'd rather die than admit it. The first day there had been one bloody rebellion when Beau swore she would cleave out the gizzard of anyone who attempted to truss her up in stays again.

But fortunately for all concerned, Griffin had heard the commotion from his study and had smoothed things over, settling the question in Beau's favor before she took a scissors to Madame Charmande's petticoats.

His lips had been curved in the slightest smile as he had paced over to her, spanning her waist with his hands. "Look you, now, Madame Charmande," he had addressed the seamstress in charge. "Have you ever seen a woman with such a willowy waist, even one who is all crammed into one of those infernal contraptions you ladies are wont to wear?"

Beau's stomach had gone fluttery, and she'd forced a cocky grin. "You can put 'em in the fire with my breeches, Stone," she'd warned. "Because the next one who comes at me with one of those torture devices will be wearing it around his throat."

With great ceremony Griffin had taken up the offensive article and left the room, holding it far from his body, as if it were a repugnant snake.

After that Griffin had poked his head into the sewing room with great regularity, giving his opinion on everything from the amount of lace to be caught at a morning gown's cuffs to what kind of edging should be sewn onto a chemise.

Beau had teased him unmercifully about his knowledge of women's intimate apparel, scandalizing the servants and sewing women alike. But Griffin had only laughed, his eyes twinkling and his mouth curving with pleasure.

Beau smiled at the memory now as the dewy-sweet breeze kissed her cheeks and toyed with the little tendrils that had escaped the chignon the quivering maid had coaxed her hair into that morning.

Stone had a beautiful laugh, she thought, trying to get a gauzy butterfly to land on the outstretched toe of her slipper. The man should definitely laugh more often. But she imagined that there was not much to be merry about in the dark, brooding study in which Stone sequestered himself for long hours every day. Each time Griffin left the dim room the muscles were tightly drawn over the bones of his face, his eyes dulled with frustration and exhaustion.

Beau sighed as a cloud darted before the sun. Blast it to hell, she was beginning to like Griffin Stone far too much, beginning to take tally of the worry lines in his brow, the grimness hovering about his mouth. She was beginning to seek the man out and try to think of some outrageous quip that might amuse him.

It was absurd, this fascination she had with him, and yet . . . every time she looked at the wardrobe now bursting with beautiful gowns, every time some servant delivered a new trinket Stone had decided no lady should be without, every time he tugged her curls or laughed at her jests, Isabeau felt something stir deep inside her. Something wonderful. Something new.

A furtive sound behind Beau made her wheel, leaping to her feet in the tall window casing. She'd half expected to find the dowager duchess gliding toward her, ready to push her out the casement. But instead there was only a scrawny maid, shaking so hard her teeth were chattering.

"You witling!" Beau snapped. "You nearly made me jump out that window, sneaking up on me like some kind of cutthroat."

"Y-yer pardon, miss. Oh, please, miss, d-don't take on so," the girl blathered, eyeing Beau's precarious perch with white-faced fear. "I wasn't sneakin', I was—was jest comin' up to give ye a message from his lordship, like he told me to do."

"His lordship?" Beau asked with a little skip of pleasure.

"Aye, miss, 'e said 'twas time t'start yer schoolin', but . . . lor' have mercy, miss, don't go divin' out onto the cobbles," the girl wailed. "My lord would be in a most terrible temper if ye did."

Remembering how she'd stopped the very same housemaid from scolding a stable lad to tears yesterday noon, Beau bounced nearer the edge of the crumbling stone ledge. With the greatest of glee she pretended to teeter there, her arms flailing in the open space. The servant shrieked as Beau started to fall, but at the last instant Beau leapt down from the ledge, landing on her slippered feet, laughing uproariously.

The maidservant's face washed a dull red, and huge, gulping sobs came from her chest. "Shame! For shame on you, miss, scaring me like that! Serve you right if my heart had jest stopped and I'd died right on the spot."

"And it would have served you right if I had cleaved your gullet clean yesterday, when you were hounding poor Martin," Beau said. "But fortunately for the both of us, the world seems a bit short on justice right now. So if you will just tell me where I am to meet my lord, you can go back to the kitchens and tell all the rest of the servants what a witch I am."

The maid was only too happy to comply.

Without a backward glance Isabeau dashed down the corridor, her skirts caught up to her knees as she bounded down the stairs two at a time.

Breathless, she raced into the rose salon, only Griffin's strong arms stopping her before she could overturn a table set with priceless porcelain. Beau gasped, laughing as she slammed up against his hard chest. And she stayed there, pressed against him, pretending to steady herself.

"Mistress DeBurgh, a lady does not charge into a chamber as if a ravening wolf were at her heels," Griffin said, placing one finger beneath her chin and tipping her head back so he could peer into her face. "A lady enters a room gracefully, a feast for the senses, a delight to the eye."

"To wait upon a husband who is a pain in the arse?" Beau asked with a wicked grin.

Griff choked on a laugh. "Absolutely not, milady. You see, the word 'arse' is not even in the vocabulary of the well-bred lady, nor, I might add, are 'damnation,' 'blood and thunder,' or any of the other colorful phrases you are so fond of."

"I see. I suppose that ladies are only allowed to say 'yes, milord' and 'no, milord' and 'whatever you bloody say, milord.' "

"Not so. You are also allowed to ask if any of your guests need tea. You are to inquire if the honorable Mrs.

Malaprop's darling boy has recovered from his bout of biliousness. Why, any number of—"

"Deadly dull things. I shall go mad being a lady, Stone. I know it," Beau cried mournfully.

Griffin laughed. "Well, perhaps we *should* leave the art of polite conversation for later, my dear, after we've tidied up some of your, er, rougher edges. We wouldn't want your reformation to be too much of a shock. Shall we begin again?"

"If my lord wishes it," Beau said in a syrupy tone.

He swept her a courtly bow. "Good morrow, Mistress DeBurgh. You are looking in tolerable good health."

Beau dimpled, quelling a giggle. "Why, my lord Stone, such a pleasant surprise! How have you been keeping yourself of late?"

"Neck-deep in trouble, I fear. And you?"

"Aside from breaking some more of that glass frippery you've got scattered all over this place—"

"*And* terrorizing the maids, *and* fleecing the footmen at dice," Griffin interrupted sternly.

Beau gave him a saucy toss of her head. "I have been doing quite wondrously well."

Griffin choked back a laugh. "We shall see about that, you impertinent baggage. Go stand over there by the fireplace so I can look at you."

Beau felt a prickle of pleasure. She knew that the blue silk set off her fiery hair to perfection and made her eyes shine.

"Hmm," Griffin murmured. "The gown is highly acceptable. Just enough galon touched about to make it shimmer. The lace seems a bit coarse, though, next to your skin. I wonder if I should commission spiders to weave a web to use as lace for your gowns, fairy princess."

"I think not. The things would be blasted sticky."

"Probably so. Well, then, the finest lace to be had must do. Let me see. Turn toward the light just a little."

She did so, feeling ridiculous.

"The face is acceptable enough, I guess. Although there is a bit too much of the devil in that smile of yours, and your eyes are full of plotting wickedness. You've fine teeth, though, and that is a definite advantage. A man grows weary of women pulling their lips over crooked ones."

"I'm beginning to feel like a bloody horse, Stone!" Beau groused.

"You've got slippers on, praise the lord," Griff said, ignoring her. "The servants were fairly kicking down walls, they were so put out at the footprints you were leaving all down their polished halls. And the maids, I hear, are drawing lots for the dubious honor of serving you. I had one give me her notice just this morning when she drew the short straw."

He considered a moment. "All in all, though, you might do well enough, I suppose, if it were not for that infernal hair."

"My hair?" Isabeau yelped in indignation, clapping one hand over the tresses that were her one vanity. "What the devil is wrong with my hair? Why, that idiot maid stuck the hairpins straight into my skull, I'll have you know, and I didn't hit her once, though I was sore tempted!"

"Most admirable restraint. But I believe it is customary for ladies of fashion to wear their hair powdered, my dear."

"Oh, no, Stone," Isabeau said, rounding on him, her good humor flown. "If you think you are going to get me to slop lard and flour all over *my* head, you are sadly mistaken!"

"Pomatum and powder are the accepted—"

"Well, *un*accept them! I'd feel as if there were *things* crawling in my hair if I mucked it all up that way."

"There is a bit of discomfort, but that is the price of elegance."

"Well, the price is a damned sight too high." Isabeau rounded on him, hands on hips. "If it was the fashion to wear a pudding bag on your head, I suppose that you would ask me to do it."

Griffin barked a laugh, his eyes shining. "Don't be ridiculous."

"It makes as much sense as flour and lard. And besides, the powder makes me sneeze and puts me in a formidable temper."

"Heaven forbid." Griffin feigned a shudder. Then he raised a finger, curling it around a wisp of her hair. "I must confess, I prefer your hair unpowdered anyway. All red and gold, with the light caught in the strands." His voice dropped low, and Beau could sense him leaning toward her.

She caught her breath, her pulses quickening, but he stiffened, then drew away. "We are never going to buckle down to our lessons if you persist in distracting me, Mistress DeBurgh. Now, you sit here." He drew out a gilt chair. Its legs were so slender it seemed they would shatter beneath the weight of a cushion.

Beau eyed the seat with doubt but then plopped down on it, tugging it forward with a horrible scraping sound. Griffin winced. It made her smile.

"Now," Griffin said in the accents of a weary schoolmaster tutoring a recalcitrant child, "we shall begin with the basic feminine responsibilities in a household of quality. As a woman you will be in charge of the home, your duty to make it a comfortable, pleasant environment for the man of your choice."

"I cannot think of a man alive that I'd choose for anything but fishbait," Beau said.

"You are to have nothing to do with securing the food for the table. You are only to oversee the serving of it," Griff said with a studied solemnity. "Now, you must be particularly attentive to any guest who might further your family's prospects."

"That, at least, stands to reason. Men are such thick-headed dolts as a rule, they'd need a woman to mop up the disasters they create."

"It is nothing to be taken lightly. Even great men of power need wise hostesses to aid them in their careers. Much of the nation's business is decided over the woman's tea cakes."

"I assure you the only thing my tea cakes would be good for would be loading up King George's cannons."

Griffin sank into the chair opposite her, burying his face in his hands. After a moment he propped his chin on his knuckles and glared at her. "This is going to get us nowhere, milady. This is to be a serious business for both of us, if you recall."

"All right, all right, have it your bloody way. I am perishing to learn what I shall get to do next. Scrub windows? Kiss my lord's boots?"

"Let's begin again. Pretend for a moment that you are the mistress of my estate. We are giving a ball tonight. First we must formally receive our guests."

"If they are friends of yours, they should know the way in, and I should think they'd be uncomfortable with all that formal shilly-shallying."

"You may dispense with the formalities on rare occasions where you are entertaining only your most intimate circle, but the rest of the time decorum is required. You see, as a lady of quality it will be your duty to entertain not only those whose company you enjoy, but also those who are socially apropos."

"Socially . . . devil in lightning! What you mean is I must be sweet-faced to people I hate?"

"You must never be rude to them, no matter how much you dislike them."

"Of all the stupid notions I've ever heard! I'll die of a stomach complaint if I have to keep all that fury bottled up inside, or else I'll explode one night and cut down the lot of 'em with my pistols!" Beau fumed, outraged. "No, Stone, I have to say it. I cannot think that going to all this work to entertain people I loathe is worth the effort. No swearing, no blood and thunder, and I suppose bawdy jests are out of the question?"

"Indubitably, my dear." Griffin pushed the delicate teapot closer to Beau's turned-up nose. "Now, if we are done with our fit of pique, you may pour me some tea."

Beau slammed her hand on the table. "Did you take some wound to the hand I'm not aware of? The pot is well within your reach."

"But you are the hostess. You must pour the tea graciously, with an elegant flair."

"I'll pour it with flair, all right. Right into your lap." Beau grumbled. She grabbed up the fragile teapot as if it were her saddle and slung the hot liquid into Griffin's cup with enough force to make it rattle against its saucer.

Some of the liquid slopped on the table, but Griffin said nothing. He merely mopped up the mess with a fine linen cloth. "Since you obviously have that skill mastered," he said, "now we shall commence with the proper way to dine. If you look before you, you will see that I had the servants make you a special place setting to practice with."

Isabeau looked down onto the setting. It seemed to be a maze of silver and crystal and china. For once in her life she was daunted. "What the blazes do you aristos do, Stone? Stick every scrap of silver you own on the table? I vow it is just so you can show off how rich you are. But if you ask me, it is like wearing all of your waistcoats at once so that people will know you've got them."

Griff pressed his knuckles to his mouth, his brows lowering in what might have passed for disapproval. But Beau noticed laugh lines crinkling about his eyes. With his other hand he scooped up a spoon, rapping on the table. "Mistress Isabeau, pay attention, if you please," he said with mock severity.

For almost an hour Griffin kept her to task, teaching her the use of every implement on the table. Though confused at first, she soon became determined to master the blasted skill and set to it with a vengeance.

At last well pleased, Griffin pushed himself away from the table. He gave a satisfied sigh. "Now, milady," he said, "is the perfect time to retire to the library for a fine glass of port."

"Stone, I believe that is the first thing you've said all day that I agree with," Beau said with a heartfelt sigh. "I'll even be the perfect hostess and fetch the bloody bottle for you if you tell me where it is."

She saw some imp of mischief in his eyes, but his face was solemn as he shook his head. "I am afraid that the tradition of retiring for a glass of port excludes those of the fairer sex. Only the men are allowed to slip off and imbibe. It is there that they discuss vital matters like politics and the happenings in the House of Lords."

"My eye they do! More likely they bandy about the charms of their latest mistresses or how much they've lost gaming!"

"A lady of quality is not supposed to acknowledge that mistresses exist, my love. But the sad truth is that we do spend most of our time talking about horses and hounds and gaming."

"There! I knew it!" Beau said, triumphant. "That is much more to my liking! I'd like to see you try to keep me from it!"

"Isabeau, Isabeau." He tsked softly. "How can you revel in hounds and horses in the library when you have to entertain the ladies in the salon?"

Beau made a face. "I don't suppose they are doing anything half so diverting."

"Why, they are sipping tea, talking."

"Bah! About what?"

"Frills and furbelows, I should imagine. Babies and governesses and the peccadilloes of their servants."

"I can't believe anyone would want to talk about such rot. Why can't the women go into the infernal library with the men? Who makes all these bloody rules? If I had to wager, I'd guess some pompous idiot of a man barred the door to the library because his wife was smarter than he. I'd bet that he was afraid his wife would make him look like a fool."

Griffin couldn't stop a laugh. "You are probably right," he admitted. "I know of several fellows who might do just that very thing."

"I shall mount a rebellion," Beau said, striking her hand to her breast. "You shall return from your port to find your wives dicing and swilling Blue Ruin, talking about ways to bedevil their husband's lights o' love."

"Is that so? Well, if you are not too wearied after your rebellion, do you think you might care to indulge in any of the usual amusements? Music? Singing?"

"I can't play the pianoforte, and the only songs I know would turn your grand ladies green."

"Then we will have to cover up this sad lack of accomplishments by dazzling the assemblage with something else."

"My skill with the pistols?" Beau asked hopefully. "I could shoot the posy off one of the ladies' bonnets. Or I could pick the buttons off a man's waistcoat at twenty paces."

"I'm afraid shooting in the house is very bad form, Isabeau. It will have to be something else." He seemed to consider the problem. "Dancing," he said at last, well pleased with himself.

"D-dancing?" Had he said drowning she could have been no more disconcerted. The thought of touching him, stumbling about as awkwardly as she had at her fencing lessons, filled her with dread. She was graceless, and she knew it. She thrust her hands behind her back, retreating behind the delicate table. "No, I don't think I—"

"Dance with me, Isabeau."

She curled her hands into fists, attempting to feign carelessness. "I've had enough of lessons for today. And anyway, I would just tread upon your toes. I'll not be responsible for crippling you."

"Despite all your bluster you're a wisp of a thing," Griffin said, his hands spanning her waist as if to prove his point. Suddenly she gasped as he lifted her high and held her there, forcing her to gaze down into those dangerously handsome features.

"P-put me down, you ruffian!" she stammered, wriggling against the grasp of his hands. "I mean it, Stone! Or you can take your 'lady' nonsense and cast it—"

He dropped her with a suddenness that made her cry out. His hands caught her a split second before her slippers slammed into the floor. "Your wish is my command, milady," he said with amusement. "I seem to remember you saying nearly those same words mere seconds before you shattered—what was it? My grandmother's Ming? I must confess, you've taken such a toll on Darkling Moor's possessions, it is hard to keep an accounting."

"This place is much too cluttered anyway," Beau said between gritted teeth. "I'm doing you a service, ridding you of old refuse that should have been thrown away centuries ago."

Griff grimaced. "I doubt many connoisseurs of antiquities would agree with you. However, I am willing to allow bygones to be bygones.

"And now, if you would honor me?" He swept her a courtly bow, extending one strong hand.

"Honor you? I'll most likely *horrify* you before we make an end to it. Griffin, the muddle I made of the silver and such will be nothing in comparison to this disaster. Jack attempted to teach me to dance once, and I was clumsy as a colt."

"Come now, at least in dancing you'll not be in danger of getting nicked with a blade."

Beau thought she'd prefer to be gazing down burnished steel than faced with the alarming charm that seemed to radiate from every pore of Griffin Stone's virile body.

But she straightened, sticking out her hand abruptly. Griff retreated a step. "Well?" she snapped. "Let's get it over with."

Griffin grinned. "Ah, such pretty manners, such winning ways! I've seen warmer eyes across a dueling field." He caught up her chilled fingers. His hand felt warm, strong. "Smile, Isabeau. The orchestra, it seems, is striking up a minuet."

Beau muttered an expletive, and pulled a face that had Griffin chuckling. But as his laughter faded he began to hum deep in his chest, endearingly off-key. And Beau thought she had never heard anything so beautiful.

With a patience that amazed her Griffin schooled her in the figures of the dance, whispering encouragement, enduring her fumblings, steadying her whenever she tripped over the cumbersome folds of her gown.

And despite herself, the tension began to drain from Isabeau's rigid arms and stiff legs. Despite herself, she became lost in the approval that shone in sea-blue eyes.

She circled, dipped, swayed, returning to slip her fingers into the grasp of Griffin's warm ones. And the regal patterns of the minuet faded into a dance more primitive, more alluring.

Their eyes locked and held; their lips trembled with a desire that made each brush of fingers across fingers exquisitely seductive.

He moved with the grace of a panther, dangerous, sensual. His dark hair swept back from his brow in thick waves that seemed to dare Beau's hands to tame them.

Beau shivered. Languorous heat stole over her, making her own movements more entrancing. She met his gaze openly. She had never been able to hide what she was feeling for long. And never before had she felt such soul-deep emotion.

Griffin's humming rasped as though he were robbed of breath, and when he turned to catch up her hand yet again the harsh sounds died in his throat.

He stood, peering down at her, his fingers unmoving, his face still, so still.

"W-what is amiss?" Beau forced the words between her lips. "Did I break your toes? I told you I would before we even began."

"No, it is just . . ." He drew away from her, and Beau suddenly felt cold. "It has been a long time since there has been dancing in this salon. When I was a child, there were grand balls held at Darkling Moor. My mother would let us sneak down from the nursery to peer at the guests, and she would always slip in here with us and dance, first with William, then with me, while the music drifted down the hall."

"It must have been wonderful," Beau said softly.

"Grandmama thought it was inexcusably rude for the duchess of Graymore to run off like a truant dairymaid. But no matter how she scolded, my mother would not listen."

"She hated your mother. The dowager duchess, I mean. I could see it when we talked. When I woke up she was bending over my bed like some old hag," Beau teased. "I'll never again torment Molly about being afraid of bad dreams, for that was a nightmare, I assure you. I thought the old witch would choke when she saw what I was wearing."

"I wager she did." Griffin gave a hollow laugh. He touched the miniature of a beautiful, smiling lady on a small table, and Isabeau's heart ached for him. "My mother caught a fever when I was six, and died so swiftly it seemed that one moment she was laughing and dancing, and the next I was staring at her in her coffin. My grandmother swept through the house burning everything my mother had touched, as if she were trying to blot out her very existence. She said it was because she feared the things were a breeding ground for fever, but even then I knew better."

"Was she jealous of your father's love for your mother?"

"No." Bitterness creased Griffin's face. "My grandmother hated my father almost as much as she hates me. But my mother . . . she loved him, and that was her greatest heartache of all." Griffin's hands fell to his side, an aura of sadness surrounding him. "My father was something of a rake, I'm afraid. Not capable of being faithful to anyone. He was fond of my mother, after a fashion. And he petted her shamelessly, with the same careless good humor he bestowed on everyone around him. But as for any abiding passion"—he shrugged—"it was not in him to give."

Beau watched him, silent. She felt as though she were peering past his blue-gray eyes into Griffin's very soul. She wanted to ask why his mother hadn't taken a fire iron to his father and cudgeled him into giving up his mistresses. But for once her first thoughts did not trip off her heedless tongue. Something in the tone of Griffin's voice held her.

"She must have loved him very much," she said, sensing he needed her to speak.

"She adored him." Griffin smiled wistfully. "Any trinket he brought to her, any gift, she treasured above all others. That was why . . ." He looked away as if to shield emotions too raw to let anyone witness. "That was why when she died I hid the gown. I couldn't bear for it to be thrust into the flames. It was one of his gifts and she had loved it so much."

Beau nibbled at her lip, remembering the glow that had wreathed her mother's face whenever her father had entered the room. Lianna Devereaux had been a beauty beyond compare at any time, but when she had gazed upon Robb DeBurgh she had seemed an angel straight down from heaven. How would those delicate features have appeared if Lianna had looked upon her husband and seen the reflection of a score of other women in his eyes? And how would that agony have touched a child who loved them both?

She stood, uncertain what to do, knowing instinctively that Griffin would not want pity or commiseration.

At last he turned. "And so, Isabeau, I think you learned far more than how to serve tea today. You will think me a tyrant for keeping you at your lessons so long."

"I happen to think that tyrants are most amiable company," she said softly.

"You are too kind. At any rate, you may be off now, and take a run in the gardens before we must face each other across a real dining room table."

Beau started to leave, then stopped, returning to stand before him. "Thank you, my lord, for the most . . . most lovely minuet I've ever danced."

"The *only* minuet you've ever danced." The soft, sad light in his eyes only made the longing pulse deeper still within Beau.

Tentatively she ran her fingertips down his high cheekbone, reveling in the feel of his jaw knotting beneath her touch. But the emotions between them were binding her into knots as well, frightening her with feelings that flooded through her like a riptide, carrying her away. And she feared that she was losing herself in them.

The need to see him smile again was fierce.

"Perhaps I shall . . . shall have to repay my debt to you by teaching you something as well." Her voice was soft and tender. "Of course, I know precious little that would be of use to you."

"You owe me nothing, little one," he whispered, leaning his cheek against her palm to trap it against his shoulder.

"Ah, but I do. What think you, milord? Have you ever considered a career as a highway brigand?"

He smiled at her. "I am beginning to believe you have already stolen something far more precious than my coin, Milady Flame." He grasped her wrist, guiding her hand gently down until it covered his heart.

Beau's throat squeezed shut with some emotion she could not name, and she fled from it, turning and hurrying from the room.

Chapter Fifteen

It was a perfect day for a battle.

Griffin shielded his eyes against the dazzling morning sun and gazed across the woodlands that surrounded Darkling Moor; the lush vegetation sparkled with morning dew. The whole day lay before him. Today he was free—no weight of ledgers or financial snarls. None of Charles's devilment. Yet today's task might prove more formidable still. More formidable, and yet more entertaining, more enticing, more hazardous to life and limb.

For today the Devil's Flame was going to learn to ride like a woman.

His lips curved into a grin, his eyes flashing to a beautiful silver mare who stood trapped out in a gleaming sidesaddle. The mare was the most spirited in Darkling Moor's stable, a mount that few females would dare to ride. And yet Griffin knew instinctively that the sleek, skittish Moonshadow would soon be looked upon with the most blistering disdain. For even that spirited beast would seem like a bumbling child's nag in comparison to the wild-eyed stallion Isabeau DeBurgh had been riding as she charged down on his coach three weeks ago.

"As if Beau will not be fair spoiling for fisticuffs even

before she leaves her chamber!" Griffin muttered to himself. She'd be outraged the instant she saw what she was expected to wear when in the saddle. He grimaced, thinking of the garments he had seen laid out upon Isabeau's bed. A petticoat of lush blue camlet trimmed in gold, a tight-fitting coat with an elegant frill of lace for her throat. And the hat—a cocky little beaver hat with a plume all dusted in gold.

It was a riding habit fit for a princess. He had seen to that, to the indignation of the seamstresses and servants whom he had charged to have it complete within a span of time that had made them blanch.

He had promised the red-tressed "princess" a wild ride over the parklands, a reward for the way she had applied herself to "fan-waving and tea-sloshing" the past two weeks. He just hadn't mentioned that when they went for this wild ride she would be in full feminine regalia on a shiny new sidesaddle he had commissioned.

Even from his own chambers he had been able to hear the outraged row she'd kicked up with the servants, but after almost a month of being without a horse he had trusted that Beau would do anything—anything to feel one beneath her again. Even if she had to be "trussed up like a cursed partridge" to do it.

Griffin warmed, remembering the first time he had seen Beau hurtling down toward his coach, her cape whipping back in the wind. She had ridden as though she were born to the saddle. And yet, if any of the London set were to see her riding that way, reckless, her slender, breech-clad legs clamped about MacBeth, they would dissolve into rigid scorn.

Griffin was determined that Isabeau would now master the art of riding in the guise of a lady—master it so well that she would again have the freedom to race headlong into the rushing winds, sailing over fences and streams and the trees that had tumbled to the turf.

If it bloody well killed them both.

He patted the neck of his own gelding, Brutus. Griffin

supposed it would be small comfort to Isabeau, but he would not be riding his first choice of mounts this morning either. His favorite blood bay stallion would have interfered with the secret part of this morning's agenda that he knew would throw Isabeau into absolute ecstasies.

Before dawn he had sent a running footman to the inn where he'd first taken the wounded Beau. The footman had carried specific orders for the inn's hostler, commanding him to prepare the night-black stallion Griffin had been stabling within the establishment's sturdiest stall these past weeks.

MacBeth. It was fitting that Isabeau should ride a stallion named for one whose hotheadedness had cost him a crown. And it would be most interesting to see what havoc the half-wild beast would wreak on Darkling Moor's stable, and on Griffin's own stallion as well.

"Most likely the pair of them will eventually cut each other to ribbons," Griff muttered, removing the tricorn from his head. "God knows I'll most likely live to regret—"

"—the day you were bloody born!"

At the angry words Griffin wheeled toward the house. The figure stalking toward him was a vision of loveliness—vibrant blue molding to delectable breasts, a tiny waist, petticoats tumbling to the ground like a waterfall. The hat brim perched on red-gold curls dipped rakishly over glittering green eyes, the porcelain-delicate features beneath flushed with a stunning beauty.

But Griff was certain that if the king's entire army had been confronted by such a scowl upon the field of Culloden, the lot of them would have fled in terror.

"My lady," Griffin said, making an elegant bow, "you look uncommon beautiful this morning."

"I look an uncommon fool, you mean!" Beau hurled him a glare. "You promised we were to go riding. *Riding,* for God's sake. I fluttered my fan and swooned and traipsed around suffocating in silk for two whole weeks. I haven't belched at the table, flung any of the servants out the window, or shot your infernal grandmother. Last night you smiled at me and told me I'd earned a reward, a respite from my labors. A ride across the heath. I was so hungry for the wind in my face I could hardly sleep last night. And now . . . now, you bloody bastard, I wake up to find that you've been plotting against me with the whole bloody household!"

She stalked over to him, nearly stomping on his toes. Her anger-flushed features were inches from his own. *"How the bloody hell do you expect me to ride in this . . . this . . . thing!"*

"Riding habit. It is called a—"

"I know *damned* well what it is called, you arrogant oaf! It is an abomination rigged up by a pack of men to keep women from outriding them."

Griffin choked out a laugh. "Come now, I hardly think—"

"Do you see any *men* dangling half-on, half-off their horse's backs in sidesaddles, my lord Stone? Do you see any men riding with their legs all tangled up in whatever the blazes this blue stuff is?" She swiped a hand over the rich fabric as if it were the most odious of rags.

"Isabeau," he began patiently, "one cannot ride astride garbed in petticoats."

"My point exactly! How the devil can one ride at all if she cannot even use the knees?"

"There is a recent invention called *reins,"* Griffin said, struggling to keep his voice stern.

"Don't patronize me, Stone!" The words were accompanied by a wallop in his chest; her small fist held a surprising strength. "If you think for one minute I am going to mince about looking like a bloomin' idiot on some . . . some half-dead nag fit only for the renderer's pot, you can go to hell."

"I had thought, rather, that we would go to an inn."

"An inn?"

"Yes. I seem to remember that we left something there. A piece of your property. Unless, of course, you had stolen it."

"Stolen it? What—" The eyes that burned with anger shifted, green-gold sparks of hopefulness, happiness, stirring in their depths as she seemed to read something in his face. "MacBeth! We can go get MacBeth?" She let out a whoop, hurling the beaver hat high.

"Yes. Providing, that is, that you make a sincere effort to ride *to* and *from* the inn in a manner befitting one of your station."

"My station?" Delicately arched brows crashed low in a scowl. "I—"

"I mean it, Beau. You are one of the finest riders that I've ever had the privilege to see. And that beast of yours—he is magnificent as well. I don't give a tinker's damn if you want to slip away sometimes and race through the woods like a wild Indian, but when we go to London"—he saw her pale slightly—"you cannot dash about St. James with your skirts flying up about your ears."

"London?" She licked her lips, the gesture her single betrayal of nervousness. "I . . . I think I rather . . . rather like it here better, even with your grandmother witching her way about. I was hoping we could postpone going there for a while yet. Ten years, perhaps?"

Griffin felt a wave of empathy, hating the thought of plunging his fresh-faced, unspoiled Beau neck-deep into lead paint and patches and Hungary water. London was a veritable sea of intrigue, and the *ton* practiced a cunning, subtle, and cutting cruelty. The most elegant society could be a poisonous labyrinth for those who were not used to watching for daggers thrust at one's back.

Sweet Christ, Griff chided himself inwardly, the girl was a blasted brigand! Surely she could dispatch a roomful of sharp-tongued misses.

And sly monsieurs? a voice inside him mocked.

But despite his niggling doubts, he reached out one hand, tugging on a bright curl. "You will adore London," he said cheerily. "I shall take you to the theater, and to Ranelagh. We shall go off to St. James and feed the swans. And if you are good . . . if you are very, very good, I might try to arrange a tour of the Tower for you, so that you can pore over the armor and swords and suchlike. I know how much you *adore* swords."

Beau's mouth puckered with distaste. "Waste of precious

energy, they are," she said. "All that dancing around, thrusting and parrying while one good shot would rid you of the nuisance once and for all. But"—she fretted her lower lip—"maybe if you took me dicing at White's . . ."

"I think not, babe. It wouldn't do for you to fleece half of the *ton* before you've been presented. It would put your prospective suitors in a very bad skin, I fear. And speaking of bad skins, I think that stallion of yours is probably flaying the flesh from every stable boy at that inn by now. I sent ahead and told them to make him ready, but I much doubt MacBeth has enough patience to wait very long."

Beau's lips compressed, her fingers fiddling with the fall of lace at her throat. "They would not be so foolhardy as to tie him, would they? I fear MacBeth has a most violent aversion to hitching places."

Griffin shrugged. "Considering how long you've been huffing about losing your temper, the poor horse could have felled the whole inn by now and torn up every bit of fencing."

Beau scooped up her hat and jammed it on her head with resolution. She started toward the mare she had previously eyed with contempt. "What are you waiting for, Stone? An engraved invitation?" she called back to him.

Griffin made a heroic effort not to laugh, managing only to give a choked cough as Isabeau hauled herself awkwardly onto the horse's back. Her petticoats snaggled about her legs as she struggled to settle herself in the sidesaddle.

If the high-bred Moonshadow had understood the king's English, she would have been outraged at the imprecations her rider uttered. Beau questioned everything from the silver horse's parentage to the depth of her intelligence. But within moments Griffin found that Isabeau had again managed to master a seemingly difficult feat, making it seem simple.

"Race you," Griff could not resist goading her, expecting some sharp rejoinder. But Beau merely gave him a look of challenge and brought her gold-plumed hat down on Moonshadow's rump.

The mare lunged forward, and for an instant Griff feared Beau was going to tumble backwards or pitch flat onto her face in the turf. But though she cursed, swore, and blasphemed in a way that would make a vicar swoon, she stayed on the horse's back. Stayed on it while urging the mare to skim, neck or nothing, down Darkling Moor's winding drive.

Griff swung up on his own mount and kneed Brutus into a run, but he held his horse back slightly while he savored the sight Isabeau made, a splash of sapphire and flame and sleek, gleaming silver on the emerald velvet hillside.

The miles that had seemed so tedious while they'd traveled within the coach melted beneath the horses' fleet hooves. The morass of problems that still awaited Griffin within the vast manor house seemed to evaporate like the morning mists beneath the sunshine of Isabeau's laughter, her teasing, her smiles. Yes, and that endearing, heart-wrenching unease that still puckered her brow, caused, Griffin was sure, by her dread of the impending trip to London.

Far too quickly the inn's ramshackle frame shone against the sky, but Isabeau fairly flew from the saddle, scarcely taking time to rein the winded mare to a halt. Griff shouted warning, tried to vault from his own mount to help her, but there was nothing he could do as her petticoats caught on the saddle. A moment later she tumbled into the dirt.

Griff was beside her at once, fully intending to ease her to her feet and brush the dirt off her petticoats. But Beau merely wrenched away from his grasp, all but flinging herself against the solid warmth of the ebony stallion prancing about in the care of a terrorized stable boy.

"Milady! Nay!" The lad shrieked, trying to guard the delicate woman from the frenzied stallion. "He nearly broke Jimmy's arm."

"Bah!" Beau said, catching at the horse's nose, forcing the stallion's massive head down until she was peering into its eyes as though it were a recalcitrant child. "It is a fine stir you've kicked up here, sirrah! Continue this way and Lord

Stone will send you off to Tattersalls, and *then* what will you do?"

Griff watched her, his heart lurching, as she reacquainted herself with her perfect mount. He'd long remember this incident—this one perfect moment.

It was as if a hand tightened about his throat, as if sea spray stung his eyes. He turned away, mumbling some excuse about having to settle his accounting within.

Beau watched him go, her cheeks pinkening with shyness. Clearing her throat, she shifted the reins again to the stable lad's reluctant grasp, bidding the stallion to behave himself as sternly as any governess instructing her charge.

"Griffin?" she called, hastening to catch up to him. But he was already beyond hearing, lost amid the bustle of morning travelers readying to be on their way.

"Griffin, wait!" Beau scooped up her skirts and rushed toward the door. Just as she reached it two figures spilled out. One was a girl garbed in garish colors, her face done up in lead paint beneath a wide-brimmed bonnet; the other was an odious teamster.

Beau gasped, startled. She attempted to avoid the ill-matched pair, but she slammed headlong into something that seemed nothing but birdlike bones, frail, trembling.

"Watch where ye're goin', doxy mine!" the man said, nearly yanking the girl's arm from its socket as he righted her. "I'd not like t'turn ye back t'Nell damaged!"

The words sliced through Beau, rapier-sharp. She caught quickly at the girl's sleeve. Beneath the brim of the huge bonnet the girl cast a mortified glance at her, her angel-sweet features awash with shame. Shame, and yet not even the slightest shading of recognition.

Molly! Beau tried to squeeze the name through her lips, but she was struck dumb. The girl tore away from her grasp, stumbling down into the stable yard. Molly raced to a waiting coach, climbing inside, slamming the door closed before the man could enter, and it was as if she would have crawled into the very earth itself rather than gaze into the face of—of whom? Her dearest friend? Her protector?

No, the face of the woman who had left her to the likes of

the loathsome beast even now digging at his crotch with blunt fingers.

But Jack . . . Jack vowed he would take care of her! A voice cried inside Beau. He promised . . .

Promised when you had crushed his pride? Hurt him? Promised when you had hurled his love back into his face?

God, I have to find her, Beau thought desperately. Molly would go back to Nell's: If Beau cut across the woods, she could reach there before Molly did.

"Isabeau?"

She jumped at the sound of Griffin's voice. He looked down at her so solemn, concerned, tender . . . so tender that it seemed the cruelest of condemnations after the bestial face of the man who had been at Molly's side.

"No, Griff . . . I cannot . . . cannot . . . stay . . . go with you." Her voice cracked, torn, ragged with a sob. "God, what have I done?"

Anguish raked through her, pain such as she'd never known. She had betrayed Molly and now must betray this dark-haired nobleman whom she had come to . . . to *love?*

She sank her teeth into her lower lip to stifle the racking sobs building inside her. And suddenly she was running, fleeing across the yard, vaulting astride onto MacBeth's massive bare back.

The stallion reared, essaying a whinny of fright as Beau's petticoats ballooned around her, snapping in the wind. The hands that had always been so skillful on the reins were shaking in a way that broke the skittish horse's trust in his rider for the first time. Her heels dug into the horse's sides with a force that sent the stallion shooting from the stable yard in a blur of equine power.

She clung to the horse's back, driving him to breakneck speed, bolting through tangled trees, over stone fences, nearly crashing into a curricle racing toward the inn. But she saw nothing except Molly Maguire's pinched face and the lewd slaverings of the man who had put her through hell.

A shout of alarm rose from behind her. Griffin commanded her to halt, but the sound only blended with the curses and shrieks of those within the inn yard. She raced faster, harder, as if she could escape the image that had seared itself in her mind, burned there with acid shadings of guilt.

With an oath Griffin flung himself onto his own mount, desperation rising inside him as he watched the half-crazed girl hurtling away on the charging stallion. Sweet God, she was going to kill herself—break her cursed neck!

He urged his gelding after her hopelessly. He knew full well he could never catch MacBeth.

. . . cannot stay . . . God, what have I done . . . Her agonized cry cut at Griffin as he struggled to keep stallion and rider within his sight. Three times she almost fell, and once the half-mad stallion nearly slammed her into an overhanging limb in an attempt to brush her from his back.

Griffin cried out a warning. He watched, desperate, as he saw Beau rein the stallion toward what seemed a solid wall of trees. The woodlands were treacherous with undergrowth, and they seemed to swallow her whole.

The sound of crashing hooves through brush, the lashing of branches against horse and rider made Griffin's hands clench tighter still on the reins as Isabeau disappeared from his sight. He drove his gelding with a savagery that stunned him, goaded by the image of her lithe, infinitely sweet body lying on the ground, bloodied, broken.

Dead.

No, Griffin told himself, a shaft of foreboding lancing deep inside him. Beau was the most gifted rider he'd ever seen. But at that instant it was as if the fates were jeering at him. A horrible equine sound split the air, and that sound was lost in a human scream more awful still.

He leaned low over his gelding's neck, plunging on down the ragged path Isabeau and MacBeth had cut in the brush. It seemed an eternity before he broke into the hidden clearing and saw the massive stallion plunging about in raw terror, some bond of loyalty keeping it from abandoning its mistress despite what looked to be some poacher's carnage scattered all about.

Griff's nostrils were assaulted by the stench of rotting flesh as his eyes swept the carcass of a lamb, its throat slit, its wool red with blood. A stag dangled, butchered, in a way that bespoke a cruelty that would have sickened Griff were he not nearly mad with fear. Like a child's doll Beau lay crumpled in the shadow of gray stone ruins.

The half-crumbling structure seemed as still and eerie as a tomb.

Griffin flung himself from his gelding's back, unable to think, breathe, his whole body shaking with fear for her as he ran to her side. He crashed to his knees, not feeling the stones cutting into his flesh, feeling nothing save the most mind-shattering panic he had ever known.

"Isabeau!" The harsh, animal cry could not be his own. "Isabeau, for God's sake!" His hand searched frantically for a pulse. Her skin was warm, but her face was a waxen white.

His heart almost stopped as his eyes locked on a smear of dark crimson upon the blue camlet. His mind raced in denial. Surely a fresh wound would be bright red—bright. The blood could not be Isabeau's.

Suddenly a shudder went through her slender body, a sob shaking her shoulders. She whimpered, and the sound of it made Griffin's own throat go raw.

"—should die . . . deserve it for . . . for what . . . I did—" she choked out. After a moment of relief Griffin's stomach tightened in knots at the thought that this broken, devastatingly vulnerable woman was his wild, bold Isabeau. He pulled her into his arms, cradling her against his chest, stroking the hair back from grimy cheeks.

"Shh, now," he murmured, sliding his hand down to check for broken bones. "I never heard anything so absurd! What the devil could you have done that was so horrible in that tiny scrap of time it took me to walk from the stable yard to the inn? You were bloody beaming with happiness when I left you, love. Babbling to that cursed man-killer of yours. I know you've a dastardly temper, but I doubt even you could have stirred up Armageddon so quickly."

She opened her eyes that were pools of pain. "I saw her, Griff. Saw her with that . . . that beast pawing her! Would have sold my soul for my pistols to . . . to blast him away."

"Of course you would," Griffin agreed, as though she were

a child, "and a mighty handy job you would have done of it."

"It is my fault . . . my fault that she had to . . . to do it. But I thought Jack was taking care of her. He promised me. Promised he would, and I . . . I trusted him." She buried her face in Griff's chest. "But the whole time I was playing at grand lady, fighting with you, kissing you, Molly was scared and . . . and alone . . . and . . . Nell was forcing her to go off with those men who hurt her."

Griffin leaned his cheek against her tumbled hair, feeling her tears dampen his shirt, sear his heart.

"Beau," he whispered, "surely it is not your fault. This Molly, Jack, Nell, whoever these people are, they have a free will, can care for themselves."

She yanked away from him, her head cracking into his jaw so hard he winced. "What do you know of it?" she lashed out, her eyes spitting outrage, her hands knotted into fists. She looked pale and sickened by something Griff could not understand. "You, in your fancy house with your servants running about to kiss your bleeding feet if you want them to. What do you know about being abandoned? Being hungry? Having to—to sell yourself in order to survive?"

Hurt streaked through Griffin. Although he could see her pain, could sense that she was beyond reason, beyond hope, he felt sick with horror. His brave, beautiful Isabeau endured a similar fate?

"Beau," he said brokenly. "Sweet God, you did not . . . were not . . ."

"A whore?" She jammed herself to her feet, stumbling, wobbling, but when Griff leapt up to steady her she ripped away from his fingers, eyeing him with such loathing his breath caught in his throat. "No, I was no whore. But only because I took up the pistols and bolted off for the highroads. If I'd not been able to ply that trade, God knows I would have been forced into the other."

Griffin's jaw clenched. Beau gave a harsh laugh. "An empty belly and a cityful of snow are even poorer bedfellows than a groping man would be."

"Then you robbed to feed yourself? To care for—"

"For myself, yes, and for Molly as well. To save her from having to . . . to go with them . . ." Beau's lips curled in a sneer, a laugh that was half sob rising in her throat. "Why the bloody hell did you think I rode? Because I had nothing better to do than try to get myself hanged?"

"You seemed to take such pleasure in running about recklessly, seemed to be so blasted proud of your father." Griff battled to defend himself, more confused than before. "I thought—"

"I *am* proud of my father. Yes, and of all the knights of the road," Beau cried. "I'm proud of them for not curling up and dying—*starving* to death—while high-and-mighty aristocrats like you bleed them dry."

The words were a knife thrust to Griffin's soul, and he stood there staring at her, watching her outrage turn to anger, then into embers of regret. The silence was crushing. Beau turned away, pacing to where a dead tree writhed skyward.

"I didn't mean that," she said at last, her voice quavering. "I mean about you. You are . . . are a generous man, so . . . giving and caring." She turned the full light of tear-filled eyes upon him, her face washed with a solemnity and an earnestness that transformed her fiery beauty into that of an angel.

"You're wrong, Isabeau. I'm as guilty as the rest of them. Sometimes"—he dragged his fingers through his hair—"sometimes I think I am worse. For I pretend to be most liberal, a blasted philanthropist dashing about with my radical opinions that all life is of value. That everyone deserves to be safe, well tended. Yet I do nothing to bring it about."

"You touch what lives you can. And you are a kind master. And me . . . look what you have done on my behalf."

"What have I done? I've managed to imprison you in a place you hate. I've forced you to change all that you are—swaddled you in skirts, made you learn to bow that proud head of yours in a curtsy to women who are not fit to wipe the dust from your slippers. Even your riding—I commanded you to do it according to *my* expectations. And never once . . . never once did I consider that you had a life before you tried to rob me. Never once did I consider that you most likely had people who loved you. Depended on you."

"I've known joy with you, Griffin Stone." There was a catch in her voice, some emotion that mesmerized him glowing even through the sorrow in her eyes. "Even when I wanted to toss you out a window you understood me in a way no one . . . no one ever has before. It is strange, is it not? We just met, but I feel as if I have known you my whole life. Sometimes, even before you speak, I know what you are going to say. And I know just how to make you angry. Just how to make you smile."

She looked down. Her shoulders stiffened as she moved toward him. Then her hands came up to frame his face. "I'll remember you, Griffin," she whispered, tears welling in the corners of her eyes, spilling from her lashes. "Always. But I have to go back, don't you see? Back to Molly, back to the only way I know to carve my place in life."

"No. Isabeau, I can't let you . . . let you . . ." Can't let you go away from me, his heart screamed, tortured by visions of her laughing, dancing in the rose salon. You will leave my life barren of joy, he thought.

"But I have to go. Molly—"

"Let me tend to Molly. Help her. I'll send you off to London and catch up with you after I've tended to things here."

"Molly is my responsibility. My friend. I must do this."

"Beau, for the love of God, let me do this for you. Trust me."

He saw the misery deepen in Beau's eyes, and he remembered that some bastard named Jack had promised to help her. Then he had betrayed her when she trusted him to care for her friend.

"Come now, milady rogue, you promised me a month, and you are a full week short of your wager. You gave me your word. Now I give you mine. I'll not disappoint you, Beau," he vowed. "I swear it upon my life."

Slowly she slipped her hand downward, her small, trembling fingers sliding into his own. She was offering him her trust, he knew, yet his whole body ached with tenderness, longing, regret.

For it was as if, in that instant, she were offering him infinitely more.

Chapter Sixteen

London's inevitable fog clung to its rooftops, the blend of smoke, soot, and moisture seeming to spew like fresh-sheared wool from countless chimneys and steeples. Inside the Stone family townhouse Isabeau paced across the music room, trailing her fingers over the keys of a gilt-trimmed pianoforte. The melancholy tones soughed like the wind upon a night road.

Beau sighed. She had been here three days watching the clocks tick away the hours, listening for any sound that might signal Griffin's arrival. He had promised to come soon, and yet it seemed as if years had passed since she'd last looked into his eyes, seen his smile, heard his solemn promise that Molly would be saved.

But the only word Beau had received was a cryptic note that had arrived by messenger two days before, hastily penned in a bold, masculine scrawl. *All is well. Things to tend to. Yr. obedient servant, Lord Griffin Stone.*

At first waves of relief had surged through her, then joy, but as the time passed with no more word of what things he had to tend to, and what the devil "all is well" meant, Beau had begun to chafe, wildly impatient, starting at the sound of every coach or rider that passed by until she felt flightier than a bee dancing on boiled honey.

Finally she had scolded herself soundly, forcing herself to ignore the clatter and bustle that surrounded the ducal residence.

But she could not so handily blot out thoughts of the man who had invaded her heart, for there were hints of him everywhere within the elegant house. The assorted bric-a-brac made her remember his expression the day she'd shattered the Ming; the silverware reminded her of their lessons in the rose salon, while every time she put on a gown she had to remember what he had said about the fabric or the trim or how it suited her face and hair.

Yet the place Beau felt most bedeviled by thoughts of Griffin Stone was in the music room, which was where she spent most of her day.

Beau grimaced. She was lonely. Her eyes shifted to the ornate fireplace. Above the carved mantel hung a portrait of a small boy beside a fat pony. The youth's round cheeks were babe-soft instead of stubbled, the chin a sweet curve rather than a stubborn jut that fair shrieked of pride, but the eyes danced with devilment, and the lips were compressed with impatience—no doubt to take that noble steed adventuring. They were Griffin's own.

He looked dashed uncomfortable in the portrait, all strangled in a white neckcloth, red velvet and gold galon swathing him from chin to knee. He seemed every inch the tiny monarch ruling over some small kingdom, choked by the myriad rules and regulations the *ton* demanded.

Beau looked deeply into those painted blue eyes, knowing the sorrow that lurked behind them. She wondered if Griffin had ever known wild abandon in his childhood. By the saints, his poor pony would most likely have shied if he'd seen her as a child—a red-curled imp pilfering some merchant wares. She wondered if Griffin had known the pleasure of Fair Day. Whether he had ever stolen a peek at a three-headed goat and shivered with delicious horror. Or whether he had watched a juggler toss daggers in a wondrous danger-filled circle.

If Jack had managed to place her in the arms of the Devereauxs, she could have shared Griffin's childhood.

As Beau wandered about the elegant townhouse these past three days, suffering the fittings of the countless London seamstresses, she felt a stirring of new respect for the woman who had borne her. And Beau felt deeply sorry for the child Griff had been. She longed to strip him of his laces, his jewels, and his title, and to take him off to revel in some merry country fete.

She loved him.

The certainty shocked her, stunned her with its whiskey-warm desires, filled her with aching and need and fiery-fierce passions.

Yet she had never suspected that the emotions the poets rhapsodized about could make her so infernally miserable.

For the man whom she loved—loved with a depth she had never known she possessed—had carted her off to London to polish her up enough so she'd not give her grandmother apoplexy when he dumped Beau on her doorstep. So he could be rid of her. Dispose of her, even as he was off disposing of the difficulty with Molly.

Beau sighed, shaking out the folds of a lilac-pink gown Madame Charmande had completed the day before. In truth, Beau thought glumly, she should be worried that something had gone amiss with Griffin's plans. He said that all was well, and yet had she not believed that was the case when Jack had left Darkling Moor that long-ago night?

Beau cursed herself inwardly. She hadn't even questioned Griffin about his plans for Molly. She had merely nodded and bundled herself off obediently into the Graymore coach bound for London.

Yet as the hours passed and her innate impatience grew until she felt she would explode, Beau felt a thread of some emotion within her so strong, so instinctive, that she could not deny it.

She trusted him.

It was strange that after Jack's betrayal she trusted this man she had not even known a month ago. It was odd that the feeling should be so clear, so undeniable. Yet it was there.

From the time she had been a child she had known that the fairy-tale love her parents shared was wondrously rare, a dream that few were fortunate enough to stumble into.

She had seen the ugly side of love countless times at Blowsy Nell's. Had seen lust, had seen jealousy so ruthless it had resulted in broken bones and dark bruises.

She had seen, as well, the breezy amours of the brigands who roved the night, avowing eternal devotion to one before racing off to another woman's bed.

Yet there was nothing ugly in Griffin Stone's smile. None of that brittle, shallow emotion that had tainted Beau's views of the dealings between men and women.

There was honor in Griffin Stone. There was strength—strength enough to lean upon if one needed it. Strength enough to allow others to stand on their own. Strength enough to leave himself vulnerable to hurt, to pain, to life.

Beau flushed at the memory of his hungry mouth on hers, his hands eager on her body, as if he were seeking something so ephemeral he did not know whether it existed at all.

He had wanted her. But he had been too honorable, too noble to follow the path to which their passions had led.

Beau pulled a face, glaring into a gold-framed looking glass that hung upon the wall. Scruples could be damned inconvenient at times. But she was glad Griffin Stone possessed more than his just share.

For without them she would never have been carried off to Darkling Moor, never have felt the brush of his fingertips against her skin as he dressed her in silver tissue, never have learned to dance while he hummed an off-key minuet.

"Where the blazes is he?" she muttered, plunking herself down upon the pianoforte's stool, her hands hitting the keys with such force that the frightful sound would have driven any music master in London to dive into the Thames.

The sound faded away slowly as she leaned her forehead against her dainty sleeves, and the confection of curls one of the servants had coaxed her hair into that morning crumpled shamefully under such ill usage. She wanted to kick something.

The sound of a soft rap at the door was flint spark to tinder, and her head jerked upright, sending her carefully arranged ribbons askew. "What the blazes do you want?"

The door swung open, and she saw blue eyes so bright with suppressed merriment she leapt to her feet.

Love should have changed the way she saw him, Beau thought numbly, should have shaped a devilish rogue into some dreamy-eyed knight. But when he stood before her she still saw the rakehell who had set the London *ton* upon its ear, the blackguard who could devastate any lady at twenty paces with his infernally brilliant smile.

She scowled at him uneasily as she faced him, for the first time having admitted to herself the depth of her feelings.

"Misstress DeBurgh?" Griffin swept her a bow, the play of his well-honed muscles beneath his perfectly tailored, travel-dusted clothes sparking awareness through every fiber of her being.

"It is about time you showed your face about here, Stone," Beau said. "I've had seven proposals and one abduction attempt, and I am eloping to Gretna Green next Thursday."

"Felicitations. Anyone I am aquainted with?"

"A count or viscount or some such. Or was it a duke? I misremember."

"Well, in that case, as a proper guardian, I shall need to provide you with a few necessaries. It seems that the seamstresses have almost finished what might serve as your trousseau," he said, running appreciative eyes over her gown. "And if the man is eloping with you—well, the bounder does not deserve to get your dowry. I shall give you pin money, of course."

"Of course."

"But the one thing every lady of quality needs, wed or unwed, is the use of a most dependable lady's maid."

"Bah! I almost wrung the neck of the last chit you tried to saddle me with. If you foist that witch with the gray hair and the comb made out of a hayman's scythe upon me again, I promise I'll—"

"Save your threats, babe. Methinks I have come upon a suitable character. One that may be to your liking."

He turned, extending his hand to someone beyond the door.

Molly stepped timidly into the grand room, her eyes round with wonder, her cheeks pink with happiness. "Good morrow, Mistress Isab—"

Her words were lost in Beau's glad cry, a blur in lilac-pink flinging itself into the smaller girl's arms. Laughter bubbled, mingled with snifflings and whisperings and hugs, until the two of them emerged from burying their faces in each other's curls, their faces wet, their eyes shining.

"Moll . . . I'm so . . . so sorry," Beau choked out. "I—oh, Griffin . . . my lord . . ." She spun upon him, giving him a fierce hug. "Thank you . . . so much . . . I . . ."

"I do not envy you your position, Molly." He gave the girl one of his most dazzling smiles over Beau's shoulder. "I would rather confront a score of Jacobite cavalry than face putting Isabeau's hair up in curls."

"Beau has faced fates as daunting as any battle on my behalf," Molly said softly. "I shall be more than happy to enter the fray upon hers."

Griffin cleared his throat. "Very well, then, I shall leave you to your reunion. But I wanted to warn you to keep your weeping brief. My cousin, Lady Charcross, has arranged an engagement for us at Ranelagh a week from now, and, we'll not want to miss it. Molly, I would appreciate it if you could send your mistress upon that outing wearing something other than doeskin breeches and knee boots."

"I shall contrive to oblige you, my lord." Molly bobbed him a most respectful curtsy.

Beau flashed Griffin a glance bubbling with merriment. "And I shall contrive to *defy* you."

Griffin clicked his tongue against his teeth, making a tsking sound. "Pray tell me again who this poor unfortunate is that you have picked for a husband. I think it only fair to warn the man."

Beau spun about, scooping up an embroidered pincushion from what looked to be a sewing basket abandoned—perhaps a generation before. She threw it at Griffin in a graceful movement.

Griffin's hand shot out, and he caught the stuffed square from the air in mid-flight, holding it aloft in triumph. "She's tossing things that are not breakable now," he said to Molly with a wink. "It is a vast improvement from the—"

"Stone," Isabeau warned, reaching teasingly for a delicately latticed basket of purest porcelain.

"I surrender! I surrender!" Griffin cried out, dropping the cushion as though she had leveled one of her pistols upon him. "I shall repair to my bedchamber, cowardly dog that I am. Just do not begin, er . . . ridding the townhouse of its clutter."

Beau brandished the fragile object, smiling as Griff made a great show of retreating, his laughter echoing in the corridor beyond.

Yet once he'd gone the music room did not buzz with chatter as Beau had expected. Silence lay between her and Molly, thick, heavy, bearing down upon Beau until she knew not what to do, what to say.

"Your Lord Stone, he is a most generous man," Molly offered.

Beau started at the broken silence, her chest seeming to constrict as Molly went on.

"I can see why you stayed with him."

"While you were chained to Nell's bidding?" Beau's fists clenched, her nails cutting into the tender flesh of her palms.

"Isabeau, I—"

"No, Molly, hear me out. I was horrified when I realized that you . . . you were still serving Nell's patrons. I thought you were taken care of, or I never would have remained."

"Beau, I've told you a hundred times that I do not want you to risk your life for me. That Owen and I . . . we are not your burden to bear."

"You're no blasted burden! I love you—care for you. Ride for you because I choose to. But after Griffin . . . found me, I saw Jack and asked him . . . asked him to see to the both of you, you and Owen. And Jack said that he would. He swore it, Molly, or I would never have stayed away. Blast, even after I saw you at that inn I could scarcely believe he would betray me."

Molly worried her pale lower lip, her gaze darting away from Beau's, the tiniest tremor besetting her birdlike hand. "Isabeau . . . Jack . . . he . . ." Molly turned away, an uncommon stiffness to the set of her shoulders. "He did not betray you."

"But I saw you—saw you there with that disgusting, pawing oaf of a man."

"But Jack did not break his promise. He came to me after he spoke with you at Darkling Moor. Told me of the vow you had wrung from him. He looked so solemn, so hurt. I'd never seen him without the flash of his smile before, without the laughter that lights his eyes. But it is gone now. It was gone even then."

Beau's fingers tightened in the folds of her petticoat, crushing the delicate fabric. "I don't want to hear—don't want to know. God, I wish that I could love him the way he needs me to, Moll, but I can't! I can't! Even that night when Jack came to my room, I think I was already half in love with—" Beau cursed, spinning away from her friend, stalking across the room to the ornate fireplace.

"With Lord Stone," Molly finished for her.

Beau nodded, her fingertips reaching up and touching the child's portrait she had come to love.

"Then you know, Isabeau," Molly said softly. "You must know why I could not hold Mr. Ramsey to his promise, even to spare myself from Nell's patrons."

"Because I rejected him? Molly, it is mad to—"

"Would you sit in your gilded room waiting while your lord dashed out to risk his life on your behalf? Would you scoop up the coin he brought back and buy yourself pasties and ale whilst a hangman's noose dangled over his head?"

Beau started at Molly's impassioned words. Before, the girl's face had always seemed so fragile, so helpless. Though Molly's rosebud-pink lips quivered and her translucent skin appeared delicate as a babe's, for the first time in her life Molly's eyes burned with inner strength and a resolve that made Beau look upon her friend with a new respect.

"You love him. You love Jack."

"Far too much to allow him to die for me. Far too much to take coin from him. Even I have some pride, Beau." The words were softly reproving. Beau winced beneath them.

"Of course you have pride. I've never thought otherwise. Moll, it is just that—that you're so—"

"So frail? So frightened? Afraid of my own shadow, not to mention anyone else's?"

"No, it is . . ." Beau gestured helplessly, groping for words. "People like you cannot be expected to grub along with the rest of us poor mortals. You are an angel. You should be tucked away, safe upon some cloud, distributing largess, playing at guardian."

"I wish I could play at guardian," Molly said, her brow crinkling, her eyes worried. "Wish I could help him . . ."

"Jack?" Beau smiled briefly at the mere thought of timid Molly assisting bold Gentleman Jack Ramsey. But Beau wiped the grin from her lips, angry with herself as she saw hurt streak across Molly's face.

"I know you think me nothing but a coward. Think me worthless in any crisis. But he has been so subdued lately. So . . . somber. I had hoped it might help him just to—to talk, to have someone listen. Unfortunately, it seems he has the same opinion of my usefulness that you do."

"Molly—"

"He'd scarce say a word to me or anyone else about whatever is troubling him. And he has become so reckless that I nearly go into apoplexy every time he mounts his horse."

"Jack has always been neck or nothing. He can fend for himself."

"Something is amiss. Something odd, different. He rides off at all hours, constantly quizzing people about things that make no sense. He asks them about . . . poachers, and knife blades."

Beau remembered Griffin's own concern with the cruel poachers whose prey had been abandoned at Gethsemane

Abbey. Griffin had set Darkling Moor's game keepers to search for them even before he'd sent her off to London. But to no avail. But Molly's voice broke through her thoughts. "Even those dandies Jack used to find so amusing make him restive." Molly went on. "Whenever anyone mentions them, his brow furrows and he grows so quiet."

"He's probably just weary of being plagued by the society rakes." Beau tried to soothe Molly's unease. "And as for knives and the like, he has always had a love affair with lengths of honed steel. It is nothing, I am certain. Maybe . . ."

She glanced at her friend, trying to decide whether easing Molly's apprehension was worth dealing her some small hurt. "Jack is just not used to his advances being rejected. Maybe he is but moping, healing up his heart enough to offer it to another"—she tugged upon Molly's curls—"a golden-haired angel who will adore him far more than the stubborn rogue deserves."

A becoming rose stained Molly's cheeks, but she shook her head. "No, I don't think he'd ever—"

"Just wait, Molly me girl. Once we've done fitting you out as a grand lady's maid the poor rogue will not know what befell him. These ribbons and laces are a blasted nuisance to me—make me feel like I'm a cursed maypole. But you . . . you'll be dazzling supreme."

"Beau," Molly giggled, her eyes regaining their sparkle, "I hardly think lady's maids trick themselves out as fancy as their mistresses. Most likely it will be sturdy, serviceable garb for me, and neat little mobcaps."

"Bah! The upstairs maids have already hinted that the high and holy ladies throw their cast-off finery to their servants. I can just see it now—a perfect confection in blue and pink done up for Mistress Isabeau DeBurgh. One with a bonnet trimmed in rosebuds. You do like rosebuds, do you not?"

"Yes," Molly said, her eyes glowing with laughter.

"But of course"—Beau mimicked a preening noblewoman—"being the paragon of impeccable taste that Mistress DeBurgh is, she will reject the gown upon the grounds that . . . that the pink is far too . . . pink, and the blue is uncommon blue."

Molly dissolved into gales of laughter as Beau minced about the music room with her nose poked into the air. The laugh caught in Molly's throat, and suddenly the girl ran to Beau, catching her in a hard embrace.

"Ah, Beau, it is so good to be with you again. To laugh and not be afraid. I don't know what I would have done if Lord Stone hadn't appeared when he did." A shudder went through her slight frame. "There was a man, an awful man with the whitest skin and the coldest eyes wanting to, er . . . engage me. I said I wouldn't. I always managed to be spoken for when he came about. He frightened me, Beau, frightened me in a way I've never been before."

"But Lord Stone did come."

"Yes, but if he hadn't, eventually I would not have been able to slip from that pale man's grasp."

"You'll never have to be afraid again, Molly. I promise. Griffin—I mean my lord Stone—he is determined to mold me into a lady of quality. And if he succeeds, although I still have my doubts, I shall always take care of you."

"Just like when you rescued Owen and me from the bakers?"

"Owen!" Beau gasped, the memory of the lanky, troublesome lad slamming into her. "Oh, where is—"

"Lord Stone took him up as well. Settled him in at Darkling Moor as a stable lad. That is what took so much time. You see, MacBeth, it seems, blames Owen for the bungled robbery, and every time Owen got near the stables the stallion pitched one of his legendary fits. But they have made their peace now and are . . . Isabeau?"

Molly's lips compressed in concern, and she peered into her friend's face, dainty fingers smoothing Beau's cheek, smearing the damp streaks that traced down from her lashes. Crying. Beau was crying.

She knew she should be bloody humiliated by dissolving into a bout of reekingly feminine tears, and yet it touched her. Touched her so deeply that Griffin had not only gone after Molly and made certain Beau had her beloved friend constantly at her side, but had also swooped the scapegrace Owen away from the harsh underworld, offering the boy the means to make his own way.

If she had not loved Griffin Stone already, she would have fallen in love with him at that moment. Her heart swelled with happiness, gratitude, until a tiny sob tore from her breast.

"Beau, you're weeping," Molly said.

"Abominable things, tears!" Beau said, taking an angry swipe at her reddening eyes. "Don't see . . . see why I should be afflicted with 'em. But Molly, I love him so much it hurts inside, when he is so kind . . ."

Molly smiled her sweet, angelic smile. "I think he loves you, too. You should have heard him upon the ride to London, regaling me with the stories of how you turned his household upside down. His eyes shone with delight. And despite his outward smiles, I fear he is a man much given to sadness."

Beau's mind filled with images of Judith Stone's icy face and Griffin's tales of his brother's exasperation.

"I'm going to make him happy, Molly," Beau said, her words as unyielding as those of any monarch vowing to reclaim a throne, "whether he wills it or no."

"He'd best surrender his banners at once and be done with it," Molly said, saluting as she had when they had been children playing at King Charles and Cromwell.

"Thank you, Moll. For listening to me. For putting up with my infernal caterwauling and . . . and not tormenting me about it."

"How do you know I shan't in the future? I need only tell Owen about it, and it would spread like brushfire."

"Do that, and our friendship is over!" Beau flung her a watery smile, then hastened out of the room.

The round-faced butler told her that Master Griffin had repaired to his chambers to refresh himself after his journey. And despite the servant's protests she swept up the stairs and down the corridor to Griffin's apartments.

Her hand trembled slightly as she touched the door handle, but she drew in a deep breath, opening the panel with surprising care.

Griffin stood before a shaving bowl bare-chested, his breeches slung low upon lean hips as he swiped a gleaming razor across the soap that clung about the square line of his jaw.

"If you have brought water for my bath, James, you're too late. I contrived to wash—"

When he glanced over and saw Isabeau the sharp blade in his hand skittered across one cheek, and a thin streak of blood welled where it had nicked his bronze skin. He dropped the implement, leaping to one side just before it struck his toes. But he scarcely seemed to notice as his hand pressed against the tiny wound. Naked longing flared in his eyes for just a moment before he shuttered it away.

One hand raked through the damp ends of dark hair that reached his broad shoulders, his fingers sliding self-consciously down the muscled planes cut with such beguiling beauty on a chest dusted with dark hair. Beau's mouth went dry as she skimmed her gaze down that unrelentingly masculine chest, tracing the ribbon of black that dipped past his navel and disappeared into the band of breeches that fit him like a second skin.

"Isabeau." Her name was the gentlest of caresses upon his lips, the tones edged with a need that stirred fire in Beau's veins. "Is there something wrong?"

"You cut yourself. I—"

He flushed. "It is scarcely a scratch. Far beneath my notice. Was—was there something you needed?"

"No," Beau managed to say. "I—I but wanted to talk with you. You've been gone an infernally long time, and—"

"Ladies do not hold interviews with gentlemen in their bedchambers. It is most improper." He crossed over to her, and she could smell the scent of soap upon his skin, the whispering fragrance of bayberry clinging damply to his sun-bronzed chest. He reached out and ran a fingertip down the curve of her nose, letting the callused pad rest for a heartbeat upon the silky swell of her lip. "If any were to see us thus, I fear you would be compromised beyond redemption. It would be a shame for such a beauty to be forced to wed the likes of me."

"Then . . . then I hope the whole world sees me. I shall usher in every vicar in London. For I should hold it the highest of honors to be at the side of such a wondrously kind man. A man who aids street urchins and shields serving maids and tolerates a pure witch of a grandmother, even though the shriveled-up harpy deserves to be sunk in the nearest river."

"Isabeau." Griffin brushed a tender kiss across her brow. "You must not drown the dowager duchess. Your word."

"No, I'll not give my word. For I might find some way to send her grace whisking off a church steeple if she ever dares again to deal pain to—to the man I . . . love." Beau felt her cheeks flame, felt the unaccustomed dewiness sting in her eyes as she gazed up into that face that was so devilishly handsome, so incredibly strong, so infinitely gentle.

She had expected some words in return, something to show her that he felt the same racing joy that she did, the same breathless wonder at having discovered something miraculous totally by surprise.

Instead she saw disbelief and sadness, and a pain that struck through to her heart.

"Isabeau."

"I love you! Blast it, Stone, I—"

"You believe that you do. Babe, it is so confusing, I know, all these feelings you're experiencing. And what with me whirling your life about like a child's top, it is no wonder you are . . . muddled. But . . . look at you, Isabeau, look." He turned her so that she could see her reflection in the glass over his shaving bowl. "You are nothing but a babe in this world. Innocent . . . so . . . so vulnerable. I know that you think you love me"—the words snagged in his throat, and she saw him battle and fail to suppress the need that was fierce in his eyes—"but you're only grateful. You don't even know me."

"I know you well enough. I know that you're loving and brave, and that you—you make me laugh—"

"Isabeau, it is hardly a measure for loving."

"No? Well, what about trembling, Stone? You make me do that, too, and Christ knows I've never been troubled with that problem before. When you're near me my whole cursed body aches, and I feel like I'll fly to pieces if you don't touch me. If you don't kiss me. But then when you do . . . I shatter like your grandmother's thrice-cursed Ming, because I want . . . need so much more. . . ."

A shudder worked through his half-naked body, the corded muscles beneath his damp skin knotting. Beau reached out, trailing her fingers in a feather-light pattern across the sun-darkened flesh, a throbbing setting up at the juncture of her thighs as she felt the spasm of his muscles beneath her hand.

"Beau, don't." His fingers held her wrist in a bruising grasp, his teeth clenching with something that seemed akin to pain. But she merely flattened her palm against the hard plane, circling the pebble-hard nub of his nipple.

"Don't what? You cannot say you don't feel it for me as well. I may be innocent of curtsying and fans, milord Stone, but where I came from, I can assure you, I did not remain innocent regarding *this.*" She leaned forward, brushing her lips across the tiny wound upon his cheek, nipping at his naked collarbone. The taste of him, the feel of his quivering filled her with a sense of power, a sense of wonder, and a stubborn resolve beyond any she had ever possessed.

"Christ!" Griff hissed in a ragged breath, hurling her hand away from him, wheeling to stalk across the room. He stood there, framed in the light spilling in from the window, his dark hair tumbled like some pagan king's, his feet planted wide. "Damn it, Beau, what do you want of me? Do you want me to snatch up what you are offering—pity, maybe, or gratitude that you mistake for love? Do you want me to bind you to me for eternity when you are scarce a child, watch you come to realize that you may respect me, hold me in some affection, but that I am nothing but the benefactor who snatched you from the highroads? I may be a bastard in countless ways, Isabeau, but I'm not bastard enough to chain you to the first man who touches your fancy, even if it is me."

"Blood and thunder, Stone, I've known scores of men, blasted hordes of them," Beau retorted, her own temper raging. "And as a sex, I have not found them a very admirable lot. I've no desire to go poking in amongst them, waiting for one of them to trample over me or grab my pursestrings or my petticoats."

"You've known brigands, highwaymen, criminals, Beau. Soon you'll be in ballrooms with the best London has to offer."

"Bah. I've seen them as well. They're the ones who toss their coin to Nell for poor Molly, then nearly run their carriages over her when they are through."

"Isabeau."

"Fine." There was a steely edge of temper in her voice, one that reverberated with danger. "You will not believe that I love you until I've dazzled half a dozen men. That is your own stupidity. But I'll humor you, Stone. Because even when you're being a pigheaded, addle-brained idiot, I love you so much I ache inside."

Beau saw him flinch. "I just don't think you know your own mind, Isabeau. And it would drive me insane if another man—" He stopped, the glint in his eye thunderous enough to satisfy even Beau.

"I've known my own mind since I was two years old, Stone," Beau said, her eyes narrowed with challenge. "And I warn you. I always get what I want."

With that Isabeau stomped from the chamber, her chin thrust in the air, her eyes gleaming with a belligerence that would have made Molly blanch with trepidation.

Chapter Seventeen

Silver lace and shining shoe buckles, glittering snuffboxes and gemstones of every size, from the vulgar to the negligible, spangled the throng of amusement-seekers who crowded about the large rotunda of Ranelagh Gardens. The myriad of colors, smells, and sounds provided a banquet for the senses. Laughing and chattering, the people plied the booths seeking tea or, for the more daring, wine, while Ranelagh House itself loomed to the north like some beneficent monarch, an ornamental lake in the distance rippling like liquid sapphire.

Oblivious to his surroundings, Griffin strode down the walk, trying to recapture the lazy aura of diversion he had experienced within Ranelagh years before when it had been but one more treasure trove of lights o' love, convivial company, and fine drink. How many times had he ambled along these winding pathways when he had been a young man eager for romances and spoiling for fights? He had embroiled himself in three duels here and had won considerable coin making far-flung wagers with his friends. But despite his wild actions, he had never felt this coil-tight tension knotting up in the core of him, this teeth-grinding, fist-clenching, tongue-tangling unease that gave him the sense that he was walking along the edge of a razor.

He scowled down at Isabeau, a muscle in his jaw working. Tonight she was a vision. She seemed alive with fire and passion and a playfulness that he mistrusted. Her flame-bright hair was unpowdered, in defiance of fashion. Her gown clung all buttery gold about her tiny waist, its embroidery of rich green lattice and dainty blue flowers accenting the creamy luster of her flawless skin. Her tight sleeves were iced in snowy lace that spilled down past her wrists, her expressive hands fluttering as she delighted in each new spectacle.

Griffin cursed inwardly, his gaze fixing on the filmy white froth. He felt the urge to rip away the delicate webbing and tuck it over the low swept bodice.

She was an infernal menace. She drew the eyes of every man upon the walk. Three dandies had nearly run over an elderly baron's wife, their eyes having goggled out at Isabeau. And one scrawny stripling of nineteen had slammed headlong into the side of a booth when she passed. She had so dazzled the cursed boy with one of her smiles—that blinding, impish smile—that Griffin had wanted to grab her and kiss her until she couldn't see or even think of any man save himself.

"Is that the sort of man you are so eager for me to become aquainted with, my lord?" she had inquired with honeyed sweetness, a slight hint of a smirk about her lips.

He had dragged every bit of self-control he had possessed to the fore and had told her she might attempt to select one not so fresh from his cradle.

"For a man who is going to such a deal of trouble to introduce me to eligible prospects, you seem to be overly particular," she had teased him. "We've been here nearly an hour, and you've not presented me to a single one." Tossing her curls until they had bounced, burnished red-gold, against her shoulders, she had peered at him from beneath her lashes. "Well, maybe I shall be pure drowning in men at the supper you and your dear Cousin What-the-blazes have arranged."

"Cousin Jane," he had snapped. "Lady Charcross. And if there was anyone here worth the cloth in his breeches, I would thrust you upon him at once."

She had laughed at him then, a light, tinkling laugh that had been full of mischief. His chest had constricted until he had nearly tumbled over a cart laden with pasties.

He glared at her, a flush mounting yet again in his cheeks as he recalled the humiliating episode, but his eyes were snared by a tiny freckle that peeked over the bodice's edging as if to taunt him, and his already aching loins tightened further still.

Blast it, she was driving him insane. And she was having a bloody rollick of a time doing it! If he could but get her to cover herself decently . . .

"Isabeau, do you not think we should retrieve your cloak from the coach?" he managed stiffly. "You appear a trifle chilled."

"Oh, no, my lord. It is a wondrous balmy night." She brushed her fingers over the bared skin of her décolletage in a gesture that all but unmanned him. "I marvel that you could suggest such a thing. You look quite . . . er . . . over*heated* yourself. You are not becoming feverish?" She turned, ignoring the crowd, laying her hand, still warm from her breasts, upon his brow, sliding her fingers in a delicately seductive path down his cheek. He drew in a sharp breath, but that proved still more devastating to his senses, for the scent of her—violets and cinnamon and sweet meadow breezes—filled his nostrils, raced through his veins.

"Damn it, Isabeau, there is nothing amiss with me that your—your *concealing* yourself modestly would not cure. As your guardian—"

"As my guardian, you ordered my gowns. All in the height of fashion. And as for what is disturbing you, look about you. Half the women here this evening have more flesh displayed than I."

"Is that so, Mistress DeBurgh? Then I had best affix my attention upon those we pass, for they must be fair naked from the waist up!" The instant he snapped out those hasty words he cursed himself for uttering them. Isabeau's eyes widened with amusement, and she collapsed into a fit of giggles. He wanted to clap his hand over that berry-red, beckoning mouth.

With delightful innocence Beau flung her arms about his neck, setting up a roar of approving laughter all around them. Her breath was moist, warm against the tensile cords of his neck, the sensitive skin about his ear. "If you *dare* to fix your gaze upon any save me, Lord Stone, I shall steal into your bedchamber tonight and cleave out your gizzard!"

Griffin let loose an oath, his hands sweeping up to clench about her wrists, drag her hands away, but the image of Isabeau slipping into his rooms, all soft and scented and hungry to love him, filled him with the even sharper vision of drifting down amongst cool linen sheets, touching her, tasting her until they were both wild with the need clawing through them.

"Fine," Griff ground out, beads of perspiration clinging to his skin. "Cleaving out my gizzard would be far preferable to this infernal torture. Mark me, woman, if you—"

"Shtone! Shtone!" The slurred cry muffled Griffin's warning. A hand slammed companionably into his shoulder as a bewigged man in a puce coat stumbled into him. The force made Beau wobble as well, and Griff's hand shot out to steady her, his fingers colliding with bared flesh that was as warm as sun-drenched satin.

He pulled his hand away as if he had been burned. In truth he had been, the sensation of her skin beneath his hand searing a molten path to his loins.

He wheeled to face the man who had assaulted him, glad to have someone to vent his fury upon. But the somewhat vague eyes peered into his face with owlish pleasure, features only slightly coarsened by dissipation, alight with surprise.

Albert Tarkington, Baronet of Vailtree, beamed with the same unbreachable good nature he had affected since they had been boys together at Eton.

Griffin stared into the countenance of his old friend, for

an instant regretting that he could not vent his frustration by challenging him to a duel—a nice, sane matching of swords to ease the fire raging inside him.

"So 'tish you, Shtone!" the plump-faced baronet exclaimed, cracking his palm again into Griff's shoulder. "Heard you were to be about, but I scarcely believed it, even if it was your own cousin who informed me. Dashed glad to see you again."

"Bertie." Griff removed himself from the man's reach.

"Ish been a thousand years since I saw you last," Bertie said. "Mished you dreadful, the lot of us did. Grieved for you when Tom Southwood told us the old duke dived for his crypt."

Griffin had a fleeting twinge of worry for Charles as he recalled Tom's enigmatic note.

Tarkington's voice dropped low, his bleary eyes earnest despite the network of red veins running through their whites. "Bleedin' good fellow, yer brother was, disregardin' the fact that he waxed a bit starshed."

Griff grimaced, struck suddenly by the odd certainty that he was more touched by Tarkington's blunt condolences than by any of the more solemn ones he had received since setting foot upon English shores. "William was a good fellow, wasn't he, Bert?" Griff said, grateful that Tarkington's customary inebriation would most likely keep the baronet from taking note of the sudden thickness in Griffin's voice.

But Bertie cleared his own rather gouty gullet and pulled a kerchief from his pocket to mop his sweaty brow. "So," he said with forced bluffness, "Janey—I mean, your cousin, Lady Charcross—said you were getting up a party tonight to . . . er, preshent some ward you were saddled with. There be half a dozen o' the *ton*'s finest awaiting yon." He gestured in the general direction of the rotunda. "Expected old Southwood to be amongst 'em, seeing as the twain o' you were ever so thick. But he just put in from the Continent this morn. Must be damned tired what with chasing after that wife of his."

"Tom is waiting upon me tomorrow night." There was a

grimness in Griffin's voice that startled Beau. "He's coming to the townhouse so that we can . . . clear up a bit of business between us."

Bertie shrugged. "Well, Southwood has more woman than he can rightly handle already, I'm told. Leavesh more pickings for the resht of us." Tarkington thumped Griffin upon the shoulder good-naturedly. "So, Shtone, tell me. Did you provide a rash of other females in addition to this . . . *ward?*"

"I fear he brought only me." Isabeau stepped toward Bertie, her eyes dancing beguilingly as she curtsied. "I fear," she continued in a stage whisper, "my Lord Stone is in a great hurry to marry me off so that I'll not be a bother to my family any longer."

Griffin went rigid as Bertie almost strangled upon his own neckcloth. His thick fingers reached up to wrench that offending garment askew. "'Zounds!" he gasped. "You . . . are Shtone's—"

"My ward," Griffin stated frigidly. "Mistress Isabeau DeBurgh."

"'Pon my soul, Griffin, can't be 'cause she's mudface that you're itching to be rid of her!" Bertie declared. "A reg'lar stunner, she be. With all that . . . that red stuff on her head."

"Hair. It is called hair."

Bertie looked mortally wounded. "I'm not *that* drunk, Shtone. You've seen me drunker. *I've* seen *you* drunker."

Unaccountably Griff felt heat steal along his cheekbones. For the first time in his life he hoped none of the stories of his wild past would be told.

"Bertie," he said, grabbing Tarkington by one meaty arm, "I hardly think it would be proper to discuss such states of indisposition with my ward present."

Bertie hiccuped, waving his other hand toward the laughing Beau. "Well, it is just that, with a face the like o' that, all peachy an' smooth, I can't see why you're making a fuss about tryin' to leg-shackle her. Why, any man without numb breeches would—"

"Any man would scarcely do for my ward." The shadow

of pleasure he had taken in seeing his old companion once again faded from Griff, leaving in its wake irritation and the fervent wish that he had never suggested taking in Ranelagh, had never dreamed up the scheme of introducing Isabeau into society, and that he had merely kept her safely locked inside Darkling Moor, bounding down stairs three at a time, sneaking licks from the sugar rock and matching wits with him at chess.

"Mr. Bertie, I regret to say that my lord is a most tedious guardian, ever preaching propriety," Beau piped up, extending a hand to the baronet's gloved one. "But I think he is somewhat of a hypocrite. The stories I've heard . . ." Her voice trailed off suggestively as she peered up at Tarkington through those thick, dark lashes. "*I* believe that his lordship wants me out of his way so that he may take his place again in society as reigning rakehell."

Albert choked out a guffaw, raising Beau's fingers to his lips in salute, and it was all Griffin could do not to knock Tarkington's hand away with one fist. "Well, I believe that there are a bevy of London's finest bucks in the rotunda believing they are to be saddled with some horse-faced girl of agonizingly good family and torturously nondescript personality. That's how it usually is when there is such a stir to send a gel off. I think they will be pleasantly surprised. If I may, milady?" Bertie offered her one puce sleeve, and she let her fingertips drift down onto it, smiling up into the baronet's face in a way that drove Griffin mad.

"Thank you, kind sir," she said, keeping pace with the nobleman as he began a somewhat unsteady course toward the rotunda. Heavenly smells wafted out, tantalizing those who would dine. The clatter of china and silver, the scraping of chairs against the floor, and the ever-present chatter seemed to lure those outside the building with an invisible thread.

Isabeau slanted a glance up at Griffin, who stalked beside them. His mouth was tight with anger, and his eyes were like twin embers, hot and furious and full of hunger—a hunger every roast capon in London could not have filled. A hunger

Beau fully intended to taunt and torment until even the most noble and saintly of men would not have the strength to subdue it. And Lord Griffin Stone was no accursed saint!

She flashed him a wicked glance, wetting her lips so they shone in the lamplight, and a delicious shiver worked through her as she imagined what it would be like when that barely leashed passion that had glittered in Griffin's eyes was loosed upon her. Devastating. Mind-shattering. Wild and wondrous and as full of danger as the storms that hurtled in from the vast oceans, his loving would be. Yet filled with such a rare, sweet tenderness it would break her heart. She was stunned as tears pricked at the back of her eyes, her smile softening with anticipation.

"Here we be, Mistress DeBurgh." Bertie Tarkington's voice jarred her back to the present, and she was surprised to find that they had entered the building. In front of her a fair rainbow of masculine forms was seated around a large table. Beau met the battery of their stunned eyes with her most winning smile, trying not to laugh as they all but tripped over one another in their efforts to secure a place at her side.

Golden-curled Adonises, powdered dandies, rugged-featured, dark-eyed paragons who reeked of the sporting set crowded near her. It was as if Griffin's cousin had managed to prepare a regular banquet of men for Beau's perusal. Whatever tastes she had been prone to would have been represented among this company. But not a one of them, from the flamboyant, bewigged giant of a man garbed in scarlet to the bookish, long-nosed gent with a slight lisp could hold a candle to the man who had already bewitched her heart.

Beau stole a glance at him, taking in his thunderous scowl. There were ominous roilings of emotion within the blue-gray depths of his eyes. They held a delicious danger, the same alluring menace that had been present when she had first seen his face across a moonlit road. And there was something about seeing him this way that fueled the imp of mischief always lurking in Isabeau's breast, making her want to prick even more relentlessly at what sanity he had managed to maintain.

She shook herself mentally. She was aware that the vague babble she had been hearing was several introductions being rattled off at once, as if she were a prize to be awarded to whichever of the candidates was first to reveal his name. She drew a fan from her pocket, unfurling the painted scene of the Muses with a flirtatious snap.

"I vow I shall never be able to keep the lot of you straight," she said, giving them her most dazzling smile. "There are so many of you, and . . . well, I regret I have not been much in polite company."

"It is a crime to keep such beauty hidden," a bull of a man boomed. "Stone should be taken up by the constable for effecting the thievery of such a delight to mine orbs."

"And such fine orbs you have, too," Beau commiserated, tapping the man on one brown coatsleeve. "I know what I shall do to save myself from this muddle. I shall call you all by what I judge to be your finest feature—that way I shall not have to trouble myself by stumbling over your titles and whatnot. What say you? Do you not think that the most marvelous of ideas?"

A rumble of laughing approval rose up from the throng of men.

"Mistress DeBurgh, you will not insult our guests by denying them their names," Griffin began in steely accents.

"Ah, blast, Stone, who the devil wants a mere name when such a beauty as this might be flattering the very deuce out of him?" a jolly lad of about five and twenty offered, then turned to Isabeau, bowing over her hand. "You may, milady, call me anything you desire, so long as you gift me with the light of your smile."

Beau giggled as Griffin nearly choked at the boy's words. She so enjoyed Stone's discomfiture that she oozed charm as she took the boy's hand in her own. "I believe I shall call you Monsieur Hands. I ask you," she said, drawing the others into her game, "does he not have a most remarkably strong set of hands? Yet well shaped. Like those of an artist. Have you ever considered taking up the brush?"

The boy looked as if someone had smeared crimson paint on his face, his lashes dropping over his eyes in a sudden bout of shyness. "I—I . . . have dabbled at it a bit."

"Then when I choose my husband I shall commission you to paint my wedding portrait. There. It is settled. And you." She turned the full force of her eyes upon a tall man whose face was sprinkled with freckles. She could almost see the poor fellow blanch and was intuitively aware that he was most likely curling up in dread, thinking she'd mention his obviously hated feature. But Beau fixed her gaze upon his nose, then clapped her hands in delight. "Hawk. Yes, sir, that is what you will be called. You boast a right noble beak, I think, and—"

"And I? What shall I be called?" others piped up as she christened them each anew, making them all blush with pleasure or chuckle in amusement. As the last youth stepped forward—with an exceedingly handsome face and form, but eyes somewhat lacking in intelligence—Beau's own lids widened with wicked excitement. Upon each one of his cheeks was a small white scar, so symmetrically perfect it was all Isabeau could do not to fall into her pudding.

Instead she fluttered her fan, inquiring with a husky breathlessness that made Griffin curse. "Oh, sir, you . . . you bear the most dashing feature of all. Those marks upon your cheeks! I vow they make you look like a bold pirate rogue, or Robin of the Hood. So . . . so masculine, so wondrous menacing. I swear it fair robs me of words to express . . ."

Monsieur Scar preened like a gamecock, fingers weighted with jewels brushing the white marks with as much pride as though they were medals of valor. "Why, Mistress DeBurgh, I would boast to you from whence these came, but I do not want to distress you."

"Distress me?" Beau said as she nibbled at the food servants had slipped onto her plate. "I shall contrive to keep my courage up. With all these strong men about me, I believe I shall manage not to quake."

She had taken them all up into her web of charm, the entire party hanging upon every word she uttered, every smile, every laugh. And with each stroke of the witty repartee Griffin's face grew darker, grimmer.

"If you are certain . . ." Monsieur Scar let his voice drop into the eerie tones Beau had so often used herself. "Even sheltered as you have been, Mistress DeBurgh, you must have heard tell of Gentleman Jack Ramsey."

"The—the highwayman?" Beau feigned a gasp, her fingers catching at her throat as if she were stricken with fear.

"Mr. Clark," Griffin's voice cut in, "I do not think my ward cares to suffer through tales that do not concern her."

"Oh, but I beg to differ, my lord," Beau said, leaning toward the youth eagerly. "I am entranced by the tale. Fair perishing to know what transpired!"

"It was a dark and stormy night, the winds rattling the tree branches like the bones of a corpse, when *he* fell upon us."

"Ramsey?" Beau encouraged.

"No," another of the party piped up. "It was Clark's governor coming to drag him home to his schoolbooks!"

But Clark ignored the gibe, pressing closer to Isabeau. "The most fearful brigand ever to slash a purse! He was a giant of a man, his horse's eyes pits of fire, his sword flashing like quicksilver against the night. Any man I know would have lost his courage at the sight of him, Mistress DeBurgh, and fled in pure horror. Any man save me."

The crowd choked and snorted and sneered at his claim, but Clark went on oblivious, not caring a fig what his comrades thought as long as he held the rapt attention of a lady.

"I have heard that Gentleman Jack is most dreadful handsome," Isabeau said, toying with the lace at her breast, "and that the women he holds at bay with his sword are more eager to surrender their virtue to him than their jewels."

"Isabeau," Griff ground out, "we do not discuss ladies' virtue at the table."

The conversation had taken a turn young Clark had not

expected, and he stammered, groping for a way to steer it back to his own heroism.

Monsieur Hawk chuckled. "Beware, Clark, lest you convince Mistress DeBurgh to scorn the lot of us and race out to the crossroads in search of this Ramsey. It would be a blasted pity were she to elude us all."

"In truth," Beau said, dealing Griffin another verbal riposte, "though Gentleman Jack seems a most daring rogue, it is another who has captured my imagination. One entitled Lucifer's Flame, Satan's Fire . . . oh, drat, what was it?"

"The Devil's Flame?" Bertie inserted hopefully. "Why, Stone, did I not hear some rumor that you were set upon by that very rogue? Janey—I mean Lady Charcross—mentioned that her servants had heard from a postilion that—"

"It is nothing but bloody rumor," Griffin growled. "You would do well not to show your witlessness, Bertie, by heeding servants' gossip."

"I say, old fellow," Bertie sniffed, "it was your cousin who—"

"My lord Stone is just attempting to be modest," Isabeau chirruped, casting Griffin a tolerant glance. "Why, it is true indeed. He even matched swords with the blackguard—"

"Damn it, Isabeau," Griffin shot from his seat, his fists clenched, "this is not amusing."

"You found it very much so, as I remember. You see," she said, leaning toward Tarkington with a conspiratorial laugh, "the Devil's Flame is a veritable tumble-nose with a sword, so my lord dealt him a lesson he will not soon forget."

"Is that so, Stone?" one of the men asked, others adding to his plea. "Do regale us."

"Oh, please, my lord." Beau fluttered her lashes, her fan dipping to accent the cleavage of her breasts. "Do regale us with your adventures."

Griffin slammed his fist onto the table, his eyes searing with such fury, such fear, that Beau faltered beneath it for an instant. "There will be no more regaling of any kind at all," he snarled. "My ward appears to be quite beside herself."

One strong hand shot out, clamping around Isabeau's wrist. "A megrim, is it, my dear?"

"I fear I have been afflicted by a most troublesome heat in the blood of late." Isabeau let desire show in her eyes, let her lips part as if in invitation. "Perhaps if I took to my bed . . ."

Fire, wind, crashing waves of need seemed to race between them. Griffin's eyes blazed so dark Beau felt her head swim. Then he was pulling her, guiding her toward the door, the objections of the party and his sharp excuses scarcely penetrating the primitive thrumming of Beau's heart.

It was all she could do to keep pace with him as he strode through the crowd that was still reveling in the night, his long, muscled legs devouring the ground in dangerous, measured strides.

"Griffin," she could not help but say, "my slippers. I cannot keep pace."

But he only swore and scooped her into his arms. She felt the power within him, the leashed savagery enveloping her in a whirl of sensation so wild, so hypnotizing that she did not know he had reached the Graymore coach until he had flung her inside it.

He snarled a command to the wide-eyed coachman and all but ripped the curtains down across the windows to veil them from prying eyes. But despite his efforts a ripple of light from the brass lamp sneaked through a tiny gap in the curtains. His features appeared so taut, so perilous in the flickering light that they seemed to be the mask of some enraged pagan god.

Beau swallowed hard, feeling like a reckless doe who has suddenly found herself in a wolf's ruthless jaws.

That racing of something akin to fear was foreign to her, more annoying than any other emotion could be. And it made her thrust her chin up in pure defiance, stifling her gasp as the coach lurched into motion.

"What the bloody hell did you think you were doing in there?" Griffin's voice cut the silence like a rapier.

"I was being charming, as you instructed. Attempting to trap some poor wretch into marriage."

"Marriage?" He gave an ugly laugh. "The way you were flaunting your charms, milady, you'd never have reached the altar. Maybe the bedchamber, or a cell at Newgate."

"You must forgive me." Beau's voice dripped insolence. "I am new at this game of flirtation."

"You underestimate yourself, milady. Half the men present were drooling upon their waistcoats over you, and the rest were plotting how to get you into their beds without having me slice them stem to stern in a duel over your honor. But then, you have no honor, do you, milady Flame? You charged into my bedchamber one day ago with vows of eternal love. And now you are slavering over anything in breeches."

"I was *what?"*

"Simpering like a cursed lightskirt, fondling their hands, admiring their . . . by God, when you raved over Minton's breeches I could have thrashed you bloody!"

"Could you have, my lord?" Isabeau knew she was courting disaster, but suddenly she was loving the menace glittering in every tensile muscle, every stark plane of Griffin Stone's body. "I think you are a liar."

"Don't taunt the devil, girl, unless you want to be sucked down into hell."

"I *am* the Devil, Stone. Sent here to tempt you. And I know full well what you wanted to do to me . . . with me . . . at that accursed supper. You wanted what I wanted, felt what I felt . . . but you had not the courage to take it."

"Damn you, shut up."

"Why? Are you afraid, Stone? Afraid to hear the truth? That you're mad with need for me, that you want to tumble me back into the sheets and take—"

She saw him shudder, fight for control. "Curse it."

"I love you. *Love you.* Is that what you are afraid of?" All taunting, all baiting had fled. Instead she was flooded with an innate understanding of the man even now battling with his conscience, wrestling with the scars slashed upon his very soul.

"What is it, Stone? Do you think once I've touched you, kissed you, felt you inside me, I'll suddenly awaken and be aware of whatever flaw it is that makes your grandmother despise you?"

"Beau."

"Do you fear I'll leave you then, hie away with some witling like Clark or Tarkington or—"

"Damn you to hell!" Griffin ground out, lunging across the seat, the suddenness of his movement wrenching a gasp from Beau's chest. "If you ever so much as look at them, I'll—"

"I don't want them. I want you, Griffin. I want you so much I can't think of anything else. Want you so much I fear I might die of it." Her hands were shaking, her voice quavering with emotion as she tangled her hands in the midnight satin of his hair. The light from the coach slashed across his face, the feral hunger, primitive fury in his features searing into Beau's heart.

With a groan of surrender he crushed her against him, his mouth crashing down on hers with a savagery that bruised, a desire so fierce it fed the flame of her own. There was no time, no place for the elegant dance of civilized mating. This was as wild as the joining of the first man and woman, and as miraculous.

He bore her down onto the velvet squabs, his hands everywhere upon her, devouring her, as though she and she alone could fill some emptiness inside him, the depth of which neither of them had suspected. Yet he filled her as well, filled her with a dizzy wonder that surpassed any sensation she had ever known.

"Beau . . . Beau . . ." He pressed his lips against her flesh as he bared it, his hands tangling in lacings, tearing them free. The satin stomacher fell away, undergarments dispatched with haste by fingers that played across her skin with the skill of a master.

Oblivious to the jolting of the coach, oblivious to the streets of London flashing by beyond their tiny haven, Beau kissed him, touched him, her hands fumbling with his shirt. Her palms collided with hard muscle sheathed in satiny warm skin, the hair-roughened plane sending fire jolting through her veins.

Cool night air kissed her breasts as he made them naked to his gaze, and his eyes went black with passion as he traced the outline of those vulnerable curves, the pink-tipped crests already aching for the wet heat of his mouth.

"Christ," he rasped, his thumb skimming across her sensitized skin. "You are beautiful . . . so infernally beautiful."

Beau moaned, arching her head back, dragging his lips down to her fevered, aching flesh. He drew her nipple into that hot, wet cavern, his tongue toying with it, his teeth grazing it, his fingers hot and insistent as he tore away the last of her petticoats.

One callused palm curved about her calf, stroking her rigid muscles, pausing to skim over the fragile skin behind her knee before he charted a torturous path along the tight tendons of her inner thigh.

Beau jumped at the sensation of his hand there, his long fingers stroking, fueling the raging inferno building in her secret places while he suckled, worshiping her breasts in the most delicate of torture. "Beau . . ." He breathed her name. "God, you feel so good, so warm . . . so cursed sweet . . ."

He was swearing at her even as he loved her, and Beau adored it, adored him, wanting to drive him to the same peak of insanity to which he was hurtling her.

She groped for the fastenings of his breeches, hungry for the feel of him naked against her, desperate to touch the unyielding lines of the body pressed so intimately against hers. After a moment the fastenings slid free, releasing him into her hand. Hard. Hot. His maleness jutted against her palm just as his finger trailed through the dewy curls at the apex of her thighs.

A shudder worked through him, and she was humbled, awed, that she held the power to bring this man such pleasure. Gently, so gently, he slipped one finger inside her, readying her for the mating to come. He toyed with her, teased her, until her whole body felt as if it were tearing asunder with the madness he was inspiring.

"Griffin . . ." She whimpered his name, arching against the exquisite mastery of his hand. She opened her thighs wider still, begging to possess him, all of him. The rocking of the coach mingled with the whirling in her head as he staked his hands on either side of her shoulders, settling his lean hips between her quivering legs.

"Isabeau . . ." he groaned. "I don't . . . don't want to hurt you . . ."

"I'm no cursed fragile flower, Stone." The words were as fierce as the passion within her. "Take me. Now."

A guttural cry wrenched from him as he thrust, burying the pulsing heat of him deep within her. Pain bit, sharp, but she gloried in it, gloried in the feel of him as he plunged again and again into her welcoming depths.

Then the stinging ebbed, flowing into a whirlpool of blue-gray eyes desperate for love, a mouth that couldn't get enough of the taste of her, a hard, masculine body drawing upon every skill it possessed to drive her insane.

It built, grew, that mad stirring in her womb, tormenting her until she clawed at the hard plane of his back, the taut curve of his buttocks, trying desperately to draw him deeper, deeper still.

Her head thrashed against the coach seat, Griffin's thrown back, jaw clenched, eyes crushed shut as the rhythm consumed them.

Then in an instant the maelstrom broke free, an animal groan tearing from Griffin in answer to her own cry of release as spasm after spasm racked her body.

He collapsed against her as they both struggled to breathe, to gather the shattered remnants of their separate souls into one.

Beau clutched him to her, their sweating, trembling bodies yet seeming as one as she stroked that fall of dark, thick hair.

"Isabeau." He breathed her name, his knuckles smoothing her cheek. "What trickery did you use to bewitch me? Did you make a pact with the dark one? Or are you some fallen angel sent here to save me?"

"I must be an angel . . . for this is surely heaven." A sound that was half laugh, half sob ripped from her, and she buried her face in the spicy warmth of his throat. "I never expected to breach heaven's gates, Griffin Stone, but if I'd . . . if I'd known it was such a wondrous place, I vow I'd have spent a lifetime at my prayers."

"And what would you have prayed for?"

"This. Only this. Always this."

Storm-blue eyes pierced deep into her soul. "I love you, Isabeau. You knew it from the first."

She nodded but could not keep tears from welling at her lashes.

"You make me burn, woman, make me ache. You make me whole in a way I've never known before." A smile broke across those strong lips, and it wrenched Isabeau's heart. "I tried to warn you. Tried to keep you safe from me. I told you that I possess a thousand flaws."

"A hideous temper and an over-soft heart."

"I'll rage at you, order you about."

"And I'll defy you at every turn."

"But I love you, Isabeau DeBurgh. More than life itself. And if you will stoop to have me, I vow I'll never make you sorry that you became my wife."

"Your . . . wife!" Beau flung herself into his arms, kissing him, laughing as she felt joy well all shimmery silver within her.

But whatever words she had been about to say were lost as she felt the coach lurch, the vehicle beginning to slow its speed.

"Blood and thunder!" she sputtered, peeking out the curtain to see the Stone townhouse looming against the night sky. Griffin cursed, the pair of them struggling madly to draw on their clothes in the confines of the coach while shaking with laughter. Desperately Griff fumbled with the lacings of her gown, the lacings he had torn in his haste to love her. It was hopeless.

His shirt was billowing in total disarray beneath his crumpled coat, his breeches scarce yanked above his hips as Griffin dug Beau's cloak from where it had fallen upon the coach's floor and swirled it around her, doing the same with his own mantle just as the coach door flew open.

If the dour-faced footman suspected anything, his expression never betrayed it, but Beau dared not glance at Griffin, for she could feel the suppressed merriment in him, the threat that either one of them might dissolve into fits of mirth at any moment.

"I trust you had an agreeable outing, my lord," the servant said with a solemnity that made Beau catch the inside of her lip hard with her teeth in an effort to keep from giggling.

"Quite." Griff's strangled reply made Beau choke.

"It is a nasty cough you're beset with, Mistress DeBurgh," the footman observed, offering his hand to help her down from the coach. "I do hope you did not take a chill."

"No. It was—it was quite warm in the coach," she managed to say, slanting Griffin a glance that made him compress his lips in a white line of desperation. His face darkened with the effort to remain sober.

Isabeau touched the footman's outstretched hand, the rest of her clothing clutched beneath the flowing blue velvet of her cloak as she attempted to descend with the regal bearing befitting the woman who was to be Lord Griffin Stone's bride. But the moment they entered the townhouse and reached the stairs they dashed up them pell-mell, stumbling against each other, tripping over their trailing garments until they spilled into Griffin's bedchamber, their stomachs aching as they fell into paroxysms of laughter.

Beau sagged against him, loving the feel of the mirth rumbling in his chest, loving the way his eyes sparkled, twinkled, bearing no more hint of pain.

"I hope you had an agreeable outing, my lord." Beau mimicked the footman's tones to perfection through breathless giggles.

"It was the most agreeable outing I've ever experienced, milady. When we are wed I fully intend to make all our journeys in coaches. I shall order a new one built with wider seats and more room. And when we plot our directions we shall always take the longest routes."

"Then you had best order locks put into the inside of the thing's doors, or else the next time your footman's eyes might pop clear out of his head. If we'd not been . . . er . . . finished . . ." Beau clutched at Griffin's shirtfront, laughing until tears ran down her cheeks. "Oh, Griff . . . just imagine . . ."

His arms crushed her to him, then he spanned her ribs with his hands, swooping her high above him. She peered down into that face, that handsome face that suddenly seemed so youthful, so brimming with happiness.

"I love you, Milady Flame. I love you, love you, love you!" He whirled her around until she was breathless, then slowly lowered her to cradle her in his arms.

"Did you mean what you said in the coach?" she said, nestling against the hard plane of his chest. "That you wish to wed me?"

"It was a temporary insanity. But I vow I never want to be sane again."

"Bah! As if you were so *before* I met you!" Beau kissed him, then pulled back. Suddenly her brow puckered with unaccustomed thoughtfulness. "Griffin?"

"What, angel." He waited for some sweet confession, some vow of the love shining in her eyes.

But her gaze glinted with mischief. "Does this mean I get my breeches back?"

"Count yourself fortunate if I allow you any clothing at all. I may keep you here forever, naked and needing." His fingers loosened the cloak's fastenings, letting it fall to pool upon the floor at her feet. "Ah, Isabeau, Isabeau," he breathed, his voice suddenly husky, his eyes firing again with hunger, hot and dark. "I want you so damned much."

His lips crashed down upon hers, their laughter fading as they delved into a joy sweeter still upon the downy-soft bed.

Chapter Eighteen

Candles blazed in a dozen sconces, holding the night shadows at bay within the Blue Drawing Room. The rattle of dice being cast on the mahogany table to the accompaniment of curses that would have made a seafarer pause seemed an absolute blasphemy set against the chamber's staid majesty.

But Griffin delighted in the colorful phrases, and in the woman who sat opposite him, her slender body gowned in an open robe of pink silk damask, a stomacher of pink ribbon and silver lace accenting the creamy smoothness of her breasts.

Griffin lounged back in his chair watching the candlelight play across Isabeau's face as she shook the bits of ivory. Her lips compressed with concentration, her eyes snapped as she cast the dice onto the table.

She cursed. The soft, drowsy kitten of a woman who had lain curled beside him before dawn had vanished, leaving in her place an emerald-eyed hoyden who positively hated to lose.

And she was losing. Badly.

"I believe you have just sacrificed your horse, Mistress

DeBurgh," he observed mildly, adoring the militant set of her jaw, the high flush upon her flawless cheeks.

"You've weighted these blasted things, Stone," she blustered, banging one fist upon the table. "Stake me if you haven't! And if you don't break them open, I shall—"

"Cleave out my gizzard? Blast me into eternity?"

"No." She seemed to be struggling to discover some threat dire enough to punish so heinous a crime. "If you don't, I—I shall never kiss you again."

Griff gave an eloquent shudder. "I surrender!" He rolled his eyes heavenward as though in supplication. "Of course, I've been attempting to do so for nearly an hour now. Believe me, nothing I could win from you is worth this much agony."

Her soft rose lips compressed into something very like a pout. "Don't be labeling *me* a spoilt babe, Stone, when you are the one who is cheating. You promised your infernal friend would be here over an hour ago to break up this game. Did you send out a bevy of brigands to delay him when you began to fleece me?"

Griff felt a twinge of conscience. His concerns about Charles and the purpose of Tom's visit should have held his attention. Instead, he'd been lost in the pleasure of Beau's company. But he suppressed the whisperings of unease, leaning over to capture her lips in a hard kiss.

"Never fear, love. I shall allow you to ride MacBeth whenever the spirit moves you. And as for Tom, I assure you he is quite safe traveling London's streets. He may appear bookish and quiet, but beneath it all"—Griff chuckled, recalling past episodes with his friend—"Southwood is the very devil of a fighter."

"He blasted well better be! I fully intend to call him out for my losses! I've not even met the man, and already I loathe—"

A discreet knock upon the door made Griff straighten. He gave permission to enter while Beau flung herself back against the cushions of her chair as though he had plotted the interruption of her tirade on purpose.

The door swung open, the butler entering. Though the old servant's eyes scanned the table, replete with its evidence of gaming, he did not so much as lift a brow, the redoubtable retainer merely clearing his throat. "My lord, the Honorable Mr. Thomas Southwood."

Griff leapt to his feet, his dice box clattering to the table as he rushed toward his friend. The man was swathed neck to knees in a flowing gray cape, his boots scuffed, his hat askew.

Ten years had done little to alter the fall of thick blond curls that tumbled over Tom's broad forehead, his studious face unmarred by lines except about the dreamy gray eyes that bore a shade of a squint, no doubt from spending too many late nights poring over thick tomes.

"Tom! God's feet," Griff cried, hastening across the room to capture his friend in a bluff embrace. "It is good to see you, man! It has been so bloody long—so much has happened!"

"Yes. Too much." There was a touch of strain in Southwood's voice. The arms that hugged Griffin seemed to tighten involuntarily.

Griff pulled away, peering into his friend's beloved, familiar face. "Tom . . ."

"So," a voice broke in. Beau confronted Southwood with a twinkling of mischievous accusation in her eyes. "You are the blackguard who has cost me my horse."

"Your—your . . . My most sincere apologies."

Griff's fingers clenched unconsciously. Tom, the ever easily ruffled Tom, had scarce blinked.

"We have been playing at dice, Isabeau and I." Griff attempted to jar his old friend into a smile. "Because you were late, she has gambled away her horse. Luckily for her, we are to be married, so she will be able to wheedle a ride astride him upon occasion."

Tom simply stared.

Griff forced a smile. "Tom, did you hear me? I am fair chafing to be leg-shackled as soon as the banns are cried."

Griff expected a reaction—disbelief, astonishment, laughter—anything except the quiet acceptance, the distracted restlessness that shadowed Southwood's face.

"Tom," he said, "I am presenting my betrothed to you. Mistress Isabeau DeBurgh. Isabeau, my best friend in the world, the Honorable Thomas Southwood."

"Oh . . . your betrothed. My heartiest felicitations." Southwood stammered. "I am most happy for you."

"You might dredge up a bit of enthusiasm," Beau teased. "I've seen cheerier countenances at bloody funerals."

Griffin forced a laugh, but the sound was suddenly, strangely hollow. He had seen Tom Southwood misted with daydreams, had seen him solemn, seen him smile, and had even been one of the few to see the quiet man whirl into one of his rare furies. But there was something, some emotion within Southwood's face now that Griff had never witnessed before. Something that made him want to glance over his shoulder into the consuming darkness beyond the glistening windowpanes.

"Isabeau," Griff said softly, "I think Tom and I need to talk."

"Grand," Beau said, sashaying up to Tom, taking his arm with that newfound ease that seemed to surround her, garbed as she was in woman's fripperies. "I would adore hearing tales of what a reprobate Griffin was before he was hustled off to the colonies. And you, my honorable Mr. Southwood, seem just the man to enlighten me."

"Tom and I have more important things to discuss than skinned knees and raucous nights," Griff interrupted. Unease made his voice harsh. "I need to speak with him alone."

"Oh, I beg your pardon," she said in a sugary voice, pressing her hand to her breast with dramatic flair. "I should not want to distract you with idle woman's chatter when you obviously have *important* matters to discuss—matters far beyond my meager powers of comprehension. I would not dream of encumbering you with my presence a moment longer."

Beau swept up to Southwood, smiling into the man's eyes. "Before I go, I think it only fair to warn you that you will not escape me so easily again, Mr. Southwood. I shall expect a full accounting of my lord's darkest secrets when next we meet."

As if suddenly startled from a bad dream, Tom seemed to shake himself, favoring her with an earnest smile. "You must forgive me for being a dullard, Mistress DeBurgh. I promise I will be more attentive another time. I am most—most happy for you and Griffin. He will need someone . . . after . . ."

Feeling an odd kinship with the studious young man, Beau stretched up on her tiptoes, brushing his cheek with a kiss. "I shall take good care of him for you," she said softly. "I promise."

Griffin watched her as she swept from the room, graceful as a wood sprite. Suddenly he wished she could weave some magic to dispel the sense of foreboding snarling around him.

"She is beautiful, Griffin. Charming. But I thank you for sending her away." Southwood's sigh of relief brought Griffin's attention back to his friend. "I fear she would have been most disconcerted when she saw . . ." His words trailed off, but the fingers of his left hand slipped the fastening of his cloak, letting that rich garment fall from his shoulders to reveal coat and waistcoat, as ever somewhat mussed, and a cravat, carelessly tied. But it was the lace that spilled about Tom's wrist that snagged Griffin's gaze, held it—for it was stained bright crimson with blood.

"What the deuce?" Griff ripped the fine fabric aside to peer at the nasty cut that bisected Tom's surprisingly muscular forearm. "How the devil did this happen?"

"I fear I ran afoul of two most unsavory rogues upon my journey here."

"This is abominable," Griff said, digging a clean handkerchief from one pocket and binding it about the wound. "The very streets of London have become a menace. Anyone can be set upon by footpads at any hour."

"These men were not stalking just anyone." Tom's voice was gentle, fraught with that quiet urgency that had given Griff pause moments before. "Whoever the rogues were who fell upon me, wherever they came from, I fear they had been searching most especially for me."

"Come, Tom. Who the devil would want to harm you? The irate proprietor of some lending library, afire for your blood because you forgot to bring back your books?" Griff cast out the uneasy jest, hoping to wring from Tom even a hint of a smile—anything . . .

But Tom only raised the fingers of his good hand, kneading the flesh at his temple. "I wish it were that simple. Unfortunately, I believe that someone was eager to stop me from coming here. From seeing you."

"I don't understand."

"Neither do I—not the whole of it, at least. Brace yourself, old fellow," Southwood said. "The news I bear—I fear it is terrible."

Griff's mind flashed back to the cryptic note he had received at Darkling Moor and his nephew's reaction to it. "Is it Charles? If that boy has been stirring up mischief, I vow I'll—"

"No, it is nothing to do with the boy, though with the company he's been keeping it is a miracle he's not neck-deep in some calamity. I fear . . . fear it is about William."

All thought, all breath seemed driven from Griffin's body. "What the devil?"

Southwood's hand came up to curve in a strong grasp about Griff's shoulder as if to steady him while delivering some hideous blow. "Griff, William . . . William's death . . . I fear it was no accident."

"No accident? He fell off his horse."

"Yes, but it was not that that killed him."

"Tom, for God's sake, what are you saying?"

"William was murdered."

It was as if flaming pitch drowned Griffin, searing him with the most agonizing pain he had ever known. "Murdered? I don't believe it. Someone would have told me. By God's blood, a duke's murder would have been splashed across every pamphleteer's ware in England. Even in the colonies I would have heard something."

"No one knows save me and the man who tended him before the burial. And I threatened to cut out his tongue if he should betray the truth. Charles, if you'll pardon me for saying so, has not the sense of a three-year-old. I feared that he would race off and do something foolish, and that you would return to find two new additions to the Stone crypt instead of only one.

"And you, loving William the way you did"—Tom fidgeted with his neckcloth—"dash it all, Griff, I didn't want you finding out such gruesome tidings from some ghoulish letter or an accounting some scandalmonger here in England had sent you. I was certain you would be returning to England to deal with William's affairs. I knew I could speak with you then."

"But why the blazes didn't you tell me the instant I was in England? Christ, I would have been clawing through every hellhole on this island to track the cursed murderer to his lair."

"I was in France with Mary Beth. I returned as soon as I knew you were in London. Yet as for that other difficulty . . . I believe I have taken care of that for you."

"The other? What?"

"Discovering who murdered your brother."

Tom's face was pale, his eyes reflecting a horror long past, yet still haunting enough to turn his stomach. "There was . . . an initial slashed into William's chest. A mark carved there with a knife or sword."

"A mark." Griff's stomach pitched, sweat beading his brow. "Cut into . . . oh, my God."

Tom turned away, his face tinged with the same sickness. "I made some inquiries, did some searching on my own," he continued. "And what I discovered was that a slash like the one upon William is a signature of sorts."

"A *signature?* Who? By God's blood, what twisted whoreson would do such a hideous thing?"

Tom reached into his coat pocket, withdrawing a pamphlet. The printing was so fresh the ink was smeared. Griff could scarcely force his numb fingers to close about it, his gaze fixing on the image inked upon the page.

"It is a famed brigand that raids hereabouts," Tom said quietly. "A highwayman by the name of Gentleman Jack."

* * *

Beau sat on an embroidered stool, sticking out her tongue at her reflection in the mirror. "I look like I'm wearing sausages on my head!" she complained to Molly, who was attempting to tame her wild curls into the latest fashion. "My hair is so stuffed up with pincushions and pillows, my neck aches!"

"This style is the height of elegance, I assure you," Molly said as she attempted to fix a particulary troublesome curl in place. "My lord Stone will love it."

"Then let him bloody well wear it himself," Beau groused. "My lord and I have already come to an understanding regarding coiffures, Mistress Maguire. And just because you are my dearest friend in the whole world, that doesn't mean you will be able to cajole me into looking like a jackanapes on the streets of London."

Beau screwed up her face with such effect that Molly dissolved into fits of giggles. "You had best not let your betrothed see you looking that way, or he might cry off the engagement."

"He could bloody well try," Beau said with great relish. "If he dared attempt it, it would be pistols at dawn for him, m'girl. And I am a *much* better shot than he is."

Molly tugged at a curl, and Beau yelped. But she had no time to think of an appropriate epithet before she heard the sound of footsteps in the hall. Hoping it was Griffin, she leapt up from the seat to the sound of Molly's exasperated cry.

"Now look what you have done!" the girl wailed as the thick mass of Beau's hair tumbled down, the pads Molly had so tediously worked into her coiffure bouncing on the floor. "You've ruined it, you ungrateful—"

But Molly's accusations were shattered into silence. The chamber door crashed open, revealing within its wooden frame a man so changed from the rogue who had bested Beau at dicing he seemed a total stranger.

His skin was deathly gray, every muscle in his throat standing out like knotted cords, every plane of his face raked with a harshness that made Beau's breath snag in her chest. He was shaking. Shaking. His eyes were like blue flame, burning, yet filled with such agony, such torment, Beau hastened toward him.

"Griff? Love, what—"

"Where is he?" His words were so cold, they seemed to freeze Beau's very soul.

"He? Who? Southwood? I've not seen—"

"Southwood is belowstairs, ordering up my horses, dispatching a footman to Bow Street with a message from me. No, it is *this*"—he waved a sheet of parchment at her—"*this* blood-hungry bastard I want—need—so I can slit his accursed throat."

Beau took a step back, stunned by the savagery in Griff's voice as he thrust the pamphlet toward her. She whipped her hands behind her back, suddenly frightened, more frightened than she had ever been in her life.

"Griffin, what in God's name is amiss?"

"He murdered my brother! Murdered him, damn it. And carved his initial in Will's chest."

Beau stared into his pain-racked features, wishing she could do something, anything to ease his anguish. "Sit, love," she said, attempting to soothe him. "Molly, bring some brandy."

"I don't want any accursed brandy. I want to know where the devil this monster dwells. This sick, twisted animal you call your friend."

Beau reeled as if he had slapped her, panic rising in her veins. "Blast it, Griff, you're making no sense. How would I know—"

"Where Gentleman Jack Ramsey makes his home?" The words were a brutal sneer, laced with such loathing, such rage, Beau's hands began to tremble.

"J-Jack . . ." Beau stammered, Molly's cry of denial seeming to whirl at her through some nightmarish mist. "Don't be absurd! Even if your brother *was* murdered, Jack would never—"

"Never have cut someone down upon the highroads? Never have slashed them, left scars on their faces to feed his cursed arrogance?"

"The *ton* bucks—they *beg* him to do it!" Beau cried. "It is some—some sort of game with them to prove their courage to the aristocratic witches they court. Jack—he would never kill—never be so mad as to carve anything upon a corpse! For the love of God, Griff, he was my protector from the time I was a child. I know him as well as I know my own soul. And I vow to you on our love, upon my very life, that Jack Ramsey did not kill your brother!"

"And the others? I suppose he had nothing to do with their deaths either."

"Wh-what others?" Molly's voice was sick, quavering. "Oh, my lord Stone, please . . ."

"The women—young girls butchered by his hand. Look you here. This friend—this *man* whom you know as well as your own soul—look at the atrocities he stands accused of."

Rage, anguish, confusion warred within Beau as Griffin's fist closed in the fall of her hair. He jabbed the piece of parchment toward her yet again, his knotted fingers making certain that she could not wrench away but would have to look upon the sheet in his grasp.

Her horrified gaze fixed upon the smeared image, a crude mockery of the merry Jack Ramsey who had taught her to ride the highroads, the Jack who had taken her to country fairs, who had taught her to ride, to shoot. An evil satyr stared out lasciviously from the page, his hooded eyes dark with evil, his smile a cruel leer. There was so much raw physical similarity that Beau did not even have to lower her gaze to read the inscription below it. Yet with a near-crazed fascination she scanned downward, claws tearing within her stomach as she read the accusations levied against her mentor.

There were accounts of the murdered women from Blowsy Nell's. Each was listed in gut-wrenching detail. Countless other atrocities were laid at Jack's feet. Betrayer, the pampleteer had labeled him—an animal whom the common folk had adored as a hero, and who had suddenly turned mad, crazed, so brutal that a traitor's death would be too easy a passing for him into the gates of hell.

Beau felt the blood drain from her face, the room suddenly seeming to wheel off its axis as she pressed one hand to her stomach, afraid she would be sick.

"No," she whispered as she read the pampleteer's exhortation that the murdering dog be run down like an animal. "Jack . . . Jack would never . . ."

"Beau." Molly's sob tore at her, and she glanced down into the girl's stricken face. "My God, they . . . they'll rend him to pieces if they find him."

"They won't have the chance," Griffin cut in, his voice rapier sharp. "It is my sword—my hand that will send that murdering bastard to the devil that spawned him. And you, Isabeau—you will take me to find him."

"No." Beau raised her eyes to Griffin's, feeling as though her heart were being cut from her breast. "Griffin, I cannot."

"Tell me, girl, where is he? In that thieves' lair you used to call home? Or some other corner of hell?"

Panic rose in her throat as she saw murder glinting in those eyes that had once shone with love. Desperate, she faced him, a lie borne of sick terror forming on her lips. "Nell's is far too vulgar a place for a man the like of Ramsey. He—he has a dozen lairs where you will never find him."

"But you must know where the murdering bastard is," Griffin snarled. "Damn it, Beau, have you heard anything I've said? Have you heard what this beast has done? To my brother—*my brother*—the only goddamned person in my life who ever loved . . . loved me until you. Or do you love me, Isabeau? Do you love me at all?"

"Of course I do! Blast it, I'd give my life this instant if it would spare you this! But not Jack's life, Griffin. No matter how much I love you, I cannot cast the life of a friend—a beloved friend who trusts me—upon your sword."

A raw animal-like sound tore from Griffin's throat as his hands clamped about her arms with desperation. "Beau. For the love of God, Beau, help me."

Tears welled in his tortured blue eyes, dampening the sharp-carved cheekbones. The mouth that had brought her such pleasure twisted with the deepest agony Beau had ever seen. And it was as if her own soul drank in that searing pain, multiplying it a thousand times over.

"Griff . . . I *cannot do it.* Please . . . please trust me . . . believe . . ."

A savage curse tore from Griffin's lips as he hurled her away from him, grinding the heel of his hand against his eyes. "Believe . . . believe in what? Love? Loyalty? Christ, I should have known that you would shield him. But it will make no odds, Isabeau. I'll drag the murdering bastard out. And I vow to you I'll kill him."

He wheeled, stalking from the room, and the chamber was suddenly engulfed in echoing, terrifying silence. Beau stared at the pamphlet she had dropped when Griff had grabbed her, her pulse leaping with alarm.

"B-Beau . . . what . . . what are we going to do?" Molly sobbed.

"Warn Jack," Beau whispered.

Warn Jack, she thought, and lose Griffin for all time.

Chapter Nineteen

Beau drove her heels into MacBeth's sweat-sheened barrel, urging the stallion toward the distant silhouette of the inn. Their breakneck pace had nearly hurled Molly from behind Beau a dozen times during their crazed flight, but she'd hung on with amazing tenacity, a remarkable aura of strength and resolve emanating from her in the hours since they had raced away from the congested streets of London and off into the countryside beyond.

Beau had pilfered a pair of breeches from Griffin's deserted bedchamber, and the fabric bagged around her waist, dampened with sweat and with the moisture that hung heavy in the night air. The comforting weight of a brace of loaded pistols pressed against her thighs. Griffin's full white shirt tortured her with the scent of him, the size of him, as if, wrapped in that flowing garment, she were lost in his very soul. Griff's face, so beloved, so betrayed, seemed to torment her from the night sky. His pain and his pleading lashed her with guilt and regret and the most soul-numbing sorrow she had ever known.

She crushed down the clawing grief welling inside her, crushed the hopelessness as she reined the laboring stallion down into the hollow that cupped about Nell's like a giant's hand.

Before she could bolt from the horse's back Molly was sliding off from behind her, tumbling to the ground a mere whisper from MacBeth's huge, slashing hooves. Beau scrambled down even as her friend was staggering back to her feet, a scrawny hostler rushing forth to take the stallion's reins.

"Moll! Beau!" the youth cried, "such a stirring! Did you hear? Hear about Jack?"

"Please, God, he has not been taken," Molly cried, her face ashen.

"Nay. But never fear. The murderin' bastard'll be found! And when he is, that handsome face he be so proud of'll be savaged so bad even the whores will run from him in terror."

"You witling wretch!" Beau grabbed the hostler by the shirt, knocking him off his feet. "You know bloody well Jack would never—could never have done the things that blasted pamphlet claims! It was Jack who found you on the road, Aaron MacGregor, Jack who cozened Nell into giving you this situation! Damn it, he should have left you to starve!"

"Maybe so, but we all know why he didna let you starve, don't we, Isabeau?" MacGregor stumbled to his feet, sputtering curses. "The twain o' you be so infernal thick, maybe ye share his twisted passions."

Beau balled up her fist and slammed into the boy's chest. With a thud he careened into the side of an abandoned keg. "Next time . . . next time I won't dirty my hands on you," she grated. "A pistol ball will do the work for me."

She wheeled, running toward the doorway, the breathless Molly at her side. "Beau," Molly said in a desperate whisper. "Oh, God, Beau, if even the people here at Nell's have turned against Jack, it is worse . . . so much worse than we suspected. I was certain he'd be here, be safe. But now—where . . . where could he be hiding?"

Beau ground her teeth in an effort to keep from screaming, Molly's fears firing the panic surging through her. "Of course he's here," she hissed as she reached for the door latch. "Nell, witch that she is, loves Jack as much as we do. She would never hurl him to the wolves."

Beau saw a flicker of hope lighten Molly's troubled gaze, saw her draw a steadying breath. Then Beau flung the door open, stalking into the dimly lit room as though she had never left it.

But inside the dirt, the danger, the suffering was clearer than ever before.

The clusters of wenching, drinking revelers she had tipped her glass with had vanished, leaving in their place huddled groups talking angrily over their tankards of ale. The laughter, the bawdy teasing had fled as well, tension seeming to coil about the room like a serpent, wrenching tighter, tighter, until it seemed to close off Isabeau's throat.

Molly gave a tiny whimper of what might be fright, but Beau gouged her with an elbow in warning, forcing herself to saunter into the chamber as if she had just ridden in from a successful night's raiding.

But as the forbidding gazes of everyone in the room turned toward her her breath caught, and she had to stop herself from clutching at the engraved butt of Griffin's pistol.

Instead she thrust her chin upward with a jocular belligerence that scorned all those who were regarding her with a mixture of trepidation and surliness. She paced toward the fire, extending her fingers as if to warm her hands.

"There she be! Jack's sniveling brat," an unwashed oaf by the name of Silas bellowed above the sudden harsh whispers. "She'll know where to find the murderin'—"

The sound of a pistol hammer being leveled back cracked through the room like cannon fire as Isabeau turned, weapon in hand. But her voice was even. "Silas, Silas," she chided. "Didn't the bitch that bore you ever warn you about casting aspersions on other people's characters? It is a most disconcerting trait."

She examined the long barrel, brow puckered in bemusement. "And you—*all* of you"—she encompassed the whole room in her subtle threat—"know quite well that I am, shall we say, somewhat lacking in patience. Now, if you wish to irritate me further with this idiocy, it is fine. They are your skins, after all, and it makes no odds to me whether or not I put a few holes in 'em."

She forced her lips into a feral grin, the grin that belonged not to Isabeau DeBurgh, but to the ruthless, daunting Devil's Flame. Her eyes were hard as she shrugged. "You will forgive me for interrupting your separate tirades, but as we are all *friends* here at Nell's, I thought it was only fair to warn you of my current temper."

Despite her casual stance and lazy gaze Beau was tense, ready, searching for anyone among the assemblage who dared to ignore her warning. But even the burly Silas had lapsed into a watchful silence, and Beau gently lowered the hammer of the pistol into place.

"Now," she said as if nothing had happened, "I'm famished. Where the blazes is . . . Nell!" She forced enthusiasm into her tones as the stocky woman waddled into the room carrying a tray laden with the choicest bits of food the establishment had to offer. "Faith, it is as if you read my very mind!" Beau said, sweeping over to take the tray. "Maybe I've underestimated your powers of sight all this time." She snatched up a crusty loaf of bread warm from the oven.

"It is not for . . ." Anger flared in the old woman's eyes, but Nell's lips clamped shut as though she feared she might betray something. Beau knew in that instant that her suspicions regarding Jack's whereabouts were correct.

"I've had a most rewarding run upon the highroads," Beau said, ignoring Nell's indignation, "and if I remember correctly, I owe you an accounting for next month's rent. If you would just come to my room . . ."

"You thieving hussy, I'll not—now give me back that tray."

Ignoring Nell's hiss of fury, Beau strode up the stairs. A wide-eyed Molly and a blustering Nell followed in her wake. When Beau reached her own small chamber she dumped the tray upon the scarred table, then slammed the door behind the other two women, all pretense of lazy arrogance and unaffected calm disappearing.

"Nell, where is he?" Beau demanded.

"He? I'd not be knowin' who you're blatherin' about," Nell said with a loftiness that incensed Beau.

"You know damn well it is Jack. Blast it, I have to help him. Talk to him. Somebody does! Christ, the lot of them below would like nothing more than to deal him a traitor's death themselves, scurvy bastards! And he cannot hide beneath your bedcurtains forever."

Nell's thin lips disappeared, loathing brimming in her eyes. "As if I'd betray my lad to you! If he hadn't been a-chasin' after to save your hide, he'd have been able to stop this madness afore it got afoot. He'd nearly mastered it, discovered . . . but then you had to blunder off, even though I warned you. And Jack—you drove him fair out o' his mind by first disappearin' and then cuttin' out his heart!"

"I love Jack! As a friend, Nell! A friend! As for giving him my heart—it is impossible, and I cannot help it. But I *can* aid him here—now. I can help him escape in a way you never could."

"The devil you say! You are nothing but another of his women, clinging to his breeches, though you've not even the decency to let 'im in yours! Go to the devil, Isabeau DeBurgh! I'll not—"

"It is Jack who will go to the devil if you don't take me to him. Is that what you want? Do you want him to be ripped to shreds by a blood-hungry mob? Do you want him to be dragged through the streets? Hurled into Newgate? Do you want his corpse to dangle, dipped in tar, above a bloody crossroads? The crowds who came to cheer my father, who loved him even at his death—they'll not be lauding Gentleman Jack Ramsey as he is taken to the gallows. They'll despise him, hate him, hurl at him their scorn and their fury. That is, if they don't savage him beyond recognition even *before* he reaches the executioner."

"Witch! You evil witch! It is because of you—"

"Fine! Shower me with blame, curse me to the devil if you wish! I care not. But damn it, Nell, take me to Jack, let me help him! It is not just the people who are thirsting for his blood, not just Bow Street. A powerful nobleman is even now mounting a search. He believes that Jack murdered his brother. Nell, he's half crazed with grief and rage, and—"

"It is he. The man you betrayed my Jack for—"

"Thunderation, I could have had Jack halfway to the coast by now!" Beau cried, grabbing Nell's fleshy arms, shaking her. "Do you want him to die? Do you?"

The old woman's eyes clashed with Beau's, and within Nell's face she saw indecision and a very real fear. The room crackled with tension, then suddenly Nell sagged, defeat clouding her features.

"All right, all right, may you rot in hell. He—he's secreted away in the smugglers' den."

"Of course!" Beau kicked herself inwardly as she remembered the small secret chamber she and Molly had played hide-and-seek in years before. "It is a perfect place to hold him until we can arrange for his escape. Moll, you run below and keep watch over the witlings at the tables while I go and make arrangements with Jack. I'll be down as soon as possible."

Molly nodded, fleeing down the stairs as Beau started to bolt toward the hidden room.

"Wait." Nell stopped her. "He'll blast you into eternity if you don't signal 'im thus. Three knocks upon the panel. Then he'll slide it free."

"Right," Beau acknowledged.

"Wait."

Beau stopped again at the old woman's bidding, turning to fling her an impatient glare. "I loathe an' despise you, Isabeau DeBurgh," Nell said softly, "but if you can spare the lad for me, I'll thank you till the day I die."

"No one's going to die," Beau said, and she slipped out into the hallway, moving stealthily through the shadows toward Nell's own opulent rooms.

Once inside she rapped out the signal and waited for the panel to slide free. It seemed an eternity before she heard the sound of warped wood protesting as it was slid back.

Light from a single candle illuminated a face so haggard, so filled with hopelessness she could scarcely believe it was that of Jack Ramsey. The dark eyes that had made countless feminine hearts flutter looked like bruised circles. His cheeks were hollow, his skin the color of tallow. Even the impeccable linens that were his passion now lay against a smudged coat, the frills as limp and lifeless as his smile.

"Beau." There was no surprise in his voice, only a pervasive sadness that cut her to the quick. It was as if he had known that despite their quarrel she would help him.

Beau's eyes burned as she reached up one hand, smoothing a lock of dull, dark hair from Ramsey's brow. "Well, what have you to say for yourself, you bumbling idiot?" she said, the gruffness of her words softened by her own tremulous smile. "I'm gone but a month, and look what an accursed mess you've made."

Jack attempted to force a smile. He reached out to her, catching her in his arms as though he were drowning and she was his only hope of salvation. "Isabeau . . . sweet God, it is over . . . over. And there is nothing that I can do to right it."

"Bah! I've yet to see the muddle we could not solve between us. Even if we can't make things right for you here in England, we've only to get you to the coast and set you on a ship bound for France or the colonies. It is about time you gave up riding the High Toby anyway, aged and decrepit as you've become."

"I wish I'd retired my blasted sword a year ago," Jack said ruefully, "before . . . Beau, I had nothing to do with those murders—Christ, those women. I would never have—"

"You don't have to claim innocence with me. If I found you bending over their bodies, your sword dripping blood, I would not believe you capable of such a horror."

"For that I thank you." He pulled away from her, turning to rake agitated fingers through his hair. "But someone has gone to a great deal of trouble to make the rest of the world believe that it is so. Someone with enough power, enough wealth, and enough cunning to weave a web around me so stealthily that I didn't even realize I was snared inside it until I was so bound up I couldn't breathe."

"Who? Who could hate you enough to concoct such a diabolic scheme?"

"I don't believe he hates me. He doesn't even know me, aside from the stories he has heard at his club or amongst the fetes of the *ton.* I was a convenient scapegoat to pin his evil upon, and it was easy—so infernally easy. If I'd only taken things more seriously in the beginning, I could have averted much of this. But I was so all-fired confident, so complacent in the common folk's regard for me, I thought that nothing could breach their faith."

"You think some aristocrat has stirred up this tempest? On purpose? I don't understand."

"It is beyond understanding, the magnitude of his perversion, his sickness. I had been attempting to uncover his plottings for weeks, since the moment I knew it was no game. And I've found all the evidence I needed to expose him, except that now"—he laughed bitterly— "now who would believe me, Isabeau? Take my word against that of a blasted marquess when I stand accused of his crimes?"

"We must find a way—find a way to make them listen."

"No, it is too late. But since my life is already forfeit, I shall have one last revenge. There is to be a ritual tonight . . . an initiation ritual where another innocent girl is to die. But I fully intend to make certain it is *his* blood that drains on the stones this night, *his* soul that is cast into hell."

"Whatever this is about I'll aid you, Jack. We'll ride—"

Beau suddenly stiffened, aware of a commotion in the corridor. Her heart leapt into her throat as she tried to close off the secret room, but the heavy panel squeaked its disapproval, the aged wood seeming to infuse steely tentacles into the guide board along which it ran.

"Damn it, Beau, push!" Jack commanded, their desperation only making the sheet of wood jam more tightly still. With one mighty shove it finally gave way, slamming into place, but not before Beau had glimpsed the doorway to Nell's chamber being filled with at least a score of burly figures that were even now spilling into the room.

Swords had gleamed, pistol barrels waved in countless hands, and Beau turned to Jack, yanking her own weapons free. "It seems we're going to be leaving Nell's sooner than we'd intended," she said, trying to flash him a bracing smile. Ramsey's sword whisked free of its scabbard, his eyes glittering, dangerous.

"Beau, I'll not let you hurl your life away for me. Surrender."

"Bloody hell! And let you claim all the glory?" The jest was filled with desperate bravado, her words drowned out as something crashed into the portal of the hidden room. The aged wood creaked, buckled, splintering in a score of pieces as the tiny room filled with men—not the surly mob from the tables below, not the cold-eyed runners from Bow Street, but rather the burly servants that had graced Stone's London townhouse—grooms, footmen—while at their head stood a hard-eyed, raging Griffin, his face deathly gray, his sword gleaming.

"You . . . you followed me," she choked out, sick with fury and grief and rage. "My God, how could you?"

She saw something fleeting within those tormented eyes, something like regret, anguish, before it was crushed into steely resolve. "How could I not? This man is a murderer, Isabeau. God knows how many innocents have been his victims besides William. But no more, Beau. No more. Ramsey, it is *my* steel you shall taste this night, you twisted, craven dog. And I defy you—dare you to carve your bloody initials upon my chest."

"I'm no murderer." Jack's fingers clenched upon the hilt of his sword. "But if you are so eager to die—"

"No, Jack." Beau clutched her pistols in trembling hands, leveling them at Griffin's midsection. "Griff, I'll not let you do this. I won't let either of you do this."

His eyes seemed to pierce her. "And what are you going to do, Isabeau?" There was such tortured gentleness in his tones, such infinite loss. "Are you going to shoot me, love? Kill me?"

His words had so ravaged her spirit she had not noticed him slowly pacing toward her until he was so near she could smell the rich scent of sandalwood and leather that always clung to him.

"Griff, do not make me . . ." Her hands quivered, her

heart threatening to beat its way from her breast. "It is lies, all lies about Jack, I swear it."

"As you swore you loved me? Strange, it is difficult to believe that now, when you stand ready to blast a pistol ball into my heart."

"I do love you, damn your stubborn eyes! Too much to let you cut down an innocent man. Too much to let you destroy—"

"Then, milady rogue, you shall have to kill me."

He stood bare inches from the barrels of her pistols, his eyes boring into hers, waiting, watching.

Beau felt as though she were being torn asunder, knowing that in his own way Griffin was trying to give her this chance to wreak her own vengeance upon him. To shoot him, to kill him if she could, knowing it would not save Ramsey from the king's justice.

It broke her heart. A sudden, ragged sob rose within her as his hands, those hands that had spiraled her into wonder, closed about the barrels of her weapons, taking them from her numb fingers.

"I hate you," she cried out, flinging herself against him, driving her fists against the hard wall of his chest. "I hate you, hate you, hate you—"

"I know." The words were soft. He did nothing to defend himself, only standing there rigid as she battered her balled hands against him.

"My lord." A voice broke through Beau's anguish. "Do you want us to take the murderin' wretch?"

"No! Don't you dare! Damn you!" Beau cried, but her protest was drowned out by Ramsey himself as the highwayman flexed his daunting sword arm.

"I'd not advise it, my friend," Jack drawled. "That is, unless you'd like to be lighter by the weight of, shall we say, one ear." His gaze fixed upon that feature, the dancing of his sword point making it obvious to all that Ramsey did indeed possess the prowess to relieve the young footman of that article.

Despite their far superior numbers, some amongst Griffin's servants took an involuntary step back. But the tension within Beau snapped wild, making her half crazed with terror as Griffin's hands closed about her wrists, pinning them against him. "Take her," he ordered, thrusting Beau into the grasp of the giant of a man who had served as his coachman. "And damn it, don't let her go."

"Griffin—for the love of God." She begged him to see reason.

But all words died. Even time seemed to freeze into a scene worse than the most hideous nightmare as menacing storm-blue eyes glanced past her to lock upon Jack Ramsey's face.

"It seems my lady could not bring herself to kill me." Griffin's voice was cold, yet wracked with hopelessness, pain. "Perhaps, sir, you would care to try."

His fingers closed about the hilt of his own weapon, and he drew the blade with a deliberateness that drove Isabeau insane.

"Griffin! Both of you! Stop! Sweet Savior, stop!" Beau fought madly against the man who held her, knowing it was futile.

"Get back, the lot of you," Stone commanded. "And no matter what the outcome, no one is to interfere."

"My lord—"

"It is madness, sir—"

"Nay—" Protests rose from the cluster of men at his back.

"Damn it, that is an order! A direct order! Any man disobeying me will be dismissed without a farthing."

"It is a most generous gesture, this matching of swords," Jack drawled, lifting his blade in salute. "It is a pity such an honorable man must lose his life over a lie."

"It is you who will die, Ramsey. For William. And for the innocents you slew."

Beau screamed as the first crack of blade against blade echoed through the tiny chamber, the two men graceful as dancers in a most deadly pas au deux. Like whipcords they coiled and struck, steel glinting as it slashed near arms, belly, chest. With each thrust, each parry, it was evident that both men were the most daunting of masters, evenly matched in this, their dicing with Dame Death.

And as Beau watched in horrified fascination, in the rawest terror she had ever known, she hated herself, hated herself because she had indeed betrayed Jack Ramsey's trust. Even though she knew Griffin was wrong, she could not bear the thought of him falling beneath the sword.

At the cost of Jack's life? A voice shrieked inside her. No, I cannot bear to lose either of them, cannot bear it.

She cried out as Ramsey's blade bit through the fabric of Griffin's coatsleeve. A small crimson stain began to spread across the dark velvet. But only the whitening of Griffin's lips betrayed his pain. Even his wound failed to slow the inexorable onslaught of Stone's weapon.

Beau shuddered. Her heart seemed to cease beating as the battle between the two men waxed grimmer, more deadly. Griff gashed Jack's taut thigh, and sweat soaked the shirts of both men. Their faces gleamed with it, their hair sticking to their brows as they battled on.

Breath rasped in their chests, the only sounds within the chamber the hiss of blades as they dodged slashing blows, the grunts and curses as the weapons crashed together.

Beau struggled desperately against her captor, seeking some way, any way to escape. But the man who bound her was diligent, leaving her no means to elude him.

It seemed the battle had lasted forever, then suddenly it was finished. Griffin hooked his blade in the handle of Jack's sword and flung Ramsey's weapon from his fingers.

The sword Jack had treasured spun through the air, skidding to a halt against one wall. Ramsey's fingers stretched toward the weapon as if some sorcery could make it fly back to his hand, but after a moment Jack let his arm fall to his side, his eyes meeting Griffin's gaze with a courage that twisted talons deep in Beau's breast.

The tiniest of smiles crooked Jack's lips as he faced his death, Griffin's blade gleaming a mere hair's breadth from his chest.

"You are the first man who has ever bested me," Jack said softly. "Perhaps it is indeed time to die."

"You killed my brother." Griffin's voice was low. "Damn you, you killed William."

"You have won the right to believe that I did," Jack said. "Wash free your grief with my blood."

Beau couldn't stifle a sob as Griffin's gaze flashed from Jack's face to capture hers with anguish, longing. "Nothing will ever cleanse away my grief now, Ramsey. No, nor cleanse away this sin. Will it, Isabeau?"

Beau held her breath endless seconds, her chest seemingly crushed in a giant fist. She cried out as Griffin cursed brutally, then hurled his own sword against the wooden panel.

"Take him," he said, jerking his head toward Ramsey. "Bind him and tie him astride a horse. We'll take him off to Newgate to let the king's courts wreak fair justice."

Beau felt her knees buckle with momentary relief at Jack's reprieve, time giving her some small hope that she could save him. If she could only reach her horse when Griffin's party rode away.

"And as for Isabeau"—Griffin gestured toward the tiny chamber—"drag that armoire over to block her inside this cranny. If you let her escape, it will cost your life."

"N-no! Griffin," Beau cried. She battled with renewed frenzy against her captor as raw terror jolted through her, flooding her with horrifying memories of childhood, of being barred within her mother's armoire, helpless, half crazed, while her beloved father was carried off to die.

"Don't struggle so, miss, I don't want to hurt you," the coachman pleaded, hauling her toward the small cubicle as four of Griffin's other servants moved to reposition the heavy piece of furniture meant to form her prison door. But Beau did fight—desperately—clawing, flailing as she was thrust into the smugglers' den.

"Keep her here a full two hours. By then Ramsey will be safely behind bars, and she won't be able to get into trouble."

"Aye, milord. But I fear we'd best take the candle," the

coachman said softly. "She might injure herself or set the place afire."

"Yes." Griffin's face was twisted with regret. He stepped into the chamber, his fingers closing about the single candlestick illuminating the tiny den.

"I'm sorry, Isabeau," he said with devastating gentleness as he stepped from the tiny room. "I'd ask you to forgive me, but I know you never will."

"Griffin." She choked out his name as he turned his back upon her. "Griffin, please . . . oh God, don't . . ."

Then there was nothing but the horrible grating sound of the armoire being slid into place, the meager light vanishing into an abyss of hopelessness and mind-shattering despair.

Chapter Twenty

An eternity seemed to creep by in the hours Beau was locked inside the tiny, pitch-dark room, bound, alone with her terrors, her furies, her fears. Helpless. Hopeless. Emotions tearing through her, as she paced the small length of floor.

Time and time again she cracked into some object, bruising her flesh, but she was so numb she scarcely felt it. Still, she had to slam her fists against the unfeeling plane of the armoire's back, had to damn Griffin Stone, his servants, and herself to hell a thousand times or succumb to madness in that tiny, windowless room.

Her captors were unyielding as granite cliffs, their gentle yet firm voices muffled as they pleaded with her to calm herself, stop torturing herself. It would all be over soon.

Over . . . as her father's death had been over that long-ago day. Over, with such grinding finality that she had never been able to make things right for bold Six Coach Robb, so that she was racked with guilt and tormented by her own helplessness against the cruelties of fate.

But this time it was not cold-eyed soldiers who had shattered the very center of her trust, her faith in herself and in those she dared love. It was the stormy-eyed man who had taken her heart. That dauntingly strong, achingly vulnerable rogue who had raged at her, laughed with her, and tumbled her back into coverlets with such infinite passion and tenderness, that she had begun to believe in miracles.

Griffin Stone had betrayed her. Betrayed Jack. Destroyed her in ways that could never be made right. Why, then, did the darkness all around her taunt her, not with Ramsey's resigned eyes, but rather with Griffin Stone's anguished face?

Beau bit her lip, driving her foot against the table leg in frustration. "Blast it, he took Jack! To Newgate, damn it! To hang!"

But how many times had she herself experienced the raw rage that she had seen in Griffin's face? How many times had her own temper broken free, lashing out at any who stood in her way?

If it had been Molly who had died so hideously, would she, Isabeau, have been able to remain calm, listen to reason, and trust?

How could it be that even now she could feel that uncontrollable tug, that kinship of souls between her and Griffin that made her feel every dagger of guilt twisting inside him, every chasm of loss and acid regret?

He loved her with a depth that had humbled her, awed her, and yet his honor, his loyalty to his brother, and his relentless sense of duty had left him no choice. No choice but to destroy the love he had shared with her. No choice but to betray her.

Beau ground her fingertips against her burning eyes, wanting to drive back the image of his face as he had stood inches from the loaded barrels of her pistols. He had faced her for long seconds that had spiraled into eternity, allowing her the chance to take her own revenge upon him, if she so chose.

It had been the most wrenching of gifts, the only one he'd had the power to offer her. But she had not been able to pull the trigger any more than he had been able to cut down Jack, because he had known how deeply Beau cared for the highwayman rogue.

No, Beau thought with sudden, stinging bitterness, Griff had not possessed the will to cut Jack down, but he had no difficulty in dragging Jack off to Newgate to face the gallows. Griffin Stone would have Jack Ramsey's blood upon his hands, even though it was not by the honest thrust of his own blade.

"Blast it, there must be something—something you can do!" she railed at herself aloud. "Think, Isabeau! Damn you, *think!*"

She jumped as there was a sudden scraping sound, a strip of light piercing her eyes as the armoire was shoved back inch by grinding inch. The brace of burly servants Griff had left to guard her stood sheepish, their eyes full of regret. "Ah, miss, miss, what did ye do to yerself?" the coachman lamented, stepping in to take up her battered hand. "Ye must let me tend—"

"Take your hands off her!" A shrill, sobbing cry rent the quiet as Molly plunged past the shattered doorway to catch Beau in quivering arms. "Haven't you already done her enough ill?"

The coachman flinched, a dull red flush creeping up his neck. "I—I was but following my lord's orders."

"Your *lord* is a monster!" Molly's face was mottled with anger, wet with tears.

"Mistress DeBurgh, he . . . I . . ."

"You've done your cursed duty," Beau snapped. "Just go now. *Go!*"

The two servants eyed each other uneasily, then one nodded, and the pair of them started toward the corridor. The coachman paused, glancing back as he fidgeted with a button upon his waistcoat. "Mistress DeBurgh, you'll look after those cuts—otherwise they'll fester and scar."

Beau's gaze tracked down to her fingers, a laugh filled with bitterness rising within her. "I've suffered far worse scars today." She hated herself for the next soft words that fell from her lips, but she could not stop them. "Take care of my lord Stone. He'll need . . ."

Someone to love him, someone to make him laugh, she

thought, someone to show him the beauty deep inside his soul.

The coachman nodded as if he had read her thoughts, then vanished through the doorway.

"Take care of that beast?" Molly's voice shook with revulsion. "Isabeau, how could you even think of Griffin Stone without loathing him? He's turned Jack over to Bow Street, to the hangman!"

"Blast it, Molly, hush! Hell will turn to ice before I let Jack hang! There has to be some way to save him." Beau paced Nell's room, drumming the heel of her hand against her brow as if to jar loose some plan, some tiny spark of hope. "That's it!" She cried out so loud Molly nigh jumped from her skin. "It's easy, so blasted easy, it might work."

"What? Beau, you cannot mean to charge into Newgate."

"Ah, but I do. Yet not the way you fear. Not in a mission to rescue Jack, but rather as a grief-ridden visitor bidding him a tearful farewell."

"I don't understand."

"Moll, something is afoot—something evil, something terrifying—and Jack has the power to expose it. He was telling me about it when Griffin came, but he didn't have a chance to finish. Jack was planning to ride tonight to expose whoever is attempting to cast him to the dogs. If I can get to Jack, if he can tell me the whole of it, I'll ride in Jack's place."

"But even if you clear him of the charges of murder, Beau, Jack's escapades on the High Toby are legend. They'll hang him and glory in it."

"Not if we can get enough coin to buy him a pardon. It is said that if you pay enough, they won't go through with execution. Instead they will deport you."

"Deport you? To where?"

Beau clenched her fists. "A penal colony."

"No! He'd be nothing more than a slave!"

"It is a damn sight better than being dead!"

Molly's eyes swam with tears, and she pressed her fist to her pale lips as if to stifle the sobs Beau sensed were battling to beat their way from the girl's throat.

"Moll." She tried to gentle her voice. "At the moment it is the best hope we have to offer him. We have to take it."

Molly whispered her agreement in a small voice, the expression in her eyes suddenly distant, as though the chamber and even Beau had spun away. "Where . . . where will we get enough coin to save him?"

Beau rubbed her throbbing temples. "I don't know. But I'll think of something after I shatter these ridiculous lies about the murders."

"By then it might be too late. The authorities—they'll be eager to see the famed Gentleman Jack Ramsey hang."

"Sweet Christ, what do you want me to do? It will be a bloody miracle if I can even reach Jack tonight and discover what I need to know to clear him. Damn it, Moll, just stay here out of my bloody way until I think of something!"

Beau hated her friend's stricken expression. Molly looked as though Beau had crushed her beneath her boot heel. And maybe Beau had crushed Molly's fragile confidence in herself. But damnation, she had to go, had to ride, or else all would be lost.

"Moll." Beau caught the girl by the arms, staring into those wide, pain-filled eyes. "There is nothing you can do to help Jack. Just wait. And pray."

With those words Beau wheeled, bolting down the stairs and into the night.

Molly stared after her as if in a trance until suddenly there was a bit of movement in the doorway. Nell Rooligan's lumpy body filled the opening.

"She's gone to aid him?" The old hag's voice grated against Molly's nerves.

"Yes," Molly said faintly, her stomach churning. "But she's going to need coin—a great deal of coin."

"You can have all I possess, but, Lud, girl, it will not be enough. And where the three o' us are to get more I've no way o' knowin'. Unless . . ." Nell's eyes narrowed. "You remember that fancy nobleman what was askin' after you so often?"

"Yes." Molly turned, her skin crawling with dread.

"He came to me yesterday askin' for you most especial to accompany him to some fete a-goin' on this night."

"A fete?"

"Aye, somethin' t'do with a bunch o' swells. Said he needed an angel o' a woman to tryst wi' a devil like himself."

Molly shuddered at the memory of those cold, soulless eyes.

"When I told him you were no longer in me employ he was real disappointed-like. I offered him the pick o' any o' my bevy o' pretties, and he chose Lisette, but I could tell he was wishin' that you were his partridge."

Molly drew a deep breath, steadying herself. "I want this one. What is his name, and where can I find him?"

"His name be Valmont Alistair, or Alistair something . . . Malcolm. Aye, that was it. He has a hunting box near that ruined chapel about eight miles from here. Perhaps he is there yet."

"Nell, I have to—to go to him. When Beau returns tell her—"

"Aye. But girl, there be disturbings this night, railings in the other world. I can feel 'em."

Molly's lips curved in a solemn, aching smile. "There is no world for me at all if Jack Ramsey dwells not within it." Nausea clenched within Molly's belly as she turned and forced her feet down the stairs into the night that Beau had always seen as a friend. Into the night that for Molly had ever been haunted with demons and phantoms preying on unwary souls.

The tiny cell reeked of despair, the light from the torch in the guard's outstretched hand dribbling over mildewed stone and filthy straw.

Bile rose in Isabeau's throat as her gaze swept the hellhole that was to be Jack Ramsey's resting place before the grave. No highwayman's cell, this, decked out with whatever comforts the brigand's coin could buy. There were no thick blankets, no tankards with fine ale, no candles driving back shadowy fears. Even the water in a pewter pitcher was scummed over, the candlelight making the liquid's surface a stomach-churning shade of green.

But Beau would have preferred to stare forever at the skitterings of rats within the straw or to gaze unceasingly into that poisonous water rather than to look at the man who sat in the cell's far corner. A huge iron collar was fastened about Jack Ramsey's neck. The shackles weighting his wrists and ankles were bound together with lengths of heavy chain.

Shadows carved deep hollows in his face, giving it the appearance of a cadaver, while a vicious purple welt slashed across his once-handsome features.

The guard grumbled as he stalked over to jam the torch base into a rusted sconce, and he wiped the drool from the corner of his mouth with the back of one grimy paw. "Ye've but five minutes wi' the murderin' scum, doxy. An' ye'd best take joy in 'em, 'cause it is said the bastard'll hang before the week be out. People don't take t'women bein' carved up, do they, Ramsey?" The guard sneered, kicking a tuft of soiled straw into Jack's face.

"Stop it, you blasted cur," Beau snapped, her fist clenching. "Stop it before I—"

"Afore ye what, missy?" The man's rotted teeth were exposed by his shiny, wet lips. "Punch ol' Barnt here into eternity? A bit o' a thing like ye? I be fair tremblin'."

"Beau, don't." Jack's voice cut through her racing fury. "It's not worth it. He'll only drag you out of here if you do, and I—I need to . . . talk with you . . . one last time."

Beau forced her fingers to relax, tamping down her temper with all the inner strength she possessed.

"Backin' down, me sweeting? It's most wise of ye."

"You've had your amusement at our cost, Barnt," Jack said. "Now leave us the hell in peace."

"Ain't goin' to be peace where ye're goin', Ramsey. Jest hellfire an' brimstone. I wonder how ye'll take to it when it is yer flesh splittin' beneath the devil's blade." Barnt chuckled.

"I can only hope that Lucifer has a good whetstone," Jack retorted with a mockery of his lazy smile. "I find dull swords annoying."

At last tired of his game, Barnt cursed, scratching his

belly as he exited the cell. He slammed the door into place, the grinding of the lock making the hair at Beau's nape prickle, her stomach lurch.

But she turned again toward Ramsey, the sight of her friend thus abused making her hands tremble.

"Jack." She croaked his name, knowing that she dared not, must not cry.

"You must excuse the accommodations," Jack said. "It seems the appointments for highwaymen and those for murderers are somewhat different."

"You'll not be in here for long."

Ramsey gave a rough laugh. "So they tell me. However, the alternative does not seem much more alluring. What think you, Beau? Do you believe in hell? I do. Now."

"Don't be absurd. You're not—not going to die."

"And how, pray tell, are you going to prevent it, Impertinence?" The use of her pet name made a lump rise in Beau's throat. "Forces far more powerful than we are tilting with my fate now."

"Well then, they had better be damned powerful, for they'll have to rip you from me at the forfeit of their lives. I've been thinking—"

"God save us."

"Blast it, Jack, I've been stewing it over in my mind ever since I rode out from Nell's, and I think there may be a way to spare you this." She gestured toward the gruesome surroundings. "You spoke of some devilment to take place tonight. You had planned to go there, to dispatch this beast who has blackened your name."

"Yes. But now it is hopeless. Impossible."

"No. I think it is almost better. Better that you are here, locked away."

"Thank you for your kind concern."

Beau went to him, knelt down upon the straw. "Listen, damn you. With you imprisoned here there is no way you could be held accountable for whatever happens tonight. I'll go back to Nell's and raise a band of men. We'll ride to wherever this . . . this ritual you spoke of is to take place, and we'll snare the blackguard who is responsible for this."

"Beau, it is not that I'm ungrateful," Jack said slowly. "I

thank you from my heart for coming here, but it is too late, my sweet. I'm a highwayman. They'll hang—"

"God's blood," Beau raged. "Between you and Molly we might as well nail the lid upon your coffin and be done with it! I'm sick to death of the both of you! Now tell me where the bloody hell this ritual is to take place, and who the blazes is to command it, before I wrap those cursed chains about your neck and strangle you myself!"

She was seething, fresh, revitalizing anger surging through her. And as she glared down at Jack she suddenly saw the tiniest flicker of what might have been hope. But the highwayman merely arched one dark brow, wincing a trifle as the muscles pulled at his bruised flesh. "Methinks," he said solemnly, touching one finger to the iron collar, "that you would have the very devil of a time finding any neck to get the chains around."

Beau balled up her fist and dealt him a thudding blow in the chest, reluctant laughter bubbling up inside her. "Believe me, I shall manage, if you don't hasten to spill the whole of it."

"It is a stable lad who told me. He had happened upon it and overheard the animals at their plottings." Jack's face went grim, sick horror seeming to cling like a web about his features. "They are a mob of aristocrats, Beau. Outcasts, hell-rakers, youths hungry for adventure and approval. There must be eight, ten of them that gather at that abandoned abbey hidden away in the wood. Gethsemane it was called before it was ruined."

"I know the place." Beau shuddered, remembering the stomach-wrenching scene within the clearing, the stench of blood, the carcasses of animals tortured, dead.

"It seems the leader dulls his followers' senses by beginning with beasts," Jack went on, "dipping their hands in blood upon the ruined altar. Once . . . once they are neck-deep in the reveling and frightened of him, he drags them deeper into horror." Jack shuddered. "Their initiation, their final ritual, is that of human sacrifice, Isabeau. Women. Young women. Beautiful women. Angels, they call them, who bear the men's pledge of loyalty to the devil. And what those girls suffer before—" Jack's mouth twisted, his face tinged gray. "They must beg for death."

Beau's mouth went dry, her nails digging deep into her palms. "Then I'll need a dozen men. At least that, well armed."

"And where are you going to get them?" Jack gave a sick laugh. "Do you think you'll find anyone to aid you in pulling Gentleman Jack Ramsey from hell's flames? When they believe me to be capable of wreaking such horrors upon innocents—"

"I'll find a way—some way." Beau's mind filled with images of Griffin, his gaze warm with compassion, raw with love for her. Love enough, she hoped, to grasp this single chance to acquit the man he believed to be his brother's killer. "Stone—he has that many men. If I can convince him to give me this chance to prove—"

"Lord Stone would lay the moon at your feet if it was within his grasp. He loves you, Beau. Yes, and despite this"—Jack jangled his chains—"Stone is a good man. Even as he was leaving me here I overheard him tell his servants he was returning to Nell's to make certain you were all right. But as for his helping me . . ." Jack leaned his head back against the wall, his eyes closing. "Your Lord Stone truly believes I murdered his brother. It would be a miracle if he agreed to such a plan."

"Even if he doesn't, I'll find some way, Jack."

"I know you'll try, Beau. I thank you for that. But if in the end you cannot bring the bastards to justice, I want you—need you to do me one last favor. Kill *him* for me."

"Him?"

"The bastard who began it. The bastard who has the rest of the idiot louts beneath his spell. The bastard who wields the knife."

"I vow it. Who?"

"Alistair, Isabeau. Malcolm Alistair, Marquess of Valmont."

Beau stared into Jack's face, feeling as though she had stumbled into a gaping, endless hole. "Alistair." She whispered the name, her skin clammy as she recalled the day she had first arrived at Darkling Moor. *He* had been there. That cold-eyed, white-faced specter who had made Beau's very flesh crawl. Was it possible that Charles—Griffin's pathetic, misguided Charles— could be snared in Alistair's web? Was it possible that *that* was the reason William Stone had been slashed down?

"Isabeau." Jack's voice tore her from her frenzied thoughts. "There is one more thing. These women—these angels the worshippers cut down—they are all alike in two features. Their hair must be honey gold. And their eyes—"

"Blue." Isabeau forced the word through stiff lips as Molly's chilling words drifted back to her . . . fears about a pale man, a nobleman with cruel eyes who had offered to pay Nell a fortune.

Thank God—thank God Molly was safe.

The rasping of the key in the lock made Beau start, and she hastily flung her arms about Jack, the harsh edges of his bindings cutting deep into her flesh.

"I'll be back, Ramsey. I vow I will," she pledged fiercely. "With the Marquess of Valmont's head upon a pike."

Aches ground deep in Beau's muscles, exhaustion dragging at her like leaden weights as she reined MacBeth into the deserted inn yard. It was as if the mayhem of hours before had been wiped away by a giant hand, only the distant rumblings of thunder hinting that a tempest was brewing. A tempest whose poison could touch all whom she loved—Jack, Molly, and Griffin as well.

Beau shivered against the wind, clambering down from MacBeth with an unaccustomed awkwardness as she prayed that Jack had not been mistaken, that Griffin had indeed returned to Blowsy Nell's. Even when she had purported to loathe and despise him, it would be like Griffin to still attempt to shield her behind his powerful shoulders. Shoulders that had borne far too much pain for their years, far too much grief, too little joy.

And now every fragile hope they had both held of finding a future together could be crushed by one blazing of the stubborness within him.

He'll listen. He has to listen, Beau raged inwardly. I'll force him to see reason.

She could not, dared not think of what would happen if Griffin denied her. She crossed to the heavy door, swung it open. The firelight from the hearth cast an eerie glow about the familiar room, gleaming upon pewter tankards, worn wood, glass hurricanes whose flames had all been extinguished, except for one that yet struggled against the darkness in a distant corner.

The tongue of flame limned the haggard planes of Griffin's face. He was here.

If Jack Ramsey's hell did indeed exist, Beau was certain the condemned could not look as tormented as Griffin Stone did now. She felt a desperate urge to fling herself into his arms, to drink in his hard warmth, his strength, to comfort him, and to have him croon to her that this night was nothing but some hideous dream.

But it was real. Spine-chillingly real.

"You're . . . you're here." Her voice quavered, her knees suddenly wobbly with relief as she hastened toward him. "Griffin, thank God you are here."

"Where the blazes else would I be? From what I was told, you bolted out of here half-crazed. I couldn't find you." Even through the accusatory tone of his voice she could hear the worry for her.

"I had to go to Jack, see him, so—"

"You went to Newgate?" Griff paled. "You little idiot! What if someone had recognized you?"

"As the Devil's Flame? Unless I was rigged out in full cloak and mask, how would they have guessed? But even if there had been a chance they would, I'd have gone there, if I'd had to, to hear the rest of what Jack had to say."

"Oh, yes, I'd wager he filled you full of claims of his innocence, his—"

"Damn your eyes, Griffin Stone, the man *is* innocent! But it is not his own life he fears for this night. It is the lives of others—others like those girls who lie murdered, yes, and misguided striplings like your Charles."

"Charles? I don't understand."

"Maybe that is because *you never bloody listen!"* She crossed to him, catching his face in her hands. "Those murders are part of a ritual, some sort of hellish ritual by men sucked into worship of the devil. The leader, he gathers up youths—youths who are lost, at odds with their families —and he gives them . . . gives them approval, goads them into doing hideous things . . . horrible things."

"And you think Charles . . ."

"I'm not certain, but saints know he's with the murdering bastard often enough! The girls—they are sacrifices, the final step in initiation, and tonight—Jack vows that tonight—"

Griffin's fingers came up, tangled in her hair. "Beau! Stop this, for God's sake! I know full well Charles is no model of honor and propriety, but he is no more capable of murdering a woman than I am. And as for Ramsey, I wouldn't believe him if he said the bloody ocean was blue."

With a sob Beau tore away from him. "Damn you to hell, Griffin Stone! Damn you to hell! You claim you love me, but you won't bloody trust me. You say you want to bring William's murderer to justice, but you're willing to let an innocent man hang! How the devil will you feel when Jack Ramsey lies dead and the Marquess of Valmont goes on murdering?"

"Valmont?"

Beau's wrath cleared. Griffin's features were hard, cold, as if carved in ice. Only his eyes were alive with blue flame. "I told you it was he! He's been master of this from the beginning—murdering and then weaving his web so that it would seem Jack was guilty! For God knows, who would believe lowling scum the like of Jack Ramsey or—or me, when Valmont's a blasted marquess? Even you won't—"

"Where?" Death flared in Griff's eyes, a killing rage that made Beau take a step back. "Where is this cursed meeting to be?"

"That abbey place where I fell the day we saw Molly—the place with the—the slaughtered beasts."

"Gethsemane."

"Jack says there should be eight of them at least. We'll

have to ride. Get your men." Beau felt a surge of dread, of resolve rising within her. "When Valmont knows he's been discovered he'll be desperate."

"Noy, Isabeau. He'll be dead." Griff took one of the pistols from his waist, handing it to her in a gesture that spoke worlds of his trust in her strength, in her courage. "I can raise a score of men within the hour. We can ride—"

A creak upon the stairs made them both wheel, Beau jumping as if she almost feared the mystical, evil Alistair had somehow crept up on them. But the shadowed face was that of Nell, eyes lost in pockets of flesh now wide, fearful, her ragged hair giving her the appearance of some ancient druid priestess.

Beau had felt contempt for the old woman's mystic ways for so long, loathing her for the ruin she had made of so many young girls' lives. And yet, as she stared into Nell's face now, a sick stirring began in the pit of Beau's stomach, drowning her in stark foreboding, for it was as if the old woman had peered into the realm of the damned.

"Nell, what is it? What the blazes do you want?"

"The netherworld . . . it is rising tonight. A nightmare . . . I had a nightmare . . . saw . . ." Nell's fleshy shoulders quaked. "She was screaming."

"She? Nell, who the blazes—"

"Molly Maguire. I saw her with—with the devil. But the face . . . it was *his.*"

"Molly is abovestairs, safe in her room, thank God! I told her to stay there. Griff and I, we have to ride."

"Nay, don't you see?" Nell's voice cracked, her aged hands plucking at her throat as though she were strangling. "Molly was desperate to gain enough coin to free Jack, and that nobleman who wanted her . . . he'd offered me a fortune yesterday to take her for his pleasure. But I didn't think . . . didn't know . . . until—until the dream."

"Molly!" Beau shouted the name, bolting toward the stairs in desperation. "Molly, get down here."

"She's gone! Gone, and I sent her. Sent them all." Nell sobbed, sinking down onto the riser. "Don't you see? She's gone off to find the marquess of Valmont."

Chapter Twenty-One

Griffin leaned low over his horse's neck, the thundering of hooves along the dark road seeming to drive cudgels of guilt and remorse into him.

What had he done? He had wanted to draw blood. Swiftly. Had wanted to rake away this fresh clawing of grief. But instead he had slashed it like a whipcord into Isabeau's face.

And now not only she, but other innocents as well, might pay the price of his folly.

He glanced at the figure beside him, her red hair streaming in the wind, her lithe body at one with the mammoth stallion she urged along the faint, pale ribbon of dirt. She rode like a demon on the night-veiled path, her uncanny skill showing Griffin as nothing else could the daring that had earned the Devil's Flame a place in legend.

But would even her courage be enough to fight the evil of Malcolm Alistair? Would her daring be able to spark life into Molly if Valmont had already begun his grotesque revels?

Griff's fingers clenched on the reins as his mind filled with images of that diabolical nobleman.

How could he have been so blind? He'd listened to no one,

heeded only his own reckless passions. And this time he feared that nothing could ever be made right.

"This way." Beau's cry carried on the wind as she veered down an even narrower fork in the road, the trees reaching out gnarled branches like fingers of death. He drew abreast of her, heard her call, "Can't be much further . . . turn into the wood—"

Her words ended in a sharp cry as MacBeth suddenly reared, plunging and neighing in fright as the moonlight revealed a grotesque sight in the pathway, a rich velvet cloak crimson with blood.

His mount collided with hers, both horses half crazed with terror, and for an instant Griff thought Beau would crash to the ground. But spurred by the evidence of Valmont's dark secrets, Beau righted herself, driving her mount into the tangle of woodland toward, Griffin was certain, a horror greater than any she had ever known.

"Beau, stop!" he shouted. "You little fool!"

With an oath he gripped his own mount's reins, urging the horse to ever greater speed. Brutus surged faster, but Beau's stallion had gained a dozen lengths over him, the beast seeming to sense its mistress's desperation.

She plunged through a break in the trees, and he could see the clearing ahead of them. It was bathed in hellish hues, orange, sulphur yellow and blood red oozing across the stone from the torches shoved in a score of sconces. The flames' glow seemed to spew from the rooftop of the ruined structure, the colors painting the sky as they spilled through the topmost section of a spire that had fallen in centuries ago.

Signs of revelry were still scattered around the abbey's gardens: tankards, silver trays of food, a scarlet cape puddled upon the earth like a pool of fresh blood. It was as if Satan himself had split open the earth and sucked all life down into his dark domain, for it was quiet, too quiet, every evil specter wandering the earth this night seeming to be poised, waiting.

Griff felt a prickling at his nape. There had been no time

to gather the men they had needed to overpower Alistair's throng. Yet this sudden feeling of being hideously vulnerable to harm was absurd, ridiculous, for it was evident that whatever evil had wreathed the ruined abbey this night had fled, leaving only its grisly aftermath.

Griff saw Beau rein in bare inches from the abbey's crumbling doorway, saw her fling herself from her mount. He called to her, commanding her to wait. But an army of demons could not have kept her from racing toward the edifice and into its arched entryway. He drove his heels deep into his horse's side, attempting to catch her, but it was too late.

She had already descended into Malcolm Alistair's hell.

The light blinded Beau, driving spikes of brightness deep into eyes already hazed with panic as she bolted through the doorway. Her fingers clenched, numb, about the butt of her pistol, her stomach pitching wildly with terror for Molly. But nothing in Beau's vivid imagination could have matched the horror before her as her sight slowly cleared.

Satanic symbols defaced the once-holy confines of Gethsemane Abbey. Crude portrayals of lurid scenes were painted over walls that had once been a glowing beacon of faith to the countryside. Every perversion that lurked in the minds of twisted men seemed represented upon the crumbling stone: a feast of decadence, a testament to bone-chilling evil.

Beau's gaze swept about what had once been the abbey's chapel, searching for some sign of life. But there was nothing save candles still burning and the sickly sweet stench of blood.

"No." Beau couldn't stop herself from whimpering the denial, but it was choked into a horrified cry as her gaze locked suddenly upon the altar. The delicate white-robed figure lying deathly still upon it was obscured from Beau's view by the veils of white that draped the aged stone—pristine white cloth now stained dark with blood.

"M-Molly!" Beau sobbed out her friend's name, hurling the pistol aside as she dashed to where the girl lay, her curls spilled out across the fabric like molten gold, her face a lifeless gray. Gray save for the streaks of blood smearing her babe-soft cheeks.

"No! Please, God, no," Beau pleaded aloud as she grabbed Molly's limp hands, her fragile wrists bound cruelly with silk cord. Warm. Her fingers were still warm, but there was no life pulsing in the hands that had softened so many of Beau's tempers, had soothed away the few woes Beau had allowed to creep about the defenses of her well-guarded heart.

She was dead.

The certainty of it broke Beau's heart, but the fates seemed to mock her. No wound marred Molly's slight, white-veiled frame; nothing seemed to bind her to the world of the dead except the cords that pinned the girl to the altar—that and her still features.

Tears streaked down Beau's face as she struggled to tear the bindings away from Molly's bruised flesh. Grief more devastating than any she'd ever known knifed through Beau, combined with a half-crazed fury that branded itself deep within her.

She heard a slight sound behind her and whirled, ready to dive for her pistol. She prayed she would find the frigid countenance of Malcolm Alistair staring back at her. But it was Griffin's face, Griffin's eyes mirroring her own stark grief.

"Isabeau." His drawn sword dropped from his fingers as he ran toward her, catching her up in his arms as if he wanted to shield her. But she didn't want to be sheltered, didn't want to be comforted, for there was no solace in a world without Molly Maguire.

She tried to battle him, wanting nothing but to clutch Molly close. But he held her tight, her tears dampening his chest as she sagged against him.

"It is too—too late," Beau choked out. "Sweet God, I was supposed . . . supposed to protect her . . . supposed to . . . take care of her. I jeered at her for—for being a coward, but she—she rode here, came here . . . to offer herself up for Jack."

"I'm sorry, love." Griff's anguished whisper was buried in the fall of her hair. "God in heaven, I'm so . . . so sorry."

Beau pulled away from the warm shelter of his arms, pulled herself from the acid burnings of grief into the cleansing, numbing flow of fury. "I'm going to kill him," she ground out. "Now, Griff. I'm going to kill Valmont."

"Isabeau."

"Damn it, I want his blood! For what—what he did to her! Look at her!" Beau spun around to where Molly yet lay, her face angel-sweet in the candlelight. "She never harmed anyone—ever."

"I'd sell my soul to bring her back to you"—Griffin's voice was thick with sorrow—"but I can't. I can do nothing but pierce Malcolm Alistair's heart with my sword for you. We'll untie her and carry her back to Darkling Moor. And then we'll ride, Isabeau. Together."

He cradled her cheeks between his hands, his handsome face taut, his eyes filled with promise. Beau felt his strength flow into her, mingled with the fiercest of loves.

She reached up a quivering hand to lay atop his and nodded.

He released her, turning back to the altar, and Beau could see the lines of his face carve deeper with compassion as he worked to slip free the knots that had bound Molly to her fate. But as he tugged at the length of cord fastened about her thin chest he suddenly froze, his eyes widening, his breath catching as he stared down at the girl.

"My God, Beau," he gasped, flattening his palm against Molly's chest. "My God, Beau, her heart—it is beating."

"B-beating? What—"

"She's alive!"

His words spiraled jubilation through Beau, and she felt as if she were tumbling, falling from a precipice. She shoved past him, pressing her own cheek against Molly's to feel the faint thrumming of her pulsebeat.

With a glad cry Beau jerked upright. She helped Griffin untie the rest of Molly's bindings as her tears coursed cheeks that had been washed with grief moments before.

"Let me get her off of this—this thing." Loathing dripped

from Griff's tones as he slipped one arm beneath Molly, intending to ease her down from the altar that had almost been her deathbed.

But at that instant the fragile lids opened, revealing eyes half mad with terror.

A scream tore from Molly's raw throat, the weakened girl struggling pitifully in Griffin's arms, her small fists flailing.

"Don't . . . don't kill me . . ."

Her cries chilled Beau's blood, and she hastened to catch Molly's face in her hands, forcing the terrorized girl to look at her.

"It is Lord Stone, Moll, and me, Beau." She tried to soothe her friend. "No one is going to kill you. It is over."

"The knife! He was—was going to—Isabeau?" Suddenly Molly fell into an incredulous silence as her gaze locked upon Beau's face. Joy that Molly still lived shifted again into white-hot rage at what she had suffered. The fury inside Beau multiplied a hundredfold at the devastation evident in those once-tranquil eyes.

With a heartrending sob Molly clutched at Beau, and Beau hugged her tight, wanting to drive back the lurking evil that had nearly consumed her. Beau stroked the spun-gold hair, but her eyes blazed with protectiveness.

Griff's voice, deep, calming, broke in. "Molly, did they hurt you anywhere?"

"N-no. They but told me what—what they were going to do to me—the marquess did. Sh-showed me the knife. Oh, sweet Jesus, Beau . . ." A sob seemed ready to tear her apart.

Isabeau crushed the girl against her. "It's all right, Molly, it's all right."

"I know you're frightened," Griffin said gently to the girl, "But we need to know . . . do you have any idea where they've all gone? The bastards that tried to hurt you? Do you know what happened to make them go?"

"I d-don't know. The last thing I remember, they were all gathered around me, leering and laughing. One of them slit his own hand and—and smeared blood on my—my face, and I screamed and screamed. . . ."

"I would have fainted clear away myself," Beau said,

gently stroking the girl's hair, "what with fiends like that waving knives in my face."

"Oh, Beau, I didn't—didn't know they would hurt me. I didn't know. . . ."

"Of course you didn't, love. But it's over now."

"It's not over until we're out of here." Griffin's voice was grim as he glanced around the crumbling chamber. "If we don't know why they left in such a blasted hurry, we've no way of knowing when or if they're coming back. Molly, can you walk?"

"I d-don't know. I—I'll try." She took a staggering step, but even with both Beau and Griffin attempting to support her, her knees all but buckled. A whimper escaped her lips.

"You're weak as a newborn lamb, lass, and no wonder," Griff said. "Let me carry you." With infinite gentleness Griffin scooped the girl into his arms. She sagged against him, limp as a child's rag moppet, her face pale as a drift of fresh snow.

She looked so small, so helpless, so fragile in contrast to Griffin's broad, muscled chest that Isabeau still half expected her to melt away beneath his hands as if by some evil sorcery. Beau shuddered, glancing behind her, the skin at the back of her neck tingling.

"Hurry, Griff. It's as if the place has eyes."

There was a sound from the dark alcove above the altar, and Beau wheeled, her skin crawling, blood chilling as a voice, whisper-soft, cold as death, echoed within the abbey.

"The devil has eyes everywhere . . . even in your very soul."

Beau heard Molly's frantic cry, saw Griffin struggle to release her and lunge for his sword. But the jewel-hilted weapon lay useless a cart's length away on the stone floor, the ominous clicking of a pistol's hammer echoing from that veil of darkness above.

"Try for the sword, Stone, and your lady will bear a most unsightly hole where her face used to be," the frigid tones warned.

Beau heard Griff's low curse, saw him hesitate for a heartbeat. Then he raised his hands, palms outward in a show of surrender as he stepped to place his own strong body between Beau and Molly and the demon lurking above.

"Valmont," Griff spat, eyes angling upward, "you murdering bastard."

"Stone, Stone, this is becoming a most distressing habit with you, always interrupting my amusements." Shadows pooled about the tall, thin body of Malcolm Alistair, Marquess of Valmont, obscuring him in what seemed to be almost the darkness of the grave. "But then, that boorish behavior seems to run in the Graymore blood."

Candlelight glinted upon a silver pistol as Valmont stepped from the darkness, dragging a weak, wobbly figure with him. The weapon was pressed tight against the soft brown curls of a gangly, broken youth held captive by Alistair's arm.

"Charles!" Griffin cried as the boy tripped over what appeared to be the robes of some strange religious order, the edges stitched in ancient symbols. The youth's thin hands were bound in front of him with silken cord, but the sleeve of the white robing him was stained an alarming bloody red. "Valmont, if you hurt him, I'll send you to the devil even faster than I'd intended," Griffin warned through gritted teeth.

Valmont moved toward the crumbling stairs, a demonic laugh escaping from his throat. It was as if the spirits that still lurked within the ruined abbey had pared away all pretense of sanity from the man's cadaverous face, leaving it stripped to the barest strokings of evil Griffin had ever witnessed. He had seen men—wicked men—lost in ravings before, had seen men possessed by an almost bestial savagery.

But the cruelty that flickered in Malcolm Alistair's eyes terrified him more deeply than anything he had ever faced, for it was cold, soulless. The marquess's eyes seemed to mirror twin gateways into the realm of the forever damned.

"U-Uncle Griff . . . I t-tried . . . to stop . . . him . . ." Charles quavered, stumbling over a piece of fallen stone. "I t-tried. . . ."

"I know, boy, I know." Griff took an involuntary step forward, fear bounding inside him, pain raking him as if his own blood was draining away beneath the death-white cassock.

Alistair gave the boy a cruel jerk, jamming the pistol barrel so tight against his temple that Charles cried out. "Don't you know by now, you stupid fool? Nothing can stop me. No one can. Not you, not your uncle, not your father."

"My father?" Charles all but whimpered in denial. "What in God's name—"

"Valmont," Griffin said. "What the devil—"

Alistair shook his head with what seemed almost regret. "It was only to be a game of cat and mouse, the notes I sent. A way to bind dear Charles more closely to me when he was starting to slip away. Why, no one had ever escaped my noose before, and I could not bear the thought of losing such a pretty player in my little game. But when Charles went to his father . . . well, I fear sobersides William was too persistent in his attempts to discover who was bedeviling his precious, cherished son."

"Oh, my God . . . my God, no . . ." A hideous sound tore from Charles's throat.

"Sometimes we are all struck with unpleasant tasks, my own. I fear I had to kill him, run him down on the road and—"

"You bastard! You bloody bastard!" Despite the pistol and the wound in his arm, the boy struggled, wild with grief, as if daring Valmont to pull the trigger, courting it.

"You craven dog! Let him go, damn you!" Griffin charged for the stairs, heedless of the pistol.

But Valmont only laughed, a laugh that echoed from hell. Then in a sick, stunning heartbeat Alistair flung the boy headlong down the risers. Molly's shriek blended with Griffin's cry of denial as Charles crashed and rolled down the crumbling stone, a horrible scream breaching his lips as his injured arm cracked against the stone edges, making them wet with blood.

Desperately Griffin flung himself at the boy, trying to

break his fall. With a thud Charles landed against him, and Griff caught him up in strong arms.

Charles struggled to right himself, but he sagged back, weak in Griffin's grasp. "Papa," Charles choked out. "Uncle Griff, he—he killed . . . my father. . . ."

"You're mad, Valmont!" Griffin roared. "I'll cleave your flesh away a sliver at a time and glory in it."

"Do not tempt the devil, Stone." Valmont's laughter echoed through the ruins. "He will tear out your throat." Alistair's cold eyes flicked from Griffin's rage-suffused features to chill Beau and Molly with that cunning regard.

Slowly, like some phantom come real, Valmont descended the stone stairway. His lips curved in an ugly half smile, the black patches affixed to his face seeming to reflect the putrid sores within his very soul.

"However, my lord," he observed, his pale tongue flicking out to moisten death-gray lips, "I find it is not *your* throat, nor that of your puling nephew, into which I am hungry to sink my fangs this night. No, softer, tenderer flesh, I think."

"Valmont, you're insane." Griff pulled away from Charles and stood. Desperately he battled to find some way, any way to reach a weapon to use against the evil marquess. But even if he had been able to grasp his sword's hilt, it would serve them no purpose, for Alistair's pistol ball would slam home before he could bring his blade to bear.

"Valmont," he said, "I vow if you hurt any one of them, I'll—"

"You'll do nothing, Stone. You'll be dead. It would be most inconvenient, after all, to have you dashing about, revealing to the *ton* my more eclectic appetites. The nobility bears such weak stomachs, I fear."

"You think they'd not investigate the murder of Charles? And my own death?"

"Ah, but I am counting on it, my lord. Why do you think I got your nephew garbed up in this little masquerade of priest's robes? You see, I had already conjured up a most pleasing account to tell to the authorities before you came to spoil it. I was going to inform them that I was riding in the woods this night when I heard a poor girl screaming. Being noble-spirited I dashed to her rescue, but it was too late. The demented duke of Graymore had already slashed her to death, as he had all the other poor unfortunates that fell beneath his blade. Faced with the ravening animal, I was so struck with outraged horror that I cut him down."

"You lying bastard," Isabeau said. "They would never believe you."

"Ah, but even if they did not, they would not dare to say it. One of the privileges of the aristocracy, I fear."

"The others . . ." Charles's voice quavered. "They'll tell the truth if I die. They ran away after I came to the girl's defense, would not kill me even when you ordered it."

"A minor inconvenience, my pet. They may not have the stomach to kill a duke, but they'll not come forward to cleanse your name, especially when it will sully their own. They are terrified of me, you see. Scared sheep devouring one another to escape the jaws of hell. But they have already passed through it. They can never escape." Valmont fingered the barrel of his pistol, his face creasing in irritation. "My disciples have always been frightened sheep doing my bidding. Always . . . until you, Charles."

Valmont's lips curled in disgust. "I fear I underestimated you, my pet. There is too much of your uncle in you."

"I'm glad of it! P-proud. Uncle Griff, I'm s-so sorry I dragged you into this . . . and the—the women. I didn't know . . . I never—"

"The problem I am now faced with is how to drag your esteemed uncle out of it. How to dispose of him, and his harlot. I fear four corpses at one time may prove a trifle messy. Perhaps if I staged it as a family quarrel . . ."

"You'll never get away with this," Beau warned. "Jack told us about your atrocities. He knows—"

Laughter rose to Valmont's lips, laughter so hideous, frigid, it seemed to cut like ice crystals, sharp into Beau's skin. "And who, pray tell, will believe a thieving rogue like Ramsey over the word of the marquess of Valmont? The accusations would be ludicrous, milady. Yes, for I"—thin lips curled back from pointed teeth—"I am such a *civilized* fellow."

"You're an animal, Valmont, a cowardly swine." Griff took a step toward the marquess.

"I would not even breathe if I were you, Stone," Alistair said softly. "It would be far simpler for me merely to pull the trigger and kill you now. And yet . . . do you recall that time you interrupted my revelings in the inn? That lovely morsel of a woman I was about to sample?"

"You were slashing her with a riding crop." Scorn dripped from Griffin's voice.

"And you took exception to my little game. Perhaps you will enjoy it more if you lie bound, helpless, like your nephew, watching while I amuse myself, not only with your nephew, but also with your woman."

Beau could feel Griffin's rage pulsing deep, could feel his helplessness, his resolve. "I'll send you to the devil before—"

"Do you not know by now, Stone? I am the devil. The dark side of your soul. Of every man's soul. Your brother knew it. And this puling nephew of yours. Charles here thought it was a grand adventure, this, did you not, Charles, my own? Thought it a lark to plumb the depths of your own debauchery. It was just that in the end, when I forced you to see the hideousness deep inside yourself, you cowered from it. Cowered. But I . . . I glory in the demons that lurk within me. Glory in wrenching them from other men's souls."

Beau averted her eyes from the pale face, trying to hold back her rising panic. But her breath caught, then her heart thudded with renewed hope as her gaze snagged upon something gleaming amidst the ropes they had torn off Molly, something half hidden beneath the veils of white yet draped about the makeshift altar. The pistol. If she could reach it now . . .

She stretched out her fingers to catch at Molly's icy hand, heard her sharp intake of breath, and she knew that the timid girl had also glimpsed the weapon.

Beau looked to Alistair again, felt the piercing of that diabolical gaze as it fixed upon her.

"You." The marquess jerked his head toward her. "It is time for our little fete to begin. But first we shall want to make certain that the other spectator of our . . . er . . . sporting is comfortably established."

"Like hell, you bastard," Griff snarled, and Beau could sense that he was tensing, knew he was preparing to fling himself at Valmont, to take the bullet before surrendering the ones he loved to the evil man's clutches. She knew Griff would do so, trusting her to reach the sword and do something.

But before Griff could move she stepped between him and Alistair, laying one hand on Griff's chest. Her eyes clung to his for an instant. "No, Griff, don't. He'll kill you," she said aloud, mouthing the word "pistol" as she prayed he would see through his own blind rage and panic, prayed he would sense in her this single frail hope.

"Such a docile little doxy you've chosen, Stone," Valmont taunted. "But then they all are before . . . before they know what I will do to them. I wonder if she'll whimper when she lies beneath my knife, offering herself up for you."

Griffin lunged, but Beau steeled her whole weight against him, blocking him with her body. "No!" she hissed. "The ropes . . . by the ropes." She felt him stiffen, her meaning suddenly clear. And in that frozen instant those despair-filled eyes shone with the fiercest of hope.

"The ropes, girl," Alistair's voice cut in. "Get them and truss his lordship up so that he can watch."

Every muscle in Beau's body thrummed, burned, ached with tension as she forced herself to affect a shiver. She looked at the gloating marquess with what she hoped were fright-filled eyes. She saw the evil man lick his lips in anticipation, and she lowered her chin, slinking toward the coils of rope, affecting abject terror.

One shot. She would have one shot, one chance. For if Valmont suspected what she was doing, if he saw her and was able to fire his own weapon, Griffin would die. Yet

Alistair's eyes were fixed even now upon her, hungering for her pain.

"M-my lord marquess." It was Molly's voice, Beau realized, stunned, as she saw her friend walking toward him like some martyred angel. "It is—it is whispered in the streets that you ply these tortures because—because you are in truth no man, not able to—to take a woman save with your knife."

Rage flashed into Alistair's eyes. The hand that held his weapon quivered as it shifted to point at Molly's breast. "You'll regret that, you crawling whore, regret—"

With a cry Beau grabbed the butt of the pistol and wheeled. Her shot shattered the night a stomach-wrenching heartbeat after Valmont's weapon spat lead. At that same heart-stopping moment Charles hurled himself toward the fear-frozen Molly with astonishing strength.

There was a sickening gasp, the thud of lead striking flesh.

Beau cried out a denial as Charles and Molly crashed to the ground, unmoving, even as Griff dived for his sword. In one fluid movement he was on his feet, spinning toward Valmont.

But Griff would never feel the primal joy of driving his blade into the body of the man who had murdered his brother, the man who had threatened the woman he loved. For the marquess lay crumpled upon the stone floor an arm's length from Charles, felled by the legendary accuracy of the Devil's Flame. In his embroidered waistcoat was a gaping, wet hole, and his eyes glazed as the lord of Gethsemane's dark revels plunged into Lucifer's arms.

Griff jammed his sword back into its scabbard. Both he and Beau moved to where Molly and Charles lay in a tangle of ice-pale skin and white robes. The girl was sobbing, hysterical, as she tore the bonds from Charles's wrists. The instant the boy's hands were free he dragged her into his arms, and Molly clung to the embroidered cassock while Charles held her against his breast. Brown curls rested upon gold as the boy choked out words of comfort.

Beau started toward them, but Griffin's hand closed about

hers. “They’ve been through even more than we, God help them,” he whispered in a voice tinged with love and regret. Beau leaned against his hard-muscled warmth, her mind still churning with images of what might have been if Charles Stone had not been so brave.

“It’s over now,” Charles crooned, swaying Molly back and forth in his arms. “It’s over.”

“No,” Molly sobbed, clinging to the boy as if he were her only haven in a world gone mad. “It is not over yet. Jack. Mr. Ramsey. He is to die.”

Beau felt Griff pull away from her, and he went to kneel beside the trembling girl. He cupped her chin, brushing back the tangle of gold from her face.

“Gentleman Jack Ramsey will not hang, Molly,” he said, his eyes burning. “Not if I must storm Newgate Prison myself.”

Chapter Twenty-Two

The corridors of Darkling Moor were cloaked in almost funereal silence but this day there would be no such rites of grieving at the estate. There would be none of the pomp and solemn splendor that accompanied a duke's passing.

Charles Stone, tenth duke of Graymore, was alive.

Alive because Isabeau DeBurgh had defied the very devil. And the man she loved.

Griffin jammed his hands deep in the pockets of his frock coat as he paced down the hushed corridors. Beau had shown unbelievable courage.

She had swept into Darkling Moor with Molly and the wounded Charles in tow, the horror of what she'd seen still etched plainly in her face. Yet she had managed the crisis like a noblewoman or a warrior queen. She had mustered the servants from their beds and scattered them in every direction on countless errands.

She had been magnificent, formidable, exuding an aura of capability and a confidence that had inspired even the most reluctant serving maid to race to do her bidding.

Griffin had watched, stunned, with a keen, bittersweet kind of pleasure. Although she wore his breeches cinched about her waist and a flowing white shirt that hid every hint of feminine curves, she had seemed the grandest of ladies.

He had seen her garbed in the finest satins and in laces a princess would envy. But only last night, when she had stood with her hair loose down her back, her hands yet stained from staunching the flow of Charles's blood, did he truly understand what a miracle Isabeau De Burgh was. The best, the brightest of both the aristocracy and the resourceful, strong-willed commoner who had been her father.

Since the day she'd tried to rob him, pistols blazing, he'd attempted to reshape her, to mold her into something more acceptable, more sedate, something as ordinary as a vapid court beauty.

And yet she had already been strong and brave and beautiful, and her fierce code of honor was far more honest than any from the stiff-necked ruling class.

He'd been wasting his time. Instead of trying to change her into some benighted, preconceived image he'd had of what a woman should be he should have been fighting like the blazes to make *himself* worthy of *her.*

Griff's mouth hardened with resolve, his eyes darkening. He didn't deserve her love. But he vowed to try, God curse it, with everything inside him. To try to make himself worthy to be her husband.

Or perish in the attempt, a voice mocked inside him.

Griffin grimaced, remembering the hellish night. He'd been so busy trying to save Jack Ramsey from the hangman's noose, he hadn't gone to Beau. But he had thought about her, hungered for her, the whole time he had been battling to secure Jack Ramsey's freedom. He'd ended up buying the man as an indentured servant for his property at Marrislea. It had taken all the might of the Stone family and a fortune that would have made a king blanch to free the notorious rogue, but Griffin had paid the sum willingly, knowing it would put some measure of trust back in Isabeau's wild-sweet eyes.

As for Ramsey, it had been as if the man could see past his torment into Griffin's own. There had been no recriminations, no righteous wrath from the bold highwayman. Jack had only said, "I lost someone once. It is hard to see through grief's flames."

They had ridden in companionable silence until Griffin had settled Ramsey in the Graymore hunting box. There were plenty of servants there, always awaiting the duke's pleasure. And Griffin had made certain they were alert, their pistols loaded and ready. Even though Griffin had been able to convince the bleary-eyed judge he'd roused from his mistress's bed that Ramsey was innocent, the country folk still believed Jack to be the blackest of murderers. And until Jack Ramsey was safely out of England, he was in danger.

At most it would take a few days to arrange his passage to Marrislea. And Griffin had already set his staff working on the myriad details involved in an ocean crossing.

The following day he had returned to Darkling Moor exhausted. But his heart had longed for Beau, his hands burning with the need to bury themselves in her hair, to skim hungrily over her soft white flesh. During the endless time that he had dashed about trying to right the disaster he'd almost wrought he had thought of her, dreamed of her. He had wanted to assure himself that she was safe, that she was his. He'd wanted them to celebrate life in the most primitive of rituals.

He had been halfway down the corridor to her bedroom when he had heard the soft tread of a sly-faced serving wench's footsteps. And as he'd met the chit's eyes he had seen the tiniest of smirks clinging about her lips. He had stopped. Awareness had struck him like a poleax to his chest.

Were the other nights he'd spent in Beau's arms being bandied about in kitchen gossip, accompanied by lascivious sniggers and speculations?

Griff had gritted his teeth, the voice of his conscience railing inside him so loudly it frayed at his nerves. *A gentleman does not charge into the chamber of his betrothed, bedding her with wild abandon when any servant might see or hear the indiscretion and spread it through half the kitchens in Norfolk before the man in question has had time to fasten up his breeches.*

He'd wanted to tell his newfound sense of propriety to go straight to the devil. His resurgent scruples were more chafing than any pentitent's sackcloth and ashes. But he'd steeled himself. Grimly he marched back to his own cold, empty bed. He had spent the night cursing himself, cursing her, cursing every servant who had ever indulged in gossip. But even that hadn't eased the fierce hunger gnawing inside him. He had lain beneath the coverlets, watching night bleed into dawn, his whole body rigid with need.

When he could no longer bear it he'd climbed out of bed and thrown on his most somber garb, resolved to bury his passions in William's forbidding study. Surely even the fiercest of sensual desires would dampen once he lost himself in the maze of ledgers and numbers and countless agricultural disasters to be found within those walls.

One last time he would attempt to gather the books into some semblance of order so the task would be less daunting when Charles had recovered from his wound and was ready to take an interest in his holdings.

Griffin strode down the stairway, gratitude flooding through him.

Charles had escaped death's jaws with only a flesh wound to his left arm. He'd have a token scar, the surgeon had claimed—just enough of a mark to impress his lights o' love with tales of his bravery. But Charles would live to be an old man now, please God. And an infinitely wiser one.

Far wiser than the wastrel rakehell Lord Griffin, who had returned to England only to create a worse muddle than the one he'd left so many years before.

Griffin sighed, feeling the crushing weight of what might have happened in the ruins of Gethsemane Abbey. But he brushed it away, his jaw tightening. For some reason God, or the fates, or sweet Lady Fortune had spared him and those he loved. He wouldn't waste more time, more energy flagellating himself with remorse. He'd make amends, and he'd be grateful, damned grateful, for this new chance.

Griffin paused at the base of the stairs, running his fingers lightly over the carvings. Even though he'd managed to wrench Charles free from Valmont, the ruin of

Graymore's estates still remained, and the restoration of its once vast fortunes would be the most daunting task of all.

Except for the prospect of facing Isabeau again and not being able to touch her, kiss her, drive himself deep inside her until she was, in truth, his wife.

Battling to crush the wild emotions, he paced to the heavy door and sucked in a deep breath, already dreading the feel of the room's dim interior closing around him. After a moment he pushed open the door.

He froze, stunned, his gritty eyes assaulted by the light of a dozen candles and the sight of a pale-faced figure garbed in a sedate blue frock coat sitting behind the desk. Dark brown curls tumbled about Charles's face, and his eyes were narrowed as he studied the massive ledger in his hands.

He was so preoccupied that he didn't even notice the door had opened. He merely chewed at the end of a quill and then scribbled some notes on a sheaf of vellum at his side.

For a moment Griffin was tempted to scold Charles and hustle him back to the sickbed where he belonged. But there was something in Charles's face that stopped him. A solemnity, an aura of resolve, as if the boy had aged a dozen years in the night he'd spent at Gethsemane Abbey.

Griff was surprised to find himself stepping back from the door, raising his hand to rap on it softly. He had to knock again before Charles looked up, shaking his head as if to clear it.

"Uncle Griffin." Charles smiled in welcome. "Come in, come in. I was just trying to wade through this muddle about the Tewkesbury estate. There has been a bit of a drought there, I fear, and they are having some difficulty with their crops."

Griffin himself had spent two days attempting to find a solution to the tenant's dilemma, but he only gave Charles an encouraging nod. "It is a puzzlement, that's for certain."

"I've drafted a note to Mr. Howell. I was thinking that we should go there, perhaps, to see what can be done."

Griff felt a fist tighten in his chest, pride and renewed hope welling within him. "I think that would be very wise, your grace."

The boy flushed. "No, I'm not wise in the least. But I'm going to try to be. Do the best I can. I know I can never fill my father's place. But he loved these lands, Uncle Griff. Almost"—the boy looked away—"almost as much as he loved me."

"He loved you very much, Charles."

"I know. I did precious little to earn his love when he was alive. But I am going to do my best to deserve it now. I'm going to find a way to reverse all the damage I've done to Darkling Moor. I'm going to make it a fitting legacy to my father."

Griffin heard the echoes of his own resolve in the youth's voice, and he felt a kinship of spirit with his nephew. The same kinship he'd felt the day he'd given a little boy a ring in a flower-starred meadow and shared his pain of loneliness and loss. Slowly Griff approached Charles, wishing he could pull the young man into his arms, comfort him, reassure him as he had that long-ago day. Instead Griffin laid a hand on Charles's shoulder.

"You'll make a fine duke. One to be proud of. I'm sure, beneath it all, your father knew."

"Do you think so, Uncle Griffin?" There was just enough childish hope in Charles's voice to wrench at Griffin's heart.

But before he could speak the study door slammed open, startling them both. They looked up, and Griffin stared into the fury-glazed features of Judith Stone.

"You!" She pointed a skeletal finger at Griffin, hate blazing in her eyes. "I might have known you would be in this room, dragging that poor boy from his sickbed when he was hovering at death's door!"

"Grandmama. A pleasant morning to you," Griffin attempted with feigned carelessness.

"Look at that child, you scoundrel! He's white as a ghost! And it is a miracle he's not in his grave after what you put him through."

"Grandmother," Charles interrupted, "what happened to me happened because of my own foolishness. If it were not for Uncle Griffin, I would be dead."

"Dead? But don't you see, Charles, he *wants* you dead!

Wants you dead so he can inherit Darkling Moor, inherit the dukedom! He's a worthless profligate! A reprehensible scoundrel, not fit to wipe the mud from a respectable man's boots."

"Grandmother," Charles started to protest, but Griffin waved a hand to silence him.

"I couldn't agree with you more, Grandmama," Griffin said. "I have been guilty of every sin you accused me of and more."

The old lady almost gagged, her face freezing into icy fury. "I'll not have you mocking me, sirrah! Not have you jeering at decent, upstanding—"

"You mistake me, madam. I am serious." Griffin glanced up at the portrait of his father, and the wastrel duke's lively eyes beamed heedlessly down from the canvas. "It is true there is a bit too much of my father's wild blood in my veins, but I am resolved to try to tame it."

"You . . . you are resolved to *what?*"

"Become respectable. A source of pride to my family. To my *wife,*" Griffin added softly, the word precious, infinitely sweet.

He was so caught in the sudden emotions that were washing through him that he did not see the dowager duchess storming toward him until she was an arm's length away.

Judith Stone's face was livid, her hand trembling on the gold head of her cane. She lashed it upward, jabbing its end at Griffin's chest. "No, no you don't, my fine blackguard! You'll not dupe anyone with this show of piousness! All of England shall see through your ruse."

"I am certain they would, were it a ruse. But you see, I am quite sincere. Committed to this course."

"Committed to Bedlam would be more fitting! Ever since you arrived here—"

"Ever since he arrived here," Charles interrupted firmly, "Uncle Griffin has been treated rudely and cruelly. Abominably. By both of us." Charles's voice held an edge of steel Griffin had never heard before.

Judith's chin dropped perceptibly, and her eyes widened.

"Look what he has done since he has charged in here! He's made our lives miserable, carrying on with his doxy beneath this very roof, ordering you and me about as if we were his slaves! No court in the world would expect you to suffer beneath his heel as you have the past month! After what happened the other night they would rip him from the guardianship in an instant."

Charles stood behind the desk, and Griffin was struck by how tall the boy now seemed. "You will cease this unseemly display at once, Grandmother," he said quietly.

"I'm well used to it, Charles," Griffin intervened. "And, I must admit, a measure of it has been well deserved. It doesn't matter."

"I believe it does." Charles looked at Griffin with a heartening steadiness, then turned again to face the dowager duchess. "My lord uncle will always be welcome in my home. The most esteemed of visitors. If you cannot keep a civil tongue in your head when he is my guest, Grandmother, you will kindly keep to your rooms."

"Keep to my rooms! How dare you—"

"Because I am the duke," his grace of Graymore said quietly, meeting her eyes.

For the second time in her life Judith Stone was rendered speechless.

The sun was waning, candles flickering in the windows of Darkling Moor, when Griffin reined his winded horse down the carriage circle. Charles had gone back to his bed hours earlier, but only after Griffin had promised to discharge a dozen duties that were preying on Charles's mind. It had been exhausting, it had been exhilarating, watching Charles come to terms with his inheritance.

The only cloud had been the expression on Judith Stone's face as she had stormed from the room. Griffin sighed, wondering if the old woman was even now barred in her chambers as if she were under siege, seething with outrage and scorn and hate.

Griffin urged Brutus into a trot as he rounded the bend. The trees parted to reveal the entryway to the estate, a blaze of lanterns. Griffin's hands froze on the reins, his lips parting in a curse as his gaze fixed on the sight before him.

The dowager duchess's traveling coach stood tricked out in full regalia, an army of servants swarming about it like frenzied honeybees, storing away what Griffin knew must be Judith Stone's treasures.

Cursing under his breath Griffin spurred his mount, dashing up the drive.

Within moments he had thrown the reins to a footman and charged up the steps into the entryway beyond.

Judith Stone, dowager duchess of Graymore, sat enthroned in a gilt chair in the green drawing room, directing the loading of her belongings with the aura of an exiled queen.

"Grandmother, for God's sake," Griffin said, stalking to where the woman sat. "What the devil are you doing?"

"I am retiring to the dower house." Her face was as unyielding as the cliffs of Cornwall. "I find it far preferable to being locked in my rooms."

"No one is going to lock you in your rooms. I am certain Charles did not mean—"

"He most certainly did! Every word of it! Did you see his eyes? The way he scowled at me? How dare the stripling brat pretend to rule Graymore? Rule me—*me!* I who was once the duchess—"

"As Charles is now the duke," Griffin said. "He is trying his best to fill his father's place. To save Graymore. But for all his determination, he is still very young. He'll need us both in the months ahead. If he is to right the Graymores' fortunes"—he hesitated for a heartbeat—"he'll need you."

The dowager duchess sprang to her feet, her face suffused with anger. "I don't want your pity. I don't want your charity. You, with your rakehell ways and your gaming and your women. You're not worthy to be Charles's most trusted advisor! You'll be a blight upon the dukedom."

"I know in the past I've been a disappointment—an embarrassment to you and"—Griffin winced inwardly—"to William as well. But I meant what I said in the study this morning. I intend to change, Grandmama. You see, I've finally . . . finally found something I love enough to change for. Finally found someone whose happiness, whose respect means more to me than all the wild scrapes and adventures—"

"That harlot you intend to marry? For *her* you will become the soul of propriety?"

"I intend to do right by her," Griffin said. "As soon as her grandmother returns I shall proffer my suit to her. Until then I vow I'll do nothing to shame Isabeau."

"Shame her further, you mean! You have already paraded her in a sheet like a common harlot, invaded her room during a bath! You have dressed her and bedded her—yes, sirrah, I know it—like some Fleet Street doxy."

Griffin met his grandmother's gaze levelly. "I would change that if I could, but I cannot. All I can do is love her, Grandmama. And that I do. More than my life."

Those words silenced the old woman for a moment, and Griffin felt a stirring of hope that he might finally, miraculously reach this woman he'd fought with, hated, defied.

"I love Isabeau," he said. "And I love this land. That is something we share, Grandmother. One thing we share. Love for Darkling Moor."

"What do you know of love? Loyalty? I would have hurled myself into Hades rather than ruin these fields. Would have allowed them to flay me alive rather than bring scandal down upon the Graymore name. While you—"

"While I would have done the same to have you look upon me with approval just once. God knows I never even hoped for love."

"Love you? A worthless profligate like that wastrel father of yours? Rivington would have brought Graymore to glory had he lived, and William . . . I could have molded him into a duke as well if his heart had not been muddied up with misplaced affections. But from the first day I saw you I knew that you would cast away every plaything you possessed to save a worthless beggar lad from harm. That you would bring shame down upon our family if by so doing you could spare a goose girl pain. For that sin I will never forgive you."

Griffin stared into that regal face, those clear, pain-riddled eyes, that thin, bladelike nose, and thanked God that his grandmother had loathed him. That she had failed to shape him into a man that was as cold and heartless as one of William's marble statues. A man that Judith Stone could care for.

For though she'd given him pain, he'd also known laughter and love. He'd known the tenderness of a child's kiss and shared sorrow and joy. Things Judith Stone had brushed aside with one sharp wave of her bony hand.

Griffin looked into her eyes, and it was as if in that instant he could see everything Judith Stone had lost.

"I am sorry for you, Grandmother. Truly sorry."

"You would be so! If I were you, I would despise someone who had so ill used me! I would plot anything, everything to wreak vengeance upon him! But this much I promise you, Griffin. I won't give you the pleasure of watching me suffer here while you pretend to be lord of the manor with that foolish Charles's blessing. I shall away to the dower house to live out my days in peace."

"In peace, Grandmama, or in loneliness? For God's sake, don't cut yourself off from this house that you love, from these lands, to spite *me.* In two years time my work here will be finished. I have complete faith that Charles will be a credit to the dukedom, and I . . . I will be returning to the colonies. To *my* life, *my* world, that I built with my own hands. Stay, Grandmother. Here, where you belong."

"I will not. It would have been insufferable enough watching that popinjay stripling posturing as duke, ordering me about as if—as if he had the right! But to suffer watching you turn respectable—" The duchess fairly trembled with revulsion. "It would give me such a putrid stomach, I should not survive the winter!"

With that the dowager duchess swept from the room, carrying away with her one last possession.

The legacy of bitterness that had tainted Griffin's life.

Chapter Twenty-Three

Salty winds swept in from the ocean, scented with the tang of adventure and freedom. Isabeau stood perched on the coachman's box, trying to lose herself in the teeming confusion of sailors and passengers, cargoes and dreams. She wanted to bury the gnawing sensation of uncertainty that had tormented her since the nightmarish evening at Gethsemane Abbey.

But even the snapping of canvas and the lusty calls of the gulls could not soothe her restlessness or the niggling sense of hurt and rejection that bedeviled her.

She glared at Griffin, who stood garbed in blue velvet, making arrangements with the captain in most lordly fashion. His mouth was as firm as a miser's pursestrings; there was no hint of his wondrous, reckless smile. His eyes were infuriatingly serious, lines carving between his brows.

He looked like a blasted undertaker, she thought, discharging his duties with such solemnity. And ever since he'd escorted her into the coach with Molly and Charles and a grinning Jack Ramsey he'd scarce deigned to talk to her about any except the most innocuous of subjects.

She had wanted to say be damned to them all, had wanted to grasp Griffin's staid neckcloth in her fist and shake the bloody bounder until he told her what the devil was plaguing him. But there had been something quelling in Griffin's face, and something fragile in Molly's eyes, that had made Beau crush her impulses for once in her life.

She grimaced, fighting down the frustration. The man looked as if half of England had sunk into the sea, not grateful that they had gotten out of that blasted coil with their hides intact.

Beau shifted her gaze to Molly. She stood silhouetted against the side of the ducal coach, her slender fingers tucked in the crook of Charles's arm. Molly's cornflower-blue eyes stole shy glances at the tall young man who was so attentive beside her. Charles looked as if he'd found an angel. The girl had all but deafened Beau that morning with chatter about the young duke, how he had been waiting at Molly's bedside when she had awakened.

According to Molly, no Sir Galahad could have begged her forgiveness more humbly, more sweetly. In Beau's current state of ill temper she had been sorely tempted to remind Molly that just the night before the girl had been willing to lay her life down for Jack Ramsey.

But even as reprehensibly irritable as Beau had been, she'd found herself unwilling to dampen the spark of life and happiness in Molly's still-pale face and in the sweet, secret smile that played about her lips.

And Beau's single pleasure had been imagining the dowager duchess's reaction to Molly as Charles's bride.

She looked away from her friend, the glow in Molly's eyes reminding her painfully of her own grating misery.

Instead, she watched Jack, who stood a dozen paces away, his eyes staring out across the wild sea, alight with the prospect of what might well prove his grandest adventure of all.

Isabeau gritted her teeth as she remembered how Griffin and Jack had earnestly plotted what was to be done with Griffin's fields in the colonies. Griff had said more to the man he had once purported to hate than he'd said to her in the past day and a half.

There had been an almost wistful look on Griffin's face

when he had described the wild lands, as if he had only recently realized how much he missed them, realized that *they* were his home, not the glittering ballrooms and grand assemblages he had been born to.

Beau worried her lower lip, wondering if he was wishing that he was the one sailing off on the huge ship, back to a life she'd never touched.

Furious with herself for mooning about like some lovesick milksop, Beau rose up on her tiptoes, determinedly fixing her attention on a grand lady wearing a most astonishing hat. The woman was shooing three strapping sons with mammoth bundles clutched in their gangly arms up the gangplank. "Blood and thunder, I almost wish I was sailing, too!" Beau gritted, shoving a wayward tendril of flame-hued hair back beneath her bonnet. "Indians and night raids would be far preferable to enduring fits of the sulks and solemns!"

Molly glanced up at her nervously, shivering as she drew closer to Charles. "That wilderness sounds positively dreadful! You'd be scalped within a fortnight, Beau, I know it!"

"I don't think even Isabeau could get herself scalped at Marrislea," Griff said, walking back to the coach. "There have been no attacks or raids of any kind since I first won the plantation dicing, and the countryside is civilized."

"Bah!" Beau cast Griff a taunting glance. "I'm certain I could roust *some*thing up with a bit of effort."

She had hoped he'd smile. He'd been so somber since the night they had battled the marquess of Valmont. She'd also hoped to goad him into gazing at her with that heated expression that turned her blood to fire, but he only regarded her with eyes as cool and aloof as those of a marble carving.

"Believe me, milady, soon you'll be stirring up enough tumult to satisfy even you," he said, flicking a bit of dust from a disgustingly plain waistcoat. "Not even the Jacobite rebellion shook the foundations of the *haute ton* to the depths that you will when you are presented by your grandmother."

"Well, that should provide *some* satisfaction," Beau snapped, leaping from her perch with a satisfying thump. "Though if Jack is set upon by pirates or colonial insurrectionists, I shall be most put out."

"Ho, there, Impertinence," Jack Ramsey's hearty voice interrupted her, the highwayman wheeling from his perusal of the confusion of the docks to swoop Beau up in a hard embrace. "I've been saddled with your mischief since you were a babe. It is his lordship's turn to keep you from getting your neck in a noose from now on. It is my advice, sir, that you populate your estates with armies of heirs. You'll need 'em, for no doubt Beau'll be losing them in the woods, or dropping 'em, or such."

Griffin's mouth compressed with such a steely lack of humor that Beau wanted to scream.

"I will not do any such thing!" Beau blustered, masking her hurt beneath a wave of indignance. But her face burned at the images Jack Ramsey had conjured—babes with Griffin's eyes, Griffin's mouth, tiny hands as perfectly shaped and long-fingered as their father's.

Yet even her vivid imagination failed her as she attempted to picture herself as her own mother had been, sweet-smiling, soft-voiced, gentle-handed in healing childish woes. She glanced at Griffin. A furrow marred his brow. She wondered what the devil she'd have to do to break through his abominable wall of silence.

"I'll not bloody lose my own babes," she insisted. "I might misplace 'em for a little—"

But it was Molly who rose, as ever, to her defense, leaving Charles's side long enough to loop one arm about Isabeau's waist. "At least they'll never be fearful of their own shadows, or shy, and—and they'll probably ride and shoot better than any other 'ristocrat babes in England."

"Such a comforting thought for my lord," Ramsey observed, chortling with delight. "Lord Griffin Stone's daughters in their satin petticoats holding their suitors at bay with German silver pistols."

Even Molly giggled at that, and Charles dissolved into

laughter, but Griffin's eyes only narrowed with patent annoyance as they flicked about the crowd bustling around them.

"The upbringing of my heirs is not a subject I care to discuss in front of the whole of London, Mr. Ramsey."

"It seems the *production* of your heirs isn't a subject you care to act on of late either, your worship," Beau muttered under her breath. Griffin's eyes snapped to meet hers, a sudden flare lighting them, then vanishing so quickly that she was certain she'd imagined it.

Damn it to hell, what was the matter with the man? Beau fumed inwardly. She knew he'd been beset by a hundred duties, a hundred difficulties since they'd ridden in from Gethsemane, and she'd tried to understand, tried to be patient, though the Lord knew it wasn't in her nature. But she had been—well, *frightened,* blast it, in Malcolm Alistair's hell, afraid of losing Griffin and a life infinitely more precious than ever before because he was in it.

She had waited for him, wanted him in her bed. She wanted him buried so deeply inside her he could touch her very soul. But he hadn't touched her, hadn't even kissed her since they'd left Gethsemane Abbey.

Why?

Sweet thunder in heaven, he couldn't be addle-witted enough to be angry about the things she'd said to him at Blowsy Nell's, could he? Even a thick-skulled, stubborn oaf of a man like he, she thought, should know that she hadn't meant a word of it. She'd been distraught with fear for Jack, and for the love she and Griffin had forged.

He should be elated that all had worked out in the end. Charles was safe, and Molly, and even Jack, free of the shackles that had bound him.

And if that hadn't been enough, at least the man should have had the good sense to dance a cursed jig when the insufferable dowager duchess had left Darkling Moor in such delicious high dudgeon. The devil knew Beau had practically been tempted to fling open the wine cellar's door and treat the entire household to a roaring drunk in honor of the occasion.

But Griffin had only viewed the happenings around him with stoic solemnity, seeming a heartbreaking stranger to Beau.

She started, her dismal musings broken as she glimpsed a sniffling Molly withdrawing from Jack's arms. The highwayman had bid the girl who had risked so much for him a tender good-bye. Jack watched for a moment as Charles hustled Molly into the sheltering coach. Then Ramsey sauntered over to Beau and cuffed her gently beneath the chin. Her eyes snapped up to meet his merry gaze. "It is time for me to go, my sweet. It seems the captain is preparing to get underway."

Beau felt a swift, crushing sensation in her chest, her throat suddenly thick, her eyes burning as she looked, for what might well be the last time, into the dancing eyes of her mentor.

For an instant she wanted to cling to him, pour out her misery over Griffin as she might have when a child. But the expression on Jack Ramsey's face and her own stubborn pride stopped her.

Regret shone in Ramsey's eyes, still tinged with a bittersweet shading of love.

Beau hurled herself against him, squeezing him so tightly Jack gasped, but his arms closed about her just as fiercely.

"You'll take care of yourself," Beau pleaded into his frockcoat. "You won't—won't get shot by any jealous husbands."

"I shall endeavor not to get shot in the back, Isabeau. But it will be a much more difficult task without you to guard behind me. I shall miss you, Impertinence." His eyes darkened, gentled. "I'll try to forget how much."

Beau could feel the weight of Griffin's gaze upon them, and she moved away from Jack's embrace.

Jack hesitated for an instant, then kissed her on the cheek and strode up the gangplank. She watched him as he reached the top, then paused, oblivious to the sea of other passengers around him.

"Ho, Isabeau!" Jack shouted, doffing his dashing tricorn in most elegant fashion. "You've not heard the last of

Gentleman Jack Ramsey, I vow!" His eyes clung to hers for a moment. Then he turned and rejoined the flow of the crowd.

She watched him until the jaunty red plume of his hat disappeared. There was a lump in her throat, a feeling of uncertainty tugging inside her.

Jack had been good to her, kind, her mentor, her friend. And yet with Griffin she had found the part of herself that could be gentle, the part that could be vulnerable, the part that could lean on someone else just a little.

Had she been a fool? Run blindly into the unsheathed blade Jack had warned her of so long ago? As she stared at Griffin's stiff, unyielding shoulders she felt as if he had somehow cut out a piece of her heart.

Furious with herself, she swiped an errant drop of moisture from her cheek, steeling herself against an unforgivable bout of tears.

Her sorrow might have battled its way to the surface despite her most vigilant efforts if she had not become suddenly aware of Griffin standing beside her.

She gritted her teeth so hard she was surprised they didn't crack.

"So he is off," Griffin said, his voice strained.

Beau jutted her chin up, stubborn. "Yes."

"Then it seems we have but one more errand to attend to. I did not want to upset you earlier, since I knew you were already lamenting Mr. Ramsey's farewell. But I received word from Tom Southwood just this morning. It seems that he and his wife were riding in St. James the other day when they saw the dowager countess feeding the swans."

"The dowager countess?" Beau echoed numbly.

"Sophie Devereaux," Griffin said quietly. "It appears that she has returned from her travels on the Continent."

Beau reached out a hand to grasp the coach wheel, steadying herself, but she felt as if Griffin had dashed her legs out from beneath her.

. . . Sophie Devereaux . . . returned from her travels . . .

No. It had been daunting enough imagining meeting this noble relative when Beau had felt confident, felt the support of Griffin's love and approval. But to do so now, when she felt so infernally vulnerable, adrift . . .

Beau tried to swallow the panic clotting in her throat, but Griffin's next words solidified it into a lump of cold, sick dread.

"I sent word to her ladyship this morning explaining your situation," Griffin told her. "As soon as we leave Molly and Charles at the townhouse, Isabeau, we will go to wait upon your grandmother."

Chapter Twenty-Four

Devereaux House was a historical treasure trove with delightful keepsakes of the noble family displayed about the grand town house. Lances that had been wielded by knights of old were clasped in the iron gauntlets of the full suits of armor that mounted guard in the hallway while broadswords and morningstar maces were affixed to the wood-paneled walls. A cavalier's cuirass was set in a place of honor, testimony to the family's loyalty to Charles II generations ago, while a most intriguing collection of pistols adorned the space above the marble fireplace.

The house might have been considered gloomy were it not for the touches of bright color, statuettes and silk drapings and porcelains that were tucked on many glistening surfaces. Numerous portraits of earlier Devereauxs regarded the entire room from richly appointed frames.

This had been Lianna Devereaux's home. She'd been a child here; it was here that she had learned to toddle along, holding onto her nurse's hand. Beau closed her eyes, imagining her mother, young and laughing and filled with dewy-eyed, romantic dreams, dreams that had come true when she was presented at court. Dozens of handsome young men had flocked around this newfound angel. But none of those weak-spined fops had done for Lianna Devereaux. No. She had somehow met bold Robb DeBurgh, and he had stolen her heart away.

And then . . . then Lianna had been flung from this magnificent house, barred from her family. She'd been abandoned even when her beloved husband was killed and hanged in chains at the crossroads. And when she, too, had died, her heart broken, the babe she had adored had been left to the mercy of strangers.

And now that babe, a woman grown, was returning to Lianna's former home. To the family that had ignored the execution of Six Coach Robb, the death of their own daughter. The people who would have left Isabeau herself to die upon the streets.

Would they fling her out the door even now? Shamed as though she were a bastard babe, returned? No doubt it had not mattered at all to them that Robb had wed his lady love, given her what little he possessed—his name, his heart, his dreams.

"I should not have come here," Beau muttered to herself, pacing the length of the room for what seemed the millionth time. "I should thumb my nose at this grandmother who cared so little for me and my parents. I should tell the old hag to go straight to the devil."

And yet, was that not what someone as snipe-nosed, as aristocratic as Sophie Devereaux would expect her to do? Wouldn't she expect her to act like the ill-bred get of a highwayman and a runaway daughter?

Beau would surprise her. She would sweep into this woman's presence like a crown princess, elegantly scornful, majestically serene.

Although underneath she was absolutely terrified that she would somehow fail the mother she had loved and the father who had been so gallant, so brave.

Beau stopped before the portrait of a prim Elizabethan lady, the painted image seeming to stare down her long nose with disdain. It was bad enough feeling like a fraud in her finest without a blasted portrait affirming her worst fears. She half expected the woman to call out to the footman and have Beau tossed out on her hindparts for daring to breach the Devereauxs' hallowed doors.

With an oath Beau paced the confines of the drawing room, cursing Griffin for deserting her there. He had insisted he needed to talk to the dowager countess alone first, to smooth the way for the meeting. But Beau had felt hurt and had chafed beneath the suspicion that he was preparing Sophie for the shock of meeting her "highwayman granddaughter" for the first time.

Blood and thunder, Beau cursed silently. She already felt as silly as an actor who'd tripped on stage. When they had reached the Stone townhouse after Jack's departure, Molly had insisted upon rigging Beau up in the finest fashion. It had taken two hours of torture, but Beau had not had the energy to protest.

Although even she had to admit that her exquisite dress—gold cloth embroidered with silver—draped her slender figure to perfection, and her hair was arranged in the most elegant style: padded and puffed and stuck into place with so much pomatum it made Beau's scalp crawl. And there was enough powder on her head to bake three loaves of bread.

Beau had worried her lower lip until it felt raw, an entire brigade of butterflies attempting to beat their way out from beneath her ribs. Even her most dangerous night raids had never spawned this awful, clawing dread within her. But on the king's highroads she'd acted instinctively, pistol in hand. The happenings in aristocrats' drawing rooms were far less predictable and more dangerous.

Unable to bear the wait another moment, she went to the partially closed doors, intending to peer through the aperture the servant had left. But just as she leaned toward it the door swept open, narrowly missing her nose.

Beau leapt back, stumbling over the hem of her gown. Only her quick reflexes kept her from tumbling backward into an ignominious heap.

Her cheeks went red as she stared at the stickpin in the footman's neckcloth. She hoped he hadn't noticed how flustered and unsettled she was.

"The dowager countess and Lord Stone await you in the

Canton salon," the servant said. "If I might show you the way?"

Beau tried to stem the wave of panic washing over her. She held her fan in a death grip and swept out into the gallery of Devereaux House with all the regal grace she could muster.

She fidgeted with the trim on her petticoats, her palms damp. Always, when she had imagined this moment, she had imagined that Griffin would be at her side, that he would be giving her his sweet, secret smile. His eyes would be filled with love, daring her to be proud because she was his lady.

She had never expected to feel so abandoned, so alone and infuriatingly afraid.

Beau winced at the footman's booming voice as he announced her.

She hung back for a moment, but then the footman was brushed aside by a solemn-faced Griffin. His severe black frock coat and silver-embroidered waistcoat emphasized the lines that carved his handsome face. His hair was brushed to a mahogany sheen, the frills at his wrists and beneath his square jaw fixed to perfection. A diamond stickpin twinkled upon his chest, but no life, no joy shone in those blue-gray eyes that had once burned with love for her. Only a steely resolve.

"Isabeau." He took her chill fingers and looped them through the crook of his arm. With a courtly bow Griffin led her into the beautiful chamber room.

In what seemed an instant, the room whirled into a chaos as at least a dozen tiny brown and white spaniels flung themselves toward her, yipping with joyful abandon. In the midst of the barking a woman of about seventy rushed forward, her iron-gray hair caught back in a fire-red ribbon, her gown of scarlet grosgrain set off by a formidable spray of diamonds and rubies, the skirts caught up to reveal a pair of boots the Devil's Flame would have envied.

Isabeau gaped as Sophie Devereaux swept her into a fierce hug.

"Child! My child! Can you ever forgive me?" the woman

cried, drawing back until Beau could see the river of tears coursing down her age-quilted cheeks. "Look at you, my dear! The very image of myself at such an age! I vow if my dastardly husband was not dead already, I should be tempted to have Lord Stone here call him out! Put him in his grave for robbing me of your company all these years!"

"G-good morrow, my lady," Beau said, her head more muddled than it had been in her whole life.

"'My lady' me again and I'll set my darlings upon you! You are my granddaughter! Mine!" Sophie's gaze shone with an almost militant joy. "He told me you were dead, dead alongside your mother. A fragile, sickly child!" The woman's chin jutted up, her mouth thinning. "But I should have known better! Any child of my Lianna would be strong in spirit, for she had the courage to tell Theodore to go straight to the devil and married the man she loved!"

The old woman caught Beau's cheeks in her hands, as if to assure herself this granddaughter was real. "Was she happy, my Lianna? Happy with her highway rogue?" Sophie asked tremulously. "After she left that was all I had to console myself with—thoughts of her joy."

Beau looked into those clear green eyes, so like her own, and felt her lips tremble. "She—she loved my father very much. And he her. I like . . . like to think that in the little time they shared they loved more than most people do in a lifetime."

Sophie dragged out a lace-trimmed handkerchief and dabbed at her eyes. "You are a good girl to tell me so. I prayed it was thus with them when I heard . . . heard that Lianna's Robb had been taken. I tried to find her, you know. Tried to help your father. But Theodore, he did all in his power to thwart me. And in the end it was too late. Robb DeBurgh was executed at Tyburn Tree, and Lianna . . . she lay dead as well. Yet most heartbreaking of all was my belief that you, too, had been swept into the grave without my ever having seen you, held you, rocked you in my arms."

The old lady turned away, overcome. Beau reached out, touching her frail arm. "Jack said that he came here after my mother had died, tried to talk to my grandfather."

"Oh, I doubt it not, but the stiff-necked wretch I was wed to was so choked up with pride he'd not have tossed you a crust to save your life. You see, he knew I loved Lianna more than I had ever loved him, and that her child would be even more precious in my eyes. Sometimes I think he drove Lianna into Robb DeBurgh's arms, just to take her from me."

Sophie smiled, a smile weighted with strength and years of sadness. "How could he have believed he could take her from me when I carried her always deep in my heart? Your father, he smuggled this to me by the hand of a servant when you were but three years old." Sophie brushed her fingers lovingly across a miniature nestled in the fabric of her gown. "It was his way, I think, of assuring me Lianna was happy, well cared for. I have never gone a day without it pinned to my bosom."

The image was painted on porcelain, surrounded by a gold wreath of wild rose and thistle. In its midst was a laughing, bright-eyed girl child with flaming red curls, an impudent little nose, and lips pink as rosebuds. She was cradled in the arms of a golden-haired angel of a woman dressed in flowing white.

Beau stared into her mother's beautiful face, her throat constricting as she remembered the last time she had seen Lianna. Her fragile, angelic face had been twisted with grief at her husband's death and pain at Isabeau's childish fury. Beau had never called her mother coward, but Lianna had known how she felt. It had been in those melting, anguished eyes, those delicate hands that had clung to Beau's sturdy fingers, as if that alone could stave off encroaching death.

At that moment Beau would have sold her soul to be able to beg her mother's forgiveness.

She felt a tear tremble on her lashes, then slip free. Tenderly Sophie wiped it away. "Enough of this weeping from both of us. This is a time for joy, my darling. You are here. Here. I shall take you with me to Italy and France. I shall show you the Continent, all the things Lianna and I were never able to share." Sophie gave a watery laugh. "And

God help the man who attempts to take you from me again!"

"But—but Grandmother, I don't—don't think . . ." Beau stammered. She glanced at Griffin. He stood apart from them, as if separated by some invisible wall.

His face was impassive, his eyes unreadable, hiding what was in his soul. She had thought that he would have told Sophie of the future. Of the love they shared, the dreams. But from the old woman's words and the bright glow of satisfaction in her eyes, it was evident that Griffin had said nothing about their love. Nor that he intended to make Beau his wife.

The joy Beau had felt, the cleansing and healing of childhood wounds shifted into a pain so deep she staggered with its force.

She wheeled on him, her eyes blazing. "Blast it, Stone, say something! Tell her—"

The dowager countess stared, taken aback, her eyes clouded with confusion. "Oh, dear, tell me I did not offend you already, child. I fear I am somewhat impetuous. If you do not care to rove the Continent, I vow I will be satisfied to keep you by my hearth fires forever."

Beau began to answer, but before she could speak Griffin broke in. "I fear Mistress DeBurgh and I need a few moments alone, your ladyship." His voice was quiet, so level she wanted to black his eyes.

"But of course." Sophie's hand fluttered to her breast. As she left the room she turned once again to Isabeau, clasping the girl's stiff hands in hers. "I am so grateful, child, so grateful I have been given this chance to know you. I just want you to know . . . this is your home now. Whenever . . . if ever you want it."

Silence cloaked the room when Sophie left it, quietly shutting the doors behind her.

Beau's hands knotted into fists, and she wanted to scream at Griffin, to rail at him. But for once in her life her ever-sharp tongue failed her.

"Isabeau, if you would allow me to explain," Griffin began.

"Explain?" She spun around to face him, certain all her anguish was writ plainly on her features. "I'll wager you'd best explain if you expect to keep that cowardly hide of yours intact! You did not tell her about us! About . . . about the promise you made me, that we would wed."

"You made that promise when you had no other choices, when I was all you knew. Now Sophie can lay the world at your feet. You heard what she said—"

"I heard a woman who is still just a stranger—a kindly one, but a stranger nonetheless—planning out the rest of my life. Well, my next seventy years are already spent, I'm sorry to say, in making your life pure torment. Have you changed your mind? Don't you wish to be saddled any longer with—"

"Damn it, Beau, you deserve a man who is respectable, a gentleman you can be proud to call your husband. You deserve to be courted and wooed and won like any other woman."

"Of all the stupid, addle-pated, idiotic, brainless bits of nonsense I've ever heard," Beau cried, her eyes snapping. "I'm not a bloody heifer at a fair to be awarded to the most aggressive bull. And as for being wooed, I thought we'd gotten *that* out of the way in the coach on the way home from Ranelagh."

"Don't you see? That is exactly what I am attempting to point out to you. I was your guardian, trusted with the task of protecting you. You should have had white lace, a wedding gown, and a bridal bed decked all in flowers. Not a man fire-hot with passions bearing you down in the seat of an infernal coach when half of London might have been looking on."

"I would not trade that night for all the insipid bridal beds in England, you lout! I learned every inch of your body in that coach, Griffin Stone, felt the power in it, the passion. We were hungering, both of us, starving for each other. And it was the most glorious feeling I've ever known. But it is obvious you have forgotten, for you've not even bothered to touch me, to kiss me, since the night we vanquished Valmont."

"Forgotten? Sweet Jesus, I've not been able to think of anything else except tasting you, touching you. But damn it, Beau, I'll not have your honor slurred by licentious servants, not have it bandied about that—"

"That I was your lover? Your mistress? That I lay tangled up in the coverlets with you night after night, learning what it was to bury myself in someone else's soul? If you want *my* opinion, you goat-brained fool, it is a little late for you to be so bloody particular!"

"Just wait one blasted minute, woman!" Griffin said, pulling her against his big body. "You may not bloody appreciate it, but I'm trying to have just a little honor, just a little restraint for the first damned time in my life! I'm trying to be a gentleman worthy enough to love you."

"A gentleman? A *gentleman!*" Beau spat the word as if it were the most infamous of epithets. "Well, if you are planning to turn into one of *those,* I shall cry off the engagement myself! If I had wanted a blasted gentleman, I would have waylaid one years ago. I could have taken any one of a dozen fops prisoner. Maybe I should go back to the highroads and try to find some other reprehensible, stubborn blackguard who loves me just a tenth as well as you once did."

She turned and stalked toward the door. In a heartbeat he was beside her, his hand gripping her arm. When he spun her to face him the raw fury, raw pain flashing across his features made her heart leap in her chest.

"Damn you to hell, woman, I'll not let you go back to that life! Not let you get yourself hanged!"

"I'd like to see you stop me! The month we wagered is over. And besides, what use would a puffed-up, pinch-nosed gentleman have for the likes of me?"

"I love you. For Christ's sake, I want to bind you to me forever." Griff's jaw was knotted granite-hard; his eyes were glittering with such fiery passion that Beau's breath snagged in her throat. "I want to make love to you every night until you can't breathe, can't speak. I want to fill you with sons and daughters. And I want you to fill . . . fill me . . . with light, Isabeau, with laughter. But I must be certain . . .

certain I can give you the kind of future that will give you joy."

"You have given me more joy than I have ever known."

"But I have also given you sorrow. Life with me would not be easy in the best of circumstances. But now, Beau, life with me will mean a future in the colonies, far away from your grandmother, from England. Far from everything you know."

"I can write my grandmother copious letters. And as for England, I've no love for a land that leaves a man as fine as my father no choice but to ride the High Toby. I'm sure the colonies cannot be *so* much different, Griffin, for they must have sunrises there, and sunsets, and midnight rides across the highroads."

Griff laughed. "I promise you there are no brigands that cut a dash as elegant as the Devil's Flame, if that is what you are asking."

"I am only asking to stay with you, be with you. I could bear losing everyone, everything, save you. I've only had three nights away from your arms, and I've never been so miserable in my whole life!"

"Neither have I!" Griffin's voice broke, filled with wonder, with sorrow, with infinite love.

"Blast you, Griffin Stone!" She balled up one fist, thumping him on the arm. "If this bout of sackcloth and ashes is what you intend to indulge in every time one of us flies into a temper, then maybe we *shouldn't* be wed! We'll spend our whole lifetime groveling for each other's forgiveness! And I'd much rather spend the hours I have with you indulging in other pursuits. Like kissing you, loving you, feeling your mouth on my skin."

She trailed her fingernails down the cord of his neck, felt a shiver of desire rack him, his hard lips parting.

"Isabeau." His fingers framed her face, and they felt warm, rough, infinitely loving. "The best thing that ever happened to me was the night you blazed down upon that coach, pistols firing. But I never thought . . . never believed that I could hold you. That any man, even one who loved as much as I did, could ever hope to catch a flame."

Tears filled Beau's eyes, but her lips parted in a beaming smile. "You know, Stone, if you'd just had the decency to shed your cloak that night upon the road, you would have saved us both considerable trouble."

"Is that so, milady?" Griff arched his brow, his lips tipping up in anticipation.

"Um-humm. You could have kept your baubles *and* your sword point to yourself. For I'd have taken one look at you, Griffin Stone, and demanded your virtue or your life."

"My virtue?"

"I would have made it well worth your while, I vow. Perhaps once we get to America I shall take to the highroads with a vengeance. Every night I shall lay in wait for you, my pistols ready."

"And once you have me in your dastardly clutches, what will you do with me?"

"Ravish you. Shamelessly. If we can but take our leave of my grandmother, I shall give you a demonstration."

Griff looked out the window to where the Graymore coach waited, his eyes aglow with the memory of their first wild-sweet loving.

He grinned.

"I am at your mercy, milady Flame."